PRAISE FOR

KILLING GRACE

"*Killing Grace* is a devilishly smart thriller. From the shadowy spyways of Saigon to the radical underground of America, Peter Prichard weaves a pure spell. With clear command of the raw emotions of that Vietnam War era, his tale of blood and betrayal, of lies and love, simply dazzles. Prepare to read past midnight!"

—Shelby Coffey, former editor in chief, *Los Angeles Times*

"*Killing Grace* is an intriguing story of Vietnam and the US, full of vivid characters, real and imagined. This will bring back memories for those who lived through the 1960s—as the author did, in the US and Vietnam—in a fascinating tale that could almost have happened."

—Adam Clayton Powell III, executive director, USC Election Cybersecurity Initiative; director, USC Annenberg Center, Washington

"In *Killing Grace,* Peter Prichard weaves a gripping tale of the Vietnam War, rich with behind-the-scenes intrigue and colorful characters who will entertain and surprise the reader until the very last page. Highly recommended!"

—Jan Neuharth, author of the Hunt Country Suspense Novels

"*Killing Grace* offers a rare window into aspects of the war not commonly seen—from stateside protests to the work of MPs in Saigon—in a driving narrative that features mystery, action, and romance. And the inclusion of women in several roles adds another intriguing element to the story."

—Nancy Smoyer, author of *Donut Dollies in Vietnam: Baby-Blue Dresses & OD Green*

"For Baby Boomers, the Vietnam War was the crucible not only of their youths, but for the American nation itself. College-aged men learned how to protest their government from the safety of academe while working-class boys got a first-hand lesson in jungle warfare, courtesy of Uncle Sam. *Killing Grace*, Peter Prichard's dazzling first novel, has been germinating in the author's mind since his own tour of duty in Southeast Asia; couple that experience with a journalism career that took him to the top ranks of Gannett and the editorship of *USA Today*, and the result is a first-rate thriller that does justice to all sides. How do you solve a murder in a war zone? Who's right when everybody's wrong? Part undercover spy story, part police procedural, Prichard expertly limns the shifting alliances and allegiances of the players in a war that America never wanted to win, but somehow couldn't quit."

—**Michael Walsh,** author of *Hostile Intent*

"The single word that summarizes my reading of Peter's book: nostalgia. It's a work of fiction, but the anecdotes are real. For veterans who served in Vietnam in 1967 or 1968—and especially for those who served in the III Corps area of operations—the images, the military slang, and the vignettes are accurate and bring back memories. For a not-too-serious, nostalgic, and fun read, get a copy of *Killing Grace*."

—**Jim Weiskopf,** colonel, retired, US Army

"The intrigue—and even romance—of Saigon at the height of the Vietnam War springs from the pages of Peter Prichard's new novel. The quest to solve two murders and stop a terrorist attack ignites the plot but also betrays the sheer folly of this tragedy and calls to account those who stumbled us into it. *Killing Grace* is a worthy successor to Graham Greene's great Vietnam novel, *The Quiet American*."

—**Eric Dezenhall,** author of *False Light*

"What this country needs is a good old-fashioned spy story about the Vietnam War. And it's finally here — *Killing Grace: A Vietnam War Mystery*. The author is the respected Peter Prichard, who was crucial to creating USA Today. He is a veteran of the US Army in Vietnam. Vietnam was far more than our brave soldiers rushing into battle on helicopters. There was another war. It was in the USA. Fellows like Daniel Berrigan, who poured blood on draft records, were determined to do what they could to end the war in Vietnam. The US government was threatened. As another example, the US Capitol was bombed in a still-unsolved mystery from 1971.

The plot involves the CIA, the US Embassy, the FBI, and a shadowy world of traitors and double agents. Of course, blood will flow. And love? A love story is required reading with stories of arms merchants and CIA agents on the loose! 'The higher you climb, the heavier you fall' is a Vietnamese proverb that will make you think long and hard as you turn the pages; it is a saying that captures the unexpected outcome of the Vietnam War. Somehow we managed to win the battles but could not win the war. Dark, entertaining, and amusing, *Killing Grace* is a Vietnam War mystery that delivers and is a delight to read. They don't write books like this anymore . . ."

—**Jan Scruggs,** founder, Vietnam Veterans Memorial

KILLING GRACE

A VIETNAM WAR MYSTERY

PETER PRICHARD

This book is a work of fiction. Names, characters, businesses, organizations, places, events, and incidents are either a product of the author's imagination or are used fictitiously. Any resemblance to actual persons, living or dead, events, or locales is entirely coincidental.

Published by River Grove Books
Austin, TX
www.rivergrovebooks.com

Distributed by River Grove Books

Design and composition by Greenleaf Book Group
Cover design by Greenleaf Book Group
Cover images adapted under a creative commons attribution license 2.0 from ©flickr/manhhai

Publisher's Cataloging-in-Publication data is available.

Print ISBN: 978-1-63299-725-8

eBook ISBN: 978-1-63299-726-5

First Edition

To the more than 58,000 American men and women who lost their lives in Vietnam.

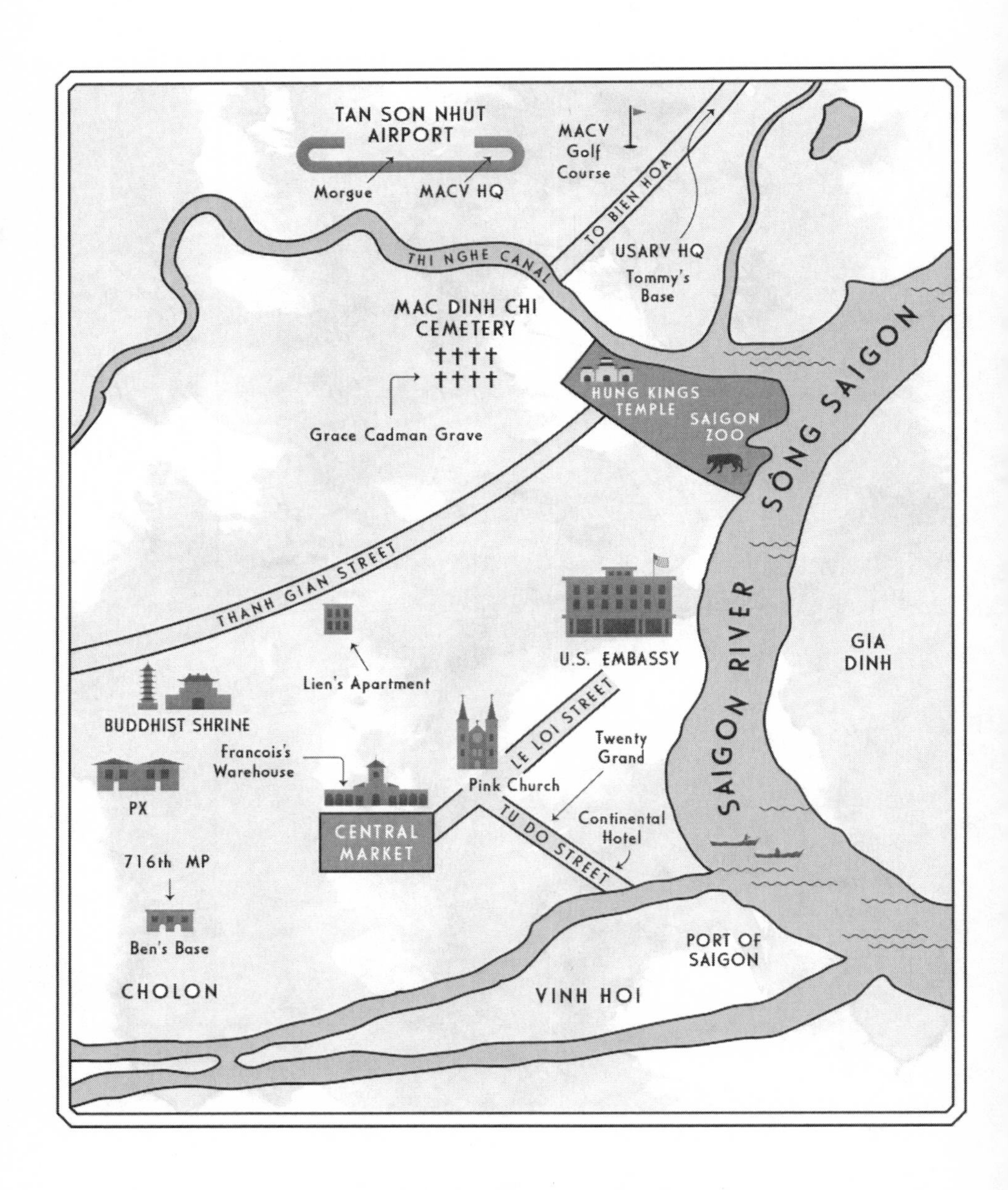

SAIGON 1967–1968

CONTENTS

CAST OF MAJOR CHARACTERS

IN ORDER OF APPEARANCE

Ben Kinkaid, a first lieutenant in the 716th Military Police Brigade

Arthur Pierpont Hopkins Senior, a prosperous Washington lobbyist for defense firms

Arthur Pierpont Hopkins Junior, a.k.a. "Hop," a Columbia history professor and founder of Rage Against the War (RAW)

Patience "Makeba" Jefferson, Hop's second-in-command of RAW

Tommy Banks, an army draftee who accepts Hop's invitation to join RAW

Grace Waverly, a Barnard student from a prominent family who joined RAW hoping to end the war

J.B. Darling, a "civil affairs attaché" and senior advisor to the U.S. ambassador

Lieutenant Colonel George Balderamos, commander of the 716th MP Battalion and Ben's commanding officer

D.B. Anderson, an FBI agent directing Operation Ricochet aimed at war protesters

Lavarious Prince, the leader of the East Coast branch of the Black Panthers

Sergeant Elijah Jackson, Ben's partner in the 716th MPs

Madame Thuy, manager of the Twenty Grand, the classiest bar on Tu Do Street

Sergeant Tran Van Duc, the MPs' interpreter

Graham Stevens, U.S. Ambassador to Vietnam

Nguyen Van Manh, Prime Minister of South Vietnam

Robert McNamara, U.S. Secretary of Defense

Le Thi Lien, J.B. Darling's assistant and interpreter

Joe Kline, Vietnam correspondent for the *Chicago Tribune*

Ned Whittlesey, Vietnam correspondent for the *New York Times*

PFC Allen Kramerwicz, a signals specialist who shares a double bunk with Tommy Banks in the USARV bivouac

Nguyen Van Francois, a.k.a. "Frank," South Vietnam's leading arms dealer

Lieutenant Nguyen Van Lu, "Lucky Lu," a captain in South Vietnam's National Police

Colonel Edward "Ned" Bier, the pathologist in charge of MACV's mortuary

Nguyen Thi Mai, Prime Minister Manh's wife and Francois Nguyen's mistress

Pham Van Phuong, Joe Kline's assistant and girlfriend

Shere Khan, the only tiger in the Saigon Zoo

1

THE GRIDIRON ONLY SINGES

12 MARCH 1966

Ben Kinkaid paused his mission to fill one hundred water glasses as the most important men in the free world swarmed through the doors of the Statler Hilton's ballroom on 16th Street. He'd taken this job as a waiter for only one night, but what a night—almost all the leaders of the U.S. government were here. The Gridiron Club's annual bash was Washington's most exclusive dinner, and the long stream of honored guests clad in black-and-white made Ben think of emperor penguins—the way they massed on Antarctic ice floes before sliding into the ocean (he enjoyed the occasional nature show).

All these men—for this press club did not admit women—preened and strutted about the room, so proud to be here. He figured it must have taken each guest an hour to wriggle into white tie, the complicated, ceremonial suit that was the required dress code. "White tie" meant a coat with long tails, a backless white waistcoat hung from a neck strap, a stiff wing collar, and five tiny studs to close up the stiff starched shirt.

Pre-tied bow ties were considered gauche, so most guests had attempted to tie their own, or maybe their wives or mistresses had done it, and many were crooked or drooping. An old-world Jewish tailor over on L Street rented the things for fifty bucks a pop—this was his high season.

The ballroom was packed to the gills. Ten long tables had been jammed in tight rows at right angles to the back wall. One hundred guests sat facing each other at each one, picnic table style. The head table had been elevated so the dozen VIPs who reigned there could look down at the hoi polloi, one thousand guests in all. Ben had spotted the uniformed heads of the armed services—a full admiral and three four-star generals—nattering away up there with that nerd McNamara. These Really Important People had seats on the dais with their backs against the wall, like gangsters cornered in a restaurant.

As Ben finished placing the silver at table two, Vice President Hubert Horatio Humphrey bounded up to take his seat. Humphrey was the quintessential hack pol who never stopped yakking. The VP was followed by two Supreme Court justices, the Speaker of the House, and the publisher of the world's most influential newspaper, the *New York Times*. The last man to take his place was the lucky correspondent from the *St. Louis Post-Dispatch* who'd ascended to the presidency of the Gridiron, the elite club that many Washington reporters regarded as their special aristocracy, the pinnacle of success. The crowd tonight included publishers, editors, reporters, columnists, and the news anchors of the three networks, along with politicians of every stripe, captains of industry, and the odd ambassador.

Ben had never heard of the Gridiron until a week ago. He'd graduated from Georgetown in 1965 but now he was adrift, the recipient of a history degree he had no idea what to do with; he'd spent most of the last year out West hiking the Rockies and teaching kids to ski. So as spring neared, he found himself holed up in his old room at his parents' house off MacArthur Boulevard in Northwest Washington, wondering what the hell to do with his life. His plan, if you could call it that, was to bum around for a few years and see where life's currents deposited him, but the Vietnam War buildup was in full swing and the draft board was on his tail. And now his father, a mid-level bureaucrat in the Small Business Administration, was threatening to charge him rent.

"A hundred bucks a month to live in my own room . . . can you imagine?" Ben had complained to his old friend Margie Prentice. They'd spent hours together struggling to paint watercolors in an art class at Wilson High. He'd asked her out for a drink to catch up. "I'm not working. I can't afford rent."

"I've got a part-time job waiting tables at some fancy dinner downtown on Saturday," Margie said. "It pays fifty bucks. Why don't you come too?"

"A one-night stand? Why not?" Ben said. "Maybe I'll meet the president."

As a gaggle of government bodyguards escorted the last guests into the ballroom, the U.S. Marine Band, "the President's Own," broke into "Hail to the Chief." The audience leapt to their feet, and Ben edged closer to the head table for a better view.

Then President Johnson parted the black curtain on the dais and stepped out with a smile and a wave. Ben was surprised by how big and imposing LBJ was in person—it was easy to imagine what a bully he could be. Everyone sat, again, and the band struck up the Armed Forces Medley, the hymns of each branch of the military. When the fight song of each service was played, veterans around the room popped up to demonstrate their loyalty—quite a few reporters had served in the Marines. They snapped off smart salutes as the crowd sang along: "From the halls of Montezuma . . ."

"Those reporters are all veterans," said the long-haired older guy who was signaling Ben for more wine. "No wonder they're all for this stupid war."

Ben glanced at the guy's place card. "Mr. Hopkins Junior," it said. The man seated across from Junior was overweight, belly hanging out, veins showing on his prominent patrician nose. A real fat cat, a Washington player. "Mr. Hopkins Senior," his card read.

"I gotta tell you, C.R.," Hopkins Senior said to the tall guy next to him, "my business has never been better." The big man's name was Smith. Ben thought he recognized him from a *Time* magazine cover. Maybe he ran an airline?

"Vietnam's heating up," Hopkins Senior continued. "Our boys are going to need a ton of gear over there—I'm trying to get the numbskulls in Congress to pay for it."

Mr. Smith just grunted, so it was hard to know what he thought.

"You're such a warmonger, Dad," Hopkins Junior said. "Haven't you figured out that Vietnam is a civil war? We got no business over there."

"C.R., have you met my son Junior here?" Hopkins Senior asked. "He's an egghead, regurgitates history for spoiled rich kids up at Columbia."

"Why can't you call me Arthur?" Junior said. Ben thought the guy was going to climb across the table and nail his dad with a right cross. But instead, he looked away and turned back to Ben.

"How much they paying you for this gig?"

"Five bucks an hour," Ben answered.

"That's not enough," Hopkins Junior said, tossing his hair like Lenny Bernstein. "It's hard work, getting food through to all these tables. What do you make of this scene?"

"Impressive," Ben said. "All the movers and shakers are here."

"Right on. Amazing that their bodyguards let them clump together in one place, don't you think?"

Ben nodded. "The reporters will have a lot to write about though."

Hopkins Junior shook his head. "No way. This thing is strictly off the record. Tonight's all about hobnobbing with big shots. These guys think they're members of some exalted tribe, better than the unlucky slobs in shoe shops or car factories . . ." Junior paused, looked up at Ben. "I'm not talking about you, of course."

"Sure," Ben said, managing not to add *you condescending jerk.* He looked around at the assembled newsmen. They were banging into one other trying to kiss up to the nearest senator, no doubt scheming about how they could hand out anonymity, play up leaks, and print rumors that would boost or destroy careers. Ben cleared his throat. "I gotta go, Mr. Hopkins. First course is coming out."

Serving four courses plus water and wine was a grind, but Ben could see how seductive it was to rub elbows with the president and schmooze with CEOs. In the days to come, these newsmen might share a bon mot or two uttered by this VIP or that with their friends, hinting in confidential tones that they were on intimate terms with these vain creatures.

In the lulls between courses, Ben watched as the august members of the eighty-one-year-old club ran through a series of juvenile skits meant to satirize the people in power. Their formula required fat men to squeeze into women's clothes and shout out appalling renditions of popular songs, their lyrics altered to skewer the assembled politicians. "The Gridiron singes . . . but never burns," the club's president had claimed.

A trio of reporters impersonating the pols they covered took the stage to proclaim they were the "Vice Presidential Beatles," the likely VP candidates for the next election: Hubert Humphrey (the incumbent), Senator Gene McCarthy, and Governor Pat Brown of California. They sang out the words in an off-key chorus:

Your pick lifts me higher,
Higher than I dreamed afore,
Just make me your Veep,
We'll surely win four more.

Ben made his way back to the younger Hopkins after the song to pour more wine for the professor, who watched the show with a sour expression.

"They're not exactly the Beatles," Ben said.

"I love the theater," Hopkins Junior said, "but this is amateur hour. The ruling class loves this shit: we decide who lives and dies, but lookee here, we can still take a joke. Fascist hypocrites, the whole damn lot of them."

Ben did think there was something showy and false about the whole thing. Beneath the corny jokes and falsetto tunes, the stench of establishment entitlement permeated the room.

"No shortage of egos here," Ben said, forcing a smile. He pointed to the two empty seats across the table. "Where'd your father go?"

"Oh, he's off twisting some congressman's arm."

"What's your dad do?"

"Arthur Pierpont Hopkins Senior? King Arthur the Great? That's what they call him down here."

"Really? Why?"

"He's the biggest lobbyist in town. He's spent his whole life bouncing back and forth between the Defense Department and lobbying jobs for the big defense contractors—Lockheed, McDonnell Douglas, Boeing, and Sikorsky. Now he helps them sell fighter jets and helicopters to the military, thousands and thousands of them. He's good at it, so he just gets richer and richer. He thinks C.R. Smith—he's Johnson's commerce secretary now—is gonna help him get a board seat at Douglas, but I'm not so sure."

The junior Hopkins sighed and continued. "You know, when Eisenhower said we should fear the influence of the military-industrial complex, he was talking about people like my father."

"Why'd you come, if you hate it so much?"

"Because my dad invited me. He's trying to atone for all the childhood outings he skipped. And I wanted to check out the crowd, see who's who. You know, research the enemy."

"What do you mean, 'the enemy'?"

"Our country's leading war criminals. The people trying to send you to Vietnam. Wise up, amigo. They're all right up there, on the dais."

Ben was surprised; besides his father, this guy must hate America too. He was no hawk when it came to the war, but like most Americans, Ben respected the nation's leaders. King Arthur and C.R. Smith got back to their seats from their schmoozing and pointed to their empty glasses.

"Come out and see my new house, C.R.," Hopkins Senior said. "I've got fifty acres in Alexandria, half a mile of shoreline on the Potomac. You can see Mount Vernon from the widow's walk. I take people up there, point down the river, and tell them, 'That's my neighbor, George Washington.' It's close to Belle Haven Country Club too. I got a case of the shanks, can't break 100 yet. Pro claims I swing too hard."

"I don't play golf," C.R. drawled, looking bored.

Ben went back to the kitchen and grabbed a tray of desserts—peach melba, he guessed. As he opened the door to the ballroom, another server ferrying a tray of glasses crashed into him. Peaches and cream and shattered crystal exploded across the floor.

"That's the entry door, dummkopf!" the head chef screamed.

Ben felt his face flush, but he managed to collect another tray of desserts and return to the fray, pushing through the correct door this time. After he'd made two trips and dropped off fifty of the small plates, he and Margie took a break in the corner of the room, up by the dais.

"Did he make you clean it up?" she asked, shooting him one of her mischievous looks. Margie was only five feet tall and barely came up to Ben's shoulder, and she bounced through life with an ever-present smile, never taking anything that seriously.

"I went right back to work, didn't give him a chance."

"Did you spill wine on any famous people? I dumped half a glass on David Brinkley." She mimed tipping a glass over his chest, laughing. "He was very gracious about it."

"I knocked over a glass of water. The guy was too drunk to notice. But I did meet a big war critic. He's the long-hair over there, bugging that server."

Hopkins Junior was twenty feet away, partially hidden by the long drapes, in an intense conversation with a young Black woman with a bright smile. Ben had seen her in the kitchen, making fun of the chef.

"That's Patience Jefferson," Margie said. "I worked a few dinners with her. She must be twenty years younger than he is. How do you think she knows him?"

"Dunno. Maybe one of his students? He's some kind of professor at Columbia. Pretty radical, I think. He was trying to get me to join him on the protest trail."

Hopkins reached behind Patience, grabbed her ass and pulled her in close, whispering in her ear. She shoved him off, wheeled around, and fled to the kitchen.

"What a pig," Margie said.

The 81st edition of the Gridiron Dinner was winding down. Ben stopped clearing plates to listen to the president, who spoke last. LBJ rushed through a few lame jokes and then turned serious—deadly, too. It was his usual pitch: the most powerful nation on earth, the United States of America, needed to keep bombing the bejeezus out of North Viet-NAAAM. He came down hard on that last syllable, drawing it out as if the country's very name disgusted him.

Ben considered what Johnson was really saying, if you stripped away the euphemisms: We're gonna blow them-there Communists to kingdom come. If we don't, they'll be landin' in Long Beach. Next thing you know, they'll be crossin' the Pedernales River, be in Dallas befo' you know it.

He couldn't fathom what the Viet Cong could possibly want with LBJ's ranch, where the president was spending most of the year lately. That long runway he'd read about in *Newsweek*, maybe?

For at least one portion of humanity, the Gridiron had done more than singe this night—the leader of the most powerful nation on earth had just threatened to incinerate every third human in Southeast Asia. Johnson had said it, but it didn't sound like he really meant it. *Curious,* Ben thought. *Is he tired of this war?*

To end the evening, the one thousand-plus trussed-up penguins in the audience linked arms, pretended they'd been best friends for years, and belted out a lusty version of "Auld Lang Syne." When the music stopped, Ben watched as the professor disentangled himself from his seat mates, unable to hide his disdain. Then Junior gave his Highness King Arthur a limp wave and got the hell out of there.

Ben walked over to the balcony that had a view of the lobby. Lots of tall men in dark suits with earpieces were shepherding their VIPs out, like courtiers protecting their princes.

Now there's a job I could do, Ben thought. *If I got into the Secret Service, would that keep me out of the war?*

2

RAGE AGAINST THE WAR

18 JUNE 1967

Tommy Banks slowed his decrepit baby blue VW for the tollbooth, lobbed two quarters into the basket, and then gunned the bug's anemic engine up the right lane of the Verrazano, his bridge from Staten Island to Neverland. He glanced up, mesmerized by the shards of light that bounced off its massive towers and gleaming cables.

My own light show. Driving high while high.

Tommy was too busy savoring his own wit to notice the car bearing down on his left, closing fast. He veered right as a black Coupe DeVille roared by; the big car missed him by inches, the driver leaning on the horn. *Fucking Todt Hill mobster. That was close.*

Tommy struggled to keep his eyes on the road. He'd gone all out to get into character but had possibly gone overboard with those last few tokes after he'd pulled out of Fort Dix. He'd thought it would be fun to mellow out, play at being a hippie for a day or two—but getting stoned before a big meeting . . . maybe not his greatest idea.

His eyes were drawn to the multicolored running lights of an oncoming semi speeding by in the opposite lane; he stared, frozen in time, a few seconds too long. Before he could react, the VW drifted right and scraped against the guard rail.

The shriek of tearing metal was deafening—his rear fender, probably.

Oh boy, but I'm still rolling.

He shoved the gearshift back up into third and fought to stay in his lane, gripping the wheel so hard his fingers turned white. *Eyes front. Focus, you idiot.*

Managing to breathe, Tommy kept the car under thirty all the way through Brooklyn, crossed the Williamsburg Bridge, and slowly made his way to the 200 block of 4th Street, the East Village. Sunday night, no traffic. He parked next to a hydrant—no meter maids around now. He ignored his shredded fender, climbed the steps to the door, and leaned on the buzzer for the third-floor walk-up.

An older-looking version of Keith Richards opened the door. "How's it hangin'?" Hopkins asked. Tommy managed not to roll his eyes, met his target's gaze without blinking, the way he'd been told. *Never hesitate, never flinch.* They stared at each other for a long moment.

"Love those wide-open pupils," Hop said. "You got an illegal smile too. You been smoking?"

"A spliff or two," Tommy said. "To take the edge off."

Hop laughed, but it wasn't friendly. His face was narrow, like a Modigliani portrait. A few wisps of hair had erupted on his chin, a goatee that didn't quite materialize. Tommy guessed he was about forty-five, but the man looked fit, like maybe he lifted weights. With his oval face and long dirty hair, Tommy decided his new professor friend resembled Christ more than any hard rocker. He found it hard to come up with a clear image of Jesus, though. He hadn't been to church in ages.

"Glad I wasn't risking my life out there with you," Hop said.

The apartment—Tommy figured it must be their safe house—was

a one bedroom, railroad style, really tight. There was a combined living room-kitchen linked to the bedroom in the back, and a tiny bathroom wedged in between.

No door to the bedroom. The window in the back looked out on a solid brick wall six inches away—the building behind them. The place wasn't much bigger than two prison cells. *No privacy. No secrets here.*

Two beat-up leather couches faced each other in the living room. They looked like moving rejects, maybe stuff they'd picked off the street. A black kitchen table with a Formica top, a small TV with rabbit ears, a portable record player, and a few shiny metal-legged chairs completed the scene. A poster on the living room wall advertised a rock concert—the Jimi Hendrix Experience. Tommy had never heard of it. Over one couch was a large reprint of Picasso's *Guernica*, the classic anti-war picture, bloody horse heads and human limbs blown all akimbo. Posters made by SDS—Students for a Democratic Society—had been slapped up on the other wall.

END THE WAR
BEFORE IT ENDS YOU

Elections Are A Hoax!

AMERIKA Out of AsiA NOW!

STOp THE DrafT! BURN YOUR CARD!

Bring the War Home!

Tommy thought the signs were amateurish. He figured a few thousand wigged-out hippie college students didn't have a prayer of derailing the great AMERIKAN war machine, no matter how admirable the idea was.

He registered a rancid smell: hash, spilled beer, pizza getting cold and old. The new Buffalo Springfield album was playing in the background, Stephen Stills singing something about a man with a gun—it added to the edgy mood.

Five people in the group. Hop was a lot older than the others, did most of the talking. "This is my friend Tommy," Hopkins said. "I met him at that protest a while ago outside the gates of Fort Myer. He's in the army now, but he's one of us."

Hop had told Tommy he was "a retired professor." He'd paused for a beat or two and added "at Columbia" to underline his status. "I'm the founder of Rage Against the War, RAW for short. We're like SDS but more militant."

"Your speech was very compelling," Tommy had said. "I learned a lot, Mr. Hopkins." *No harm in laying it on.* Hop's current crew consisted of a disheveled young man with stringy black hair and three twentysomething women. *This is RAW's brain trust? They're kids, just like me.*

One of Hop's disciples was a striking Black woman dressed in denim—all black Levi's—and her hair was styled in a bold Afro, à la Angela Davis. She looked to be about five-eight, muscular, strong, and curvy—a warrior in fighting trim. She was holding a laundry basket full of white shirts that looked identical to the one Hop was wearing. Like an emcee introducing a rock act, Hop extended his hand toward her. "Give it up for Makeba." The woman glared back at him, her eyes fierce.

"You'll have to cut Makeba some slack," Hop said. "She's pissed because I make her iron my shirts. We have a chain of command here. Chores are good for discipline."

"You think we're your fucking maids, Hop?" Makeba asked.

Hopkins shrugged, ignoring the menace in her tone.

Tommy's gaze moved to the pretty blonde on the far end of the couch. She had a Twiggy-style pixie cut and her knees were drawn to her chest—a defensive posture.

Hop interrupted Tommy's too-long gaze at the blonde woman: "Say hello to Grace." He loved being in charge.

"Hi, Tommy," Grace said, with a half-smile.

Tommy nodded at her. Grace was very fair; with her creamy skin and long neck, she reminded him of a swan. She wore a blue-and-white tie-dye T-shirt over tight jeans that showed her long legs. He thought she was around his age, maybe twenty-two.

"And that's Deborah." Hop pointed at the woman with frizzy red hair stretched out on the opposite couch, one blue-jeaned leg thrown over its arm, a provocative pose. A young man in a suede vest and an SDS headband stood next to Deborah holding a hash pipe. A boy, really: he was still fighting acne. His greasy dark hair touched his shoulders.

"I'm Carleton," he said. He took a long drag on the pipe, then offered the dope to Tommy. "This is good shit, man."

Tommy sucked on the joint and held it forever, savoring the rush. If he smoked any more, he wouldn't be able to string two sentences together. How could these people organize anything?

"Hey, man," said the pixie blonde, Grace. "You, new guy . . . Tommy . . . Why is your hair *so short*?" She kept twisting the tendrils of her own cropped hair—a nervous tic, maybe.

"Not my idea. The army cut it off. I'm just finishing training, at Fort Dix."

"So why are you here?" Carleton asked. "What are you—some kind of secret agent? Come to turn us all in?"

"Nah," Tommy said, trying to sound more confident than he felt. "I'm just an unlucky guy who doesn't want to bleed out in the jungle. I'm one of your biggest supporters."

"Fort Dix, that's way out in Jersey, right?" Carleton asked. "Where they sending you next?"

"Vietnam. Looks like everyone in my unit, we're all going . . . over there." A bead of sweat ran down his back. *Change the subject.*

Carleton shook his head, feigning sadness. "You poor dumb shit."

"I get that a lot," Tommy said, trying to keep it light.

"Why would you let them *do that* to your hair?" Grace asked. "And how'd you end up in the army? Did they cut out your brain too?"

"No choice, we all got buzz cuts," Tommy said. "I haven't had much free will lately."

"Hold on, Grace," Hop said, cutting off the argument.

Father Hippie knows best.

Tommy shook his head, kept schtum. Carleton handed the pipe to Hop but he shook his head, passed it on to Grace. *So their leader stays sober. Another reason to be careful.*

Grace drew deeply on the hash, then spit it out with a harsh cough. The tension left her face and she dissolved into the couch, headed for dreamland.

No bra, Tommy couldn't help but notice. Peaceniks weren't usually his type, but this girl had a bold spirit, looked eager to test the limits. Very different from the proper, buttoned-up girls he was bored with meeting. She seemed ready for anything.

"Did you see what the Vietnamese generals did to that guy Diem a couple years ago?" Carleton asked. "They offed their own president. Those South Vietnamese, they're all crooks over there. And now Johnson wants us to spill our blood to keep the new assholes in power. What's that about?"

Carleton had swallowed whatever line Hopkins was feeding him.

Tommy smiled. "You know what LBJ says: If we don't stop the Cong in South Vietnam, they'll be in Santa Monica soon."

"That's ridiculous," Hop said. "Our so-called leaders are delusional pricks."

"Right on," Carleton said, turning back to Tommy. "You believe that shit Johnson says?"

Tommy held up his hands in surrender. “Hey, I read it in the newspapers.”

They all laughed, except Makeba, who eyed him skeptically. “So you enlisted?”

“No, no—got drafted,” Tommy said. “Had no money for law school.” He tried another smile. “If I’d met you a year ago, Makeba, maybe I could have married you, had some kids. They don’t draft fathers, you know. I coulda gotten out of the whole thing.”

Makeba laughed. Maybe she was human under that forbidding exterior. “Marry you? Fat chance, white boy. Anyway, how the hell you going to help us?”

“You heard me, Makeba. I’m here because, just like you, I hate this war. Like Hop says, who wants to die for this? What are we fighting for, anyway?” Tommy tried singing the line from Country Joe’s latest hit, but his attempt to not give a damn landed as a toneless chant.

Makeba laughed: “Tell you one thing, private—you can’t sing for shit.”

“Easy, girl,” Hop said. “Think about it. Tommy’s free ticket to South Vietnam is no tragedy. Not yet anyway. It might turn out to be an opportunity. Like our new friend said, we all hate this dirty war. Tommy could be useful.”

“That’ll never happen,” Makeba said, her voice rising. Her Afro seemed to vibrate around her, like a strange halo. Tommy wondered if she was Hop’s girl.

“If we really want to shut the war down,” Hop said, “we’re going to have to do more than march.” Hop was getting warmed up, showing his true believer colors. “We can wave signs until our arms fall off, but peaceful protests won’t change much. We’ll feel good about ourselves, but for the army it will be business as usual. They’ll keep bombing villages, killing babies, and drafting peace-loving guys like Tommy. We need new ideas.”

“Yeah, like that monk guy, that crazy Buddhist,” Makeba said.

"What Buddhist?" Grace asked, still fussing with her hair.

"I think she means the one who immolated himself," Tommy said. "A few years ago. In Saigon."

"What's immolated?" Carleton asked. He could barely talk, his eyes half open.

"The Diem regime persecuted Buddhists," Tommy said. "When they marched for the right to practice their religion Diem's thugs opened fire, killed a bunch of them. Then another monk—Thich Quang Duc—shows up downtown. He drops a cushion in the street, sits down in the lotus position. His helper pours a five-gallon can of gas over his head. The monk says a prayer, lights a match, and poof—burnt himself to a crisp. Nothing left but charred bones. People stood there sobbing. The press loved it—the photos were all over."

"Oh, I remember that," Grace said, standing up, her eyes shining. "That monk was so courageous. He took nonviolence to a whole new level. You have to admire him—what he was willing to do for their cause."

"Right," Tommy said, admiring her idealism but not seeing much courage in this group. *These guys are no match for those monks.*

Carleton looked at Hop, his mouth open. "Um, Hop, you thinking we need to do stuff like that?"

"Nah, of course not Carleton, we're not Buddhists." Hop's eyes had a dreamy, faraway look, which worked with his messianic schtick.

Tommy caught Hop's eye and forced a smile. *I'm with you all the way, man.*

"There are a thousand ways to get headlines," Hop said, nodding back. *Right you are, Hop. You have no idea.*

3

YOUR NEAREST BUNKER

15 JUNE 1966–21 JANUARY 1967

"Have you thought about enlisting?" Ben's father had asked.

They were on their second beer at a Baltimore bar before an Orioles game. Jim Palmer was on the mound for the O's tonight and Brooks Robinson was playing third. Ben was excited; the O's had made some good moves and the season was young. Palmer looked like a great pitcher and hope was alive. But then the news came onto the black-and-white TV over the bar, crushing his mood. Cronkite was reporting the weekly body count: "153 American soldiers were killed in South Vietnam this week . . ."

Like many college boys in the mid-sixties, Ben Kinkaid never dreamed his country would force him to go to Vietnam. After graduating from Georgetown in 1965, he'd left town in the fall to ski bum around the Rockies. The war was rarely front page then; the army had enough bodies for its new adventure on the far side of the world.

But one fine January day in 1966, after another sparkling morning on the mountain, Ben had returned to his group house outside Aspen to discover a letter from the District of Columbia draft board. His student deferment had expired, he'd been reclassified 1A. His first thought was how naive and feckless he was: if he'd been smarter, faster, and better organized, he could have found something to do that would have gotten him out of this damn war.

He'd gone home to deal with it, and now he and his father sat on the worn barstools, their eyes fixed on the television as head shots of dead young men rolled by on the screen. So many faces, so many lost. Guys his age, cut down in their prime. On Friday's newscast, Cronkite ran the pictures of every soldier who'd been killed, a regular feature. The room had gone quiet; even the regulars had stopped talking to respect the dead.

Faced with the same fate, most of Ben's Georgetown buddies had gone on to graduate school—law, business, or medicine. Congress and the Selective Service System, led by the inscrutable General Lewis B. Hershey, still allowed deferments for that. As far as Ben could tell, his friends weren't really interested in those careers, just desperate to escape the draft. But Ben knew he was way too impatient to devote his life to the boring intricacies of the law or the mind-numbing routine of an office. And he was mediocre at science, so medical school was out. Besides, he hated hospitals.

His situation made him think harder about a career and what to do when he grew up. As a kid, he'd always liked cop shows—*Dragnet, Highway Patrol, The Streets of San Francisco.* The heroes on those shows—played by Jack Webb, Broderick Crawford, Karl Malden—were great. They made police work look interesting. Locking up bad guys would be exciting, and maybe he could make the world safer—that would be more satisfying than following his father into some boring desk job at a federal agency.

"And that's the way it is . . . ," Cronkite said when the pictures finally stopped.

"What a waste," Ben's dad said, shaking his head. "I hope they know what they're doing. If you did enlist . . . maybe you could ask for a non-combat job? Logistics, headquarters support, even the MPs. You might snag something interesting. That'd be a hell of a lot safer than being a grunt or a lieutenant in the infantry." He gestured at the TV. "Those young louies are getting blown to bits over there. Most MPs probably get posted to Saigon—the city looks relatively safe, at least on the news."

Ben frowned, took a long pull on his Falstaff. "Dad, why would I volunteer for *anything*? You trying to get me killed?"

"No, no. Just the opposite. I'm trying to save you—you probably can't escape the draft. But if you enlist, you have a shot to control your own destiny. The army's on-the-job training would be a bonus. Look, if the MPs will take you, you'll find out if you like police work. You're always talking about it."

Ben let his dad's advice marinate for a while. The longer he thought about it, volunteering to be an MP didn't sound so dumb. He'd imagined a hundred ways to avoid the draft and come up with nothing. He longed to discover that he had some lifesaving medical malady but he was a healthy young man, damn it. He didn't wish for anything serious, just some nuisance ailment that would let him escape the long arm of the draft: flat feet, a mild case of asthma, those would do.

To add to the capriciousness of the system, Congress had decreed that teachers would lose the deferments they'd had for years, unless they taught math or science. The Soviets were supposedly ahead of the U.S. in the space race, so emergency improvements were needed in science education—*we can't kill any more math teachers!* No help there.

Ben was lousy at math and unimpressed with teachers' salaries. Some of his friends had hastily married their high school sweethearts and promptly produced a kid or two—a growing family was good for a 3-A deferment. But all Ben had in the girlfriend department was a string of carefree girls he'd met bartending in Aspen—he couldn't think of anyone who'd be willing to embark on a quickie marriage with the likes of him, a gangly, slightly awkward guy who ran around quoting famous people.

Ben knew one Wilson High classmate who'd opted for the ultimate dodge and deserted the States for Canada. The rub there was that moving to Canada to avoid the draft was illegal. Even if this absurd war finally ended, you could be left with a felony conviction and no guarantee you could ever come home. It seemed inevitable that he was going to be dragooned into the army and deposited in Southeast Asia, where there was a strong possibility he'd expire in some godforsaken rice paddy.

There might be some circumstances that would require him to risk his life for his country, but this murky war didn't fit that bill. There was no way he could sit around and passively await his fate: he needed an escape hatch, and he needed it now.

So far he'd rejected every idea his father had come up with. *It's the 1960s, Ben,* his friends always said, *Never trust anyone over thirty.* He stared at his father now—looking older than his forty-seven years, his hair gone completely gray, the result of decades of pointless bureaucratic battles and the struggle to make ends meet on his meager salary. His dad's goal was to put in his thirty years at the SBA, jump on that pension, and move to Florida. Ben knew his dad couldn't help him get out of the draft: he was a mid-level civil servant and his political influence was zero. So when every other door seemed to close, Ben reluctantly followed his father's advice and enlisted.

"You feel good about the MPs?" his dad had asked when Ben told him he'd been accepted.

"There's nothing to feel good about," Ben said with a shrug. "But at least I'm not in the infantry."

His dad reached up and touched Ben's cheek. "If they shoot at you, don't forget to duck."

Ben completed basic training and Officer Candidate School at hot-as-hell Fort Polk, and MP training at Fort Hood, which included a basic criminal investigation course. In January 1967, he shipped out to Saigon with the 716th MP Battalion for his 365-day tour. There were more than 300,000 American troops in the war zone by then; the big brass had decided they needed to send in the MPs to provide security and a semblance of law and order.

His first taste of the chaos of war came the night he arrived in Vietnam after twenty-four hours of travel from California, crammed together with two hundred other nervous soldiers on a chartered 707. The pilot had warned them that the plane would have to bank steeply before landing, "in case there's ground fire." Several white-knuckle moments later the jet dropped from the sky in a steep dive, the nose rising at the last possible moment. They hit the runway hard, wheels smoking. Ben thanked God that he'd survived the landing, unfolded his cramped limbs, and descended the mobile stairway onto the steamy tarmac.

An eerie yellow light surrounded the field. Even though it was one in the morning, it was still very hot, high eighties and incredibly humid. Five minutes on the ground, and he was already sweating buckets. The air was thick, tangible, a pungent concoction of smells: cooking fires, strange spices, rotting vegetation, raw sewage, jet fuel, cordite. He could taste every breath.

Every few seconds, there was a loud whoosh off to the north, followed by a hollow-sounding *crump* when a shell exploded out in the dark jungle. Artillery. Not that far away.

"Ours or theirs?" asked the lieutenant colonel who'd stepped off the mobile stairs ahead of him. He'd stopped to talk with the sergeant in charge of transport who was there to meet them.

"Ours, sir," the sergeant said, saluting. "Fire suppression. Plus H&I—harassment and interdiction. We know Charlie's out there, sir. We're just not always sure where, exactly. So we just fire away and hope we hit 'em."

Off to the left, twenty meters away, Ben noticed a loose-knit group of about thirty GIs waiting near the runway. They looked bone tired, worn out, maybe even bored—a sharp contrast to his jumpy group. A few were lying on their backs on the tarmac, their heads propped on their steel pots, trying to doze. Ben guessed they'd just come from a firefight; their dull green camouflage uniforms were torn, smeared with mud, and adorned with talismans. Feathers and ribbons were pinned to their clothes, messages were scrawled on their helmets. *Fuck the VC* was a popular one. Several wore crucifixes. Most hadn't bothered to shave.

"Vietnam's over for them," the private first class next to Ben said. "Those guys are going home."

"Lucky bastards," Ben said.

The transport sergeant turned his attention to his gaggle of newbies. "Here's the drill, men. We don't expect trouble tonight. But if Mister Charles decides to rocket us you men need to know, it is *imperative* that you know the answer to one question, just one—where is my nearest bunker?

"Look behind you. The entrance to your nearest bunker, your home away from home, is right over there, to the right of them latrines. If we do experience incoming fire, stay calm. Keep your head down. Cover your head with both hands, get as low as you can, and then run—run like hell for that there bunker. You troops are in-country now—you got to always know where your bunker's at."

Ben and the others who'd dropped to this little corner of hell turned to stare at their personal bunker. There was a pause, as the new guys took in the sergeant's advice, which Ben thought was absurd. Covering your head with your hands wouldn't stop a thing.

"Are there bunkers everywhere?" someone asked.

A burst of spontaneous, hysterical laughter erupted from the dirt-spattered vets who'd moved closer to them, lining up for their flight back to the world. "No, but Charlie's got a special hidey-hole for you, troop," one of the homebound men said. More laughter—it was the funniest thing they'd ever heard. In an hour they'd be out over the Pacific at 37,000 feet, laughing it up onboard their Freedom Bird to safety.

As a line of army buses arrived, the sergeant took attendance. When he heard "Second Lieutenant Kinkaid!" Ben shouldered his heavy bag and climbed onto the first bus. It resembled a school bus, except it was camouflage green and heavy mesh screens had been welded to the windows. He took a window seat, anxious to see what the country looked like.

The road to Saigon was jammed, mostly military traffic and Vietnamese on motorbikes dodging the U.S. Army's big deuce-and-a-halves. No streetlights, but there was enough light from the ubiquitous cooking fires to see that they were traveling through a vast shantytown—it seemed to go on for miles and miles, in every direction.

There were thousands of people living out there—maybe tens of thousands, huddled in makeshift shacks. Their homes were a bizarre mixture of cardboard, scraps of corrugated steel and flattened beer cans, cobbled together with duct tape. *They must be refugees.* Whole families—often three generations, babies, parents, grandparents—squatted by the side of the road as the mama-sans tended fires and stirred their rice.

They were all dressed in black. Every single person, except for the naked babies. Ben had read that the VC always wore what looked like black pajamas—it was their uniform. *Are all these people VC? How do we tell the good guys from the bad guys?*

After about half an hour they reached Saigon. The scene along the road reminded Ben of a Bosch painting: thousands of the damned, camped overnight on their journey to the underworld, waiting to cross the Styx. Once a colonial backwater, Saigon had become a crowded, hectic, crazy place—it was the most chaotic city Ben could imagine. Everything about it was a shock to his system: the smell of burning charcoal, the stench of human waste, the little kids running alongside the bus in the dark of night, trying to sell the new GIs warm Cokes. On the ride into town the bus was quiet, no one said a word. What if those kids carried grenades instead of Cokes?

During his first few weeks in-country, Ben discovered that U.S. forces faced a raft of problems: constantly changing Vietnamese governments, the inability to tell friend from foe, and pervasive corruption. Even so, after a month or two, ensconced with his fellow officers in their comfortable barracks—the building had been a rich rubber merchant's villa when the French had run things—Ben settled into a routine. He showed up on time, kept his head down, and followed orders. He was a quick study, and after a couple of months he got his First Lieutenant bars.

He'd tacked a 1967 calendar on the wall over his bunk. Every night before he turned in, he dutifully crossed off the day, drew a big "X" through it. Maybe his father had been right about the Saigon people saw on the news: despite the chaos, many days the city seemed relatively safe. Ben began to dare to think his tour might turn out okay. Was that possible? Could he survive his year in hell, go home in one piece?

4

WARRIORS FOR PEACE

18–25 JUNE 1967

Tommy had left RAW's apartment around two a.m., relieved he was sober enough to block out the bouncing lights and find his way back to Fort Dix. As Hopkins had prattled on about Vietnamese history deep into the night, he'd struggled to stay awake. It reminded him of lectures in the halls of Fordham, when he amused himself by ranking the best-looking girls in the room (in RAW's safe house, it was Grace).

Hop's recap started with the first full-scale invasion of Vietnam in 111 B.C., when the Chinese established the Han dynasty. Then two brave natives, the Trung sisters, threw the hated invaders out in 40 A.D., only to be crushed two years later by a larger Chinese army. Waving a tattered drawing of the two women, Hop shouted to underline his point: "The Vietnamese *hate* invaders. They're a very valiant people."

The messianic RAW leader had adopted the pompous tone of a know-it-all academic; he'd been a full professor but had ditched Columbia to join the revolution full-time. The little voice in Tommy's head couldn't resist a dig: *So Hop, you gave up tenure? For this?*

"For centuries, the Vietnamese have repelled their enemies," Hop continued. "The Trung sisters were Amazons, man. Heroes, skilled in the martial arts. They captured 65 cities from the Chinese. Imagine that! Here we are, two thousand years later, and the Vietnamese people still celebrate the Trungs—it's inspirational."

Hop obviously got off on hearing himself talk. But Tommy had to admit, it sounded like the history of Vietnam—or Annam, as Hop insisted on calling it—was always the same old story. Every so often new invaders would arrive, followed by a new struggle to evict them. Over the centuries, Vietnam had been ruled by the Chinese, then the Mongol hordes, and then the Chinese again, until the French started a colony there in 1858.

In 1940 the Japanese invaded; Vietnamese partisans, led by Ho Chi Minh, fought to repel them. The French returned in 1945, and Ho's National Front went to war with them. After the French lost Dien Bien Phu in 1954, the Viet Minh kicked them out for good. North Vietnam declared independence, and the country was partitioned. Ho's Communists ruled the North, and Ngo Dinh Diem and his fellow Catholics came to power in the South.

"Now it's America's turn to screw up," Hop said. "Make no mistake. History will repeat itself." He paused to look at Tommy. "They probably didn't get around to teaching you that up at Fordham."

What an asshole. He's lucky I didn't bring my bat.

"The U.S. Army isn't about to enlighten you either. All the invaders lost. That's what will happen to Ameri-*KA* too." Hop shouted out the last syllable, embracing the fascist spelling the radicals favored—Ameri*ka*. "We'll have to get out, too, in the end. RAW can make that exit happen faster; that's our opportunity.

"When Ho fought the Japanese in 1944," Hop continued, waxing poetic about his communist hero, "American Army Rangers fought beside him. The man's well-educated; he admires the patriots of the American Revolution. In 1776, the British were the most powerful army in the world, but George Washington and a few ragtag farmers kicked their asses. Ho has always admired how the Americans defeated the British. Did you know, when Vietnam declared independence, Ho copied part of our Declaration?"

Hopkins pulled a wrinkled document out of his pants pocket. "Listen to this. These are the first lines of the Declaration of Independence of the Democratic Republic of Vietnam: 'All men are created equal. They are endowed by their Creator with certain inalienable rights, among them life, liberty, and the pursuit of happiness.'"

"The Vietnamese are just like us," Grace said, her face aglow. "They want their freedom. That's all any of us want. Why can't we see that, and just leave them be? Live and let live."

Tommy didn't think ending the war would be that simple, but he was impressed with Grace's passion. Freedom was what he wanted, too, but that wasn't where fate had been steering him lately. Hop's riff on Amerika's oppression of the freedom-loving people of Vietnam was nothing new. When Tommy was in his teens, living in a Hell's Kitchen tenement, his postal clerk father routinely lectured the family about America's sins: "What this country needs to do," his father liked to say, "is share all of its bounty with all of its citizens. Not according to their abilities, but their needs."

Classic Marxism, Tommy had learned later, when he'd scored his scholarship to Fordham. The agendas of these socialist do-gooders sounded fine in the classroom, but he couldn't see how America would ever voluntarily become an egalitarian place through some kind of peaceful revolution. When it came to combatting the evils of capitalist colonialism, Tommy was more inclined toward direct action. *But it's too early to talk about that.*

Before they split up, Hop had announced his strategy for the next rally, planned for Washington Square on the Fourth of July. They'd attract a lot of students, a big crowd. He wanted to copy the tactics of the civil rights marchers and provoke the cops into beating up the SDSers and the RAW protesters.

"We'll invite the Black Panthers too," Hop said. He predicted that the press would play up any violence that occurred—the front-page pictures of injured protesters would jump-start their cause.

"You lead the way, Tommy," Hop said. "Grace will go in right behind you. Shove your peace signs right up in the pigs' faces."

"Great idea, Hop," Tommy said. He gave Grace a thumbs-up, and she smiled back at him. Finally, the pretentious professor had said something that made sense. Partnering with this dishy girl was something to look forward to—maybe they could have some fun before the army shipped him out.

Makeba chuckled when she heard Hop's plan. "Yeah, I like that, white boy," she said. "We'll see how brave you are going up against New York's finest. Those fuckers are mean; they'll bust you up the side of the head before they even look at you. But it will be good to have the Panthers on our side—those brothers are serious."

As the meeting ended, Tommy had persuaded Grace to meet him that coming Sunday at a coffee shop across from Washington Square to discuss tactics.

He got there early and took the window table that looked out on the park. Grace waltzed through the door right on time, wearing blue jeans, a jean jacket, and a single strand of pearls. She scanned the room, pushed her hair from her eyes, and smiled when she saw him. He got to his feet and held the chair out for her, the way they did it in old movies. Chivalry might be dying, but Tommy enjoyed pretending he was the gallant hero in an old movie.

"That's a good French restaurant across the street," Grace said.

"Do you live near here?" Tommy asked as their coffee came. Grace took cream, three sugars.

"Yes, we've always lived in Manhattan. My dad was an intelligence officer in the war. With the OSS. Then he went to work for Chase Manhattan."

"Isn't that the Rockefellers' bank?"

"Yeah, my dad's a big Republican. He's a deal maker—you know, acquisitions, real estate, that kind of thing."

"So your parents must be rich, right?"

"I guess. Does it matter?" she asked, tugging at her pearls. Tommy thought they looked real, but what did he know.

"Do they know you're a part of RAW—in the movement?"

Grace laughed. "They have no idea what RAW is. They think I'm going back to Barnard in September to study English lit, the romantic poets. They'll freak out when I tell them I'm quitting."

"I'll bet they will," Tommy said. "It costs $5,000 a year and they've already paid for two years." Columbia cost a bundle, so Tommy hadn't bothered to apply.

"So what? They have the money. All they care about is appearances. They want me to finish and go get a job as a gofer for some horny old man in publishing or something. My father thinks about two things—his bank and his sailboat. My mother's into fashion and hosting parties at the house in Watch Hill. She's still pissed I didn't follow her to Sweet Briar. They don't give a damn about real issues. The last thing I want to do is be like them. Romantic poetry's not important. I want to make a difference with my life. Hop taught me that."

"What's the deal with you and the professor? Are you guys an item?"

Grace shrugged. "I mean, we've dated. But Hop says it's not the right time to get super attached, any serious romance will mess up the movement."

"How's that?"

"Well, if you care more about your boyfriend than ending the war or neutralizing the pigs, that's a problem. We have to keep our priorities straight. Don't get me wrong, he likes me. And we're close. But he says it's better for the cell if we share what we have. Hop thinks we should share *everything*, you know what I mean?"

"Like in a commune?" Tommy asked, raising an eyebrow.

"That's the general idea." Tommy sensed she wasn't going to give him a lot of detail. "So if anybody gets too close, too touchy-feely, too worried about what your honey wants for breakfast—then Hop changes things up. Sometimes he passes us around. Not all the time, only once in a while."

Tommy shook his head. He would never share Grace with anybody. Not even once.

"Hop says we can't get too dependent on each other. SDS, RAW, the movement, our cause—all of that has to come first."

"So he forces you to sleep with other people? Even if you don't want to? Hell, you should call the cops."

Grace kept fiddling, pulled at her hoop earrings.

"No, it's not about force. Not really," she said, with a sly smile. "I mean, it's our choice, isn't it? This is the sixties, Tommy. Free love, the pill, flower power. You can read, right? Anything's possible. In RAW we're soldiers too: warriors for peace. If we're serious about ending the war we have to do whatever's necessary, for the greater good."

Maybe Grace is stronger than I thought she was.

Prettier too. He fought off an impulse to move across the table, nuzzle her long pale neck and eat her up, right there, in front of everyone. He paid for the coffee and they walked back down Broadway to Washington Square, chatting about singers they liked. Grace had just seen Bob Dylan at the Green Door, had a little crush on him. She crooned a line from his song, "The Times They Are A-Changing," stretching out the words.

"You have a good voice. You should be in a band."

"Oh, you're so nice, but singing's not my future. We're way too busy now."

They stopped on a park bench to watch some beatniks recite poetry. A guy called Ginsberg was doing a reading, an anti-war poem with a strange title, "Wichita Vortex Sutra #3," about a bunch of Viet Cong dying painful deaths in the red mud.

Tommy didn't want to dwell on that picture. They moved to the other side of the square, tried to work out where the police would set their barricades on the Fourth.

"What should we yell?" Grace asked. "To get the pigs riled up." Her face lit up, as if she'd been waiting her entire life to sling insults at cops.

"I guess 'Make love not war' won't do it."

She laughed. "Nope. They already think we're just crazies who want to wreck the system. They're not interested in peace. Most of them like beating us up."

"How about 'Drop acid not bombs'?"

"Good one, but they'll just laugh. "How about 'Fuck the pigs'? That'll push their buttons. Maybe we'll get lucky, and they'll do something stupid."

"This could get serious," Tommy said. "I don't want you to get hurt. You sure Hop knows what he's doing? He's practically begging the cops to attack us."

"He understands another peaceful parade won't accomplish much," she said, nodding. "We need to go to the next level. I'm ready. We're bombing children over there, for crying out loud!"

Maybe Grace was naive about the war and the real risk that the police would beat their brains out, but she was brave. At least he'd be right beside her, maybe he could protect her. They'd had a course on hand-to-hand combat at Dix, where he'd learned how to blind the enemy by jamming your middle fingers into their eyes. But these cops wore face shields, so that wouldn't work.

They sat down on a bench near some chess players. Grace reached over, ran her fingers over Tommy's hand. He took the chance and put his arm around her, basked in her scent. She moved closer and whispered, her warm breath in his ear. "Relax, Tommy. Go with the flow. This will be fun."

If getting beaten and arrested is fun. Tommy leaned in, kissed her softly. "I don't know, Grace. I think this is better."

5

SHADES OF GRAY

24 JUNE 1967

J.B. Darling squatted behind his golf ball on the ninth hole of the course still maintained by MACV (Military Assistance Command, Vietnam) and tried to get a read on his five-foot putt. He thought it would leak a little right, in the direction of the Saigon River.

"Don't bother," Lieutenant Colonel George Balderamos said, pulling his sweat-soaked shirt down over his bulging paunch. "I got two putts from ten feet to win, so that's a gimme."

"Thanks, I guess," Darling said, picking up his ball and hearing his knees creak. "That squat made me feel like one of those mama-sans chewing on her betel nuts by the side of the road. Got no idea how those women stay down in it so long. This is three wins in a row for you. You're not spending enough time at work."

"Right," Balderamos laughed. "And if I keep giving you five-footers, you'll never make that putt when it matters."

"Mr. Darling," as he was known to friends and colleagues in Saigon (he never used his first name), understood that it was a violation of the ancient rules of golf to pick up a five-foot putt. But every duffer did it, and what was life all about anyway? It was about competing shades of gray. When faced with a decision, ninety-nine percent of the time Darling just picked the shade that seemed most promising in the moment. If he had learned anything in his long career, it was that there were no moral absolutes.

Darling watched as the colonel's ten-footer for birdie teetered on the left side of the hole and dropped.

"That's a thirty-five," Balderamos said. "My handicap must be down to about one."

"You got time for one pop?" Darling asked. Balderamos was one of the last people he wanted to spend time with, but it was hard to find regular partners; most Americans had gotten very busy as the war raged on. Besides, he could be useful.

"Sure, if you're buying," the colonel said. "I always got time for you. We MPs need to have a good relationship with the civil affairs attaché."

Darling laughed. "I like your discretion, Colonel. Some people just love to gossip about who's who over here."

"That's not me," Balderamos said. "They don't put you in charge of Saigon's MPs and the C.I.D. if you can't keep a secret. And I like having friends in high places."

Darling threw his putter on the ground in front of his ten-year-old Vietnamese caddie, who scrambled to pick it up. He mopped his face with his sweat-soaked towel and glanced up at the gathering dark gray clouds. The monsoon season had started; it was ninety-five degrees and would rain buckets soon, ruining the creases in the fresh khaki pants his maid had carefully ironed this morning. He hated looking messy.

He jammed a thick wad of nearly worthless Vietnamese scrip—the equivalent of fifty cents each—into the hands of the two young caddies. They looked happy enough; if he gave them any more, the other golfers would scream that he was destroying the system.

Darling and the colonel walked on to the clubhouse, the gracious villa that faced the ninth green. They took a table under a ceiling fan on the second story veranda that looked out to the wide brown river as it meandered through the city on its way to the South China Sea. *Sông Saigon*, the locals called it.

"This is the first war I've been in that has its own golf course," Darling said. He ordered them gin and tonics and took a moment to admire the vintage sepia-toned photos that graced the walls. The scenes were of French expats strolling Saigon's broad avenues back in the 1930s. These stylish Frogs were turned out all in white and appeared to be on Easy Street. That version of the city looked so inviting—quaint, exotic, peaceful. The Paris of the Orient, they used to call it. He wished he'd lived here then, had been a merchant prince in that quiet colonial world, instead of a frazzled combatant in a complicated war.

"You gotta love the French," Darling said. "They knew how to enjoy life in the colonies. And these villas—such a sense of permanence. This one was built at the turn of the century."

"But it's so damn hot," the colonel said, downing his highball in two gulps. He reached in front of Darling and palmed half the peanuts from a glass bowl. "I can see why they left."

What a slob. "Yeah, but they took siestas then. Life was slower," Darling said, picking up the bowl. "More peanuts?"

The colonel shook his head, his mouth still full.

Darling cleared his throat and got to the point. "Could I ask a favor?"

"Sure, but don't think I'm giving you any strokes."

"I'd never ask. But I might need some help, to listen to a few people. It's gotta be done quietly, a special job."

"Discretion's my middle name," the colonel said, looking thrilled to be asked.

Darling stifled a laugh. *How'd this bozo ever make colonel?*

6

OFF THE PIGS

04 JULY 1967

It was the Fourth of July, and Tommy was up early on his rare day off. He never slept well in the barracks at Dix—their bunk room was noisy and their NCO tormentors kept too many lights on. All night long you could hear men coughing, snoring, bed clothes moving, the occasional cry of someone's nightmare.

At 0700 he was in his VW on his way to Manhattan and wishing he had a coffee. It was hot and overcast, but at least it wasn't raining. He was in no mood to go march in another downpour; the drill instructors did that to them every time it rained. Part of him wished he had the balls to pick up Grace, spirit her away, and rent a room somewhere.

The RAW cell members had assembled in Washington Square with a large group of SDSers to double-check their tactics. When Tommy arrived, Hop handed him a long two-by-two wooden beam. "Staple your sign to this. Some people use plastic, but it's flimsy. If you're gonna mix it up with riot police, your wooden beam's the better choice."

Tommy spotted Grace standing next to the makeshift stage that had been mounted on sawhorses and walked over, "Who are all these people?" he asked.

The crowd looked like they expected a rock concert. Tommy took in all the long hair, bandannas, flowing skirts. People had brought their guitars and their dogs and were passing joints around, right out in the open.

"Those are the SDSers," Grace said, touching his shoulder. "We don't know most of them. Isn't it exciting? Things keep getting bigger and bigger!"

She handed Tommy a heavy-duty stapler and they began attaching their "PEACE NOW!" signs to the wooden posts.

They heard the roar of motorcycle engines over on Broadway. A convoy of twenty Black men riding Harley Davidsons came rumbling down the avenue. They rolled over the curb into the park and pulled onto the grass right in front of Hop, revving their engines.

The big, bearded guy on the first bike dismounted and extended his hand. Hop hesitated for a long moment and then took it.

"Lavarious Prince," the man said. He had a deep voice; if he'd been a preacher he wouldn't need a mic. "You Professor Hopkins?" Lavarious asked.

Tommy guessed Lavarious was at least six-five—broad shoulders, built like an NFL tackle. He looked primed for combat in his black leathers with silver buckles. He'd topped it off with a red beret that sported the Panthers' symbol, the clenched fist.

Lavarious pointed at the improvised sawhorse stage. "So is that your . . . ?" he asked.

Hop nodded.

Lavarious grinned. "Looks like it could collapse."

"No, no, it'll be fine," Hop said, looking uncertain now. "Thank you for coming, Lavarious. Here's the agenda: I'll speak first and then introduce you. You've got three minutes to touch on your points, then you throw it back to me. I'll rally the troops and then we march through the cops, down Broadway to the federal buildings."

"That's your plan?" Lavarious asked, frowning. "You kick it off, talk for as long as you want and then feed me a few crumbs? A whole three minutes? You gotta be shittin' me." He opened his arms to his fellow Black Panthers. "Me and the brothers got an entire program to talk about: full employment, better education, safe housing, an end to police brutality. I can't do that in three minutes."

"This protest is about the war," Hop said. "We can't waste time on full employment."

Tommy nudged Grace and whispered, "Hop's over his head now. That Panther might kill him before the cops even get here."

"You're right about that, sunshine," Makeba said. She'd moved in close, right behind Hop—she couldn't stop smiling whenever Lavarious spoke.

"The cops are here," Grace said, pointing to the vans and mounted police officers arriving across the street.

"I respect your position, man," Hop said to Lavarious. "Really, I do."

Tommy noticed that the professor reserved the use of "man" as a form of address only when talking to Black people—it showed he was hip, and oh so sincere. It was only natural that the competing agendas would clash, and now Tommy was watching it happen.

"You think we want to hear some two-hour speech on Vietnam?" Lavarious asked. "How too many White people are dying? What about the Black people who are getting killed every day, right here at home? What about Emmett Till and all the rest? You give a shit about those brothers?

"As for Vietnam, we got one demand: Black men should be exempt from serving. Period. Why should we support the military of a hostile nation, the nation that enslaved us? It's been a hundred years since Emancipation. You're the history expert, so you know that. And you still don't treat us as equals. I got two words for you, Professor: Fuck you and your war."

"Lavarious, Lavarious," Hop said, shaking his head. "Listen to me . . . We understand that Black people have suffered a lot, but we need to stay on point here."

"I'll show you what's on point," Lavarious said, wrenching the portable bullhorn out of Hop's hand.

Hop tried again. "Of course we understand that the racist pigs have enslaved you unfortunate Black people for far too long," he said. Tommy had to admire Hop's ability to be so condescending. He apparently had no fear that these "unfortunate people" might kick his ass around the block. "Listen, my friend, don't lose sight of what our real goal is today—we need to turn ordinary Americans against the war. Don't you get it? The Vietnam War is a racist thing too. Black men are getting drafted, wounded, and killed at a much higher rate than Whites. The United States Army thinks you *negroes* are just cannon fodder."

Lavarious towered over Hop, grabbed him by the shoulders, pulled him in close, and roared, "Fodder? We're *Black men*, you honky!"

"My fault," Hop said, wiping spittle off his cheeks. "But you must see it . . . You all are the real *victims* of this war. That's why I should speak first. This illegal war is America's number one issue. Ordinary Americans need to hear how we can end it. We're Rage Against the War, man. We gotta get the public on our side."

"You just spouting bullshit. No way I'm speaking second. That war you been raving about is 12,000 miles away. We gotta get people to care about racism *here*. I mean, now we have the vote, yeah, but we got no real power. Whitey has all the power. We got to burn Whitey down.

"We got to arm ourselves, fight back, and bust the system. So fuck your war protest."

"I understand, Laborious," Hop said, so rattled now that he butchered the man's name. "But we'll have more impact today if we present a unified front."

Tommy wondered if that was possible.

"What universe you in, ofay? You gonna tell the brothers what racism is? You just an arrogant, stuck-up prick. Stick to lecturing about what you think racism is at your lily white uni-ver-sity, Hopscotch."

"Yeah, Hop," Makeba said, shaking the end of her peace sign dangerously close to her mentor's eyes. "You out of your depth here. Way, way out."

Lavarious turned, bumping Hop out of the way with his shoulder. No spoiled prig who'd parachuted in from his Ivy League tower was going to censor him. He leapt onto the stage with the bullhorn to address the crowd.

"The Black man—the Black man!—he's a prisoner in his own land!"

Tommy put his arm around Grace as they watched the scene unfold. "Lavarious is on a roll," he said.

Lavarious started to chant and the crowd picked it up:

"The Revolution has come.
Time to pick up the gun!
Off the pigs! Off the pigs!"

Tommy looked over at the line of cops. They'd moved into the square, the blue line of riot police standing shoulder to shoulder with their big black truncheons, and the mounted policemen backing them up. They were all focused on Lavarious—Tommy figured they were itching to attack him. The big man kept talking:

"This is just a warm-up, my people. Listen up, pigs! We comin' for you!"

Lavarious grinned, tossed the bullhorn at Hop's head, and joined his brothers for a last-minute pep talk.

Hop watched him go, shook his head, and sighed. Tommy walked over and patted Hop on the shoulder. "He's never gonna do what you want."

Hop glared at him. "No shit, Tommy. Aren't you observant? Let's hope the uppity negro keeps it to ten minutes."

By noon the battle lines had formed, both sides itching for action. Tommy stood in the midst of a few hundred protesters massed in front of the makeshift stage the SDSers and RAW had thrown together. They started with protest songs, the Pete Seeger favorites: "We Shall Overcome," "Turn! Turn! Turn!" and "If I Had A Hammer."

Carrying their signs, Tommy and Grace moved to the front line of the demonstrators. "Hold it like this, Grace," Tommy showed her, holding the beam out in front of him at a forty-five degree angle, like a knight wielding a lance in an ancient joust.

"I think we're outnumbered," he added, pointing to the rank of police officers who'd formed two solid lines on the south and west sides of Washington Square.

Grace grabbed his arm. "Now I'm not so sure how much fun this is going to be," she said.

"They're probably scared too," Tommy said, patting her hand.

Besides their sidearms, the cops carried riot batons and pepper spray. Tommy noticed most of them had gas masks hanging from their saddles—he guessed the cops must have tear gas canisters somewhere. A few men stood at port arms with rifles; he couldn't imagine that they'd ever use them.

Lavarious arranged his Panthers in a military-style formation in front of the stage and grabbed the bullhorn, which Hop hadn't touched since Lavarious threw it at him.

"Brothers and sisters, a great man once said, 'Power cedes nothing without a demand.' In our world, Whitey has the power, all of it! And Whitey will never give up a thing—not one! It's time to grab that power, rip it OFF these honkies.

"So let's start, right now, right here! Join me when I say:

"End racism now!
"Black jobs now!
"Safe housing now!
"Black Power now!"

With one voice, the crowd rose to the moment, the chant reverberating across Washington Square. Grace pointed to the curious shoppers who'd stopped across the street to see what the ruckus was. "They're paying attention," she said. A few parents hustled their children away from the scene.

"The Revolution is here!
"It's time to pick up the gun!
"Black Power now!
"Off the pigs! Off the pigs!"

The crowd picked it up, screaming "Off the pigs! Off the pigs!" The mass of demonstrators jumped up and down with their signs and began moving toward the police line, gaining momentum. Tommy and Grace were swept into the maelstrom.

"Wait, wait, my people!" Hop yelled into the bullhorn. His voice was small, muffled—Tommy could barely hear him. He fumbled with a switch, tried to turn it back on.

"This is an illegal protest." The words boomed across the park from the cops' truck-borne sound system. You could probably hear them in Brooklyn. "You people have no permit. You are breaking the law. Clear the park now! Or we'll clear it for you."

"Here they come," Tommy said. Instead of waiting to see if the ragtag crowd of hippies would back off, the line of riot police advanced across the park, clubs at the ready. A small contingent of Black Panthers, armed with End Racism Now! signs, charged the cops' left flank. The vanguard surged forward and smashed their two-by-two shafts against the shields and helmets of the police. "Let's go!" Tommy yelled—he and Grace sprinted after them.

He glanced back and saw the rest of the SDSers charge, everyone caught up in it now. The demonstrators plunged ahead and collided with the police, swinging their wooden beams against the cops' shields. In his peripheral vision Tommy saw a big cop brush Grace's stick out of the way with his left hand and whack her with his baton. Two blows to her body, one to the temple. Grace collapsed in a pile at his feet.

"Stay down!" Tommy yelled. He charged the bully cop, his beam extended as far as he could reach. Lavarious arrived before he could get there, hit the cop with a rolling cross-body block and bowled him over. The cop started to get up but Makeba swung her sign like a baseball bat, nailing the officer on the side of the head. Several protesters rushed in, kicking him while he was down. Tommy dropped his sign so he could help Grace.

Grace rolled in the grass, moaning and holding her head, blood running down the left side of her face. Tommy picked her up, grabbing her from behind, and half-carried, half-dragged her to safety across 12th Street. No cops in this direction. He held her against the wall of an apartment building, pulled off his T-shirt and wrapped it around her head to stanch the bleeding. He hugged her for a minute or two, feeling her rock against him, and then they limped north, up Broadway.

"Tommy, I think you saved me," Grace said. She was still crying, but managed a weak smile.

"Lucky we got out of there. They could have killed you! We need ice."

He bought two bags at a deli on 13th Street and they sat down on the curb to rest and take stock. The riot continued; they could hear shouts and sirens in the distance. Grace's wound was still bleeding. He dabbed at it with his shirt: "You need to go to the ER."

They got a cab up to Bellevue where the on-duty doc, a young woman close to Tommy's age, used twelve stitches to close the swelling wound that zigzagged down toward Grace's cheek. No concussion though. "Your friend just needs rest."

Grace sat shaking on the examination table, touching her big bandage. "Is this going to scar?"

"Maybe a little," the ER doc said. "But just a thin red line, I think. Makeup will take care of it, or you can grow your hair." She left to deal with a stabbing.

"Those cops are such bastards," Grace said. "I can't believe they did that to us. They're like Nazis."

"Do you want me to take you back to 4th Street?" Tommy asked.

"No, I won't get any sleep there. I better go to my mother's."

"Where's she live?"

"Gramercy Park. Not far."

"Ritzy. You want them to see you like this? What will you say?"

"Nothing. They're traveling. In Europe. Will you stay with me, Tommy?" Grace reached over and kissed him on the cheek, her hands on his head, lingering there.

"You bet," Tommy said. "Whatever you need, I'm there."

He looked down at their clothes. They were both smeared with blood, her blood. *We're like brothers in arms.*

7

THE TWENTY GRAND

06 JULY 1967

Ben and his partner, Sergeant Elijah B. Jackson from Queens, New York, were heading out of MP headquarters for their jeep when Lt. Col. George Balderamos bustled in, fifteen minutes late for the pre-curfew briefing.

"Listen up men!" the colonel yelled to the thirty MPs standing around the small room packed with radios that was the MPs' TOC—Tactical Operations Center. "As you've all heard, the Roxy Theater on Tu Do Street was bombed at 2300 last night. Three GIs died, a lot more were wounded. This happened while we were supposedly enforcing the curfew. Nobody saw a thing, nada, zilch." He glared at Ben and Elijah. "I know you'd rather play at being a detective, Lieutenant, but that's not your real job."

Balderamos was the commanding officer of the 18th MP battalion, a lifer who'd signed up for the army when he was eighteen to get out of

Puerto Rico. He was only in his late thirties, but he was already twenty-five pounds beyond his ideal weight and losing his hair.

"Your number one mission is to enforce the curfew," the colonel said. "*Strictly. No exceptions.* From 2200 to 0600. So why was a movie even playing that late? Why were there American soldiers in there watching the damn thing? Why didn't you ass wipes shut it down?"

Silence in the room. After several dress-downs, Ben and the others had learned it was better to let the colonel have his little fits, wait him out.

"I got three years to go in this army," Balderamos said. "Then I'm retired, out of here on half pay, moving back to Dorado Beach. There's no way I'll let you clowns spoil the pinnacle of my career. So when you get out there tonight, make damn sure there's not a single soldier left in the bars come 2200 hours. Got it? You're dismissed."

Ben fought back a laugh, gave Elijah an eye roll.

"You think Baldy lost his hair or his balls first?" Elijah asked when they got outside. The colonel was famous for rarely leaving the safety of the office, except to suck up to his superiors at the daily MACV briefing—the five o'clock follies—or hack around the army's golf course two afternoons a week with some embassy guys.

"His balls had to be first," Ben said. "Baldy's no leader. He's starting to look like a fat monk, but he's not one of the benign ones."

Elijah laughed. Ben's partner had a big personality, his smile could warm up a room. Back in New York, Elijah had tested into one of the city's most elite schools—the Bronx High School of Science. Since he was almost six feet tall and 180 pounds of muscle, he'd earned the starting safety slot on the BHS football team. He graduated with honors but skipped college and joined the army.

"Why'd you enlist?" Ben had asked him on their first patrol.

"There was no money for college," Elijah said. "My dad left us when I was three. My mom was a maid for this rich lady out in Manhasset. We had a three bedroom in Far Rockaway. We lived with my grandma—she's the secretary at our local A.M.E. church. Love that place. I sing bass in the choir. Or I used to."

"Did you want to be an MP?"

"Nah," Elijah said. "My experiences with cops haven't been exactly positive. I was into computers in high school. Wanted to work on IBM mainframes. The recruiter told me they'd send me to school, teach me how to program them."

"But they didn't."

"You know the answer," Elijah had said. "The army needs bodies behind rifles, not keyboards."

After Baldy's speech, Ben and Elijah made a modest effort to follow his instructions and headed over to Tu Do Street in their jeep.

Hundreds of GIs were crowded into the twenty or so bars that lined the street. Every few minutes a wave of drunken soldiers would burst out through the doors, spilling the drinks in their hands as the bar girls climbed all over them.

"Looks like the party has already started, boss," Elijah said as they idled at the curb. "Where you wanna start?"

"Let's hit the Twenty Grand. It's a tad more civilized."

"Nothing on this street is civilized," Elijah said. The Twenty Grand was Tu Do's biggest bar, at the epicenter of the action. It was cleaner and more upscale than a lot of the joints; the polished mahogany bar was sixty feet long and the drinks cost twenty percent more than the tawdrier places, but there were comfortable chairs and the Grand booked the best Vietnamese cover bands.

Elijah drove their jeep up onto the sidewalk; they climbed out and pushed through the swinging doors to find themselves in the middle of a fist fight.

"You're five hundred bucks short!" a burly master sergeant yelled as he grabbed a short, big-eared private by his collar, lifted him off the floor, and threw him across the room. The hapless GI slid to a stop when he banged his head against the bottom of the bar.

"Whoa!" Ben yelled. The sergeant turned toward the door just as Elijah tackled him, driving his shoulder into the guy's neck. Ben pulled the private to his feet, jammed him up against the bar, and handcuffed him to the brass rail that ran along the top. The crowd backed off as Elijah put a chokehold on the sergeant, dragged him across the room, and dumped him in a lounge chair and stood over him, his hand on his .45.

"This party's over!" Ben yelled to the crowded room. "It's 2230, you're all breaking curfew. Get the hell out of here, back to your hooches."

Nobody moved.

"Get moving! Now!" Elijah shouted. His deep baritone filled the room, got the crowd moving. "Before we call the calvary and ship every swinging dick here to the LBJ Ranch." That was shorthand for the Long Binh Stockade, where the MPs stuffed the curfew breakers who were dumb enough to get violent.

The GIs mumbled their goodbyes to the girls and began straggling out.

Ben leaned over the bar. "What's going on here, Madame Thuy?" The handsome woman in a pristine white áo dài with gold trim shook her head. Ben was a regular at the Twenty Grand; he often stopped for a drink in the early morning after a graveyard shift, liked to chat with Thuy. She knew all the Saigon gossip, had run the place since the 1950s when the French were still here.

Thuy gestured toward the man Ben had cuffed to the bar. "This one not so smart," she said. "He talk this master sergeant into writing him an order for second R&R, then he go spend two weeks in Hong Kong with his buddy. So first he break R&R rules and now he AWOL too. But he forget to pay sergeant all the bribes before he leave, and now he broke. He spend everything he have on Chinese girls in Kowloon. Those girls more expensive than ours."

"He got two R&Rs?" Elijah asked from a few feet away. "Where do I sign up for that?" To boost morale, the army had decreed that during his yearlong tour, every GI was entitled to an all-expenses paid six-day trip to the Pacific paradise of his choice—Bangkok, Hong Kong, Honolulu, Penang, or Sydney. Ben figured it was just another way the army liked to screw with your head, plucking you out of a combat zone and flying you to a beach for six days. But every single soldier took one. It subtracted six days from the time the enemy had available to kill you. R&Rs were so popular now that bent NCOs were selling them, apparently.

"Thank you, Madame Thuy," Ben said. "I appreciate the straight story."

She smiled at him, and Ben wondered how old she was. Fifty? She was still very beautiful. He walked over to the master sergeant, who was still rubbing his neck. "How much did you charge that troop for the second R&R?"

"A thousand bucks," the sergeant said, scowling. "I would have let the second five hundred go, but when he decided to take his buddy with him the lieutenant wouldn't sign the order unless I gave him a bigger cut."

"What the hell are you running, a crime syndicate?" Ben asked. The scope of corruption never ceased to amaze him. It reached from the highest-ranking ARVN generals and government officials down through the ranks and infected transactions at every level. The police, civilians, now even American soldiers—it seemed as if everyone was working some scam to profit off the war.

"Okay, Madame Thuy, we're going to throw these lame fools in the jeep and drop them off at the LBJ, let the JAG lawyers sort this one out. But please . . . just try to respect the curfew, will you? Makes our jobs a lot easier."

"Oh I try do that, Lieutenant Kin-Kay," Madame Thuy said with a wink. "But I have to make living, you know."

8

ADVENTURE TOURISM

06 JULY 1967

Two days after the Washington Square protest that had devolved into a riot, the RAW cell's members met with twenty SDSers who fought the cops with them, everyone crammed into the tiny 4th Street apartment. Grace sat in her same spot on the beat-up couch; she had a black eye in addition to her stitches but seemed in good spirits, and she lit up when Tommy came through the door. Looking around the crowded room, Tommy noticed a long brown leather case propped up in the corner. He decided to say something before Hopkins could get rolling.

"Well, that was a disaster," Tommy said, looking straight at Hop, trying out his *no fear* face.

"It certainly was," Hop said, surprising Tommy by agreeing. "We may have to reexamine our plans for joint actions. Maybe the Panthers aren't the best fit for us."

Makeba gave Hop one of her looks, brown eyes flashing. "That's bullshit, Hop. You just don't like Lavarious stepping on your toes."

It occurred to Tommy that if the Panthers got more involved with RAW, Makeba might turn on Hopkins.

"Sorry, Makeba," Hop said, "but this alliance isn't working. The Panthers want to reform our entire society, while we just want to end the war. Very different goals. I—scratch that, I mean we . . . we managed to get some attention on Saturday, it just wasn't the right kind."

The headline in the *Daily News* on Sunday morning was "Thugs Run Amok in Village." The *Times* had been more temperate: "Black Panthers Disrupt War Protest March." The subhead read: "Fifteen Students, Three Officers Injured; Police Struggle to Keep the Peace."

"No real discussion of the war," Hop said, waving the *Daily News* cover. "Not much about SDS, and those lazy reporters still don't have a clue what RAW is. The *Times* printed the Panthers' demands, but not ours. That asshole Lavarious knew exactly what he was doing. He was chanting 'Off the pigs' before I could even open my mouth. All he ever wanted was a riot."

"But so did you," Tommy said. "Lavarious took what he wanted when he had the chance. Just like most people."

"He won't be taking anything from me next time," Hop said, his face flushed. "Because there's not going to be a next time."

"I hate to admit it," said Makeba, "but our sunshine soldier here is right. That brother is a force of nature. Don't blow him off, Hop. The man's got charisma—a lot like you. He can help us. We just need to show him some respect."

"What an idiotic idea," Hop said, rolling his eyes.

Makeba flinched.

Not a good idea to insult her.

"There's gotta be other ways to get attention," Tommy said, gesturing at Grace. "Why not have Grace talk to the press, do some interviews while she's all bandaged up. Let the reporters see what those vicious pigs did to her."

"I love that idea," Grace said, getting to her feet. "Let's show the world that women aren't afraid to fight for the cause too. Remember the Trung sisters."

"All right," Hop said, a bit too reluctantly. "I'll arrange something." Grace glanced at Tommy, caught his eye with a little smile. He wondered if Hop noticed, he didn't want him to think they were an item. Deborah, the redhead Tommy had met his first night in their safe house, reclined on one end of the couch, her usual spot. She stared at Grace; maybe she'd picked up the covert smile.

Hop said RAW's members had to discuss strategy and dismissed the SDSers. Tommy watched the ragtag group—many nursing injuries—drift out.

"I have to say this, Hop," Deborah said when they'd left and it was just the six of them again. "That was a dangerous scene in the park." Tommy had noticed Deborah didn't speak often, but when she did it was something worth listening to. "Those pigs on horseback nearly trampled Carleton and me. We got gassed, too. We won't be able to stop anything if we're dead."

"Yeah," Carleton said with a dreamy smile, "that was far out." It was only ten in the morning and he was already high.

"Took a whole day for my eyes to calm down," Makeba said. "At least tear gas is color blind. The cops were coughing so hard I thought some pig would croak right there."

"Listen, *Patience*," Hop said, the wise father lecturing his kids, "being in the movement means we have to take a few risks, even suffer a tiny bit. Get over it."

"Who's Patience?" Tommy asked.

"I am," Makeba said. "My mother's idea. That's what it says on my birth certificate, Patience Mae Jefferson. By the time I was five, Mom was long gone. My grandmother in D.C. raised me. She loved African music, especially Miriam Makeba. So when I turned eighteen, I changed my name—to just Makeba, no last name."

"That's cool, unique," Tommy said. He wanted to ask what happened to her mother, but not now. "So Hop, what's that?" Tommy nodded toward the corner of the room. "In the long leather case?"

"A prized possession. It's a shotgun. My father gave it to me for my sixteenth birthday. A hand-me-down, but a good one. Made in Italy by Beretta, the oldest corporation in the world. An over-and-under double barrel, very valuable. Pop used it to shoot skeet. Sometimes pheasants, but mostly sporting clays."

"What you use it for?"

"I'm working on that."

Tommy thought about probing but didn't want to press Hop with all the others here. "Did I tell you my news?" Tommy asked. "I got my orders—I'm shipping out to Nam in two weeks. There's got to be some way I can help you guys."

"We need to stay in touch," Hop said. "I'll keep you up to date, give you a number to call too. They let you use the phone, right?"

"I guess. The army doesn't care much about our personal communication needs. I'll probably have to call collect."

"That's no problem." Hop never seemed to worry about money. "If you sense any opportunities over there, give me a jingle. Maybe we can send a courier, nail down the details."

"A courier? To Vietnam? Are you kidding?"

"Why not?" Hop asked. "I read in the *Times* that South Vietnam is still a tourist destination. Twenty thousand vacationers a year, in spite of the war. They call people who go over there 'adventure tourists.'"

"That's one way to look at it," Tommy said. "It ain't Disneyland though."

9

PROUD TO SERVE

10 JULY 1967

Ben had been in-country nearly six months when Lt. Col. Balderamos announced that the Secretary of Defense, the Honorable Robert McNamara, was flying in for one of his periodic briefings and a tour of outlying bases.

The colonel had been in the office since 0700 but hadn't stirred from his desk. His bulky frame was bent over the latest edition of *Time* magazine, the nation's leading newsweekly. *Time* arrived in the office from the States on Thursdays, and Baldy usually studied it for at least an hour. "That's how he knows what to say to the VIPs he plays golf with," Elijah had said.

At 0800 Ben and Elijah stood stiffly at parade rest in the colonel's office—chins up, shoulders back, hands clasped behind their backs. No particular reason to do so, other than the colonel's penchant for spit, polish, and rigid bullshit. They kept quiet while he explained the mission: "The secretary likes to see how the war is going, firsthand."

To show how serious he was about McNamara's visit, the colonel stuffed the magazine (which he never shared) back in his top drawer.

"The DOD needs extra bodies—additional security when the secretary goes visiting. So I'm nominating you two swinging dicks."

Ben and Elijah would be part of McNamara's entourage and travel up country to III Corps with the secretary of defense, the U.S. ambassador, MACV's commanding general, Prime Minister Manh, and the international press corps.

Ben suppressed a smile—it would be fun to get out of Saigon for a day. He was grateful for the relative safety of his usual assignment, but curfew duty could get boring.

"Don't try to take any initiative out there, Lieutenant," Balderamos said to Ben. "I realize that because you went to a fancy college—Georgetown, was it?—you think you're a whole lot smarter than the rest of us. But remember this, *Kinkaid*. Your hotshot college don't mean bupkes over here. So when you're out with the secretary just do what you're fucking told and keep everyone happy. If the DOD guys want you to bring them coffee, smile and go get it. If they want you to wipe their asses, smile and go get the toilet paper. Of course you won't find any TP out there—just a scrap or two of an old newspaper. And be careful," he said with a laugh, "the ink on it is runny.

"Your motto is just smile. *Comprende*, Lieutenant?"

"Yes, sir," Ben said. He looked at Elijah and they saluted the colonel and left. It was better to keep face time with Baldy to a minimum.

At 0600, two days later, Ben and Elijah joined the DOD security detail at Tan Son Nhut and watched the sun rise, an hour before Secretary of Defense McNamara was scheduled to land. The plan called for the secretary to confer with Ambassador Stevens at the airport and then fly on to Cam Ranh Bay to inspect the huge logistics base American forces were building there. After a short speech to those troops, they would helicopter to the market town of Ban Me Thuot and then drive the last fifty kilometers to visit a strategic hamlet.

The strategic hamlet plan was modeled on Sir Robert Thompson's strategy in the 1950s, when the Brits beat back a Communist insurgency in Malaya. It called for the U.S. to arm the inhabitants of remote villages and train them to resist attacks. The VC frequently infiltrated small settlements and then kidnapped or murdered anyone they suspected of collaborating with the enemy; the dissenters were often buried alive. American planners assumed that once a hamlet had been fortified, it would be much harder for the VC to seize it.

If the enemy did attack, villagers could radio for help and the insurgents would be met by overwhelming force from ARVN or American troops. This way the allies would be able to deploy conventional forces to defeat guerrilla tactics. A promising idea, but Ben wondered whether it would work in practice.

That morning the crowd on the tarmac at Tan Son Nhut had swelled to one hundred and fifty. There was a ton of security: plainclothes DOD men augmented by MPs and the Vietnamese National Police, dubbed the "White Mice" for their dazzling, short-sleeved shirts. They were feared and hated and known for torturing prisoners. Sometimes, after the VC had spilled their guts, the White Mice shoved them into helicopters and chucked them out the open gun door at 3,000 feet to finish the job.

Ben noticed a lot of armed Americans who were obviously part of the security detail, but he had no idea who they worked for. He'd discovered there were thousands of mysterious American civilians working in Vietnam.

Nguyen Van Manh, the South Vietnamese prime minister who was always being interviewed in *Stars and Stripes*, the army's newspaper, emerged from a hangar to join several generals and a gaggle of other bureaucrats waiting for the secretary. The press corps was penned up behind a temporary barrier; Ben guessed McNamara didn't want to take questions.

"This looks like a classic clusterfuck to me, Lieutenant," Elijah said. "Most of these bureaucrats are just in Nam for the hazard pay."

"You know what the great Admiral Hyman Rickover said about bureaucracies, Elijah?"

"The submarine guy? No, Louie, I ain't got a clue. I wanted to be a computer guy, not a historian. What difference does it make, anyway . . . sir?"

"He said, 'If you're gonna sin, sin against God, not the bureaucracy. God will forgive you, but the bureaucracy won't.'"

"Good one, sir."

Ben suspected his habit of quoting great leaders could be annoying, but Elijah usually indulged him. He hoped it wasn't because of his rank.

The day before, Ben had talked Balderamos into adding the MP unit's interpreter, ARVN Sergeant Tran Van Duc, to their assignment. Duc was a tidy, fastidious man who'd grown up in Cholon, the ethnic Chinese suburb of Saigon. He was in his late twenties, spoke serviceable English, and had a wry sense of humor.

"How's your war going, Sergeant Duc?" Ben had asked Duc, not long after they'd met.

"Oh, Lieutenant Kin-Kay, my war number ten! Very bad."

"Why is that? I mean, you're bopping around Saigon with me and Sergeant Jackson. You're not trapped in a combat unit crawling through elephant grass every day."

"You not know how ARVN soldiers treat me. My war terrible. It because I am Chinese. That why they hate me."

"So what? You grew up in Vietnam, right?"

"True," Duc said. "But you no understand. All Vietnamese hate all Chinese people. Because of past."

"What past?"

"Chinese invade Vietnam, beaucoup times. Vietnamese people, they never forget. So all ARVNs hate Sergeant Duc too. My job always number ten. Hard to be good interpreter. Every day, ARVN call me Chinese scum."

"They do?" Ben said. He had no idea that the South Vietnamese hated the Chinese. For years he'd heard prominent politicians in the States, from the president on down, drone on about how a monolithic force of Vietnamese and Chicoms threatened South Vietnam and by extension, America. That was the domino theory: If South Vietnam fell, Cambodia would be next, then Laos, Thailand, and the rest of Southeast Asia. That's why we were here. How's that happen if the Vietnamese hate the Chinese?

"When you were growing up, did you trust the U.S. government?" Ben had asked Elijah after Duc had gone home.

"Not exactly," Elijah said. "You've noticed that I'm Black, right, Louie? We're living a different experience."

Ben had grown up pretty much believing whatever the U.S. government said. He'd assumed—without thinking much about it—that America's leaders told people the truth, at least most of the time.

"Why didn't you trust them?" Ben asked, realizing that it was probably a stupid question. When he'd come of age in the late fifties and early sixties, the District of Columbia was in many ways a segregated city; Ben didn't know many Black people.

"Take your pick," Elijah had said, with a rueful laugh. "They said we were free, but they wouldn't let us vote. We still can't get loans, it's hard to own a business, our schools are shit, and sometimes the cops beat us up for fun. That's still the way it is. So no, I don't always trust the government."

"Then think about what Duc was saying," Ben said. "Hell, if our government's lying about its rationale for a major war, what else would they lie about?"

Back on the tarmac at Tan Son Nhut, Ben studied the crowd of VIPs as they waited for McNamara to arrive. He was glad they'd brought Duc along—maybe he could tell them something about what the ARVN bigwigs really thought. He was beginning to understand that in this ever-more-complicated conflict, everyone had an agenda.

Ben spotted U.S. Ambassador Graham Stevens, a tall, spare New Englander; he was in an intense conversation with a trim, forty-something American with a buzz cut. The civilian (if he was one) wore khakis, aviator sunglasses, and a white, short-sleeved shirt with little ruffles down the front, one of those Cuban numbers you never tucked in. Ben walked over to one of the DOD security men. "Who's the guy in the powwow with the ambassador?"

"Not sure. Has an office right down the hall from Stevens though, so he must be somebody important."

Tran Thu Do, the ARVN commanding general, joined the Americans. There were no introductions, they all knew each other. Prime Minister Manh spoke some English and smiled a lot at the ambassador. The mysterious American summoned a woman standing nearby, perhaps an interpreter: "Lien, could you join us, please?"

An attractive young Vietnamese woman in a white áo dài and black silk slacks hurried over. Her hair was in a short bob, the style well-educated Vietnamese women in the South Vietnamese government had begun to adopt. General Do paused every few moments as she translated.

Ben moved closer to watch. The woman was calm, very self-assured, and as she spoke, he was struck again by how bizarre the Vietnamese language sounded to Western ears; one word with the same letters could mean six different things, depending on which of the six tones the speaker imparted to it. As the ARVN officer went on, the American civilian in the frilly shirt who'd been jawing with the U.S. ambassador looked skeptical, maybe even contemptuous.

Then the DOD public affairs officer who'd been busy shooing

the press away from the brass announced that Secretary McNamara would land in five minutes. Ben and Elijah hustled to their assigned positions. They heard a roar to the north. Two F-4 Phantoms swept in low over the field, followed by five Cobra attack helicopters. They clattered over the airport's perimeter in a tight line, machine guns at the ready. Ben watched, awed as usual by the display of American air power. *Thank God we control the skies.*

Two minutes later, a blue-and-white Boeing 707 dropped out of the clouds in a steep descent, banked a sharp right, and landed hard with its wheels smoking. The 707 taxied right up next to their security line. Ben's gaze settled on the words emblazoned on its fuselage—UNITED STATES OF AMERICA—the most powerful nation on earth. He shivered at the sight; he was proud, at least in this moment, to play his small part in his country's service.

The secretary emerged from the door of the plane and paused at the top of the mobile staircase to wave at the crowd. Then he jogged down, looking fresh and rested in his starched khakis with the American flag embroidered over his heart. His hair was slicked straight back and parted near the middle, the way men styled it in the Roaring Twenties.

With his rimless glasses, McNamara had the determined, bulldog look of an accountant eager to scour someone's books for tiny discrepancies. He'd apparently been a "whiz kid" in his previous job as CFO of the Ford Motor Company, and Ben thought he looked the part.

Ambassador Stevens stepped briskly forward to welcome him, and then Prime Minister Manh saluted and shook the secretary's hand. Manh was decked out in a white leather flight jacket, black pants, and red socks, matched by a red kerchief around his neck. *Time* magazine had said Manh often resembled "a saxophone player in a second-rate nightclub." Ben thought that was about right.

After a short meeting in the nearby hangar, the trio reappeared and climbed aboard the lead C-130 for the flight north. Ben, Elijah, and Duc found places in the rear of the aircraft in the olive-green hammock-style seats that hung from the bare steel of the fuselage. As Ben struggled to clip his safety belt, the young female interpreter slipped into the seat beside him. Duc said something to her in Vietnamese; she responded warmly, and they chattered away like warblers. Ben thought the singsong tones of the Vietnamese language were charming when you took the time to listen.

"You two know each other?" Ben asked.

"Yes, we go same school," Duc said. "For English."

"I am Le Thi Lien," the woman said. She held her head high, sounding formal and proud. Lien extended her hand. Ben took it, touched the ends of her fingers. He bowed briefly, the way he'd seen other Vietnamese do when introduced to a stranger. He caught a bit of her scent—jasmine, maybe? Lien looked cool, smooth, composed. She wore a touch of lipstick. *Beautiful.*

"Who do you work for, Lien?" he asked.

"Mr. Darling. He is civil affairs attaché, with USAID, in U.S. Embassy." She nodded toward the guy up front in the Cuban shirt who was still next to the ambassador.

"Have you been to Cam Ranh Bay before?"

"Oh, yes. Mr. Darling and me, we travel a lot. All over Vietnam."

"That must be interesting."

She nodded. "Yes. It is. When there is no danger, of course."

"Is Mr. Darling a good boss? A good man to work for?"

"Of course." Lien smiled, the kind of smile that suggested she knew a lot more about her boss than she was ever going to tell Ben or any other American . . . or maybe any other human.

"Mr. Darling very good to work for. He is—*comment dit-on, en Anglais*—hard? No, demanding. Yes, that right word. Mr. Darling very demanding, and that is very good."

"You speak French too?"

"*Mais oui.* I enjoy learning languages."

Smart woman. Ben hadn't met a single American who spoke Vietnamese. The C-130 began its takeoff roll, and as the engines roared and drowned out conversation, Ben leaned back, closed his eyes, and daydreamed about what he could do to get to know Lien better.

10

HELLO, SUNLIGHT

15 JULY 1967

His last week in New York, Tommy wanted to take Grace out, go somewhere special. She told him to pick the place. He didn't have much money but thought he could afford hamburgers at Sardi's. Maybe they'd go late, see some stars. He could show her the caricature of Ted Healy on the wall; Tommy loved the Stooges, always laughed at their gags. Or maybe he'd point out Al Capone's picture. He thought it was funny that America's most famous criminal was up there with the famous actors; sometimes he imagined his face up there with Capone's.

Saturday after ten o'clock, and Times Square was crowded with theatergoers streaming out of the Broadway shows. Grace had said she'd meet him there, and the joint was jammed. Tommy wanted to sit somewhere quiet where they could hear each other, so he played the big shot, slipped the maître d' a tenner, and asked for a booth way in the back. It worked, just like in the movies.

Grace must have figured it was an occasion because she'd shed the hippie garb and was dressed in a short, black skirt, a tight, cream-colored blouse, and black fishnet stockings that showed off her long legs. She passed by the bar like a model on a runway, and men twisted on their stools to check her out. Grace smiled back at them, loving the attention. Tommy thought she looked like Eva Marie Saint in *North by Northwest*—the train scene when Eva Marie crawled into the upper berth with Cary Grant. He wondered if he'd ever be able to take Grace on a long train trip—they'd never get out of bed. She slid into the booth beside him; he'd had half a beer, felt brave, reached over and touched her cheek.

"You're looking beautiful."

"Aren't you the gentleman tonight? That's so nice. You know, Tommy, you'd be a real dreamboat if you'd just humor me and let your hair grow. An inch, maybe. Or two or three? I mean, you're nice-looking and all, but that hair!"

"First Sergeant would never go for long hair," he said, offering a mock salute.

"Such a killjoy," Grace said. She ordered a vodka martini, extra dry, up, with olives, the sophisticated New Yorker on the town. Tommy wanted to promenade down 5th Avenue with this dashing girl on his arm.

There was a commotion near the entrance, and he looked over. Kurt Weill's widow, the singer Lotte Lenya who was starring in *Cabaret*, had walked in. The bar crowd jumped to their feet and started clapping; they must have caught her act. Lotte threw her admirers a line from "So What?" one of the musical's famous songs. Her deep voice was unforgettable.

"This is a cool place," said Grace with a grin. "Thanks for taking me."

Tommy raised his beer, a toast. "Here's to the rest of 1967. Let's hope it's a good year, for both of us."

"It will be a great year if you can survive this awful war. I hope we can get RAW going and help end it."

"Maybe we can. What's Hop done since the debacle in the park?"

"Look," Grace said, "it's our last night together. Let's not waste it."

"I know." He caught the invitation in her eyes, began imagining how delicious they could make it.

"Aren't you scared, about going over there? I would be."

"Sure, a little. But I'm a clerk. I'm going to be a REMF. I should be fine."

"A what?"

"A REMF, a Rear Echelon Mother Fucker. That's what the guys in the infantry call us. We don't really fight. Ninety-five percent of the time, anyway. I think we'll type a lot, push paper around."

"But you'll still be in danger, right?"

"Most clerks make it home."

"You better make it. I like being with you."

"Really?" Tommy wanted to hear more. The idea he might actually have a future with a girl like Grace thrilled him. "Do you think we have something special here?"

"I think you're special, Tommy. You're brave. Not many people ever have the guts to talk back to Hop. And you rescued me, saved me from those Neanderthal cops.

"Anyway," Grace said, "you know how Hop always says RAW has to bring the war home?"

"Easy to say. Not so easy to do though."

"Hop has this dream. He thinks we need to do something big, something dramatic."

"Like what?"

"Disrupt some event, something big. We'd get huge headlines, be on the national news. Ordinary people will notice. They'll start to focus on this awful war, instead of thinking about what they're going to buy for the grill this weekend. But we'll need some help."

"What kind of help?"

"He mentions you a lot. He must think because you'll be in Nam, you'll be able to use your access to . . . you know . . . help get us what we need."

"I have no idea what I could possibly do, but I'd love to help. Any idea what he's talking about?"

"He hasn't said. He wants to keep things compartmentalized. 'Do you have a need to know, Grace?' That's what he always says. Honestly, sometimes I wonder if he even trusts me. But from the way he goes on about it, I think he wants to make some grand gesture—in New York or maybe Washington, he grew up down there. Or it could be that football game you guys care so much about . . . is it the Super Bowl? Something like that."

"Wow, he thinks big."

"Yeah, always. Look at this." Grace smiled and dug a thick blue Pan Am packet out of her big leather purse. "He bought me these tickets."

Tommy read the itinerary: New York—Los Angeles—Honolulu—Manila—Saigon.

"What? He's sending *you* to Saigon? That's a terrible idea. Sending a woman into a war zone? He must be out of his mind. When is he talking about?"

"In December. I'm going as a tourist, but I'll be a member of the Bertrand Russell Peace Initiative." She clapped her hands together, obviously proud to be asked.

Tommy saw he wouldn't be able to talk her out of it. She was practically giddy.

"Do you think you'll be settled into your army job by then? So you'll be ready to help us?"

"What's this Bertrand thing?" Tommy asked.

"It's another part of the movement. Bertrand Russell is a famous philosopher, a big promoter of peace. It's an international coalition—he's English, you know—so people from around the world are coming to a huge protest next year in Saigon. I'm going to sign up some students and Buddhist monks. I'm sure they'll march with us when they see how committed we are."

"I should be squared away by December, but it'll be tough for me to join any peace protest. I mean, they'd court martial me! Listen, Grace, do you think it's really a good idea, to be running around in a war zone? Like you said, I'm not sure anywhere's safe over there."

"If you can take it I can, Tommy. Besides, anything for the cause, right?" She waved the plane tickets and laughed. "I can't wait to show this to my folks. It will be the last straw. They'll disown me. Mom and Dad are so far right they voted for that fascist Goldwater. Can you believe it? So of course, they hate my politics. They think we should carpet-bomb Vietnam like that idiot LeMay suggested. We can't even watch the evening news together!" Grace paused and took a deep breath. "Anyway, Hop says Saigon's not that dangerous. He thinks I'll be fine."

Hop thinks this, Hop thinks that. I'm sick of hearing about Hop.

Grace leaned back in her seat, smiling again, giving him that look. She stretched her leg out under the table; her stockinged foot moved up his thigh, her toes searching, moving against his groin. It had the desired effect.

"My parents are traveling again, Tommy. I'm alone in that big house, surrounded by pictures of warmonger politicians. Let's hurry up and eat and get over there. You deserve a proper goodbye."

Tommy's goal on the cross-country flight from New York to Oakland was to get sloppy drunk. The coach section was full, but after he accidentally blurted out, "Do you know how long it takes to fly to Saigon?" the American Airlines crew took pity on the draftee in dress khakis who looked shaky. The sight of another scared troop shipping off to a combat zone awakened their generosity.

They moved him to first class, where he stretched out in the big seat, assumed his best *don't-mess-with-me* look, and downed scotch after scotch as the Great Plains, golden with fields of midsummer wheat, passed monotonously below. Just when he was drunk enough to ask for the stewardess's phone number, she cut him off. "I think you should take a break, Mr. Banks."

His head pressed against the cold window, Tommy dozed off somewhere west of Denver and didn't come to until the pilot announced they were on final descent into San Francisco.

Before he'd drifted off, he thought about Grace and their last night together. Her parents' townhouse was huge; he'd never imagined her family was that rich. They'd shared a glass of wine on her living room couch, next to end tables full of framed photos of her parents (a very handsome couple) posing at posh events with politicians—John Lindsay, Jake Javits, Nelson Rockefeller, Richard Nixon, President Eisenhower. Nary a Democrat in sight. Tommy wondered what Grace would say if she saw the prints of Marx and Engels his father had tacked on the walls of their two-bedroom walk-up, his idea of a spruce-up.

But any thought of politics vanished when Grace moved onto his lap, gently kissed his ear, giggling while he struggled with the buttons on her blouse. When he'd managed to finally unfasten her bra, she grabbed him by the tie and led him upstairs, where she peeled off his army-issue boxers and ran her fingertips down his body, red nails tracing light circles on his thighs. Then she shoved him down on the big bed, pinned his arms over his head, and straddled him. She let her hair fall across his face, brushed her nipples against his lips, took him inside her, and made short work of his excitement. Later, stirring in the small hours of the night, they had made long, slow love. She held him in place, her strong fingers embedded in his bottom. He thought he'd satisfied her that time, maybe, but didn't ask. He didn't know if he wanted to hear the answer.

Lying beside Grace while she slept, he thought about how much he would miss her. For months he'd been trapped by forces beyond his control—the army and his other problem. Since the day they'd met, seeing Grace was the only thing in the world he had to look forward to. Without her he wasn't sure he would have made it this far; he would have said adios to Del and decamped for Canada or deserted to Sweden, anything to get out of the war.

When the plane landed, Tommy was still reeling from the whiskey, but managed to shoulder his seventy-pound puke-green duffel bag and stagger out of the airport to the street. He hailed a cab and passed out. Forty minutes later the cabbie shook him awake; they'd arrived in front of a warehouse near the base of the Bay Bridge. The big sign read, U.S. ARMY OAKLAND PORT OF EMBARKATION. He'd never seen a barracks remotely like this: it was a massive building right on the waterfront, bigger than any arena or convention center.

Inside, there were thousands of bunk beds, two deep in long rows. After a ten-minute walk, he found his, Number 1179. There was no place to lock up his stuff, so he hung his duffel bag on the bed pole and collapsed. The next day, the sergeants switched on the bright lights in the barracks at 0530. By 0600 the troops had made their beds—square corners, hospital style—and assembled in their crisp khakis in a rutted parking lot.

The NCO on duty called the roll. As each soldier heard his name, he yelled back, "Present, First Sergeant!"

The men whose names were called marched off to a different building. The First Sergeant announced they'd be quarantined there for two days; the army feared that some GIs might bolt forty-eight hours before their all-expenses-paid trip to Nam, so they had locked them all down. Take no chances.

No one called Tommy's name; it was a Sunday, just a few officers and noncoms around to watch a couple thousand men. So, Tommy thought, why wait around and get assigned the usual chickenshit, time-filling duties—picking butts or scrubbing toilets? Maybe he could play hooky, walk right out of the Oakland Army Terminal. For a day, anyway.

He spotted a clipboard on a nearby desk and grabbed it; it was a long list of names, arranged by rank and serial number. He pressed it up against his chest—carrying a clipboard signaled authority—set his features in the most serious expression he could muster, and strode off, another army clerk on some vital bureaucratic mission. It took him a few minutes to get to the other end of the barracks where a corporal sat guarding the exit. Tommy flashed the list in his face: "First Sergeant told me to walk this manifest over to Building 793."

The corporal barely looked up from his sports page, nodded at the door. Outside, Tommy drew a deep breath—freedom—and threw the clipboard in a trash can. Minutes later he was in a taxi headed toward Berkeley.

"Where to, pal?" the driver asked. He looked to be in his mid-forties and sported a little porkpie hat, like the funny toppers Kerouac and his crowd wore.

"I'm out for the day, never been to California. Looking for some fun, an adventure. Is there anything doing around the university?"

"At Berkeley? Always. Tons of stuff. Could be a concert. Could be a poetry reading. Could be a nude teach-in. There could even be a riot—those can be entertaining."

Tommy liked cab drivers who were talkers; he always learned something. "What would they riot about?"

"They'll riot over anything, pal. They hate LBJ. They hate Ronald Reagan. They hate J. Edgar Hoover. They hate the Vietnam War. They hate the bourgeoisie. They hate cops. They hate people with suburban houses and two-car garages and kiddie pools. They hate people who wake up on Monday thinking about which deodorant they're going to buy on Tuesday. And thank God, they hate bras.

"You name it, they hate it," the cabbie said. "Not dope, though. They love their dope, love anything that'll get you high—grass, hash, speed, those little purple pills, lysergic acid diethylamide, the chemists call them. Called LSD on the street. But I think there's some music in Provo Park today."

"Cool," Tommy said. "Sounds like a scene. Let's go there."

"On our way. But can I ask a question? You planning to show up at Provo in that uniform?"

"Sure was, why?"

"Cause those hippies, they hate soldiers too—of course they do. Listen, I'll drop you in the center of town. The Diggers have a free store down there, lots of clothes in it, maybe you can get something else to wear."

Half an hour later, U.S. Army Specialist Four N.T. Banks emerged from the clothing store wearing a long shirt from South India. It was like a tunic, but the longhair who'd picked it out for him insisted it was a dashiki blouse. Very colorful. But it did the trick, extended down past his knees, covered everything but the last few inches of his khaki trousers.

The day had turned out to be nice, sunny, almost 80. Following the siren sound of rock music, he walked east on Center Street until he came to the park, which was overrun with concertgoers. White, Black, and Asian partiers, no one over thirty, Tommy guessed. The men had long hair and lots of the women had ditched their dresses for bikinis and put flowers in their hair. He watched, entranced, as they grooved to the music, danced, and flashed peace signs. Several people blew soap bubbles, translucent spheres of dancing colors that glistened on the breeze.

He groped his way through the crowd toward the front of the stage, where a band he didn't know was playing an endless riff on a song he'd never heard. There was a tall, young blonde woman on stage dancing barefoot, her eyes closed, arms over her head, lost in the jam, moving with the music. She didn't appear to be in the band, just some girl who'd jumped up there. He noticed her armpits were hairy. Exciting, in a primitive way. As Tommy fixated on the blonde, a skinny White man with dark glasses, his tight curly hair molded into a big Afro, bumped him from behind. He was holding a small purple pill in his palm, like an offering. "Hey, brother, you wanna get high?"

"What is it?"

"A magic potion, man. Only two bucks."

Hell, why not escape for a while? I'll probably die soon anyway. "Lay it on me." Tommy handed the guy two dollars and popped the pill.

"Groovy, huh?" The hippie swayed in place, his head thrown back, trying to match the dancer's moves. The music seemed to go on and on—no breaks for this band. Eventually Tommy found himself in the front row, engulfed in the beat and grooving to the music, checking out the dancing women all around him. How long had he been here? An hour, two hours?

Waves of color—red, blue, then a long rolling rivulet of fuchsia, an ocean of purple—flowed out of the guitars and down over the crowd. It was gentle, warm, sensual. Tommy felt his whole being let go; he was surfing, gliding over the crowd on a carpet of color. The sun glowed on his face as the lead singer, a fine-looking woman, broke into another number:

Hello sunlight
Come in sunlight
Before I die I want the sun
To shoot down on me.

Then things got really fuzzy. Later—he had no idea how much—he came to lying on a bare mattress on the floor, disoriented, weak, and wasted. The sun was just coming up, feeble light breaking through a dirty window.

Looking around, he saw the room was a crash pad, bodies scattered everywhere. He was in his T-shirt and boxer shorts. His uniform was balled up on the floor—he must have ditched it at some point. His khakis were covered with crusty dark stains. He looked closer and saw his uniform shirt was covered with the same indeterminate substance—it was red, or reddish brown. *Is that blood?* It couldn't be. He looked down at his body, examined himself, but saw no cuts, no wounds. He didn't appear to be hurt, just dazed. His mouth was incredibly dry.

One other human was awake in the pile of sleeping partiers. He was sitting with his back against the corner of the room, smoking a cigarette. Tommy thought he could be the guy who sold him the pill.

"Don't sweat it man," said the dealer, if he was one. "I know what you're thinking, but that ain't blood. When we figured out what you had on under that blouse—you were in your U.S. Army uniform! Far out, man—that takes balls.

"Some peaceniks in the crowd—the Up Against the Wall Motherfuckers—they attacked you. Said they were going to cover you in the blood of the innocent people of Vietnam. So that's what they did. But don't freak out. It's Campbell's tomato soup, man. It was a symbolic thing. Harmless. You're not allergic to tomatoes, right?"

Tommy had no memory of any of that but thought he should say something. "Power to the people, man."

"Right on, brother."

Tommy shook his head, struggled to his feet, and managed to pull on his uniform pants, which were still damp, reddish. He grabbed his rumpled dashiki, jammed it over his head, stepped over several sleeping bodies, and limped out the door into the sunshine. *Now what? I can't go to Nam looking like this.*

11

PULL YOURSELF TOGETHER

16 JULY 1967

Blinking in the sunshine and still wearing his dashiki and soiled khakis, Tommy found a phone booth outside the commune where he'd passed out. He dug out the number and called Del, who told him to cab it to his office. As he walked toward Del's corner office, Tommy struggled to keep his eyes front as he passed a bunch of guys in suits who were pointing at his shirt.

"What the hell happened to you?" Del asked when Tommy sat down in front of his big desk. Tommy took in the big American flag tacked to the wall, next to a big black-and-white portrait of some middle-aged bureaucrat Tommy didn't recognize.

"I went to a rally," Tommy said, feeling sheepish. "In Berkeley, yesterday. It was all about peace and love. They figured out I was a soldier and poured blood over me but it's just tomato soup. You don't want me back in the barracks looking like this."

"I guess those hippies weren't as stoned as you thought they were, Banks," Del said. "You realize you're AWOL now, right? If some nosy lieutenant finds out about your little escapade, he could fuck up the whole mission. You *want* to end up in Leavenworth, is that it?"

"No, sir." Tommy figured he'd better be contrite and cooperate, there was no other choice.

Del paused to adjust his suspenders and tugged at his bow tie. Tommy figured Del was about fifty, a tall, tough-looking guy with military-style hair who wore cowboy boots, which had to be a dress code violation.

Tommy had gone to that Berrigan anti-war thing outside Baltimore on a lark, hoping he might meet some pretty protesters. He didn't think the FBI would be there taking pictures. He'd worn his army uniform with his name tag on it. Big mistake. Burning Selective Service records was a felony. "Punishable by thirty years in prison," Del had said later. "If you don't play ball, we'll throw you in Leavenworth."

So stupid. But he won't ship me to prison now, I'm too valuable.

"We don't have much time," Del said. "What have you found out about RAW?"

"I made it into their group. They trust me. They think they can use me, in Vietnam."

"You've been running around with that Waverly girl, right?"

"I've met her, yeah."

"Cut the bullshit, Banks, you've done a lot more than meet her. What'd you get up to after you left Sardi's, huh?"

"How'd you know about that?"

"We know everything about you. Remember that. So what are they planning?"

Tommy shrugged. "Something big, that's all I know. I don't even think Grace knows, at this point."

"We need you to find out. That's the whole point of you now, Banks.

Otherwise we will pack your ass off to federal prison. And stay off all the drugs . . . what the hell is it with that hippie shirt?"

"It's a dashiki," Tommy said.

"I don't give a shit what you fucking radicals call it." Del got up from his desk, opened a nearby closet, took out a fresh khaki uniform on a hanger, and dropped it in Tommy's lap.

"From now on you'll do what I tell you to. Get your ass to the men's room and put this on. Have you still got your name tag? Do you realize what an idiot you are? Pull yourself together before you get yourself killed. We've got a car waiting. Your plane leaves from Travis AFB in three hours. You're gonna be on it."

12

LET SLEEPING DUCKS LIE

10 JULY 1967

Secretary McNamara stood on the porch of the concrete house USAID had recently built in the freshly designated Strategic Hamlet of Nham Ko and yelled, as loudly as he could, "Let me extend a warm welcome, from the people of the United States to the brave and independent people of South Vietnam."

Ben figured summoning that much volume must've been hard. He imagined that a bureaucrat as important as McNamara always had access to a top-of-the-line audio system, but his handlers had neglected to pack one. The Americans who'd tagged along to see him cut the ribbon to open the place baked in the sun and hoped the rains would come soon.

"Make no mistake," the secretary shouted, "by every quantitative measure, the USA and its allies are winning the Vietnam war."

It had been a tiring day. They'd been up before dawn, waited around, flown to Cam Ranh Bay, listened to speeches, helicoptered to Ban Me

Thuot, heard more speeches, then bounced over rough roads for fifty kilometers to this "model" hamlet, a cluster of straw huts and some new cement houses near the Cambodian border.

They had seen very few people along the route, always a bad sign. Ben and Elijah rode in the lead jeep, their eyes constantly on the tree lines, M16s at the ready, safeties off the entire time. But they had continuous air cover—Piper Cub spotter planes and helicopter gunships buzzing over their heads—and the VC had left them alone. Now it was after four, the sun was still unbearable, and everyone was soaked with sweat—except for the Vietnamese.

Looking calm and dignified, Lien stood next to Prime Minister Manh and General Do to explain anything they couldn't follow, while Sergeant Duc listened nearby. General Do, the ARVN commander, was a big man, barrel-chested and six-foot-three, very tall for a Vietnamese man. People claimed that the politicians made Do a four-star general because he was the tallest officer in the entire South Vietnamese army; they thought his imposing presence would impress the Americans.

Ben thought that sounded harsh but could be true. Who knew how you got to be a general over here?

Except for the villagers, the secretary was preaching to the choir. Everyone who'd traveled up from Saigon had gathered in respectful rows in front of the little house. Behind the core of outsiders there were forty or fifty locals, farmers dragged in from the rice paddies and forced to listen to the generals and politicians. Most were barefoot in black pajamas and wore conical straw hats—called *non la*—to fight the sun. Some of the government flunkies tried to push the villagers forward and get them to tune in to the speeches, but it was a losing battle.

Ben noticed a large, muddy pond behind the farmers. It looked man-made, formed by a stream that had been dammed. A well-worn path led through the tall grass to a six-foot wooden plank that extended over the water—a round hole a foot in diameter had been cut in the far end. Fish surfaced underneath it, slurping up whatever was floating there. They looked like carp.

"Prime Minister Manh up there, he's a lot like me." Ben turned to look at the bedraggled American with a notebook who'd engaged him. He was sloppily dressed and carried a prominent beer belly.

"But he doesn't look anything like you."

"Oh, we got one thing in common, Lieutenant. Like me, the Prime Minister hates being out here in the country, in the field. He just rotates from his villa in Saigon to his villa in Vung Tau. Beautiful beach—you been down there yet? Manh helicopters back and forth every week. Keeps a mistress, maybe more than one, in one of his other houses. Hasn't fired a shot in anger for years."

"And you are . . . ?" Ben asked, guessing he must be a reporter.

"Sorry. Joe Kline, with the *Chicago Tribune*. At least I'm willing to admit I hate leaving Saigon. I'm a lot more comfortable in the bar of the Continental Palace, truth be told."

"So why'd you schlep out here today?"

"My big editor in Chicago wants some color from McNamara's visit. My bosses are hot to trot on the McNamara story. People in Washington say he's going to quit the cabinet pretty soon—they say he's lost his faith in the war."

"He doesn't sound that way today," Ben said.

"What people say, what people do . . . two different things," Kline said. "You see that province chief up there behind him, Nguyen Van Dinh? He's one corrupt son of a bitch. You know when they built these quote-unquote 'fortified' hamlets, they started requiring ID cards. So Dinh, he makes the ARVNs deliver the whole supply of the new ID cards to him, personally. Now those farmers over there have to produce an ID to get past the perimeter, just to get inside their own village where they've lived and farmed for generations.

"But instead of giving the cards to the villagers, Province Chief Dinh makes everyone buy them, 100 dong per person. Every resident has to have one, and a lot of these people have big families. So that's a ton of money for them . . . it really pissed them off."

"You get that story?"

"No, my buddy over there, Whittlesey. He had it first. It was in the *Times.*"

Kline indicated the guy in the front row, close to McNamara—a trim, jittery correspondent in an immaculate camouflage jungle suit who was taking copious notes. Ben had noticed him at Tan Son Nhut.

"I followed up on it though. Sent my assistant up here to Ban Me Thuot to grab a few quotes, get the same story."

Elijah thought that was strange. "If you're back in Saigon most of the time, what can you report on? Just the MACV briefings mostly?"

"Yep. The five o'clock follies. I got a front row seat for the daily body counts. McNamara spent his whole career as a bean counter. He wants to quantify everything, so he's really big on body counts. Of course, nobody has any idea if they're accurate.

"General Westmoreland wants to keep McNamara happy, so Westy wants big numbers too, wants 'em bad. That's how they measure success. So now everybody up and down the line inflates their body counts, to show we're winning. It's just a numbers game, this war. Except there are no jackpots. Westy flies back to D.C. every couple months, recites the numbers to Congress, and says he sees light at the end of the tunnel. According to the big brass, we've never lost a battle out here. We may be losing the war, but we never lost a battle."

"Right," Ben said, trying to process Kline's burst of cynicism while Elijah just shook his head. "What's the story on that American civilian?" Elijah asked. "The guy with the crew cut sucking up to the ambassador?"

"Name's J.B. Darling. Says he's an ag guy, with USAID. No way, GI. . . . I figure he's CIA."

"Why?"

"You never see him with anyone but the ambassador, or the general staff. He travels a lot . . . nobody knows where, exactly. Lots of shadowy guys in plain clothes always queuing up to see him. They ain't rice experts, I can tell you that."

A line of Vietnamese women walked toward them, carrying water back from the village well. Each one balanced two buckets hung from the ends of the bamboo pole braced across their shoulders. Idiot sticks, the GIs called them. Ben hated the phrase, felt for them. Bent under the load, they were trudging back to their thatched huts.

"These people thought that they owned this land," Kline said. "The Viet Minh had a program back in the early 1950s, gave each family a plot of land to tend. The farmers got deeds and everything.

"Then Diem came to power in 1955. He canceled that deal and gave all the land back to the big owners and the generals. Some of them own thousands of hectares. Now the farmers have to pay those guys back rent and the government back taxes. It's the little people who always get screwed."

Ben nodded. The tiny women passed by them, their buckets looking extremely heavy. "Why are they hauling water? In the briefing, the bigwigs said they have running water here."

"Just in the concrete houses," Kline said. "USAID only paid for pipes to the new houses. If the villagers want water from those new pipes, they have to pay for that too. All the money goes to Dinh and his cronies up there. The usual suspects." Kline gave the Vietnamese VIPs a dismissive wave.

They heard a splash in the pond behind them and turned to look. A peasant squatted on his haunches at the end of the plank and centered himself over the hole. Ben couldn't believe it, but the man appeared to be defecating. Several fish broke the surface of the water, lapping it up.

"What the hell?" Ben asked, frowning.

Kline laughed. "That's how the farmers restock their protein supply. This way they never have to buy fish food. Fish get fat, the farmers eat the fish, then the farmers shit some more to feed more fish. It's a closed circle—kind of like recycling."

"You kidding me? These people eat those fish? From that pond?"

"Oh yeah. They're not the only ones, pal. Where you think all that mahi mahi you see on fancy menus in Saigon comes from?"

"Remind me to never order it," Ben said.

"You think they feed their chickens their own shit too?" Elijah asked, looking peaked. "Should we be eating that street food, Lieutenant?"

"We can't live on MREs every day, Elijah."

The speeches were winding down. To show his independence, Prime Minister Manh had skipped the free ride on the C-130 from Tan Son Nhut and flown solo in his own jet fighter to Ban Me Thuot. Manh kicked things off with a short speech in English praising South Vietnam's alliance with America, and then McNamara joined him. His DOD handlers had suggested that to curry favor with the Vietnamese, the secretary should end the day by yelling 'Long live Vietnam' in the natives' language. Dinh, the crooked, puffed-up province chief, had loved the idea.

Looking uncomfortable, McNamara reached over and grabbed the prime minister's hand. They raised their arms up in the victory gesture and McNamara shouted out his few words of memorized Vietnamese.

The military and the American bureaucrats offered limp applause—they had no idea what he'd said. A wave of laughter passed through the crowd of Vietnamese standing behind Ben. Manh shook his head and smiled broadly; next to him Lien stared at the ground, expressionless.

"What's so funny, Duc? Did McNamara get something wrong?"

"Oh yes," Duc said, still giggling. "He say it very badly. The secretary, he try to say 'Long live Vietnam' but get his tones all wrong. Instead he say, 'The southern duck wants to lie down.'"

Ben choked back a laugh. "Maybe that's not so crazy, Duc. Most of these people look overdue for their siestas."

13

REMF

03 SEPTEMBER 1967

Tommy's first brush with death came six weeks into his tour. Woozy after several drinks, he'd just left the Enlisted Men's Club when the first round hit: a white flash and a deafening explosion. As he dove into the bunker, another NVA rocket landed twenty meters away. The man right behind Tommy screamed when the shrapnel sliced through him. They dragged the man behind the sandbags, but he bled out in minutes. Tommy covered his ears and cowered in the dark as explosions rocked the earth for hours, shaking him to his core.

When the rockets finally stopped, Tommy crawled out of the bunker, walked back to his tented bivouac, and climbed into his top bunk without bothering to undress. His bunkmate, PFC Allen Kramerwicz of the Signal Corps, was snoring away in his lower bunk, probably too stoned to wake up. Tommy lay awake until four in the morning, listening for more rockets or mortars.

Even before his first brush with death, the nights were the worst for Tommy. He was in this hellhole because he was being blackmailed, but he'd assumed—*what the hell was I thinking?*—that when Del and his minions had made him their mole, he'd serve out his time at some sleepy stateside post, preferably close to Grace in New York. He'd never dreamed they'd dump him in a war zone.

Tommy was no warrior, just a lowly logistics clerk, a Rear Echelon Mother Fucker. But it had become frighteningly obvious to him how simple it was (incredibly easy, really) to get yourself killed in this stupid war, and the incident or accident that happened to do you in could occur in about a thousand ways. Fear of rockets and mortars was at the top of his list, but there were so many options.

You could be run over by a deuce-and-a-half driven by a drugged-up eighteen-year-old private on the Tan Son Nhut highway. Or, hitching a ride on a Huey, you might trip over the machine gunner, tumble through his door (which was always left wide open—God knows why, and plummet a thousand feet to your death in triple-canopy jungle. You could get cut down in the chow line by an NVA sniper, pulverized in a plane crash, or mowed down by some crazed comrade who'd had too much to drink and gotten it into his head that you'd *disrespected* him. *Put the gun down, man, it was a misunderstanding!*

Or, and this was perhaps more likely in Tommy's case, you could catch the latest virulent strain of the clap from some young *Co* down on Tu Do Street and die an agonizing death in an Okinawa hospital as your brain disintegrated. It was mind-blowing when you stopped to think about all the ways you could buy the farm, bite the dust, peg out, croak—and Tommy was just a typist, for fuck's sake. The situation made him feel helpless, furious that his fate was so completely out of his control. The endless routine wore him down, ate away at his soul. All you could do was try and endure it, check off another twenty-four hours, count down every minute you had left in this awful place. He hated the army's hierarchy, hated being told what to do every minute of every hour. Powerless to do a thing about it, Tommy felt his rage build.

The next morning, after only a few hours of sleep, Tommy was at work in his office as usual by 7:30 a.m. Six days a week, eleven hours a day, Tommy was incarcerated at his desk, which was a short walk from his hooch. His bunkmate, Kramerwicz, worked a long day too, sorting intercepted telephone and radio traffic the army collected from antennas and wiretaps.

Tommy had been in-country nearly two months, and from day one he'd had a ton of work, yes, but it was all incredibly tedious and dispiriting. He got through the long days by rerunning memories of Grace—their nights, mostly—over and over. He missed Grace so much: he thought about her, dreamed about her, went over every minute they'd had together. Was this insane war going to ruin that too?

His desk was in the center of the procurement section of the huge new USARV logistics facility at Long Binh, twenty klicks northeast of Saigon. It was his bad luck to be seated only a few feet in front of his supervisor, First Sergeant Frank Moseley. Tommy hated being so closely monitored. After a week in-country, Tommy had asked why certain forms had to be typed twice.

"Shut your mouth and do your job, Banks," the first sergeant had said. "You haven't been here long enough to ask questions."

The mountain of paper on his desk was overwhelming and the routine was stultifying, but when Tommy thought about his place in the bigger picture, a huge arms depot was a good place to be. He kept his head down and just typed, completing thousands of forms in his laborious, two-finger hunt-and-peck style.

Tommy was one of thousands of clerks whose mission was to support the hundreds of thousands of U.S. troops flooding into Vietnam. And "support" meant that it was Tommy's job to order every item the newest Nimrod Colonel or Dimwit Captain could dream up, and then follow up later to see that everything arrived safely. *Allegedly* arrived safely, because so much materiel was washing up on Vietnam's shores now, no one could keep track of where the hell it all went. The items he requisitioned ranged from the latest and greatest weapons the arms merchants could imagine—RPGs, M60s, Bouncing Betties, Claymores—to all the comforts of a suburban home for the poor suckers out in the field. It was comical, some of the stuff the army was importing. *Can you believe this? Some major in III Corps needs a Ping-Pong table.*

At the biggest bases, soldiers routinely had access to hot food, cold beer, and ice cream. Many got to shop in PXs the size of department stores. They drank in officers' and enlisted men's clubs, played basketball in their time off, read a daily newspaper, and listened to a Top 40 radio station. They could watch movies at night and order cheeseburgers at a cafe. Booze was flowing everywhere, and it was dirt cheap—a beer cost fifteen cents.

Even combat soldiers were served hot turkey dinners on holidays, transported to the boonies by helicopter. There were even days when a grunt might survive a hellish firefight in the morning, hop on a slick back to a secure base that afternoon, down a few beers, enjoy a steak dinner, and then head out on a dangerous helicopter assault the next morning. The contrast between combat and relative calm was mind-bending.

Then there was R&R, the free, six-day trip to the tropical paradise of your choice—Bangkok, Penang, Sydney, Honolulu. What could be better? Tommy thought this mini-break was another distortion of reality that added to the craziness. The typical American soldier wasn't focused on winning the war; he just marked off the days, hoping and praying to get home in one piece. Then he could try to forget about it, which wouldn't be easy.

Leaning back in his chair, Tommy regarded the pile of paper he'd already processed that morning, amused by the variety: two thousand gallons of dehydrated ice cream; seventy-two flamethrowers; three thousand frozen turkeys, to be delivered without fail before Thanksgiving; one hundred thousand condoms, in six different colors; thirty-five armored personnel carriers for the Air Cav up in III Corps.

At least Sundays provided a break from the monotony. Tommy spent his days off perusing the hundreds of stalls in Saigon's black market and then went larking with the B-girls down on Tu Do Street. But he wasn't a free spender like the other GIs. They'd think nothing of dropping fifty bucks on the watered-down drinks at the Twenty Grand or the Monaco, and never even get to first base. *Later, GI. You buy me one more Saigon Tbe. Then we fuki fuki.*

On this humid Sunday, Tommy found himself wandering through the market again, drinking in the sights and smells. It was fascinating, and for a moment he was almost happy. Almost, anyway. He stopped at a meat market to drink in the savory scent of a dozen roasted ducks strung up in a long row.

In the stall next door, ancient mama-sans were hawking American canned goods: SpaghettiOs, baked beans, corned beef hash, pears, mixed fruit in sugar syrup—all of it sourced from USAID shipments intended for field kitchens. He held up a can of Hormel all-beef chili.

"How much?" he asked the mama-san, who was chewing betel nuts, the red juice staining her chin. The nuts were addictive and supposed to give you a mild high. He hadn't been adventurous enough to try them, not yet. He was cautious about ingesting anything Vietnamese.

"Ten P," she said, holding out ten fingers. "Very special price. For GI only." She smiled, revealing the few rotting red-stained teeth she had left. He put the can back.

Anything you could think of was on sale here. Every kind of food, from fresh mangoes grown in the Delta to fine chocolates hand-crafted in Brussels. Big ticket items too, like used cars and new motor scooters. Michelin tires, Swiss watches, diamond rings, radios, record players, console televisions, books, magazines, chess sets, wine, and champagne. *Anything you want, special for you, Number One merchandise, GI.*

Tommy straddled a brand-new, blue-green Vespa on offer, fired it up, and twirled the throttle. *Five hundred, beaucoup value, American dollar only, GI!* He fiddled with complicated SLR cameras from Nikon and Canon, new models from Tokyo not yet available in the States. Dozens of stalls peddled clothes: Hawaiian shirts, Levi's, and Panama hats. He tried on a few motorcycle jackets with mottos in bright red cursive letters aimed at GIs: *When I die, I'll go to heaven, because I've spent my time in hell.*

Tommy continued his stroll, browsing cases of bladed weapons—knives, machetes, swords. He guessed there had to be much more dangerous things for sale here somewhere, stuff that he might have ordered on his own typewriter. Wandering aimlessly, he squeezed though a line of stalls selling cheap dishes and toys made in China. Their long tables butted up against a warehouse-like building.

He spotted an unmarked door at one end of the building and moseyed over. *Why not?*

He knocked. No answer, so he pushed on the steel door, put his shoulder into it. It gave way, and he found himself in a dark, smoke-filled room. The air smelled thick and sweet. Tommy paused to get his bearings. He couldn't see much but knew at once there were other humans in the room; he could hear breathing and sucking sounds, like someone pulling on a straw. Dim light filtered in from high, skinny windows; as his eyes adjusted, he realized he was smack in the middle of an opium den. Just standing there, he picked up a nice buzz from the fumes. Maybe twenty customers, mostly older men, huddled around the room over their pipes, doing their best to suck up nirvana.

Picking his way so he wouldn't trip over anyone, Tommy spotted another door in the back, also unmarked. A brothel? Or maybe a secret casino? *Give it a shot.* Out of curiosity, he tried it. Hell, he'd come this far. It was locked. He knocked lightly. A bolt slipped, the door eased open, and a very large man glared down at him.

This mountain man didn't look exactly Vietnamese—maybe he was a Montagnard, from that tribe up by the Laotian border. Tommy held the man's gaze and gestured with his head as if to enter. The doorman—obviously a bouncer-type or bodyguard—looked him over, shoved the door open, and raised an eyebrow to the middle-aged man behind him, ensconced in a bright red armchair in front of a very tall black curtain. The chair was mounted on a platform a foot above the floor and centered in the pool of sunlight that emanated from a high window. *Like a warlord on his throne.*

"Welcome," the stranger said with a tight smile.

14

THE EEL

03 SEPTEMBER 1967

"May I offer you tea?" the regal man in the chair asked, gesturing for Tommy to sit in the chair that faced him.

His host was wearing a Nile-green sharkskin suit, a starched white shirt, and a narrow black tie. The suit was so shiny, Tommy imagined it could have come from the skin of an eel. Well, maybe a hundred eels. The man's hair was pomaded, slicked straight back from his forehead, and he was nurturing a wispy goatee. He looked vaguely Vietnamese, but maybe not quite; something else was mixed in there. A pretty strange cat.

"We have for your pleasure many varieties—oolong, Formosa, even English breakfast."

"Sure, whatever. I don't know much about tea."

The man smiled. "Then the oolong, I think. The black dragon leaves. They yield such rich flavors, very good for the digestion."

"And you are?" Tommy asked the man.

"Some customers call me '*l'anguille*,'" he said.

"Is that French? I don't know it."

"Oui. It means 'the Eel'."

There were several porcelain jars with Chinese designs on the table next to him. The Eel dipped his fingers into a jar, extracted a few dark leaves, sniffed them, rolled the mass into a tight sphere, and placed it in a silver tea ball. As if he'd been cued, the thug who'd been guarding the door threw the black curtain open and appeared with a pot of just-boiled water. The Eel lowered the silver container into the steaming water and paused over the tea, savoring the aroma.

After a minute or two he took the infuser out, waited a moment, and then slipped it back into the hot water.

"We steep the tea three times. The rule of threes, you know. It helps unfurl the leaves, release all the flavors, the very essence of the tea plant." His English had an accent, but Tommy couldn't place it. European? French, perhaps.

The bodyguard hadn't bothered to close the curtain. Tommy looked into the dimly-lit space beyond it and realized the place was overflowing with guns—wall-to-wall weapons arranged on long wooden tables. Maybe fifty or sixty tables, each one about twenty feet long, jammed together in tight rows, with barely enough room to slide between them.

"*Choi oi*," Tommy said, using the pidgin Vietnamese exclamation for amazement. He glanced at the Eel and his bodyguard, who seemed unfazed that some strange American had wandered into their candy store of exotic munitions.

There were hundreds—no, maybe thousands—of weapons here. The tables in front of him were piled with long guns—shotguns, double barrels, and sawed-offs, next to arrays of automatic rifles of every conceivable design. There were M-1s, M2s, M14s, tons of M16s and Soviet AK-47s.

Many GIs wished they could carry the AK-47—it rarely jammed, unlike the early M16s.

Machine guns too: ancient American-made Browning Automatic Rifles from the 1940s and brand-new M60s. All kinds of rocket-propelled grenade launchers: M7s, M8s and M79s, the modern model issued to U.S. and ARVN troops. There were Communist versions too: the Soviet-made RPG-2s, also known as B40s, that every convoy traveler feared. He spotted dozens of WWII-vintage bazookas alongside brand-new flamethrowers and many types of mines—conventional pressure detonated models and dozens of the deadly Claymores, designed to cut down the unlucky targets with showers of shrapnel.

There was new technology too: in the back Tommy saw several shoulder-fired FIM-43 Redeye heat-seeking anti-aircraft missiles—they could take down helicopters and low-flying aircraft.

All sorts of pistols: Colt .45s, Colt Python .357 Magnums, Smith & Wesson .38 Specials, lots of Lugers, and several .22-caliber silencer-equipped models designed for up close and personal work by the Special Forces, Navy Seals, and tunnel rats.

"May I?" Tommy asked, standing up.

The Eel nodded and Tommy strode over to look at the more esoteric models the VC used, Czech and Polish machine pistols. An entire table was devoted just to derringers, from antiques to more modern versions. He paused to handle a very odd pistol with two long barrels but no trigger, wondering how it worked.

He made his way toward the back of the building where the ceiling rose even higher and the heavy ordnance was displayed: recoilless rifles and quad machine gun rigs meant for jeeps and all kinds of mortars. There were two huge pieces of serious artillery parked in a far corner—self-propelled U.S. Army howitzers, 155s. The left side of the warehouse was reserved for ammunition, from big artillery shells right down to .22

caliber cartridges. It was a stunning collection. A lot of effort, to get all this stuff. The Eel's arsenal seemed to include everything the U.S. Army had. Tommy wondered how much the owner had spent, and which ARVN generals had taken the bribes.

The Eel noticed Tommy's expression and smiled at him. "You think this is, I think the word is, *impressive*?" his host asked, pouring more tea.

"Impressive? Way beyond that. It's unreal."

"Can you tell me, *mon ami*—why did you knock upon our door?"

Clearly, the man had known immediately that Tommy was not an MP or some kind of undercover American investigator. *Or else he wouldn't have let me in.*

"Curiosity, I guess," Tommy said with a shrug. He figured it was best to keep things casual with a major arms dealer. "I'm always wondering what's behind closed doors. And I may be interested in some of your merchandise. But tell me, papa-san, why did you open your door for me? You don't do that for everybody, right?"

"Don't call me that; I am no papa-san. Perhaps I should brew more tea, if we are to talk business. Why did we let you in? I think it was your eyes, my friend. They have a lean and desperate look. And I never turn away business."

"'Yond Cassius has a lean and hungry look.' That's Shakespeare," Tommy said, proud that he'd learned something from all that reading at Fordham.

The Eel gave a thin smile, but said nothing.

Tommy moved to another table and picked up a Marine sniper rifle, a Winchester M70 bolt action 30.06 with a cool night vision scope. He cradled it in his arms, sited it down the aisle, checking the magnification. Too much gun for his purposes. Maybe something smaller.

After handling lots of options, Tommy settled on a Ruger Standard .22-caliber semiautomatic pistol, with a hundred rounds of ammo.

Probably more than he needed for his particular mission, but you never knew. He handed the man fifty bucks, tucked the weapon in the small of his back under his T-shirt, and emptied the boxes of shells into a clear plastic bag. His host didn't count the cash, just handed it to his bodyguard: "We will meet again, perhaps?"

"I hope so," Tommy said.

"Most people call me Frank," the Eel said as they parted. "Anything you want, just ask."

Tommy felt good about the day. He'd stumbled upon a major arms dealer who would probably sell anything if the price was right. Having access to this shitload of arms was a good break. Maybe he'd never need them; maybe they'd back down, forget about involving him in whatever they were planning. But if things did start happening on that front, now he knew where to go.

Tommy ducked out of the den's doorway, smoke wafting out behind him. He blinked in the bright sun, made his way slowly out of the market, and then sat down to rest on a bench beside the river, pausing to admire the day. The little Ruger felt good, snug in the small of his back. Like an old friend, like security.

15

MRS. GOULD'S SUNBIRD

15-17 SEPTEMBER 1967

The memory of what Vietnamese farmers fed their fish put Ben off street food for a while, but he still loved his coffee. Several weeks after Secretary McNamara's visit, Ben woke early and walked to his favorite brasserie—Le Petite Bistro—near the new U.S. Embassy on Thong Nhut Street. American and Vietnamese office workers swarmed the cafe before work for a quick coffee and one of its famous croissants.

He was relaxing at a table on the sidewalk, enjoying the morning and his cafe au lait before it got hot, when a trim, young Vietnamese woman drove up, parked her Vespa, and headed for the counter. She wore French designer sunglasses, and when she pushed them up into her hair, he recognized her. "Hello, Miss Lien," he called out. She looked up, surprised, then made her way to his table. He stood, bowed, and extended his hand for her light touch. "Would you join me?"

She had a pink flower in her hair and wore a pretty necklace with a dragon motif. He knew nothing about jewelry but noticed small bright stones embedded in it—diamonds? He guessed it was expensive.

"Your necklace, it's beautiful."

"It was my mother's."

He read the indecision on her face, whether to keep talking or keep on trucking. Vietnamese women and men almost never sat together in public. "Do you have time for coffee?"

A pause. "Perhaps. Mr. Darling traveling today."

"You didn't go?"

"It is Friday. He go Vung Tau. With friends, for weekend. To rest, I think. Or maybe swim, at beach."

At least Darling hadn't invited Lien to go with him. Or maybe he had, and she'd declined? Today she'd worn an aqua áo dài and white silk slacks. Ben couldn't stop admiring her trim figure, her immaculate style. "Well, Lien, if your boss is away, it's a good time to play. For a little while, anyway." He was blabbering and was surprised at how nervous she made him. "Please, take a break. Just for a few minutes."

She hesitated an instant, then gave in and sat down. He signaled for the waiter. "What kind of coffee would you like?"

"Vietnamese coffee, with sweet milk." Before he could say anything, Lien ordered it in rapid Vietnamese.

"That was a good trip the other day, with Secretary McNamara," Ben said.

"Oh, yes. Mr. Darling very pleased. He think new hamlet strategy will be—what is your expression in English—a turning?"

"Right. A turning point." He was eager to know whether Lien agreed with her boss. Most Vietnamese were very careful when they talked to Americans and routinely hid their true feelings. They were caught between two sides and their lives were often a balancing act.

"For the war, right?" Ben asked. "Those fortified hamlets, they'll help our side, reduce support for the VC in the rural areas. Is that what you think too?"

Lien lowered her eyes; perhaps she wasn't used to being asked for her opinion. Or she was deciding whether it was safe to talk about anything besides the weather. She was good at looking neutral.

"*Oui, peut-être.* Perhaps." She turned to him with a mischievous smile. "Yes, some Vietnamese say your new hamlets will be turning point, for sure. Maybe change everything. For *southern ducks*, anyway."

Ben laughed, thinking Lien was right. The hamlet idea sounded promising but he guessed it would never work in a war where allegiances shifted hourly. Out in the countryside the VC occupied whatever territory they wanted whenever they wanted to, and then vanished before American troops arrived.

Many settlements were quite remote, so the VC could easily enter them at night. Instead of attacking, they often offered villagers help. They even brought nurses and medicines to treat the sick. When they confiscated rice as a "tax," they promised to pay it back—and sometimes they actually did. They were good propagandists too: VC cadres never missed a chance to remind the rural people how deeply corrupt the Saigon government was, a reality the locals witnessed every day.

"The 'southern duck,'" Ben said. "I wonder if any of McNamara's staffers were brave enough to tell him why the natives were laughing. Maybe we shouldn't speak languages we don't understand."

"Yes, Lieutenant. I think it much better if Americans never learn our language. Then Lien have good job forever."

"Where do you live?" Ben blurted the question without thinking.

She hesitated again, met his eyes for a long moment before answering. "On Thanh Gian Street, near Buddhist shrine. I have apartment there."

A nice neighborhood. He and Elijah had driven through it several times; a lot of ARVN generals had villas there. Ben was mildly surprised Lien could afford it on an interpreter's salary. Where would she get that kind of money? It seemed more likely that B-girls would live there. There were ten thousand prostitutes in Saigon now, and a popular girl could clear $200 a month, four times the salary of a government worker.

"Do you get weekends off?"

"Only Sunday. But this week Mr. Darling say Saturday too."

"What do you like to do on your day off?"

Lien laughed. It was a pleasant, soft laugh, suggesting she richly enjoyed whatever she did in her spare time but didn't have much of it. "Usually I go zoo. I like to look at birds, see their pretty colors."

She'd actually revealed something; maybe he was getting somewhere.

Ben took his chance, blurting out. "Would you go to the zoo with me?"

She lowered her head and brushed back her rich, glossy hair with her hand. Was she embarrassed? Considering the idea? Afraid to be seen in public with an American? Or was there a boyfriend?

"When?"

His heart leapt.

"How about tomorrow?"

Another long pause while she thought about it.

"Okay."

Yes! "I'll come to your apartment."

"No," she said quickly. "I meet you there. At zoo."

"All right. When?"

"At nine, in front of Hung King Temple, by bronze elephant inside main gate." Lien took a last sip of coffee and got up to leave, smoothed her áo dài, erased a few wrinkles. He thought everything about her was gentle, delicate—like a lotus flower. She was petite, composed, and soft-spoken, and seemed incapable of doing anything clumsy or awkward. He was slightly amazed that she'd go out with a pushy American MP she barely knew.

"Then I will see you tomorrow, First Lieutenant Kin-Kay," Lien said, reminding him of Sergeant Duc.

"Please, just call me Ben." He stood and bowed from the waist again, his hands clasped in front of him, his best prayerful gesture. She returned the little bow, her eyes laughing.

At least she finds me amusing.

Ben found it hard to believe that Saigon still had a zoo. The South Vietnamese had been fighting the VC more or less nonstop since the country was partitioned thirteen years ago—how could they afford workers and money to maintain a zoo? It wasn't much of a zoo though. So far he'd seen a single giraffe, two scruffy water buffaloes homesick for their paddy, and a weary elephant.

Almost shaking with anticipation, he'd arrived early to check things out. The driver of the pedicab had pedaled three sweaty miles for a measly thirty dong, about twenty-five cents. The zoo and botanical garden occupied thirty hectares off Le Duan Street, south of where the Thi Nghe Canal emptied into the Saigon River. The park was well tended; there were lots of ancient gardeners pruning branches and tidying bushes. Its broad gravel paths were lined with majestic banyan trees and thickets of indigenous plants, perfect spots for a VC sapper squad to hide.

Waiting by the bronze elephant in front of the temple, he passed the time studying a mangy tiger imprisoned in a small cage twenty meters away. The tiger kept licking the bars; maybe they were salty, the residue of its keeper's perspiration. But at least she was safe. Out in the field the GIs or ARVNs would have hosed her down with their M16s, riotous target practice.

He worried Lien might not show, but at exactly nine a.m. she stepped from a taxi in a white silk áo dài and matching pants, elegant as ever. They touched hands and bowed gently to one another. "Hello, Lieutenant Kin-Kay," she said, her tone bright. "It is beautiful here. I am happy not to be working."

He was relieved she didn't seem nervous—just a bit resigned, maybe. Ben knew that South Vietnamese women who dated GIs attracted a lot of criticism. Many Vietnamese assumed that any woman who went out with an American must be a prostitute, and they weren't shy about saying so. He felt lucky that Lien had opened a small window into her life, and he welcomed any scrap of attention she might grant him. She linked her arm with his and they set off to view the tropical birds. As they passed the stone dragons flanking the entrance and fell in behind several mothers shepherding small children, Ben thought Lien looked almost happy.

"What kind of temple is this?" he asked, taking in the cavernous room with its twelve pillars and a central shrine inscribed with names. "Is it a religious site?"

"No. It called Hung Kings Temple. Those kings our ancestors, of all Vietnamese people. We have thousands of temples dedicated to them. But this one French build in 1920s to honor all Vietnamese soldiers who die in Great War, fighting for France. We call it Temple of Remembrance."

"You mean World War I?"

"Yes. Twelve thousand Vietnamese killed in that war, fighting Germans for French Army. It probably just an estimate, you know."

"Really?" Ben had no idea that Vietnamese soldiers had fought for France in WWI. "Did they volunteer?"

"Oh no, Kin-Kay. No Vietnamese volunteer for that. Many were workers, on rubber plantation. They caught, rounded up by colonial authorities. Then shipped to Europe, forced to fight in war."

"Another reason to love their masters," Ben said, shaking his head.

"Yes. Some people say that the independence movement in Annam become much stronger then, because French force so many Vietnamese into their army."

They passed a pleasant hour looking at the birds. It was a good collection, fifty or more species inside a high netted area. The birds were relatively free, with a decent amount of airspace to fly around in, at least for short distances. There were several feeding platforms and a few pretty bird baths with small sculptures on them. A plump green bird hopped along the ground a few feet in front of them. It was very chatty—its call sounded like "Re-up! Re-up!"

"What's that one?" Ben asked.

"Oh, you GIs say it the 'Re-Up Bird,' because of way its call sound. But that bird never recruit anyone. Real name is blue-eared barbet."

"I'm calling it the blue-eared Barbie, that's easier to remember."

Lien stopped for a long time in front of a striking bird, the size of a cardinal. It was deep scarlet on top, bright yellow below. It had a blue patch under its eye, a curved beak, and a long, bluish tail.

"Is this your favorite?" Ben asked as she pressed her forehead against the cage.

"Yes, that one called Mrs. Gould's sunbird." Lien pointed to the exhibit label written in Vietnamese and smiled up at him—a rueful smile, he thought.

A larger bird, similar to a turkey with a white crest, foraged nearby. "That one is Edwards's pheasant," Lien said. "You see, Kin-Kay? We Vietnamese not allowed to name our own birds. That pheasant in danger, very few alive now."

"Unusual names. Who was Mrs. Gould?"

"Famous British bird lady in 1800s. She also illustrator—*Birds of Europe*. Big book, very beautiful. I show you sometime, in library. She very good artist, good as your Mr. Audubon. Even better, maybe. Mrs. Gould's bird, its colors so bright. It loves sunlight. It fly all over jungle, wherever it wants, to drink nectar. When I look at it, I always think of freedom."

"If you could change the sunbird's name, what would you call it?"

"*Su tu do.* That Vietnamese word for freedom. No freedom now for this bird. Same-same our people."

"But you're free, Lien. Aren't you?"

"No, no, Kin-Kay. Like tiger you see back there, Lien trapped, in cage. All Vietnamese trapped. Just like we in prison. In invisible cages. Of our war, your war."

Ben couldn't think of a thing to say that would help Lien feel better. What she believed was sad, tragic, and true; he'd been in Vietnam almost eight months, and he wasn't sure that either side could ever win this war.

They strolled through the lush landscape of the botanical gardens. She led him to a bench beneath some banyan trees where they sat for a long while. Lien told him about her mother, an art teacher; she had died a couple of months ago. Cancer. It had been a long, painful ordeal; it broke her heart to see her mother suffer that way.

They went to a nearby cafe and lingered over lunch and then Ben hailed a pedicab.

"Where shall we go?" he asked.

"My apartment. It is cooler there." The old man stood on the pedals and strained to pull their weight, short of breath in the high heat of the afternoon.

She frowned, shook her head: "Pedicabs no good, Kin-Kay." Lien was very sensitive to anything that suggested, even in the slightest way, that one human being was subservient to another—that was repugnant.

It was one of the things he admired about her. "Next time we'll take a taxi," Ben said. "I promise." Feeling braver, he reached across and took her cool hand in his, stroked her wrist. She smiled and lowered her head, but didn't pull away. Things were moving fast but Ben understood that the war accelerated all kinds of things. Why wait when you could die at any moment?

Lien's apartment was very neat, spartan, nothing out of place. Not much decoration: a couple of oil paintings, by a Vietnamese artist he thought. They were a little abstract, shades of green on green, the verdant, picture poster shades of Vietnam. Rice farmers toiling on a sunny morning, misty mountains in the distance.

"You like? My mother paint them."

"They're beautiful."

On a table against one wall, Lien had created a shrine. Like an altar, surrounded by fresh flowers and small bowls of fruit. Two framed photographs of her parents were in the center, behind vases that held joss sticks. Her handsome father looked very formal in a dark suit and tie and a Homburg hat; he was probably trying to fit in with the French. Facing the camera, her mother looked proud, dignified, almost defiant—chin up, shoulders back. A strong spirit, like her daughter.

In the picture she had on the dragon necklace he'd seen Lien wear, and her eyes were kind. He imagined Lien kneeling at the altar, hands clasped in prayer, honoring her parents and all of her ancestors. A beautiful ritual, an act of love.

The place seemed almost too neat. If he didn't know better, he would have guessed it had been scrubbed, wiped down, as if to conceal whatever had gone on, had been there earlier. He noticed a couple of lighter rectangles on the wall where pictures might have hung but had been taken down. Why? He caught himself: *Come on, Ben, it's your day off. Don't think like a cop every minute of every day.*

As the afternoon waned, they sat on her balcony, drinking white wine. They watched the sun sink into the river, savoring the twilight. Later she took his hand, kissed it lightly, and led him back to her small bed. Everything about her was so gentle, so delicate. He helped her undress, and they made slow, passionate love that lasted into the red dawn.

16

YOU DON'T OWN ME

08-09 DECEMBER 1967

"It's been a long night, boss," Elijah said as he pulled off the Long Binh Road at 0200 and braked their jeep to a shuddering stop next to the ramshackle bar's front door. Its big sign read: *The Little Country Inn—RELAX HERE.*

Ben and Elijah had drawn the graveyard shift again. No gunfire tonight, just depressing examples of what lonely GIs did when they were out looking for love in all the nasty places. So far they'd broken up three fights, stopped a young sergeant from strangling the B-girl who'd refused to sleep with him, and transferred a troop who'd overdosed on heroin to the infirmary.

"I'm beat too," Ben said. "Let's call it a night after we shut this dive down." Four hours past curfew, and The Little Country Inn was still going full tilt.

No fancy bedrooms here. The place was another lean-to thrown together with corrugated steel scraps and duct tape. The proprietors had installed a sound system and a twenty-by-twenty dance platform in the middle of the dirt floor, where drunken GIs clamped their bar girls in death grips and slow danced to Barbra Streisand's song about lonely people needing people. Not Ben's idea of an "inn."

Ben spotted the pretty young blonde at a corner table right away. Outside of the occasional glimpse of a nurse or a Donut Dolly—college grads dispatched on one-year tours to comfort the wounded and boost morale—GIs never ran into American women in-country.

This woman was doing all the talking, to a rapt audience of three enlisted men. Ben figured they were REMFs: their uniforms were clean, and they appeared sane, no thousand-yard stares from these guys.

"Let's check that group out, boss," Elijah said, gesturing toward the girl.

"The Viet Cong are not Communists!" the woman said, her voice rising. "They're nationalists. They care about Vietnam, not China."

The woman's willing acolytes nodded away, yielding to the dedicated revolutionary. Ben wondered if the men agreed with her or were humoring her because she was beautiful.

"I'll bet you boys can't even tell me what the National Front is fighting for," she said. "Come to think of it, I'll bet you can't tell me what *you're* fighting for, either."

As Ben and Elijah approached, the three GIs stopped drinking to stare at the MPs. The wiry specialist on the left—his name tag said *Banks*—looked around the room, searching for the nearest exit.

"Would you pigs like to join us?" the woman asked, chin up. "I'm buying."

Ben wanted to just throw her out but thought better of it. "You sure you want two animals at your table, ma'am?"

"Please, Lieutenant, have a seat. I'm giving these good-looking boys a seminar on Vietnamese history," she continued. "It's a short course, but very persuasive. You might learn something."

"No, thank you, ma'am." Ben wondered if he should keep calling her that—she was no matron—but "Miss" seemed too dainty a word for this creature. "We're on duty. But I'm sorry to say that your teach-in is over. It's four hours past curfew, and I'd rather not have to arrest your friends."

"Oh, aren't you sweet?" she said, grasping his arm with a flirtatious smile. "I'm Grace."

The girl was certainly a looker: her sleeveless green dress was tight in all the right places, and her short hair fit her personality. A large peace symbol dangled from a leather cord around her neck, and Ben noted that she'd treated herself to a pedicure.

He sighed and removed her hand from his arm. Elijah jumped in. "If you don't mind me asking, ma'am, why are you here? In Vietnam, I mean. Do you work for USAID or something?"

"Oh no, soldier boy. I'd die before I'd take any of their dirty money."

The man next to Grace, Banks, reached out for Grace's hand. "Look, let's just leave so—"

"Tommy!" Grace said, shrugging him off. "These guys deserve to know." She looked at Elijah. "USAID is actually a CIA front. They should rename it U-S-A-I-T, the United States Agency for International Terrorism. But I wouldn't expect *you* to know that."

"Then who are you?" Elijah asked. "And why are you here?"

"I'm just an American tourist trying to learn, firsthand, what my country's up to," Grace said. "I needed to see the war for myself. And I have to tell you, Sergeant, my trip has been eye-opening. I had no idea of the amount of damage Ameri-KA is doing here, to the Vietnamese people. It's a humanitarian disaster."

She grabbed her large peace symbol and waved it in their faces like a credential.

"I guess you could call me a peace tourist. A patriot for peace."

A tourist? In Vietnam? Ben tried to hide his disdain. Why would any freedom-loving American travel 12,000 miles to the other side of the earth to visit this God-forsaken country that was pretty much a total war zone? To take pictures? To adopt small children? To be journey-proud and tell your hippie friends back in the world that you'd been swanning around South Vietnam?

"How'd you say you got over here?" Elijah asked, trying his best Kodachrome smile.

"I flew on an airplane, of course. How'd you think I got here?" Grace laughed. "That's not illegal, is it?"

Elijah paused, looked at Ben for relief.

Ben shook his head, tried again. "So you came by yourself?"

"No, I came with a group—the Bertrand Russell Peace Initiative."

Specialist Tommy Banks cleared his throat and gestured toward the exit.

"Who the hell's Bertrand Russell?" Elijah asked.

"I have to take a piss," Banks announced. Ben noticed his shoulder patch, the USARV Logistics Command at Long Binh. Banks started to get up, but Ben put a hand on his shoulder and pushed him back down.

"Stay here, soldier." He felt Banks twitch, his upper body rigid. Men at other tables turned to look, expecting a fight. A few got up and began to filter out.

"We're a group of right-minded people trying to put an end to this awful war," Grace said, rolling with her argument.

Does this woman ever shut up?

"We're on a fact-finding mission. We're going to report back to the American people about the best path to peace."

"Well, when you locate it, will you let the rest of us know?" Ben asked. "But right now I need to see some ID. For all of you, please."

Grace handed Ben her driver's license. Her name was Grace Waverly, and she lived at 311 East 19th Street, New York, New York. The three soldiers' papers said they were all stationed at Long Binh, the big supply base down the road. Ben studied their ID cards, which looked legit. He made a note to run Specialist Four Norman T. Banks through the system; this Tommy guy seemed a bit shifty.

"All right, men, it's your lucky night. I've never seen any of you out after curfew before, so get the hell back to your barracks before we lock your asses up in the LBJ."

The trio looked relieved. No one wanted to spend what was left of Friday night in the Long Binh Stockade. They pushed back their chairs and stood up.

"But I'm not finished," Grace said.

"You are now," Ben said. "Look, ma'am, you're not subject to our rules but this area isn't safe. Not at this hour. Maybe not at any hour. What's your plan?"

Grace mustered up a pout. "I suppose I'll just catch a cyclo back to my hotel, the Continental Palace. Do you know it?"

"We're heading back downtown," Ben said. "We can give you a lift."

She shrugged. "Sure. Just let me wish Tommy good night."

Grace took a long step toward Specialist Banks, stretched up on tiptoe, grasped his face with both hands, and covered his mouth with a long, probing kiss. "That's so you don't forget about me, baby."

"Please, Grace," Banks said, his face flushed.

Ben thought even the B-girls looked put off by her antics.

They walked out to the jeep where Ben moved to the back seat for the ride downtown and Grace Waverly climbed into the front with Elijah. The woman didn't look dangerous, but you never knew—he hadn't frisked her, he'd keep an eye on her. As Grace settled into the seat, she gave them a glimpse of her creamy white thighs, a provocative—and probably deliberate—move. During the whole maneuver, she never stopped talking:

"Vietnam is such a lovely country. But just imagine how much more beautiful it would be if you just stopped killing each other. Have you been to the Central Highlands? So many shades of color, the greens, the yellows, the paddies, the mountains. I loved the morning mists; I visited all the pagodas, they're beautiful. Hue is such a fascinating city."

"We don't have much time for sightseeing, ma'am," Elijah said.

Ben leaned forward between the front seats. "So tell me, Miss Waverly, did you meet Specialist Banks over here?"

Elijah guided the jeep to the right edge of the road, making space for the parade of army deuce-and-a-halves rumbling north.

"Oh no," Grace said. "Tommy and I have been together for a few months now. We met in New York and went to a rally together."

"You mean a war protest?"

"Of course. He was in the audience, wanted to see what we were about. Tommy's brave. He knows how dangerous it is for a soldier to be against the war. Back home we're trying to do everything we can to end it. But so far it's not enough."

"What's 'not enough' mean?" Ben asked.

"Well, demonstrations are fine, but we have to do more. Hop always says we need to be in the headlines. Otherwise, the politicians will never pay attention."

"Who's Hop?" Elijah asked.

"Just a friend. He's one of the leaders of RAW. Have you heard of us?"

The MPs shook their heads.

The dense cordon of shacks along the road thinned as they neared downtown Saigon. Despite the late hour, a few young men on mopeds sped back and forth, enjoying the chance to go flat-out when traffic was light.

"We've been in all the papers," Grace continued. "RAW stands for Rage Against the War. So, now you know. We're all students, or we were. We believe the Vietnam war is brutal and bloody and unjust and hateful. It has to be stopped. By any means necessary."

"Any means necessary?" Ben asked. "That sounds extreme."

"We just have to end it, that's all. I'm meeting with student and Buddhist leaders tomorrow—oh, I guess it's today now. We're organizing a huge 'Peace Now!' march. The press is very excited about it. I'm so glad I came out here. You can't believe everything you read or see on TV, you know. The generals, they keep saying we're winning."

Ben had heard this spiel before. He gazed up at the night sky, took a deep breath as she continued.

"But just look around. I mean, look at all the refugees living in squalor along this road, the constant bombing, the defoliation, Agent Orange, the hundreds of body bags coming home, week after week. And all these ordinary Vietnamese people, they're caught in the cross fire. I mean—what's it all about, Alfie?"

Ben watched Elijah shift in his seat, hoped he wouldn't go over the edge and drive off the road listening to this woman.

"Look at you, Sergeant. You're a Black man. Back home in the States, your people can't even live where you want to. So you tell me—why are you fighting this White man's war? Against brown people, by the way. Light brown, I guess. What color are they? They're not White, anyway."

Elijah turned to Miss Waverly and gave her his best *would you please shut up* look. "You want to know why I'm here?" Elijah asked her.

Grace stared back at him.

"My country asked. So I answered."

Ben stayed silent. He was beat, end of a long shift, no point in getting into it with her. He watched the road, made sure they gave the Vietnamese families huddled by the side of the road a wide berth. They dropped Miss Waverly at the Continental.

"I do hope we'll meet again soon," she said. "I'd love to continue our conversation."

Ben couldn't imagine anything he wanted less.

Miss Waverly held out two fingers and flashed her flirty grin. "Peace, my brothers."

As soon as she'd passed through the hotel's sand-bagged entrance, Elijah started laughing. "That woman is a trip. Thank God she's gone; I thought I was going to have to gag her. She's got balls though, coming out here by herself."

"Roger that," Ben said. They drove to HQ to do their paperwork, and Elijah went off to bed as the sun came up.

Ben hated his frequent turns on the overnight shift—he was always so wound up afterward. It took a long time to come down; even if he caught a few hours of sleep in the morning he would be awake again by noon, groggy and blinking in the brutal heat.

He decided to wind down with a gin and tonic, so he headed for Tu Do Street and his favorite seat at the Twenty Grand. Lien had told Ben that "Tu Do" meant "liberty," or "freedom." But now Saigon's most famous street had become the Avenue of Whorehouses. When the locals renamed it they probably weren't thinking about that kind of liberty.

Ben settled in at the far end of the bar next to the stage. Only eight in the morning, but an all-girl cover band was warming up. Saigon was a twenty-four-hour town now, and these early morning singers were enthusiastic. A tall Vietnamese woman in a leopard print two-piece bathing suit and thigh-high lace-up boots crooned a Dusty Springfield number, "You Don't Own Me."

Ben thought the Co had talent; she sang Dusty's song with a lot of passion. He wished Lien could hear it, but he'd never bring her here. She had this crazy dream about freeing all the girls from the sex trade. Her plan was to round them up from the bars and then ship them to nice houses on an old rubber plantation outside Vung Tau. She'd find a like-minded donor and together they would start a special school for bar girls.

Lien had mentioned her friend Francois, said he had money and good intentions, but Ben was skeptical. Once the girls were safe, she'd get them into a school, steer them toward better lives.

Sometimes Ben wondered what Lien saw in an evolving cynic like him. They'd been seeing each other regularly, every Sunday for almost three months since that first day at the zoo, and he liked it. She had urged caution a couple of times: *Don't get too attached Kin-Kay. Love in war hard to find.* It was possible she was just using him. But for what? If she was, he didn't care; being with Lien was something to look forward to.

Over in a far corner a tall GI had a small Co—five feet tall, maybe—pinned against the wall, his back to Ben. The American towered over the girl, his right hand clamped on her left breast. Not a gentle gesture—the way he was squeezing her implied ownership. The Co looked over his shoulder at Ben, her eyes flat. *Don't mistake this for love*, she seemed to say.

He drained his drink and got up to go; maybe he could doze off for an hour or two before it got too hot. He threw some Vietnamese scrip on the bar and turned to leave. He felt a nudge, something silky but firm slid against him, and then Lien's warm breath was in his ear: "Hello, soldier."

"I thought you hated this place, *em*," he said, using the Vietnamese term of endearment.

She slid into the narrow space where he stood between the stools. Lien's áo dài was a bright white, and she had a red bougainvillea blossom in her hair. She looked fresh, beautiful, ready to make her way through the sea of corruption they were swimming in. Her tunic was long, but tight enough to invite attention. She leaned against him so she fit between his legs and her breasts brushed his chest.

"I do hate bar, Benjamin. What you see happen at Twenty Grand awful. But I need to tell you something, so I come anyway."

"You're right, Lien. This is a sad place."

"You learn lot about Vietnam, Lieutenant Kin-Kay. In short time.

But I have advice for you. About that American Co you spend all night driving around."

"Really? You mean Grace Waverly? We just met her. How do you know about that?"

"Time to go. Glasses have ears here. Come," she said, taking his hand. "We go Continental, sit outside."

They found a table under the awning outside the grand hotel, which opened onto Dong Khoi Street near the opera house. Just two middle-aged Vietnamese men in the Continental's sidewalk cafe at this hour, both alone, nursing coffees. The men didn't look prosperous enough to stand the hotel's prices. Pedicab drivers on their break? Or sappers, casing the joint? White Mice, working undercover? Ben's wheels were turning, but there were no hefty satchels under their chairs. Nothing to suggest they were toting bombs around, which was always possible lately.

Ben steered Lien to the last table on one side, as far away as he could from the coffee drinkers. He recalled what his OCS instructor had said about how to avoid getting mowed down by a bomb: *Keep your distance. Remember, every foot counts.*

Lien saw them too, but didn't look worried. She ordered a coffee and Ben settled for another gin, which cost twice as much and wasn't as tasty as the Twenty Grand's version.

"Too early to drink. Why you do that?"

"We had a long night. It helps me sleep."

She smiled. "I help you sleep. My method much more healthy for you than gin-tonic. But maybe no time now for us. So this American Co, you think she tourist?"

"That's what she says. Now, how'd you find out about Grace so fast?"

"From my boss, Mr. Darling. He notice when she come here, a week ago, on flight from America. He say this Co very bad news, she buy things on black market, should never come Vietnam. And she talk a lot. Too much."

"That's definitely her," Ben said. "How does he know all that?"

"They watch her. Maybe hear her talking, don't like what she say, you know?"

They? Ben saw Lien tighten up. She never talked much about her job, what else she did besides translate. They'd never discussed how kosher Mr. J.B. Darling's agriculture credentials were, or how he really spent his time. But it was obvious now that Lien was involved in some kind of intelligence work for the Americans, and she knew that he knew.

"Why bother with surveillance?" Ben asked. "If she's just some hippie peace marcher?"

"I don't know. But they bother. They write reports."

"Strange."

"I need to tell you this, Benjamin. If you see this Co again—be careful. It could be dangerous. You understand?"

"Okay, Lien." Ben didn't want to press her. "The girl doesn't seem like much of a threat, but I'll tread lightly." He smiled at her. "You look very beautiful today, by the way."

Lien liked that and held his eyes as she sipped her coffee.

They finished their drinks and chatted about what they might do the next day—another Sunday with Lien. He savored every single one. She wanted to show him the big Buddhist temple; he'd look at anything, just to be with her.

Lien sighed as she gazed into her empty cup. "I must go to work now," she said.

Ben got up and pulled out her chair. As she rose, he leaned in behind her, pulled her closer, and kissed her lightly on the cheek. She pulled back; Lien didn't want to advertise that she was consorting with an American soldier, especially at a sidewalk cafe.

"Too much gin, GI!" she said, her hands pushing lightly against his chest. But she was still smiling. He watched as she strode off, another serious Vietnamese bureaucrat on her way to the office.

17

PARADISE

14 DECEMBER 1967

The opium business was a sideline for Francois. The Eel had learned, over the years, that it was a distasteful form of commerce: getting people hooked, working patiently with a new user to acclimate him to the lifestyle, seducing him until he became a slave to the drug. It was a sordid affair, but it gave him a power over people that could be useful. Francois stuck to recruiting men; women asked too many questions. He had watched the bodies of his addicts shrink, seen their desperation when they couldn't get their fill. It was sickening, the lengths they'd go to. They would beg, borrow, steal—or even kill—to catch one more hit, to feel the forbidden poppy pulse through their veins again.

The profits were fine, but the trouble that could ensue once he'd turned a user into a hapless beggar—or even worse, a violent criminal—was unwelcome, a distraction from where the real money was: his highly profitable trade in stolen goods. So he'd ignored the temptation to expand. He kept the den next to his warehouse small and the users limited; every new smoker had to be approved, personally, by Francois.

He thought about this when Mr. J.B. Darling of the U.S. Embassy telephoned to ask him to dinner. "I'm working a new irrigation project near Vung Tau," Darling said. "Perhaps you can help me with it."

Such obvious bullshit, but Francois accepted the invitation. He knew who Darling was. Francois made it his business to know who was in and who was out, even among the Americans. The only irrigation project Darling would care about would be a remote carp pond where he could drown the odd VC. And his reference to Vung Tau—was that deliberate? This *bâtard* could make any threat sound casual.

Saturday night they met at one of Francois's favorite spots, l'Eau Vie, a small restaurant run by French nuns along the main road to Long Binh. Francois had arrived very early. In return for a "donation," a sister he knew helped him place his little recorder under their reserved table. Darling had come alone, but Francois clocked the Czech pistol he'd sold him right away, a bulbous hump beneath his ever-present Cuban shirt. The "attaché" was wound up tighter than an alarm clock, his eyes darting around as he checked out the other diners. "This is good," Darling said as he sat down. "I can see the whole room."

It was a quiet place, low light, very discreet. They'd dined on pâté maison, fresh mussels, duck à l'orange, potatoes au gratin, and a green salad, complemented by a Cru Beaujolais. "Your food is excellent," Francois told the sister who'd served it.

"It must be," she said with a smile, "or we wouldn't fulfill our vows."

After his third glass of wine, Mr. Darling began to relax, got down to what he'd come for.

"We really appreciate the help you've given us in the past, Francois. Your work's been superb—our country owes you a great deal. I suspect we may need a couple of other things done. Then private lives can stay private. The minister will never suspect you . . . find out what you're up to every Sunday. I know how much you appreciate discretion."

I knew it, Francois thought. *He wants more.* He wondered if it might be time to treat his friend to a taste of the poppy. Otherwise, these little errands for the Americans were going to go on and on, maybe become a long-lasting commitment—he hated that possibility. It was his own fault; he should never have let that nosy American specialist in. Francois had become a player in their idiotic scheme, it would be hard to say no to Darling now. He didn't need anyone babbling about his business or his Sunday meetings. Maybe he would help them again. But just one or two more. Every deal had its limits.

"May I interest you in an unusual dessert, Monsieur Darling? Some after-dinner relaxation?"

"What would that involve?" Darling asked, his tone urgent. His antenna was humming again, the man was preternaturally suspicious.

Francois chuckled: "*Non,* mon ami, this is nothing to do with pretty young bar girls begging for their Saigon *The*. What I am proposing is just a calming influence, a break from our everyday worries."

Minutes later, after a short taxi ride to the market, Francois helped Darling recline on a large pillow alongside a low table in the far corner of his den. The paraphernalia was already arranged on the table; his servers were efficient.

When he'd started out, Francois had studied various ways to entice new users; just one puff, that was all it took. Even the educated people were vulnerable. They knew—in theory, anyway—that it was a ferocious addiction that could destroy their lives, but they'd try it anyway. A lifelong habit would start out as a lark; the user told himself it was just one time, a happy experiment.

That first hit was always, unquestionably, the best feeling the novice would ever feel. Every single soul that Francois captured with the drug had never experienced that kind of timeless pleasure, relief, and relaxation beyond all care. One *yes*, and then the poor fool always came back—twice, three times, forever. Soon once a week became once a day. Eventually the user was rendered useless, trapped by the entropy of the pipe.

"Do you know any of our Vietnamese proverbs?" Francois asked. "I like this one: *Happy hours are very short.* That's why we must seize what small pleasures we can."

As he settled in, Darling was a bit jittery. "I'm not so sure about this," he said.

"I am surprised you would say that," Francois said. "You're a very disciplined man. You can handle it. If I thought this was dangerous, I would never have suggested it. Look around, you are quite secure here."

The room was very dark and they were in a corner, hidden behind a thick curtain. The other customers were deep into their highs. Whenever he helped someone smoke, Frank made a ceremony out of it. He carefully shaped the opium into a small nugget and placed it on a slim palm frond, heating it over the flame of the lamp until it softened. Then he transferred the little pyramid of dope to the pipe, placed it perfectly over the small hole in the stone surface of the bowl and warmed it again until it became a golden, bubbling mass. He used his small steel pick to fashion a hole in the apex of the pyramid, clearing a path to inhale the sweet smoke.

Francois helped Darling hold the pipe, guiding him so he could extract the precious gentle vapors at just the right time. Darling drew so deeply on the pipe that his cheekbones emerged. This was the sweet spot.

"Do you smell it?" Francois asked. "Like hazelnuts."

The rich aromas of the night floated over them: the scent of the drug, the cooking fires of the market, the dank rot of the nearby river.

Francois watched the poppy do its work: Darling reclined, his face softened. "It feels . . . wonderful, marvelous," he said.

Mr. Darling had been relieved of his duties, carried off on a gentle zephyr. All pleasure and pain were hypotheticals now, passing fancies on the wheel of time as he drifted through the universe wrapped in the warm womb of the opium.

"They call opium the celestial drug," Francois said.

"Yes, yes," Darling said. "I needed this; I have so many worries."

"Now you have tasted paradise, mon ami. Do you know the Coleridge poem?" Francois recited the first few lines:

In Xanadu did Kubla Khan
A stately pleasure dome decree.
Where Alph, the sacred river, ran
Through caverns measureless to man
Down to a sunless sea.

Francois had taken just one quick drag on the pipe and expelled most of the smoke before it ever reached his lungs. Darling didn't notice the fakery; he was sunk, consumed by the drug. Gently, precisely, his host prepared another pipe.

Darling looked weightless, like a child floating atop a gentle wave. To speed his journey—and because he loved reciting it—Francois returned to the Coleridge:

Beware! Beware!
His flashing eyes, his floating hair!
Weave a circle round him thrice
And close your eyes with holy dread
For he on honey-dew hath fed
And drunk the milk of Paradise.

When it was time to wrap up this friendship, Francois intended to follow the poet's advice.

18

RECKLESS

09-10 DECEMBER 1967

Tommy slept in the Saturday morning after the two MPs had spoiled his night with Grace at The Little Country Inn. Too many tequila shots followed by too many cans of "the beer that made Milwaukee famous." He was parched and his head throbbed.

When he finally got to work after eleven, it didn't help his hangover when First Sergeant Moseley strolled over and sat on the edge of his desk.

"Indulge me, Banks. Why are you four hours late?"

"Forgot to set my alarm. What's it to you, anyway?"

Not a smart response. Moseley moved in, two inches from Tommy's face. "What's it to me?" he yelled, spit flying. "I'll tell you what you are to me, Banks. You're a fucking newbie specialist who's apparently dying to become a private. You're an inconsequential bug that I'm about to crush. Like a fucking mosquito!"

The first sergeant extended his hands, wound up, and cuffed both of

Banks's ears with a deafening slap. Tommy wiped Moseley's spit from his eyes as his ears rang.

"Don't you *like* your job, Banks? How about a change of scene? I can fix you up with the Air Cav. It's one phone call. Like every other swinging dick out there you'll be jumping outta slicks into firefights, walking point all day in the boonies. Think you'd get a kick outta that? You say you're bored typing. Wanna live a life of danger? I don't think so. So smarten up and get your skinny ass in here on time, or you'll be pounding paddies and ducking bullets all day. You read me, troop?"

"Yes, First Sergeant. I understand, First Sergeant. I love my job. It's just fine, it's hunky-dory. So sorry I was late, First Sergeant. I apologize."

Tommy's liver was still swimming in alcohol and his hands shook. He felt sick and pissed—pissed at the whole world. He despised Moseley, detested groveling, hated Vietnam, and couldn't believe he hadn't found a way to be alone with Grace last night.

But he and Grace certainly couldn't get it on in the hooch that was now his home, his top bunk three feet above that snoring Kramerwicz. No one from RAW had bothered to call or write, to let him know a single detail about Grace's arrival. Those assholes. If he'd known when she was coming, he could have found her a room closer to Long Binh. Hop had promised to stay in touch. There was going to be a communications *protocol,* but he had to learn about it from Del. That prick Hop couldn't be bothered. Or didn't want to tell him. Maybe the pretentious asshole was still sleeping with her.

Before the MPs had discovered them, Tommy and Grace had arranged to meet this afternoon in the Central Market, but now he'd have to work late. He waited until Moseley left for lunch and used the first sergeant's phone to call her room, keeping his voice low.

"Hello, *Norman,*" Grace said, laughing. "Why didn't you tell me that was your real name?"

"Did those annoying MPs tell you?" Tommy asked. "I never use that name, I hate it."

"But I love it!" Grace said. "Specialist Four Norman T. Banks. It sounds kind of swanky."

"I have to work tonight," Tommy said. "Can we meet tomorrow instead?"

"Sure, let's have breakfast at the hotel. 8:30 . . . on the roof. I'm meeting a reporter."

"Why? You think that's wise?"

"Why not? He's very intrigued by the movement. His name is Joe, Joe Kline, with the *Chicago Tribune*. He's very sweet. He wants to write about RAW."

Sunday morning Tommy took the bus downtown but got caught in all the military traffic. He was forty-five minutes late by the time he cleared security and found the elevator to the Continental's terrace. Grace and Kline had already eaten and were deep in conversation.

"Oh, Joe, you're so clever!" Grace said with a laugh, touching the guy's hand. Joe smiled dopily.

Tommy struggled to contain himself. Not just because Grace was such an obvious flirt with every male she ran into. That he could stomach, but she was reckless. Lately, Grace had been so indiscreet—with words, with people, with anything. Her behavior could endanger Hop's whole operation. But then, did he really care? His current strategy (or was it only a hope?) was to do the bare minimum for Del and then escape this cockamamie arrangement, try to live his own life.

"Oh, hi, Tommy," Grace said, getting up to greet him. He was afraid she'd assault him with another sloppy kiss in public so he extended his hand toward her. Grace giggled and shook it. "Meet Joe Kline," she said.

The reporter struggled to his feet; Tommy noticed that his tropical khaki shirt had lost a couple of buttons, revealing the pale overhang of his belly. Joe's glasses had heavy black frames and thick lenses that exaggerated his bulging eyes, and a web of veins crisscrossed his florid nose. *A drinker*.

"Grace is my second cousin," Tommy explained.

Grace's eyes danced. "Well, *Cousin* Tommy, Mr. Kline is very interested in RAW. He says the peace movement is getting bigger every day in the States—he's seen all the polls. He thinks we actually have a chance now to help end the war."

Kline stared at Grace, hanging on her every word. Tommy noticed the wine-red stain on his wrinkled pants. *What a loser.*

"That's right," Kline said. "The draft's very unpopular now. American casualties keep growing, week after week. The new Gallup Poll shows the majority of young people have turned against the war. But tell me, Banks, what are you up to over here?"

"I'm just a clerk."

"Where?"

"Out at Long Binh. We help with logistics."

"Big place. Whole lot of logistics out there."

"Everything from tanks to turkeys."

"Right," Kline turned away, started to work his source. "So, Grace, I'd like to do a long feature about your movement. Why you came to Vietnam, who started RAW, what you all hope to accomplish, how you think you can change pro-war attitudes among the public. Our readers will want to know what you've learned from your fact-finding mission here."

Tommy winced. *Fact finding? This idiot must think she's an ambassador or something.*

"I'd love that," Grace said, touching Kline's forearm, holding on a little too long.

"Why don't we have dinner?" Kline asked, looking bedazzled. "At La

Dolce Vita Wednesday night. The four of us—my friend Phuong will join us. You can give me more background, some color. I want to paint a picture of the protest movement."

"Sure, Joe," Grace said. Tommy mouthed a silent *no*, but she missed it. "It's a date."

"I'm sorry, but we have to go; we're late," Tommy said. Despite his recent misgivings, Tommy was determined to have some time with Grace alone. "I promised Grace that I'd show her the sights—you know, the Pink Church, the pagoda, the Presidential Palace."

As they got up to leave, Tommy noticed a Vietnamese man with sunglasses at a nearby table looking at them. He had a newspaper in his hands but he didn't seem to be reading it.

"Show me your room first," he whispered to Grace when they were in the elevator.

It was on the seventh floor. Grace had barely closed the door when he turned to her and began kissing her neck, breathless.

"Tommy, I—"

"You should learn not to talk so much." He shoved her against the wall and found the zipper of her sleeveless dress as she wrestled with her bra. Then he lifted her off the ground and she scissored his hips with her long legs, holding him fast.

Later, as they lay in bed, her head on his shoulder, Tommy said, "Be careful what you say to that reporter. We don't need any extra attention."

"Oh, Norman, I'll be long gone by the time he writes anything. You need to trust me." She climbed on top of him, took his wrists, pinned them over his head. "I know exactly what I'm doing."

"I hope so," Tommy said.

19

THAT FAMOUS COMMUNIST DUDE

09 DECEMBER 1967

Ben woke with a start in the afternoon, bathed in sweat and tangled in his mosquito net. He'd had a nightmare. His mouth was dry, and he could smell the sour alcohol on his breath. *Why'd I have that second drink?* Specialist Banks was still on his mind, so he decided to eat something and then drop by the office around 1900 to make a call. One of his buddies from MP school, First Lieutenant Steve Orsino, was still a trainer at Fort Dix and might have some info on Banks. Maybe he'd catch Orsino at his desk. It was Saturday morning in New Jersey, eleven hours earlier than Saigon time.

"Steve-O, can you hear me?" Ben shouted into the phone. As usual, the connection to the States was less than optimal. The line made deep moaning noises; he imagined the satellite signal vibrating up and down around the world to link up with the East Coast.

"You're loud and clear," Orsino said. "You been keeping your lovesick grunts away from all the bar girls?"

"Never happen, GI. A man's biology is a powerful thing. When you coming out to join us? We're having a blast."

"Right, Ben, I'll volunteer tomorrow. It looks to me like you guys have all kinds of blasts. Speaking of sappers, don't let Charlie blow you to smithereens while you're at the movies. So what's up? You can't be calling just to shoot the shit."

"We're hoping you can run a check on a guy we ran into after curfew last night. Specialist Four Norman T. Banks. He looked shifty; I didn't like his act. He arrived in-country in late July. His last posting was at Dix."

"Okay. I'll ring you when I have something. In the meantime, stay away from strange packages."

Orsino called an hour later. Elijah was back in the office, and Ben held the phone out so he could hear.

"I knew you'd mix me up in something dodgy," Orsino said. "This troop, his history's unusual. He grew up in Hell's Kitchen, in a three-room pad, a tenement on 9th Avenue. Father's a retired postal worker, mother's a seamstress. Banks graduated Fordham in '66 with high honors. He was a languages major, took a lot of Russian, minored in English. He sold hot dogs in Times Square for a couple months, then got drafted in January. In college he backpacked around Europe one summer, said he wanted to polish his languages. Claimed on one form to speak fluent Russian. When the army found that out, they asked him if he wanted to do the language school in Monterey."

"Nice gig. Safe too."

"Yeah. But here's the first odd part. He turns it down, opted for Advanced Infantry Training instead. Pretty strange. He had to know that's like volunteering for Nam. Then—this is really crazy—after a month in A.I.T. at Fort Polk he goes on weekend leave in April and gets himself arrested in his uniform at an anti-war rally someplace outside Baltimore. For burning draft records. The event was a bunch of protesters destroying Selective Service files, yelling about how the war is so wrong, so immoral, so criminal, blah, blah. Two Catholic priests led it, the Berrigan brothers—you remember? Asshole should have been court-martialed at a minimum, but he wasn't. Got no idea why. Then two weeks later, he gets new orders, transfers to logistics school at Fort Dix. I mean, how does that happen?

"Once you're in the infantry, you're a grunt for life—you don't get out. That's my experience anyway. Every soldier I've ever heard of who went to Fort Polk for AIT ended up pounding paddies in Vietnam—always, man. No exceptions."

"I know," Ben said. He'd hated Fort Polk.

"But this freak gets out of a court-martial *and* the infantry," Orsino said. "So, I called our MP office down there in Louisiana, asked what's up. They said the orders to transfer Banks back to Dix came from on high, direct from the Pentagon. He doesn't look like a kid who'd have any political influence, so I don't get it. Giving him a free pass out of the infantry like that, to be a clerk—that doesn't sound like the army I know and love, not at all."

"That's definitely weird."

"One more thing. While he was at Dix, he got into a scrap with some corporal. They're playing softball on a Sunday, start arguing over a play at home. Banks accused the guy of disrespecting him, then beat the shit out of the troop with a baseball bat. The man has issues. Our guys wanted to Article 15 him, but then his orders came in for RVN and the C.O. said forget about it, ship the scumbag out. Don't know if there was any outside influence involved there, but like you say, it's weird."

"That's very helpful, Steve-O. We got an opening for a good investigator. If I request you, the brass will probably listen."

"Sorry, GI" Orsino laughed. "Got my hands full here, trying to stop the privates from shooting each other in the ass so they don't have to join you in paradise. Appreciate your interest in my career, but it's a moot point; next month I'm out of the army."

"Really? What's next?"

"I scored an interview with DOD security at the Pentagon. I'll probably end up babysitting the secretary."

"Congratulations, Steve-O. That sounds like a great gig, twenty years, and a solid pension. Good luck, and thanks again for your help. Over and out."

Ben hung up, turned to Elijah. "So what'd you make of that?"

"Something's off," Elijah said. "Your buddy's right; everybody from Fort Polk ends up over here. Why would Banks volunteer for the infantry if he had an offer for language school? He doesn't strike me as the gung ho warrior type . . . What's his name again?"

"Norman Thomas Banks," Ben said.

"Norman Thomas? Like that Communist dude in the fifties?"

"Yeah. Well, Thomas was definitely a socialist—maybe a Communist too; he had a ton of lefty connections. But he usually described himself as a socialist and a pacifist. Ran for president a few times but didn't get far. Maybe Banks's parents are Reds too."

"That chick Grace called him Tommy," Elijah said.

"Norman must not like being Norman. Start a file, Elijah. In case we run into him again."

20

ONE WORM

11 DECEMBER 1967

The exit of the worms began when Bing stepped on the manila envelope someone had shoved under his door Monday night. He'd just returned to his flat, the top floor of a lovely old French building on Hai Ba Trung Street near the Caravelle Hotel; he loved its high ceilings, the spacious, airy rooms, and the primo view of the big river.

Bing had acquired his taste for all things French when the company had posted him to Paris for two years, just before this hellish assignment. He'd furnished his place in the colonial style: rattan chairs, cushions adorned with images of tropical plants, a mahogany bed with a canopy and a king-size mosquito net. Vintage photos of 1930s Paris graced the walls; most days Bing wished he'd been born French.

It had been a long day. Almost Christmas, but no letup at the office. He scrounged the last piece of ice from the box, poured a large vodka, and sank into the chair that faced the big window, open to the sounds and smells of the street. His ceiling fan stirred the languid air, but it was still too hot to move much. He regarded the envelope on the periphery of his vision. No address—another reason to fear it.

He waited a while, took two big pulls on his drink, and tried to relax. It was no use. Cocktail hour was ruined. He lifted the envelope by its edge and shifted it slightly, listening for sounds of moving metal or granules sliding around. Nothing. The thing looked and felt as if it contained paper, just paper. He ran a letter opener carefully along the edge and slit it open. A white business envelope fell out. "BING" was written on it, in big block letters. He knew right away who'd sent it—the only person who still called him by his childhood nickname. *Look on the bright side . . . it's not a bomb.*

The second envelope contained tear sheets from a three-year-old news magazine. The cover photo showed a grim-looking second lieutenant wading through a rice paddy. "DIRTY WAR IN VIETNAM," the headline read.

Then he realized that the piece his old friend wanted him to see was not the cover story about some nobody soldier, but an inside feature that idealized the bucolic lives of Vietnamese rice farmers.

Why send me this? The photo showed a mama-san sitting in the traditional way, squatting on her haunches in the red dust in front of a kettle of soup, the phô that Bing abhorred and avoided religiously. That was because most pots of phô were infused—inevitably, in his experience—with a hefty dose of E. coli. His pen pal had highlighted a single sentence in the article: One worm may damage the whole cooking soup.

"So goes the well-known Vietnamese proverb," the magazine's man on the scene had written. His love letter to the peasants continued:

"Hai stirs only the very best herbs into her phô, as she fights to feed her six children in a rickety lean-to in the Mekong Delta." Hai and Mai, Phan and Pham, all these damn names sound alike.

There was a handwritten message on a card stapled to the article: "Thought you'd get a kick out of how our intrepid reporters portray life in the countryside. Loved the proverb, too. So true."

He read it again. It was obvious, from the way the message had been delivered, that his master back in McLean intended to keep his hands clean. Bing had been afraid something like this might happen, because leakage was inevitable when an operation went on this long. So much was documented. Too many players, too many cables, too many readers. But the crux of the matter was not up for debate. He hated resorting to this, but here it was. They would have to act, and it had better be soon.

We can't ignore the worms.

21

A RIGHTEOUS CAUSE

13 DECEMBER 1967

"The food's very good here," Joe Kline said, knocking back his second Johnnie Walker on the rocks. Tommy and Grace were at La Dolce Vita waiting for Joe's girlfriend of six months to arrive. Tommy drummed his fingers on the immaculate white tablecloth. He had a lot to do, didn't want to waste time listening to Grace hold court for Joe and his girlfriend, but Grace had insisted.

"What's with the stupid headgear?" Tommy asked, pointing to the wide-brimmed black hats the waiters wore.

"The owner's a Venetian expat," Joe said. "He wants them to look like gondoliers." He pointed to the menu. "I can recommend the spaghetti Bolognese."

"*Buona sera*," they heard the maître d' say. "Would mademoiselle like a table, or does she desire to sit at bar, like grown-up boom-boom girl?"

"Oh, there's Phuong," Joe said, getting up.

A beautiful Vietnamese woman in a deep-red áo dài with intricate gold stitching was glaring at the maître d'. Tommy thought she looked like a French model, the way her hair was pinned up. She said something sharp in French to the man and made her way to the table.

What's she see in this Kline character? Tommy thought.

Joe held a chair out and Phuong sat down.

"So nice to meet you," Grace said. "What did that snooty maître d' say to you?"

"He think I am bar girl, *putain*, so he say I not belong here," Phuong said, shaking her head. "I explain I work for Joe, but he not listen. He not understand. Vietnamese all in same boat. Soldiers, clerks, cyclo drivers, hooch maids, B-girls—we all depend on war to survive."

"So how'd you meet Joe?" Grace asked.

"I needed an assistant," Joe said. "Phuong fit the bill. She speaks good English, and she can type. Her parents didn't love the idea. At least not at first."

"Why not?" Tommy asked.

"They say I am—how do you say? A kept woman?" Phuong reached into her purse, pulled out a cigarette and a long holder, and lit it.

"My mother, she go on and on: 'Phuong—what would grandmother say? He not your boyfriend! You are paid companion. You no better than a common courtesan!' But my parents change tune when I send money."

Tommy took another slug of his bourbon, surprised at her candor. "How much do you give them?"

"Three thousand dong a month," she said. "They retired schoolteachers. It take them one year to make that much."

"The *Tribune* pays well," Joe said.

"Now my mother say she happy I live off only one American, instead of sleeping with three hundred a year, like the others do."

Joe chuckled, apparently content to be the sugar daddy for this beautiful, straight-talking Co.

"Every month I save money," Phuong said. "When war over I open dress shop, at nice end of Tu Do Street, where old French shops are. I call it Spring Moon, it sell only the best clothes, be *très chic*."

"What a wonderful vision, Phuong," Grace said. "Imagine what that would be like, if the war was over and Tu Do Street was lined with elegant shops."

Joe took his glasses off to clean them with a napkin.

Phuong looked at him as if he'd spilled phô on his shirt. "Why you have that ugly tape on them?" she asked.

"Dropped them at lunch and then stepped on them," Joe said. "Had one too many martinis with Whittlesey at the Continental. He was celebrating his big scoop for the *Times*, the page one lead, about that village our boys burned down up north the other day. The Zippo job. The captain said they had to destroy the place in order to save it."

"That nothing to celebrate," Phuong said. "Where those people go now?"

"I guess they'll have to camp out," Joe said. "Down here with the rest of the refugees."

"Maybe better they just die, like a million others," Phuong said. "So, family torn up, they cannot grow rice no more. They far away from their ancestors now, cannot honor them." Phuong's voice rose to match her indignation and a tear ran down her cheek.

"They go live some metal hooch by side of road," she said. "They have no money, no jobs, nothing. You think you win their minds that way? Win their hearts?"

"Maybe we should just win your mind, Phuong," Joe said. "Think about it: there are fewer VC down here in Saigon, it has to be safer than out in the boonies."

Phuong, tight-lipped, refused to answer. She wasn't giving an inch.

"You're even more beautiful when you're mad," Joe said, reaching out to touch her. "All that emotion looks good on you."

Phuong shot him a furious look, batted his hand away.

"That didn't come out quite right," Joe said. "Let's order, shall we?"

The waiter took their orders.

"Grace is the American peace activist I was telling you about," Joe said after the waiter left. Phuong's face was fixed in a frozen smile, but Kline pressed on.

"She's from New York, biggest city in the U.S. of A. Very exciting place. I'm going to bring you to Times Square someday. We'll see Broadway, the Statue of Liberty, take the Circle Line cruise around Manhattan, the works."

No reaction.

Joe gave up and turned to Grace. "So tell us, what'd you do today?"

"Oh, Tommy and I went sightseeing. Out to the Buddhist temple. They have the heart of a monk displayed there—a real human heart. It's preserved, suspended in some sort of chemical. It belonged to the monk who burned himself to death a few years ago, in that protest. It's in a glass case, like a Christian relic. I cried when I saw it.

"I suggested they should add pieces of the Vietnamese babies we've murdered to their exhibit."

Tommy tensed up. *Here we go. Can't we just eat?*

"The guide's English wasn't so good," Grace continued, "so I tried gesturing, but it got complicated trying to describe 'body parts.' Those American officers, the ones who do those stupid briefings every day, they have some nerve. Do you know what they call all the Vietnamese civilians we've killed? They call them 'collateral damage'—as if they weren't even human! As if they—"

Joe held up his hand. "Easy, Grace. There's enough tragedy to go around. The VC kill civilians too. Especially the ones who support us. They bury them alive—that's their preferred method. Now, let's talk about the food."

Phuong wasn't having it. She leaned closer to Grace: "You not like this war?"

"I despise it. Don't you hate it, Phuong? Most of our boys don't want to be here, and you Vietnamese don't want them here either. They're forced to kill women and children, burn villages, make refugees, poison the land.

"All this destruction!" Grace said, tearing up.

Tommy thought she might break down completely any second, make a scene. Then they'd never get to eat.

"Our government claims we're making South Vietnam *safe for democracy*," Grace said. "No way. This war is all about corruption. Your politicians, your generals, they steal from the U.S. and then they make their own people—*your people*—pay bribes to get the aid that was meant for you in the first place. A few Vietnamese get filthy rich and the rest of you suffer. Can't someone do something about it? I mean, it's your country, Phuong."

"I see, Grace. You very *emotional* about this," Phuong said. "But what can one person do? We stuck in middle—both sides do horrible things to Vietnamese people. In South regimes change all the time, but every new one bad as the last. Almost everyone corrupt in Vietnam now."

"Some Americans, those of us who really *understand* the war," Grace said, puffing herself up, "we think we can end it. The group that I'm with, RAW, we have lots of ideas how to get our boys home."

"So enlighten me," Joe said. "How can RAW do that?"

"Bring the war back to the streets. If ordinary Americans see that Vietnam has a cost, a high price they'll have to pay, they'll think twice about electing the war criminals who support it. Our campaign has many fronts: marches, protests, sit-ins, shutdowns, direct action."

"What's 'direct action'?" Joe asked. He opened his notebook and started writing.

A group of South Vietnamese officers came in, laughing with their glamorous wives. They settled in at the large table next to them. Grace fixed them with a hard stare. "Oh 'direct action'—it's just a phrase, Joe. It involves export-imports."

Tommy bumped her shin with his foot, shot her a warning look.

"But let's not talk about this here," she said with a nod toward the ARVN officers, in an unconvincing attempt at discretion.

"You could be our herald, our messenger," Grace said, reaching over to cover Joe's hand with hers. "In a week or two I'll give you more details. It's a righteous cause, you know. Very righteous."

22

FAITHFUL UNTIL DEATH

16 DECEMBER 1967

Three days later, Tommy met Grace in the lobby of the Continental. She looked delicious in a short frock with a bright poppy print.

"Nice dress," he said.

"It's Marimekko," Grace said, kissing his cheek. "From Finland."

"Let's stay outside," he told Grace. "Who knows who's listening around here." While he was rummaging around the Eel's warehouse, Tommy had seen several listening devices for sale.

The rains had stopped and the sun was out, so they set out for a long walk along the esplanade that ran beside the river, all the way up to the Thi Nghe Canal. It was late afternoon, a few precious degrees cooler; Grace held Tommy's arm with both hands and leaned in so her cheek touched his shoulder, the way she'd seen a few Vietnamese couples promenade before dinner. It felt good to think he could take care of her, be her protector. It was his duty—despite her flaws, he thought he was in love with her.

There was a sign on the bank where the two waterways met and the river widened—*Sông Saigon*, it read.

"What's that mean, Tommy?"

"I think it's the name of the river—in Vietnamese."

Grace smiled, touched the sign. "That's the way I feel when I help these people, the ordinary Vietnamese. I feel like I'm singing their song, the people's song."

"You're such an idealist."

"What else can we be? If we don't live our ideals, we're as bad as the war criminals." Her tone changed, suddenly serious, all business. "Did you look at that list I gave you?"

"Yeah. It's very ambitious."

"How so?"

"Some of the things you want, they're big—large, awkward, and heavy. It's hard to schlep them around Saigon without anyone noticing. I'll have to involve more people, and I'm gonna need more money."

They turned left and stopped to rest in the Mac Dinh Chi Cemetery, two blocks south of the canal, not far from the U.S. Embassy. There were long rows of gravestones and mausoleums, but the French planners had allowed for open space, too. Tall kapok trees lined the wide paths, and the tropical plants were heavy with red and yellow blossoms. Grace led him to a bench facing a stone that was slightly larger than the others—the memorial of a prominent person, maybe. After they sat down, she reached over and grasped Tommy's face with both hands.

"But you'll be able to get everything on it, right?" she asked, her eyes hard.

"I think so. I'm meeting my supplier tomorrow."

"Oh, can I go with you?"

"Too dangerous. You can't be seen anywhere near that place. My guy—let's just call him the Eel—he's real skittish. It's bad enough that he might be seen talking to me, let alone to a female American tourist."

Tommy imagined how that conversation would go: *Ah, Monsieur Tommy, I see you have brought a friend. Who might this belle femme be? And what about sécurité?*

"I guess I do stand out." Grace dipped her head, as if she'd made a mistake in fourth grade, been momentarily embarrassed for mispronouncing something in front of the class.

"I got a solution," Tommy said. "We could dye your hair black and buy you a straw hat, the cone-y kind all the peasants wear, find you some black pajamas. Then you'd fit right in. The mama-sans in the market would peg you for VC."

"I prefer those pretty silk outfits," Grace said, stroking his cheek.

Now that the deal was moving, Tommy was starting to worry, fret about the details. He was trapped; he'd have to keep helping them, there was no way out. "What about money? I'll need a lot."

"Don't worry, the cash is on the way. I'm picking it up tomorrow, at the American Express office."

"Where does Hop get it all?"

"A lot of people hate this war, honey. They're happy to help. They just want to be quiet about it, that's all."

Sometimes Tommy wished Grace was a bit less passionate. She was easier to love when she wasn't consumed by the crusade. She wasn't going to tell him who was financing RAW. Were her parents involved? Highly unlikely, given their politics. It surprised him when she did manage to keep a secret. But he wasn't interested in being that useful to his masters anyway. *Change the subject.*

"What'd you think of Joe's girl?" he asked.

"I liked her. The ordinary South Vietnamese people, a lot of them take the long view. They know the war has to end someday, and they'll have to figure out the future for themselves. They're not all lackeys doing America's will, like the National Front says."

"Do you think you told Joe too much?"

"Honey, we have to keep him excited. He thinks he's got a big scoop."

"You're not going to tell him I'm in on it, are you?"

"Oh you're such a worry wart. Of course not. You're just my cousin, looking out for me while I'm here. Now, have you heard of something called the griddle club? Hasn't Hop told you what the plan is?"

"I haven't talked to Hop," Tommy said, his voice rising. "What the hell is the griddle club, some pancake contest?" He got up from the bench, started pacing. "Hop said he'd let me know when you were coming. He blew me off; he's totally unreliable."

"That's not true, Tommy. He cares about you, about us, but he has a lot on his mind. Did you know Makeba left RAW? She ran off with that hunk Panther, Lavarious. They live up in Harlem now, gonna do their own thing."

"I wish I had a smoke," Tommy said, sitting down.

Grace stroked his hand, tried to calm him. "You don't need to know *everything*, baby. We have to compartmentalize—isn't that what the spies always say?"

"I'm taking a lot of risk just to be kept in the dark."

"Don't be annoyed, Tommy. You know I can't tell you exactly what Hop's plans are. Not yet, anyway."

"After I left, did you sleep with Hop?"

She reached over, took him in her arms. "Don't you think we should live in the present, enjoy the moment? That's what the Buddhists do."

That wasn't the answer he wanted. Her reluctance to be straight with him rankled; he couldn't save her if he didn't know their plan. Grace liked skating on the edge; Hop knew that but shipped her over here anyway, into even greater danger. Now Tommy was caught in the middle, helping the assholes on both sides push the woman he cared about toward the abyss. Sometimes he wanted to drop everything, go AWOL, and take Grace with him. *Like that's going to happen.*

"At a minimum, Grace, I need to know my deadline. All this stuff won't get back to the world in a day or two."

She let her head rest on his shoulder, ran her hand under his shirt. "Just make sure our boxes get to that dock in Baltimore in the new year, before the fifteenth. Have you found a way to ship it?"

"That timing's aggressive. My man claims he's got the logistics covered though."

"That's great." She reached into her purse and gave him a page from a note pad. It had a phone number on it with a New York area code. "When you're ready, call Hop at this number."

She took a breath, leaned back, and looked across the quiet cemetery toward the canal. "What a peaceful spot. It's like an oasis, a sanctuary."

Grace kicked off her shoes and walked over to a gravestone. She looked at it for a while, let her fingers run over the letters, and read the inscription out loud:

GRACE HAZELBERG CADMAN
1876–1946
TRANSLATOR OF BIBLE INTO VIETNAMESE
"SHE WAS FAITHFUL UNTIL DEATH"

"Isn't that interesting?" she said. "Grace Cadman—I wonder what this Grace was like. Do you think she was a missionary? That's what we're doing too. When it comes to our cause, our work for peace—we'll be 'faithful until death.'" She gave him a kind smile, and his heart softened. That was the woman he loved.

"I'm so glad I made it to Vietnam and you're here to support me," she said. "You're happy about it too, aren't you?"

"Oh I'm overjoyed to be here," Tommy said, with a wry look.

She laughed and punched his shoulder.

"Okay, okay . . . seriously, I'm with you Grace, all the way. But you realize January 15 is only a month away."

"So little time," she said, standing up. "You better get busy." Grace did a little pirouette away from the gravestone, slipped into Tommy's lap, and pulled his head down so she could kiss his ear. "You taste good—maybe it's time we got back to the hotel."

They walked out to the street and he hailed a passing cyclo. Tommy put his arm around her, held her close as the driver pedaled them home through the warm night.

23

FRESH COCONUTS

17 DECEMBER 1967

"Call me Frank," his new arms merchant friend had told him, but Tommy couldn't get the eel image out of his head. The guy had been a big help, bless him. He'd loaned Tommy some muscle and together they'd loaded a lot of weapons, securing the crates to the jeep with heavy canvas straps. Night after night, Tommy had been rushing around town after curfew carrying large amounts of cash, adding to his anxieties. When he brought up his cash flow problem Del had understood, had been very responsive really. Between what Grace came up with and what Del's people deposited in dead drops there was a lot of money left over, which was coming in handy now.

Tommy watched as his supplier's fingers flew over the abacus to tally the current subtotal. When he came up with the number, Tommy handed him five plastic bags stuffed with hundred dollar bills. The Eel thumbed a few stacks and jammed it all in his suitcase.

"Merci," the Eel said.

"I'll need a copy of the shipping manifest," Tommy said. He studied the form the Eel handed him. "Coconuts, Republic of Vietnam, 12 containers" was printed near the top. "Looks good. But I'll need a few extras."

"Mais oui. What extras?"

"Four more Claymores, one AK-47, and one RPG launcher, with twenty grenades. And that Winchester M70 sniper rifle over there. See if you can pack everything in one box, with a separate shipping form." The Eel looked up, a question in his eyes, but he didn't ask.

Except when they were aimed at him, Tommy was quite fond of the Soviet-made RPG-2 rocket launchers the VC used; they were light, portable, and powerful. For what he was thinking, Soviet-made weapons were appropriate.

"Is possible. But it will cost you," his new friend said.

"My sponsors have the bread."

"Bread?"

"Sorry. The money. We have the cash."

"Oui, you have no shortage of that. Don't tell me from where it comes; I don't want to know."

It was after midnight when Tommy left the Eel's warehouse and headed south to the port—it had taken longer than he thought to load his borrowed jeep. He'd turned off the headlights, so when he whipped around the corner onto Cong Hua Street he didn't see the MP checkpoint until he was on top of it. He jammed the brakes and managed to skid to a stop, inches short of the metal barrier. A big sergeant slowly lowered the M16 he was pointing at Tommy's head to waist level, but his finger was still on the trigger. His partner had assumed the shooter's stance, his Colt .45 automatic trained on Tommy's chest.

"You in some kind of hurry, Specialist?" the sergeant asked. Tommy guessed the guy was at least six-five; he looked the type who would enjoy busting a few heads because he could.

"That's right, Sergeant—I'm running late; the ship's leaving tonight." He could hear the stress in his voice. "I'm a courier, for MACV, need to get this shit down to the port ASAP. The colonel says it's a high priority delivery."

The Eel's helpers had wrapped the goods in black plastic, concealed in a dozen wooden crates labeled "Fresh Coconuts, Produce of South Vietnam, Always Fresh, Always Sweet." The problem was, if Mr. Customs Man in Baltimore ever bothered to crawl deep into the ship's hold to take a closer look at this fruit he might pick up a distinctive scent. But not the sweet milky smell of tropical coconut, no. Questions would be inevitable: *Is that gun oil I smell?*

Tommy pulled his briefcase close, flipped the latch, and reached inside. "Hold it, troop," the guy with the .45 said, moving in so his big pistol was six inches from Tommy's head. "No sudden movements. Just take whatever it is out—real slow."

Using his thumb and forefinger, Tommy extracted the USAID paperwork he'd concocted as the cover story for his latest errand. He'd typed it a few hours earlier and forged Lieutenant Nelson's signature. Sergeant Mountain Man turned his flashlight on it, scanned it quickly, and handed it back. "This looks legit. But why no headlights, Specialist?"

"The White Mice at the checkpoint on the main road said there were reports of snipers down here." *Not the worst lie.* When the White Mice had stopped him, Tommy didn't say a word, just threw wads of twenty dollar bills at them. They laughed hysterically and waved him through.

"What's under the tarp?" Mr. Forty-Five-Automatic asked, waving his weapon at the jeep's bed.

Tommy offered up his friendliest smile. "Twelve crates of coconuts, can you believe it?" he said. "The USAID guys in my unit told me to rush 'em down to the port. It's their new program, to push coconut milk as an export, back to the States. Our ag guys say it'll give the local farmers a boost, a new income stream besides rice."

"Why the hell are coconuts a priority?" the sergeant asked. He walked back, pulled back the tarp and nudged a couple of the boxes, which had been nailed shut. Tommy had left a dozen coconuts out in the open in two burlap sacks in case something like this happened.

"Beats me," Tommy said. "I guess the colonel owes somebody a favor."

"Okay," the sergeant said, picking up a coconut. He rapped it against the tailgate to see if it was ripe, like he was picking fruit in a market. "You got a big load here; you care if we keep a few of these?"

"My coconuts are your coconuts," Tommy said, forcing a smile. "Just don't put too much rum in them."

Sergeant Mountain Man laughed, lifted the barrier. "Turn your lights on, troop. Driving blind, you could have an accident. That's a lot more likely than finding a sniper down here."

"Roger that. Thanks," Tommy said, driving away.

The contraband carbines in the crates were nothing special, but he knew they could do the job. The M2 was fully automatic: its gently curved banana magazine held thirty rounds, enough to do substantial damage before you had to reload. The good part was that these weapons were old models, easier to get now that MACV was phasing in the M16. His most recent worry was that he didn't have enough guns. To make this collar look like a big deal, a major bust that the press would cover—and maybe the TV networks too—Del and his boys would need to recover a shitload of munitions.

He thought the additional heavy ordnance Grace had asked for would fit right in: a box of grenades, some rocket launchers, a few machine guns, a flamethrower or two—he would have thrown in a 105mm howitzer if he could have properly disguised it. The bigger items were hard to move but nice to have. Del was probably itching to stand Hop up next to a huge weapons cache and pose him for the photographers, then stuff him into one of those big black Fords they liked so much. Tommy thought that scenario sounded hunky-dory—the two-faced professor deserved it. Even Walter Cronkite would have a wet dream over this story. Hop would get his fifteen minutes of infamy.

Procuring it all had been a nightmare. The Eel didn't have everything Tommy needed; he'd been forced to branch out. It was almost a full-time job, to bribe all the guards at the ARVN storage depots the Eel had steered him to. So far he'd been lucky. Just like the drama tonight, the MPs hadn't sussed him out—they always bit on the rush order story. And nobody ever ID'd uniformed couriers.

"How long will it take, for all this to get stateside?" Tommy had asked.

"Three weeks, at most," the Eel said. "When do you need your gifts to arrive?"

"They say the drop-dead date is January 14, so it has to be on the dock at the Port of Baltimore a few days earlier. To be safe, it has to sail now, this week."

"I have arranged for a quick passage. But what is so important about that date?"

"They haven't told me."

"*Sécurité,* I see. Of course. One cannot be too careful."

Tommy shook hands with Frank, gave him his best *I'm serious* look, and let the eye contact last. It felt good, to be armed and dangerous.

24

THE FOREST DIM

23 DECEMBER 1967

When Grace got back to the Continental Palace late Saturday afternoon the clerk at the front desk handed her the key and a brief message: *Meet me 9 p.m., the usual spot. Next to G.H.C.—T.* Tommy usually phoned, but maybe today they wouldn't let him. His sergeant was so strict.

It was a beautiful day—dry, not as hot as usual. She thought it would be fun to walk out along the canal to meet him. Maybe after they talked they could find a secluded spot somewhere. Lately it had been hard to get together as often as they wanted to—Tommy's days were busy and most nights he'd been working on the shipment. Her flight to New York was only a few days away; she wanted to spend as much time with him as she could, before this delicious adventure ended.

Her visit had gone well. Vietnam had been wonderful. She and Tommy had accomplished so much. They had a chance to make a difference, to stop the destruction of this beautiful country. They could save lives: of soldiers, and civilians too. It would require breaking some eggs, sure, but if you truly believed in justice, you had to do what was necessary. Sometimes violence was required. That was the truth behind every revolution; Hop had taught her that.

Grace had grown to love Vietnamese fashion, so she left the hotel early to check out the best Vietnamese dress shops, the ones Phuong had shown her at the nice end of Tu Do Street. On the way she noticed hundreds of people hurrying to Mass—it dawned on her that tomorrow was Christmas Eve. But it didn't feel like Christmas; it was so hot and there were no decorations in the streets. *I should call home tomorrow. Might as well celebrate, buy myself something.*

In one of the nicest shops she'd settled on a pair of black silk slacks and a lovely, deep blue áo dài with an abstract gold design stitched into it. She added a gorgeous silk scarf to cover her hair, and some kitty heels. The outfit looked like something the prime minister's wife would wear—that woman was so fashionable, with her big sunglasses. Grace thought Tommy wouldn't even recognize her. *I look like one of those glamorous Cos he's always admiring.*

She set off for the cemetery, walking along the river toward the Ben Nghe Canal, where scores of sampans were moored on top of one another. It appeared you could step from one to the next and walk across the canal that way. There were a lot of people about, but the scarf hid her blonde hair and no one stared at her. It was a relief, to be out of her Western clothes. She felt more comfortable, less alien.

Thousands of people lived on these little boats; she supposed it was a better existence than crouching under a piece of ragged steel by the Tan Son Nhut Road. The river was pretty, and you didn't have to worry that an out-of-control army truck might wipe out your family.

She saw mama-sans bent over their pots, stirring the evening rice, while their children played a noisy game of tag. They leapt from boat to boat, laughing aloud in the thrill of the chase. Grace expected their mothers to scold them, warn them about falling overboard. But they just watched and smiled, didn't seem to mind at all.

They were such a gentle people, there was a sweetness about them. They didn't deserve this. Sometimes, when she reflected on what RAW was planning, she felt a pang of guilt. Were they really on the right path? But then she remembered all the children who would be saved when the war finally ended, and that made her feel better about all the hard things they needed to do. Maybe they needed to inflict some violence to cancel out greater violence.

By the time she reached the cemetery, it was almost dusk. A few days ago she'd started a novel, *The Quiet American*, by Graham Greene. She'd never heard of the book before she came out to Saigon, but found it very insightful. She liked the way Greene's narrator had summed up Pyle, the American intelligence agent: "I never knew a man who had better motives for all the trouble he caused."

Grace thought many Westerners in Saigon were like Pyle—they'd never understand the roots of this war. The soldiers, the diplomats, even the newsmen—they were so sure of themselves. They didn't understand Vietnam's history, its language, its traditions, or its people. *We have no idea how ignorant we are. Ignorant and arrogant.*

She found Grace Cadman's grave just as it was getting dark. She sat down on their favorite bench, leaned back, and listened for the evening birdsong. She heard a lot of trilling but couldn't identify it. Were there nightingales in Vietnam? Grace had studied nineteenth century British poetry at Barnard, and she loved Keats; she'd been carrying a small book of his poems with her on her trips around the city. There was still enough light to read a verse or two:

O for a beaker full of the warm South,
Full of the true, the blushful Hippocrene,
With beaded bubbles winking at the brim,
And purple-stained mouth;
That I might drink, and leave the world unseen,
And with thee fade away into the forest dim . . .

There was a rustling in the bushes behind her. She turned lazily to look, hoping to see a nightingale.

25

THE AFFAIR

24 DECEMBER 1967

His driver was too cautious. On Sunday nights Francois was always in a hurry, trying to get to Mai's villa outside Vung Tau as soon as humanly possible. Traffic was horrendous at any hour but tonight was an even bigger tangle—it was Christmas Eve, and thousands of Catholics were rushing to their ancestral homes for the holiday. The one-lane road that led to Mai's house was jammed with minibuses, cyclos, and the occasional wandering water buffalo, slowing progress to a crawl.

"Can't you go around them?" Francois demanded, but his driver shook his head. *Perhaps I need a new driver*, he thought.

He wished he could command a helicopter, like Prime Minister Manh, who happened to be Mai's husband. Francois hated wasting time in the car; it was hard for them to be together now that she was in the papers all the time. Photos of Mai and the minister were even showing up in the Western magazines.

Reporters couldn't resist fawning over the dashing couple that was supposedly going to transform South Vietnam. Some writers had started comparing them to the Kennedys—journalists could be so stupid. But thankfully, Mai was often alone in the beach house. The minister had his regular meetings on Mondays in Saigon, and he traveled frequently around the country to inspect ARVN units and meet with province chiefs.

The minister loved visiting the provinces in person—that was the best way to collect the necessary bribes. Necessary, because the ministerial lifestyle was not cheap. There was a lot to look after: the big villa in Saigon, the Vung Tau hideaway, a rubber plantation, and thousands of hectares of prime rice-growing land in the Delta, all purchased by his dummy corporations. Francois found it surprising that the minister hadn't tried (at least not yet) to make an "investment" in Francois's off-the-books operation. Minister Manh had to know how much money "the Eel" was making—the arms trade was another potential honeypot to siphon. It was probably just a matter of time.

As soon as her husband left on Sundays to fly to the city, Mai would dismiss the servants and prepare for her lover. The anticipation was hard for Francois to take; his body ached thinking about her. He always brought a gift; this time a pair of delicate earrings, gold with rose-cut diamonds, fashioned by French jewelers in an antique style. He knew Mai would love them. They had a routine. They would share a light supper and a good bottle of wine—the minister had an excellent cellar—and retire to the second floor bedroom with the long view of the sea and the islands.

Francois loved watching the light play on the big statue of the Virgin Mary that rose over the harbor. He never tired of studying Vung Tau's hilly coastline. And then there were the long, languorous nights, when they couldn't get enough of each other. These moments with Mai were the only times Francois ever relaxed. He needed these little breaks;

things were always so tense in town. Especially lately, he'd been under such pressure.

Once Francois arrived, they never left the house. Francois's driver, a big Montagnard called Thi, would drop him near her villa and then decamp to a small hotel in the town. Thi certainly knew who lived there, but Francois had made it clear that anyone who ever said *one word* about his secret life would be *oh so sorry* he'd ever been born.

On Tuesdays they parted. An ARVN helicopter would arrive around 1900 to ferry Mai back to Saigon for her official duties and her afternoon *mah-jongg* games. Then Francois and Thi would brave the treacherous roads back to the city.

His arrivals were his favorite moments. On this warm fragrant evening, he waited until his car was out of sight and then knocked lightly on the ornate door. Mai opened it and embraced him. She wore a long silk robe and her feet were bare; she had nothing on underneath. They settled together on the large chaise on the bedroom balcony, drinking the sea air. He poured white wine.

"How are you, *ma chérie*?" he asked.

"I am fine. The minister is very unhappy though. He thinks there may be a coup. He is nervous."

"Everyone in Vietnam is nervous, Mai."

"I know. But your business, it is good?"

"War is always good for business. Now, I've brought you something."

He produced the red velvet box. She frowned, concerned, but then caught the mischief in his eyes. Francois wasn't about to do anything foolish; they both knew a future together was impossible. She smiled and opened it. "Oooh la la, so beautiful!"

Mai crawled over him so she could put the earrings on and see herself in the mirror. She let her robe fall open and teased him with a little twirl, twisting her gift so the jewels sparkled.

Not long after Mai and Francois had begun their affair, they'd spent a week together in Paris; Mai wanted to see the latest spring fashions. While he gambled away his afternoons at Longchamp (his horses always lost), she went to all the haute couture shows. Francois loved Paris. It was a playground, a place to indulge his love for French food and culture. His mother, Amalie, was a devout Catholic who'd grown up in Lyon. Amalie's father, Paul Rousseau, was a wine exporter; some of his best customers were expats living in Annam.

In 1915, when Amalie was seventeen and the Great War had decimated his business, Rousseau moved the family to Annam. Amalie had hated Saigon at first, but then one Sunday a handsome Annamese man asked her to be his doubles partner at the Club de Tennis. Nguyen The Truyen was the eldest son of the manager of the Banque de l'Indochine, and had studied two years at the Sorbonne. Truyen was charming, ambitious, and spoke excellent French; it also helped that he espoused the ideals of *liberté, égalité et fraternité,* especially around Amalie's parents.

Amalie pestered her father for months until he agreed to the marriage. He did so reluctantly because he knew the challenges mixed-race couples faced. Francois had inherited his Catholic faith from his mother and his talent for driving a hard bargain from his father, who became a successful banker.

During their evenings in Paris, Mai and Francois liked to stroll the Left Bank and stop at fashionable cafes. Many Vietnamese were exiles in the City of Light; Mai and Francois often crossed the street so they wouldn't face them. To avoid recognition, she wore a silk scarf and large tortoise-shell sunglasses, copying Jackie Kennedy. They discovered a bohemian spot favored by students and dined at its communal tables twice, a respite from room service. Francois thought it had been the best week of his life.

He had realized then that Mai liked hiding, being undercover. The Vietnamese had nourished secret societies for centuries, and a taste for covert action was embedded in their culture—they were always dealing with invaders. Mai knew he was a bad boy, but she loved the drama of their clandestine meetings. She couldn't stop seeing him—the risk was intoxicating. She moved away from the mirror and perched on the side of the recliner, breaking his reverie. Her robe fell open as she studied one of the earrings, turning it over in her hand.

"It is old, no?"

"They're French. Eighteenth century, I think."

"Where did you get them?"

"A woman from Nha Trang brought them to me. The Americans bombed her house. An accident, but now she has no house to go home to. She's selling everything she has left, moving to Saigon."

"*C'est triste.*"

"*Oui, oui—la sale guerre.* Our dirty war, our war of a million tragedies. Is the minister really worried?"

"Yes. He does not trust the generals. He says they are hungry for power."

"A good distraction. Your husband will be so busy warding off his enemies, he will not notice us."

"I hope so. What is the news from the market?"

"The same. They are all after me now, ma chérie, they all want a piece of me. They want me to, well . . . *plus ça change, plus c'est la même chose.*"

She laughed. "Greed is always with us."

A vision passed in front of him: the rifles, the mines, the machine guns. The careful way they had packed them, the money changing hands, the cranes swinging the long wooden boxes onto the decks of the freighter.

The night before he'd dreamed he was trapped in the dark hold of the ship. The minister and Darling had him pinned against the steel floor. Darling towered over him with a crowbar and wrenched the crate open. The American swore and ordered Francois to crawl into the box on top of the body. Her eyes were wide open. She stared up, asking why.

26

AMERICAN MERMAID

25 DECEMBER 1967

"Merry Christmas," Ben said as he answered the phone, no joy in his voice.

"Kin-Kay, how are you? Lieutenant Lu here. I have special present for you. We find body, in river. This morning, half hour ago. Young woman, blonde. Very unusual. Can you come see, right now? Pier 7?"

Lieutenant Nguyen Van Lu—"Lucky Lu" to the Americans—was the senior White Mice officer on duty Christmas Day. He'd won the Saigon lottery a few years ago but elected to keep his day job.

Ben had worked with Lu before, interviewing VC bombing suspects. The national policeman was a flamboyant dresser who wore two .45-caliber revolvers on a wide ammo belt, like a gunfighter in a B-Western. But once you got past the nickname and the cowboy accoutrements, Lu was a serious, thorough cop.

As far as Ben could tell, Lu wasn't bent, but he had a mean streak. Several times Ben had to walk away while Lu and his White Mice colleagues worked over a VC suspect. It was SOP for them: they would hook the bare wires of a field telephone up to the guy's testicles and turn the crank, shock the shit out of him.

Ben figured whatever the VC confessed to after that would be worthless; the prisoner would say anything to make the torture end. He couldn't stop Lu from abusing prisoners but hated the screaming, wanted nothing to do with it.

Ben and Elijah were down at the dock in ten minutes. The White Mice were still waiting for a body bag, so the woman had been left face down on the pier, naked, not even a poncho to cover her. Vulnerable, alone, and very dead. Ben knelt and rolled her over; he winced when he saw her face. He'd half-expected this, but it was sad anyway.

"Fisherman find her," Lu said. "About an hour ago. He anchored in Thi Nghe Canal, where it meet river. Body bump into his sampan. She spill his coffee, I think." Lu grinned.

Ben didn't think it was funny.

"We untangle her from fishnet. Very *difficile,"* Lu said.

"We know her," Ben said. "Her name's Grace Waverly. She's a tourist. From New York."

"A tourist? From U.S.? What she do here?" Lu asked.

"She was a war protester, a peacenik," Elijah said. "Sure was a pretty peacenik though."

Ben studied the body, which was partially covered in a blanket of seaweed. Her pale skin was a sharp contrast to the twisted web of iridescent green. The body seemed in good shape, hadn't been in the water long. No obvious wounds, bruises, or contusions. No marks of a ligature around her neck. No defensive wounds, no signs of a struggle. Could she have drowned? Shed her clothes, gone for a swim in Sông Saigon?

She was from Manhattan, so maybe she couldn't swim. But an accidental drowning seemed implausible, unlikely. Grace was a healthy woman in her prime; it was hard to believe they were looking at a natural death.

"Maybe she was drunk," Elijah said. "Fell in, an accident."

"You think she fell in?" Ben knelt to pick at the seaweed on one of Grace's legs, pinched some of it between his fingers.

"How'd she get seaweed all over her? No weeds in this part of the river, in the channel, or by the pier."

Elijah lifted more of the green tangle away from Grace's arm. "Like an American mermaid. But a dead one."

Ben pointed to a tattoo, newish, on the inside of her wrist.

"A mermaid with a peace symbol on her wrist. But I don't think this was a peaceful death. I can't tell you how she died yet, but something's not right."

Lu looked back up the river. "Current and tides very strong here. Maybe she go in way upriver where more weeds grow, no dredging up there. Currents pull her down here."

Ben nodded. "If she was drunk and fell in—an accident—she'd still have some clothes on, right? At least her underwear. It would be really weird to go skinny dipping around here, with so many people nearby. Maybe the pathologist can help us." He looked at Lu. "Whose case is this, anyway?"

Lu thought about it. "Lucky say this girl your Christmas present, Kin-Kay. She American. You know her, you meet her before."

"But she's a civilian, we don't usually mess with civilians, unless they work for us."

"I no want no new *dinky-dau* case, Kin-Kay," Lu said, using pidgin Vietnamese for *crazy*. "Lucky have enough problem, try to stop VC who blow up our soldiers. Your U.S. doctors have more equipment than Vietnamese, better tests.

“So you MPs take lead. Lucky be your consultant, your Number One advisor. But there is good news, Kin-Kay. Lucky work for you for free.”

“That’s a relief,” Ben said. “Most of us over here are broke and out of luck.”

26

DOCTOR DEATH

26 DECEMBER 1967

Maybe it was because it was the day after Christmas, or because the flow of body bags had been held up somewhere, but the flood of casualties to the army's morgue at Tan Son Nhut had ebbed, at least for one day. Out in the hall Ben pressed his nose against the thick window with the view of the autopsy room and squinted to read the toe tags: a sergeant killed in an ambush, a second lieutenant with lots of shrapnel wounds—he wondered if it was a fragging—and a couple of grunts, one killed on a patrol and the other in a drunken argument in his hooch. Ben offered up a small prayer for the dead.

They'd driven out there to check with the doctors and planned to go up to Long Binh later to chat up Specialist Banks. Ben knocked on the locked door to the autopsy room and took a quick step back when MACV's chief pathologist, Colonel Ned Bier, barged through it. Ben and Elijah snapped to attention and saluted.

"Dr. Death," Ben said. "What are you doing here?"

Colonel Bier didn't observe many military customs but managed a desultory salute. "I know you're surprised to see me in the lab, Lieutenant. Usually I'm stuck at my desk pushing out the paperwork. But yesterday you sent me this weird case—a young American woman, my goodness me! Why is this case so out of the ordinary, do I hear you ask? Because she expired while seeming to be in tip-top shape, the pink of health. No apparent wounds on her, at least none I can discern. Now that's strange, says I—an obvious anomaly.

"We death doctors always enjoy a good anomaly, makes our dreary jobs so much more interesting. I thought it was worth getting involved, that's all."

Ben stepped forward, shook his hand. "Glad to have our very best on it, sir."

With his shaved head, hollow cheeks, and skeletal build, Dr. Bier reminded Ben of a Halloween ghost, the malign variety. Bier led them inside to the gurney where Grace Waverly lay, looking beatific under a heavily starched sheet—the smell of the chemicals was overwhelming. He drew back the sheet, consulted his clipboard.

"I won't be able to answer all of your questions, but I already know one thing—your girl didn't drown. No water in her lungs. Dead before she ended up in the water. The White Mice who delivered her, they said she was a tourist?"

"That's what she told us, sir," Ben said. "The whole thing's unusual. We ran into her a couple weeks ago, out after curfew with her boyfriend and two other REMFs in a bar near Long Binh. She said she was a peace activist, kept going on and on about what a big mistake the war is."

Dr. Death offered a rueful smile and swept his hand across the room, taking in the rows of bodies waiting to be dispatched to their final destination. "This war? A mistake? Golly gee, that's news to me."

Ben smiled. He loved the 1950s phrases that were rattling around in Bier's brain. "Could she have fallen? Hit her head maybe, then ended up in the river somehow?"

"Anything's possible." Bier stood behind Grace, held up her head and parted her shortish hair. "Nothing showing on her head though. No wounds, bruises, or defensive injuries. If she was attacked, you'd have to assume she would have made some noise, yelled, screamed, ran for her life, done something.

"There are a lot of sampan people out there, up and down the river and jammed up in the Thi Nghe Canal. I estimate she went into the water around 2100 or so. It was still early. If there was a struggle people should have seen or heard something, noticed the commotion."

"Good point, Doc," Ben said. "We need to do more interviews. Are the blood tests back?"

"Some are. So far, nothing unusual. I did find evidence of recent sexual activity, but no sign that it was forced."

"What's the cause of death?" Elijah asked.

"Appears to be cardiac arrest."

"But you said she was healthy."

"Yes. Arteries in good shape. No signs of heart disease, but her heart shut down. Her lungs are clear, she was a fit woman in her twenties—she should have lived to be eighty."

"So it's suspicious."

"Suspicious? I don't know for sure, yet. Certainly odd though. Fishy, that's the better word, don't you think? When she got here she was naked. Did you find her clothes?"

Elijah was walking around the body, studying Grace. "Yeah, they were all on a bench in the Mac Dinh cemetery," he said. "She was wearing an áo dài. Folded very neatly. The dress looked brand-new, with her purse on top. Two hundred American dollars and her credit cards still in it.

Maybe the perpetrator, if there is one, tried to make it look like suicide. No note though."

"What tests are you waiting on?" Ben asked.

"The tox screens. From her blood and heart tissue."

Elijah looked up from his examination. "So she didn't drown. Maybe had a heart attack, but she seems healthy. What else could she have died of?"

"Could have been poisoned," Bier said. He hung his clipboard back on the wall. "But no signs of an injection, no needle marks. We looked between her toes, too, and under her armpits. Sometimes addicts jab themselves there. Trying to hide it, you know. This one doesn't look like a user though, and there was nothing suspicious in the stomach contents. She had noodle salad for lunch."

"Are there poisons that are hard to trace?"

"A few. Cyanide, the old reliable, comes to mind."

"But she'd have to shoot it up or swallow a pill or something like that, right?" Ben asked. "You would have found something, right?"

The pathologist nodded. "Cyanide doesn't last long in the blood but they got her out pretty fast and we took our samples right away. Maybe we'll get lucky, pick up something."

Colonel Bier's face dissolved into his famous smile, which reminded Ben of Vincent Price in one of those old horror movies. He looked tired, too.

Dr. Death warmed over.

28

THE CODE

26 DECEMBER 1967

They left Dr. Bier to his bodies and went off to find Specialist Four Norman Thomas Banks. It was 1900, and except for the bored PFC starting the night watch at a desk by the front door, there was no one left in the massive logistics office. As they approached, the private threw his *Playboy* magazine under his desk and hustled to his feet to salute.

"You seen Specialist Norman Banks?" Elijah asked.

"Banks? Don't know him, Sergeant. A couple thousand people work here. You could try the Enlisted Men's Club."

It was a busy bar. GIs lined up, two to three deep, queuing for beers and mixed drinks. The mixed drinks were ridiculously cheap, fifty cents for a martini with the top shelf booze. As they walked around the room checking faces and reading name tags, the crowd parted—MPs in the house. They found Banks by himself at a table way in the back, his head in his hands, drinking scotch on the rocks.

"Specialist Banks. Mind if we sit down?" Ben asked.

Banks looked tired; his eyes were bloodshot and his fatigues were rumpled. If he didn't know better, Ben would have guessed he'd come in from a patrol.

"Why not?" Banks said. "It's still a free country, right? Semi-free, anyway."

"Drowning your sorrows?" Banks didn't look up, so Ben got right into it. "Where were you on Saturday night after nine?"

"Me?" Banks asked, looking around for the exits. "Why do you give a shit where I was?"

"We're following up on something in the city."

"I was in my rack. Until zero dark thirty, anyway. That's when we got rocketed. I was in the bunker for a couple hours, hunkered down next to Kramerwicz. Ask him; he goes out of his mind if our shoulders happen to touch when we're down there."

"Who's Kramerwicz?" Elijah asked.

"My bunkmate. The guy under me." Banks looked from Ben to Elijah, searching their faces. "Why you hassling me? What happened?"

Elijah took out the snapshot of Grace, a copy of her passport photo. "You know her, right?"

"You know I do. She was with me when you asswipes kicked us out of The Little Country Inn the other day."

"How well do you know her?" Ben asked.

"She's my girlfriend. I know her pretty damn well—so is that a crime?"

Combative guy; Ben tried the gentle route. "When's the last time you saw her?"

"Couple of days ago. We have a date tomorrow night, then she's heading back to the States on Thursday. I wanted her to stay longer, but she can't."

"I'm sorry to have to say this, Specialist Banks, but your girlfriend isn't going anywhere. She's dead. She died—on Saturday night."

"What? What'd you say?" Banks rose out of his chair, his face contorted.

He shook his head, waved his arms around, a disjointed, spastic gesture. The other drinkers turned to watch, curious about the commotion.

"Your girlfriend. Grace Waverly," Ben repeated. "She's dead, unfortunately."

"Condolences," Elijah said, mechanically. He stepped around Banks and got behind him, just in case.

"How did . . . what the fuck happened? An accident? Was it one of those out-of-control ARVN trucks?"

Ben thought Banks's reaction appeared genuine. Either he was a good actor or he hadn't heard she was dead.

"We're not sure what it was. The Marine Patrol and the White Mice found her body in the river Monday morning. We don't know the cause of death yet. She was an American, obviously, so we're following up, working the autopsy."

"Autopsy? You're gonna cut her up? Grace, dead? She was young, healthy. How could this happen? Do you think . . . could she have been killed? Was she murdered?"

"This is Vietnam, man," Elijah said. "Anything's possible."

"But why? Why would anyone—?" Banks's eyes bounced around the room.

It looked as if he'd remembered something, realized why someone might hurt Grace, do something evil to her. He pivoted away and pulled at his face with his fingernails. Ben thought he might draw blood. They waited for him to say more, but Banks groaned, collapsed in his chair, and began sobbing.

Ben plowed ahead. "The White Mice found her purse. In a cemetery, the one called Mac Dinh Chi, near the Thi Nghe Canal. Her clothes were there too—a Vietnamese dress, an áo dài. It was neatly folded up on a bench. You ever been there?"

Banks wiped at his eyes. "Maybe. We go for walks along the canal sometimes."

Ben thought Banks was lying. Or at least holding something back. He reached into his pants pocket and slid a piece of paper across the table.

"We found this in Grace's purse. You got any idea what it is, what it means?"

The list of numbers read:

48 512s

24 617s

12 213s

06 312s

03 212s

Banks stared at it. His face was blank, but Ben thought his eyes registered the numbers—he'd seen the list before.

"No idea," Banks said. "They look like random numbers to me."

Elijah pointed to the second column of figures. "These ones here, starting with the 512s, they have anything to do with serial numbers? With requisitions? Is this a logistics thing?"

"No, no idea . . . I don't know!" Banks's voice rose and he wept; Ben thought he was going to sink to the floor and start wailing, the way Vietnamese mothers collapsed when their kids were slaughtered.

"How'd you say she died?" Banks asked. "Where were her clothes? Were they next to the other Grace's stone?"

"What other Grace?" Elijah asked. "Who you talking about?"

"Grace Cadman. She was a missionary, a dead missionary. From South Africa. My Grace, she liked that lady's gravestone."

"Why'd she like a gravestone?" Elijah asked.

"I dunno, she was into the inscription or something. Grace is a romantic, and it said something about faith. We sat and talked on that bench there, maybe a couple times."

"What bench?" Ben asked.

"The one next to the gravestone, idiot," Banks growled. His girlfriend's death was sinking in.

Ben weighed how much more they should tell him. "I mentioned she was wearing Vietnamese clothes. Why would she do that?"

"Those couldn't have been Grace's clothes; she'd never wear that shit."

"Did Grace have any other friends?" Elijah asked. "Were there other guys, other boyfriends?"

Banks thought about it. "Well, Grace knows lots of people. She's curious. She talks—I mean, she talked—to students, soldiers, reporters, monks, all kinds of people. She was planning that march, for peace. She liked Vietnam."

"Well," Elijah said, "looks like Vietnam didn't like her."

Ben decided to end it, let the news marinate for a while, they could hit Banks up again tomorrow.

"We'll need to talk to you again. Here's my card. If you think of anything, any detail that might help us, call my office. Anytime."

The crowd parted again as they left. "He seemed surprised, boss," Elijah said. "Maybe he didn't know she was dead."

"Yeah, that's what I thought too. It sounded like he was in love with her. Maybe he's not our answer, and we got more work to do."

When he heard their jeep leave, Tommy drained his scotch and hurried back to the hooch, a five-minute walk.

Kramerwicz was lying in his bunk with an eight-track tape deck in his lap playing the Beatles—"Sgt. Pepper's Lonely Hearts Club Band." The volume was turned up and the scent of marijuana lingered in the air. Banks ripped the player out of his hands, threw it across the room.

"Hey, that's my music!" Kramerwicz yelled.

"I need a favor, asshole. You were in the bunker last Saturday night, right?"

Kramerwicz recoiled, looking terrified.

Tommy stepped in close, grabbed him by the ears. "Listen up. If the MPs start asking questions—where I was when we got hit Saturday—you tell them I was in the bunker too. Huddled up right next to you. You got enough brain cells left to remember that?"

Kramerwicz made a feeble attempt to push Tommy away, but didn't answer. *Zonked-out pothead, totally unreliable.* Tommy yanked him up by the shirt, pulled out his Ruger, and stuck the barrel in his bunkmate's ear. "So where was I? When we got rocketed?"

"You were with me, Tommy," Kramerwicz said, his voice shaking. "We dove into the bunker, sure—we were down there together."

Banks released him, took a wad of twenty-dollar bills from his wallet and stuffed it in Kramerwicz's fatigue pocket. "Don't say anything different. This is for your trouble. Keep you in dope for a month."

"Okay, okay, that's cool, man. Just chill."

Tommy pocketed his Ruger and walked away, wondering whether Kramerwicz could keep his mouth shut.

29

UNACCEPTABLE

27 DECEMBER 1967

Ben was surprised when Lt. Col. Balderamos decided to do the Wednesday morning briefing himself; he often left them alone to plot their patrols. The number of VC terrorist incidents in Saigon had doubled recently, and the MACV brass had noticed. *You MPs have to fix it.* So the colonel spent an hour of their time strutting around the room reciting the obvious and shoving photos of bloody bodies in their faces. Last night the VC had pulled off two car bombings and one drive-by shooting. An American colonel had been wounded.

"Too bad it wasn't our colonel," Elijah whispered to Ben.

"This is totally unacceptable, people!" Balderamos shouted. As their C.O. waved the offending reports around, two pages floated away to a soft landing at Elijah's feet. Ben noticed the colonel was sweating lightly, his head had begun to glisten. Their fearless leader was losing more of his hair, probably from the stress of reporting an unending stream of bad news—war crimes in the big city—to the higher-ups.

What the hell did it mean anyway, to label something "unacceptable"? That it couldn't happen, just because we don't like it? Did Baldy believe that if he kept calling terrorism *unacceptable*, that would prevent future attacks? Nonsense. If the VC intended mayhem to erupt, it usually did.

The MPs and the White Mice could make it more difficult, but nobody could completely stamp out terrorism—not even the Israelis could do that. Ben figured what Balderamos actually found unacceptable was all the shit raining down on him from his betters. The generals groused that the streets of Saigon were no longer safe for GIs—on foot, in jeeps, or even in convoys. It was always about the crisis of the moment. A typical bureaucrat, the colonel could be counted upon to panic about whatever complaint the generals had lodged with him yesterday.

"We need more checkpoints, gotta keep the killers out of the central city. Double up on your patrols. Stay alert. Watch for suspicious packages, cars, objects in the road, bad actors in black pants out after curfew. You know the drill."

Now that he'd established Priority Numero Uno, the colonel turned to subjects he was less interested in. "So Kinkaid, what's up with the dead hippie girl?" When Ben had offered an update on Grace's death yesterday, the colonel had ignored him.

"Truth's always stranger than fiction, right, sir?" Ben said.

"Spare me your bullshit quotations."

"Yes, sir. Truth is, we don't know a lot. Marine Patrol found her body in the river near the port at 0600 Christmas Day. Naked, covered with seaweed. Preliminary autopsy shows she didn't drown. Dr. Death says she was dead before she went in the river. No visible wounds or bruises. We'll know more when all the tox screens come back. Her clothes and purse were found a mile upstream, in the cemetery next to the Thi Nghe Canal. Everything was neatly folded, on a bench.

"We're talking to a MACV clerk out at Long Binh. He knew Miss Waverly. He says she was his girlfriend. We're checking where he was Saturday night and looking for anyone else she hung out with."

"Was it a robbery?" the colonel asked.

"She had two hundred bucks in her purse. And her American Express card was still there."

"Useless to a VC. You won't see any Victor Charlies waltzing into the Amex office, Kinkaid. Strange that the cash was still there though, maybe something spooked the perp. How long had she been here?"

"About three weeks."

"Don't spend much time on it. Investigating the demise of some stoned hippie civilian is not a priority. It's her fault, she was an idiot, traveling to a war zone. Some people have shit for brains."

"Yes, sir. You're absolutely right, sir." Ben and Elijah threw the colonel their crispest salutes and left the briefing room as fast as they could. When they got to their lockers to saddle up, Elijah was still hot.

"Shit for brains?" Elijah said. "He's the buffoon."

"Judge not . . ."

"I like judging." Elijah checked his weapon, shoved a fresh clip into his M16. "I especially like forming my own opinions about field grade officers who don't know jack shit."

"Let's go find Banks again," Ben said. "Ramp up the pressure, see what he's hiding. Then do a stroll-through on Tu Do Street around noon, hit a few bars. It's possible some Co will remember Grace. Maybe the B-girls talked to her, saw her meet someone. Maybe we'll catch a break."

30

DEUCE-AND-A-HALF

27 DECEMBER 1967

Ben and Elijah put the checkpoints on hold and drove out to Long Binh again, but Banks wasn't there. "Claimed he had to do an errand for Lieutenant Nelson," First Sergeant Moseley said. "That lazy asshole is always MIA. His head is too." They left Moseley their office number and hustled back downtown to start checking the bars.

No joy at the first three. The Cos weren't having any of it, ignored Ben and Elijah's questions. The girls simply laughed when the MPs flashed the photos of Banks and Waverly.

You buy me beaucoup Saigon The, Mister MP, then I tell you all about American girl. She stay my house. Last night. I cut her hair. For free. Now she my Number One girlfriend. For sure! I see you laugh, but I no like men anymore. You believe me, right, Mister MP?

These B-girls were beyond world-weary, cynical to the core. Ben guessed that an unending stream of sexual transactions with soldiers might put them off men for life, but the money was good and most of the women had few alternatives, it was a matter of survival. It was only 11:30 a.m. but The Monaco, the A Bar, and The Ritz were already packed with GIs wasting money on Saigon The, hoping to get lucky. Most were only lucky enough to catch a dose of the Saigon Rose—STD was the number one diagnosis in the army's infirmaries these days.

As they exited The Ritz the usually cheery Elijah was frowning, shaking his head. "I don't know, Louie, these girls—they get younger and younger. It's depressing."

"For sure, GI," Ben said. "Let's try the Twenty Grand—Grace seemed partial to the classier places."

"So to speak," Elijah said.

When they came through the Twenty Grand's open door the big crowd edged away from them, retreated toward the back of the big room—MPs always *Numbah Ten* for business. Ben thought he'd start with the boss, Madame Thuy. She'd served him a dozen times after his overnight shifts. The MPs slipped onto the two stools in front of her.

"Hello, Madame Thuy."

"Lieutenant Kin-Kay, why you come here? Too late in day for your gin-tonic. And you have girlfriend now. Miss Lien, she very nice girl. Very pretty, very smart. You no need come Twenty Grand, no need my Cos. Saigon streets *très dangereuse* now. You GIs better off stay home in your tents; you safe there."

Ben guessed Thuy was about fifty, but it was hard to tell. She was rich and often wore expensive French designer clothes, as if she didn't want to fess up to being Annamese. He didn't know if she owned the Twenty Grand or just managed it, but she had a lot of sway over what happened there.

Over her many years in the bar business, Thuy had acquired a hard veneer. Her eyes were watchful, and sometimes resentful: dealing with

B-girls and their French and American customers for three decades would harden anyone's heart. But Ben had given her a lot of business and never hassled her; he hadn't rousted many of her customers either—maybe Thuy would humor them, throw them something.

"You ever see this American Co? In here? With this guy?" He handed her an enlargement of Grace's passport picture, along with a small head-shot from Banks's ID card. He wished they had a better pic of Banks.

"Not him, no. Thuy never see that GI. But American girl, yes, she come here. Always sit in corner, over there. Have long talky-talky with civilian. Two, three times. He fat American, older."

"You remember anything else about him?"

"His shirt always dirty. Messy, sloppy man, with thick glasses. Thuy not know his name. He always have notebook, write beaucoup notes. Maybe he reporter?"

"What color were his glasses?"

"Black, with thick frames. They broken. He use white tape, hold two eyes together."

"To hold the lenses together?"

Thuy nodded.

Elijah turned toward Ben. "Joe Kline?"

There was a flash of movement in the long mirror on the wall behind Thuy. A motor scooter pulled up, braked hard and slid to a stop directly across the street. A trim woman in a white áo dài and big sunglasses jumped off and began waving vigorously at them. What was that about? The Vietnamese never used urgent hand gestures to call people to them, that was considered an insult. Their movements were always subtle, respectful. It was very unusual, a bold signal like this. Elijah recognized her.

"Lieutenant, that looks like Lien."

Madame Thuy looked up, out the door. "Yes. You see, Kin-Kay? Your girlfriend no want you in Twenty Grand! This no place for boyfriend with wandering eye." She smiled broadly at him.

Lien saw that they'd recognized her, stopped waving.

"Thanks, we'll catch up with you later, Madame Thuy," Ben said. Thuy smiled back at him. Maybe she was still innocent enough to appreciate what Ben hoped was a love affair, even if it involved an American.

They jogged across the street. "Lien, what's going on?" Ben asked.

Lien shook her head and tugged at her sleeve. She looked agitated.

"Twenty Grand, it not . . ." She stopped in mid-sentence, turned her attention off to her left.

An ARVN deuce-and-a-half, its cargo bay covered by a large piece of canvas, rumbled down Tu Do Street. It was going fast, much faster than usual. When the vehicle reached the Twenty Grand, the driver whipped the wheel hard left and crashed the big truck through the bar's front door.

A slight pause, and then a blinding flash: a bright orange fireball shot out of the bar and pulsed skyward, like a rocket launch gone south. Then the shock wave—invisible, white-hot—bowled them backward into the dusty street, followed by the concussion of an ear-shattering explosion. Holding his bleeding ears, Ben rolled back and forth in the dust. He tried to get up but a wave of weakness washed over him and he collapsed. Moments passed; it was quiet, eerily quiet. The world had stopped. Ben looked over at Elijah. His partner groaned, but managed to get to his knees. A woman near them screamed, breaking the silence.

Ben and Elijah staggered to their feet and ran toward the scene. A chorus of shrieks and wails rose from the rubble, the cries of Vietnamese women and American men trapped in the firestorm.

Ben whirled around, looking for Lien. Her scooter was on the ground but there was no Lien anywhere, just a few shell-shocked civilians peeking out from their broken storefronts at the carnage.

31

ANOTHER MAN'S NOSE

27–28 DECEMBER 1967

Ben edged as close to the fire as he could, looking for survivors.

"That looks like Madame Thuy," Elijah said, pointing to a woman's arm that was pinned under the bar. They lifted the heavy piece of charred mahogany off her and Ben knelt, felt for a pulse in her neck, shook his head.

The sapper attack had wiped out the Twenty Grand. In the end, seven GIs had been killed and twenty wounded. Twelve Vietnamese women had also died, including Madame Thuy. Lt. Col. Balderamos showed up five minutes after the fire brigade.

"What are you two doing here?" the colonel demanded. "Where the hell you been?"

When Balderamos was angry, a rosy flush migrated from his cheeks to his forehead and up onto the crown of his bald head, like a house finch getting his color in spring. They hadn't organized any anti-terrorism patrols or new checkpoints, had wanted to use their time to trace Grace's movements. In retrospect, not so smart. The colonel probably thought they'd stopped for a midday drink. Ben decided to just take the heat; Balderamos got a kick out of hearing people say that he'd been right all along.

"Sorry, sir. We were here following some leads on the Waverly case."

"Forget it, Kinkaid. We're here to protect soldiers' lives. You know we can't waste resources on some dipshit hippie who offed herself. And you two can forget about rescuing anyone. Leave that to the firemen."

Ben wasn't really listening. *What happened to Lien? Was she wounded? Did she just walk away? I have to find her.*

"Shut down the street!" the colonel shouted. "Go door to door. Figure out where the hell that truck came from and who drove it. Indulge me, *Lieutenant*. Do some real police work for a change."

"Yes sir, roger that, sir," Ben said. "You're absolutely right, sir, safety is job one." *Where did I get that bullshit?*

Ben and Elijah spent the rest of the day establishing a perimeter, combing the scene, and interviewing witnesses, all the tedious but necessary grunt work involved in a bombing investigation. The colonel hung around, so Ben couldn't leave. Eventually Balderamos rushed off to placate his superiors at the five o'clock follies, so Ben and Elijah sat down against the pock-marked wall of the Pan Am ticket office for a water break. Elijah took out Grace's mysterious list of numbers and studied it again.

"If we assume for a minute that these numbers involve some kind of smuggling operation . . . ," Elijah said, pausing to think about it. "Guns, weapons, could that be it? I mean, she is some kind of radical. But how would they get weapons?"

"I don't think they're stealing rice," Ben said. "There's the black market, and Banks is in logistics; he'd have chances to make things go missing. He could redirect shipments, bribe the ARVNs, that kind of thing."

"We need to find Banks," Elijah said. "Then check the Central Market, quiz some of them big traders. You can buy anything down there."

When they were stymied on a case, they tried to pause and posit all the obvious unanswered questions; the exercise often pointed them in a new direction—sometimes even the right one.

"Look at this mess," Ben said, watching rescuers poke through the smoking wreckage. "Why did Lien show up here?"

"If she hadn't we'd be dead."

"No doubt. But I don't get how she knew we were here. Was she just passing? This bomb—did it have anything to do with our case? You think Lucky Lu found out anything about Grace?" Ben asked.

"We got a lot of people to talk to," Elijah said.

It was almost midnight before they knocked off at the bomb scene. Ben took a chance and dropped by Lien's apartment. He knocked a long time, called out, but no answer. Was it a coincidence, that Lien happened to drive by? At that exact moment? No, she'd roared up on her scooter, in a hurry. She wanted to get them out of the bar and across the street. Did she know there'd be an attack, decide to rescue them? But how did she know?

Ben slept poorly. His ears were ringing and he ached all over from the concussion of the blast wave. He fell out of the rack before dawn, drained a tasteless instant coffee, and was back in the office by six.

Lien had told him, several times, never to call her at the office. "I am busy. Mr. Darling not like personal phone calls. They keep us from important work."

He waited until seven, called Darling's office. She answered.

"Lien, are you all right?"

"I am fine, Benjamin. How are you?"

Ben exhaled. She'd escaped.

"Thank God," he said. "I was so worried. I'm okay. My head hurts, my eardrums are damaged, but I'll live."

"Yes," Lien said. "I saw you and Sergeant Elijah get up to search scene. Sorry, I couldn't stay there. Mr. Darling say he need me in office all the time now, too much going on."

So she cares more about him than me?

"I have to see you. Can we meet up tonight?"

Silence. Lately she had been too busy to go out, have dinner, do anything. The war had ramped up; Mr. Darling was very stressed. Many reports had to be composed, telexed to Virginia. *Very sorry, Benjamin, Lien have no free time today.* She seemed to be distancing herself from him, and he didn't know why.

"What you want?" she asked.

"Is this phone . . ."

She interrupted him: "Okay, nine tonight, where we always go."

"All right. See you then."

The faux temple near the zoo's entrance was closed, but the keepers never locked the main gate. He sat down on the steps in the moonlight to wait. No security here, but it didn't matter. He looked over at the tiger's cage and wondered whether Shere Khan could tell the difference between a VC and an ARVN, and then Lien touched his shoulder. "Hello, soldier."

He hadn't heard a thing. She must have come from inside the zoo, but he'd noticed no movement at all. How could she be so silent, especially in an áo dài? He should have heard silk rustling, something—maybe he was still in shock, or his hearing was really screwed. She sat next to him, took his hand, and let her head rest on his shoulder.

"Sorry Lien so busy. War get in way."

"Yes. I've missed you."

"I miss you too Kin-Kay. Bombing awful. Too many people die. Madame Thuy, she tell me you and Sergeant Elijah coming to her bar yesterday. That why you see Lien before bombing."

Lien had anticipated his question. "She phoned you?"

"Oh, no, I see her Tuesday morning, at Twenty Grand. Madame Thuy old friend. Very sorry she die. She very good woman. Thuy a patriot, for all Vietnamese people."

"But we never told Thuy we were coming to talk to her."

She touched his face, looked up. "Vietnamese always know where American soldiers go. You already know that, Lieutenant Kin-Kay." Lien's smile was magnetic; she enjoyed teasing him.

But that's no answer. He and Elijah had decided on the spur of the moment to ignore the colonel's orders and go question bar girls Wednesday. They hadn't told Thuy or anyone else. Were they followed? Or was there a mole in their office? Something was off—Lien was lying.

"You figure out yet, who kill Grace Waverly?" Lien asked.

"No. We're working on it. The bombing set us back."

"Very sad, this bombing. So many people, their life ruined. Sometimes things get started, they go too fast, like big train. Lien try, but train very hard to stop. You collect things wise people say, Benjamin. Do you know famous Vietnamese saying? 'You cannot breathe through another man's nose.'"

"I don't think so," he said. "What's that mean?" She put her arms around him, pulled him down to her chest and stroked his face, as if her tenderness would salve his wounds. He realized she was avoiding his questions, but so what?

"To Vietnamese, it about freedom. For centuries other peoples occupy our land. They breathe for us. Vietnamese people, most people, in every land, they just want to breathe free—live free. That what I always tell you."

Ben didn't get everything Lien was trying to tell him, but he didn't like the sound of it. Would he and Elijah ever solve any of this? *If the good Lord's willing and the creek don't rise.*

But the creek was running pretty high.

32

SECOND SOURCE

28 DECEMBER 1967

When Joe Kline got home it was past midnight. Phuong was curled up in red silk pajamas on the couch, reading. She looked delectable but deep in thought, entranced by her book.

"What are you reading, Phuong? It must be very interesting."

"*L'Étranger,* by Camus. A Frenchman. You have read it?"

"I've heard of it, yes, but no, I haven't read it."

Joe had joined the *Tribune* as a copy boy right out of high school, his uncle got him the job. He knew his South Side education was inferior, especially compared to some of his snooty colleagues, like Ned Whittlesey of the *Times*. But Whittlesey didn't have a beautiful, well-educated girlfriend who spoke fluent French and was learning English.

"What's it about?" Joe asked.

"How you say, in English? Aloneness? It about being all alone, by yourself. The narrator, Monsieur Meursault, he stranger to this life. He believe in nothing. He think rules of life, social conventions—all useless. He kill a man, but not regret it. Then he look forward to his own death, to execution."

"Sounds depressing."

"Yes, *un peu.* But it's fascinating. Some people we meet here like him. War make them that way. Why you home so late?"

"Work got busy. Sappers bombed the Twenty Grand, several GIs and Madame Thuy were killed. The VC who did it wore an ARVN uniform. Then I worked on that story I told you about, the one that involves Grace. Finished a draft, made a lot of progress."

"Yes, I hear about Twenty Grand—bombing big tragedy. But Joe, I no trust Grace. She talk too much. She like to play bad girl, live dangerous life. Dealing with Grace is *beaucoup risques,* I think."

"Yes, there's some risk, but she's giving me a big story. It's important news, my editors in Chicago will love it. It will win a prize, I think." Was that bad luck, to lust after a prize? But most journos couldn't help it, striving for praise was in their blood. He didn't think he should tell Phuong much about the story; she was better off not knowing.

"I brought it home." Joe showed her the big envelope, along with the cassette of his interview with Grace. Phuong looked up from her book, took a long look at the package and the tape, uneasy about what was coming. "Why you bring that here?" she asked.

"Because I need your help. I can't send this to Chicago—not yet. I need to protect it. Hide it. Just for a few days, while I tie up a few loose ends. When you go to Vinh Long Saturday to see your parents, could you put this in a safe place?"

He handed her the package. She balanced it on the tips of her fingers as if it might explode, weighed what to do.

"Okay," she finally said. "But Phuong not like Grace—I no like crazy errands, no like danger. Phuong not your spy."

"Thank you—I know it's a bother. You know I would do anything for you. Don't worry, nothing bad will come of this. Where will you put it?"

"Under table. Under shrine to ancestors. While my parents sleep."

Later, Joe lay in bed, wide awake, poring over his day. Phuong was deeply asleep, curled against his back, her arms around his waist. He craved the warmth of her hug, didn't think he could live without it. He just needed one more source, one more person to confirm all this, on or off the record, then when the hippie girl gave the go-ahead he could publish, make it all happen.

33

THE COFFINS

28-29 DECEMBER 1967

"I was sorry to hear about your girlfriend," Kramerwicz said.

He and Tommy were in the chow line in the USARV mess hall.

"How'd you find out about that?" he asked.

"It was in *Stars and Stripes* this morning," Kramerwicz said. "They said an American tourist drowned."

"Don't believe everything you read," Tommy said.

"Hey, I met this guy who got the greatest TDY assignment ever," Kramerwicz said, reaching for a second chocolate pudding.

"No shit," Tommy said. "You're usually so stoned I'm surprised you can remember anything."

"You should smoke some with me," Kramerwicz said. "It might calm you down. So did you know they let guys have a quick trip back to the States? They have this rule, the body of every poor SOB who dies over here has to be accompanied, taken home to his mother? My buddy did it and went home for two weeks. Got to see his girl and everything, after he dropped off the poor guy."

"How's that work?" Tommy asked, suddenly interested.

"You just apply for it, I guess," Kramerwicz said. "At the morgue, out at Tan Son Nhut."

Why not? What have I got to lose now?

Early the next morning, after he'd told Sergeant Moseley he had a stomach bug, Tommy was filling out a form at the morgue.

The warrant officer in charge had explained there had been a few instances where the morticians had misidentified a body. Weeks passed before the foul-up was discovered, and then the army had to inform a nice family in Ohio they'd buried the wrong man. Tommy could imagine that conversation:

We're sorry ma'am; we thought this other guy was your son.

But where is my son?

Not the easiest screw up to forgive. To prevent further embarrassment, the army tightened the process, even sending fingerprints to the FBI to make sure every battlefield casualty was identified correctly. Each soldier's body was placed in an aluminum coffin and an American flag was draped over it. Then the coffins were loaded into the holds of the huge Air Force cargo planes that carried the soldiers' remains back to the world. Nearly 20,000 men had been killed; the army had run short of officers to accompany the bodies home, so they'd started using enlisted men too.

Escort duty might be morbid, but Tommy figured it was a shrewd move, another way to add a few more safe days to your tour. He hoped to escort a body headed for the East Coast. He'd be on official business, the notification of next of kin. No one would make the connection.

Tommy finished the form and walked over to the window that had a view to the morgue. The place was in chaos, bodies everywhere, not enough morticians to deal with the flood of casualties. He saw several high steel tables with random body parts on them. Technicians hovered over the hard cases, trying to find scars or birthmarks to help with the ID. The techs looked short of people, equipment, everything.

After a forty-minute wait, the warrant officer returned to inspect his application. "Thanks for volunteering, Banks. You're in luck. I had this lieutenant scheduled in a couple days for this job in Maryland, but he bought it yesterday up in Cu Chi. If you can get this signed and back to me this afternoon, I can get you on the next flight. You just need your supervisor to sign off, give permission for a fifteen-day TDY assignment."

"Can my duty sergeant sign it?"

"No. It has to be an officer. Get the guy in charge of your logistics section to do it."

Tommy took the form back to Lieutenant Nelson's office. He liked Nelson—for an officer, he was a laid-back guy. A couple of months ago he'd bumped into Nelson outside the Officers' Club. After five minutes of small talk, Nelson got up enough nerve to ask Tommy if he could score some grass for him—he'd have to be discreet about it. *Happy to oblige, sir.*

Then Tommy took a chance and asked Nelson if he could borrow his jeep, he needed it for some logistics errands. "Why not?" Nelson said. Since then Tommy had been using it on his nightly rambles around Saigon procuring weapons—Nelson had no idea what was going down. "Could I ask another favor, sir?"

"What is it, Banks?"

"I made a mistake, sir. The other day, I had to return this weapons shipment back to the Port of Baltimore. A small one, an M79, some Claymores, and a few rifles." Tommy pulled the shipping manifest he'd created out of his pocket, pointed to the details.

"When that crate arrived the stevedores dropped it while they were unloading the ship. They dinged a couple of guns. I shipped 'em back, but I forgot to get your signature for the return on the paperwork."

Nelson scanned the form, scribbled his signature, and handed it back.

"Thank you, sir. Just one more thing. My mother is very ill, in Baltimore. I need to go home. She might be dying."

"I'm very sorry to hear that, Banks. That's sad, of course. But how you gonna manage that? You can't go home until you've served out your year. Unless she dies, then we can get you two weeks compassionate leave."

"I found a way, sir. I've volunteered for some TDY—body escort duty. I'm accompanying a fallen soldier back to Hagerstown, Maryland, to notify the next of kin. I'll have a couple of free days in the area, enough time to see my mom, then be back here in two weeks or so. I need your OK though."

"Show me."

Tommy pushed the application across the table. Nelson read it and gave him a knowing smile, the same one he'd flashed when Tommy handed him his big bag of dope.

"Sure, I'll sign. This is a sweet deal; I might try it myself sometime. Where'd you say you applied for this?"

When they were finished, Tommy was the one who was smiling. *I'm starting to get how it all works over here.*

Now that his trip home was lined up, Tommy figured it was time to get Del into the act and stitch up Hop. He went back to the office, told Sergeant Moseley he felt better, had to catch up on his work. He waited until everyone had left and then dialed the emergency phone number.

Del answered right away, he was an early riser, already in the office at 7:15 a.m.

"I got you that appointment, to pick up your friends," Tommy said. "Sunday night, January 14, at the Port of Baltimore. Hopkins and his crew will be there. Be in place before six."

34

DON'T LEAVE US HANGING

30 DECEMBER 1967

The walls of Dr. Death's office were lined with diplomas attesting to his medical qualifications, but the quirky touch was his collection of skulls. Dozens were displayed on shelves on three sides of his office, their empty eye sockets trained on Ben and Elijah. Men, women, and children were all represented, recent finds and ancient artifacts, complete with museum-quality labels. There were skulls from Nepal, the Congo, Tasmania, and Colonel Bier's favorite, a Neanderthal from a dig in Uzbekistan. He took it down from the shelf, handed it to Ben.

"Don't drop it. The guy who sold it to me said it's 40,000 years old, supposedly."

"It should be in a museum," Ben said. He used both hands to return it to the colonel. "Is it legal, to own something like this?"

"No idea. Got no time for technicalities in the middle of a war."

Elijah's face lit up, a eureka thing. "Now I get it. *Dr. Death* is about more than autopsies."

"It's true, sergeant—skulls are my hobby. Did you notice those depressions?" he asked, turning around the Neanderthal's skull. "Right here, in the cranium? Most of these guys were victims of violence. They fit right in with the job."

"'Alas, poor Yorick! I knew him, Horatio,'" Ben said.

"'A fellow of infinite jest, of most excellent fancy,'" the colonel said, eliciting a smile from Ben. "But there are no Danish skulls here, I'm afraid."

Elijah looked unimpressed. "I wish you guys would speak English."

Ben laughed. "I keep trying to tempt the sarge with great literature, but I'm failing."

"The last tox screens came back," Colonel Bier said, raising an eyebrow. "For your pretty tourist." Ben and Elijah waited.

"I like this case. This young lady's death is quite interesting, a break from trying to identify all my young men who've died too soon. The news is, the lab found trace levels of cyanide—in her blood and also in her heart muscle. A small but significant amount. This wasn't a heart attack, mind you. Not a natural one, anyway."

"So she was poisoned?" Elijah asked.

"Most people have minuscule amounts of cyanide in their system—it occurs naturally in the environment. But Miss Waverly's lactate numbers were five times the normal level, a clear indication she'd ingested a big slug of the stuff. I would estimate, based on the levels still in her blood, that she received a dose of five milligrams per liter, which would be fatal. And instantaneous. So yes, suspicions confirmed. She was murdered."

"But how?" Ben asked. "You said there were no needle marks."

"And we didn't find any poison darts or blowguns." Elijah was fond of old movies. "You're both correct. There were no darts, no needles. But I've thought of at least one other way the poison could have entered Miss Waverly's system. It involves a gun, of sorts."

"Don't leave us hanging," Ben said.

Dr. Death smiled his creepy smile again. "She could have inhaled it. We also found trace levels in her lungs. Cyanide breaks down in the body fairly quickly, but the amount left in her lungs suggests strongly that she inhaled it."

"How could that happen?"

"I've done a little research." Colonel Bier pushed a skull out of the way and extracted a thick medical book from the shelf behind him: *Strange Occurrences in Forensic Science.* He opened the heavy volume and pointed to a large photo of an odd-looking weapon, like a big pistol with two long barrels; each barrel had a lever attached at one end. No trigger, and no obvious place to insert a bullet.

"What's this?" Ben asked.

"It's a cyanide cannon. A KGB agent, a man called Bohdan Stashynsky, used it. Twice. Once in 1957 and again in 1959. He assassinated two Ukrainian nationalists with it, fervent anti-communists living in Munich. Walked up to them in broad daylight with this contraption hidden in a rolled up newspaper. Afterward, the victims' friends told the newspapers that Khrushchev had ordered the hits."

"How's it work?"

"You insert the cyanide capsule here, stuff one in the end of each barrel, see? Like a muzzleloader. The shooter—or should we call him the sprayer?—points it at the victim's face and then pulls back and releases these two spring-loaded levers. The piston inside smashes the capsule, and *voila*, a lethal mist is sprayed in the target's face.

"Your victim inhales it, and the cyanide shuts down the mitochondrial electron chain that allows her body to derive energy from oxygen. Her heart shuts down, in a matter of seconds. Instant death. And it leaves a very tidy scene, with no time for the victim to struggle or fight back."

"So how would our perp get this gun, or even know about it?" Elijah asked.

"I can't be sure," Bier said, "but it does suggest, possibly, that an intelligence service could have been involved. Who knows, maybe even two. It's the sort of thing they'd know about. This weapon, it's easy for them to like. Exotic, a quick killing, no obvious marks.

"Upon receipt of this body, most pathologists would look no further, simply assume that the person died of natural causes, a heart attack. That wouldn't make sense given her age, but pathologists are busy people, especially in war zones. We like to declare a cause of death and move on."

Ben was impressed. "Why'd you say there might be two intelligence services?"

"It's a KGB weapon. The VC and the NVA get a lot of their armaments from the Soviets. They undoubtedly get intelligence advice too. Or, if like me you're a mystery buff—I know you're a big reader, Kinkaid—maybe our side did it and decided to use a Russian weapon, to throw you local gumshoes off the scent."

"But why would our side kill her?" Elijah asked.

"Who knows? You guys are the detectives."

"You're not bad yourself," Ben said. "Thanks for your thoroughness, Dr. Bier."

The good doctor extended his hand toward the large window that looked out upon his many bodies, alone on their shiny steel tables.

"It's a dangerous world," Bier said. "Watch how you go."

35

JUMPY

30 DECEMBER 1967

The MPs had skipped breakfast, so on their way out to Long Binh they stopped at a stand on the side of the road for pork and funny noodles. In their travels around the city they'd sampled a lot of Vietnamese street food, grown to like it. Ben had even become an enthusiastic consumer of nuoc mam, the pungent fermented fish sauce the natives poured over everything (most soldiers hated the smell, couldn't stand to look at it).

Elijah inhaled the aroma of a skewer of meat fresh off the smiling mama-san's charcoal grill. "Caramelized pork—a man's got to love it. These ladies, they got this sweet, salty, fatty thing down pat, man. When I get home to Queens, I'm gonna rent me a storefront, open up a Vietnamese restaurant."

"You love to cook, Elijah," Ben said. "You figure out how to copy this street food, you'll have lines out the door."

"And we'd be washing it down with cold beer instead of warm Cokes. Six-pack of Schaefer's, some spring rolls, this noodle dish, I'm in heaven, man."

They found Banks's alibi, PFC Allen Kramerwicz, inside one of the many CONEXes the Signal Corps had installed next to the busy Long Binh construction site. Five enlisted men were inside, sweating in front of big electronic consoles. It was a very tight space and the A/C couldn't keep up with the heat; it had to be 100 degrees.

Earphones on, Kramerwicz was hunched over his machine, working to maintain radio communications with troops in the field. The system relied on signals bounced off the atmosphere and it often failed: temperature inversions in the tropics and dense triple canopy jungles swallowed radio beams. Ben asked the specialist to step outside the stifling steel box so they could talk.

Kramerwicz was a little skinny guy—nervous, jumpy, not quite all there. There were open sores on his face, like he'd been scratching at his acne. His eyes were bloodshot and he looked strung out; Ben pegged him for a drug user.

"We're investigating a suspicious death," Elijah said. "Got a few questions, if you don't mind."

The specialist struggled to fire up a cigarette with his Zippo, a skull and crossbones decal stuck to it. With the breeze and his shaking hands, he couldn't get it started. Ben played good cop, leaned over and cupped the flame until it took. His sensitive nose registered the scent of marijuana from the man's fatigues.

"Sure, ask away," Kramerwicz said, taking a long pull on the cigarette, steadying himself. "I got nothing but time. Good to see the sun."

"Long day in there, right?" Ben said, slipping into Mr. Empathetic. "Listening all day must get pretty tedious."

"Gives me a hell of a headache. Only one hundred nineteen days left. One hundred eighteen-and-a-half, now. I'm getting short." Under one hundred days left in your tour made you a short-timer.

Elijah homed in on him: "Last Saturday night, you guys got rocketed, right?"

"That was scary. I thought we were screwed but then Spooky showed up with his great big Gatling gun, rained hellfire down on Charlie. I love seein' those tracers, man. Better than the Fourth of July."

"What time was it, when you got hit?"

"About midnight."

"You know this guy?" Elijah showed him Banks' picture.

"Sure. That's Tommy. His crib is the bunk above me."

"So when you ran for the bunker, was Banks with you?"

Kramerwicz paused, sucked a deep drag, looked down, didn't make eye contact. "Oh yeah, right. He was there." He ran his hand across his mouth, maybe another tell that he was lying.

"I remember now. When we went through the door, Banks was right there behind me. We hunkered down together in the bunker, shoulder to shoulder. Tommy was shittin' his pants, we all were. I mean, those 122s, they musta hit us with fifty rockets man. Blew away some of the new construction. Explosions were so loud my hearing's screwed. We were down there forever, stuck under all those sandbags. It must have lasted three hours. Only one guy got hit though. That's what I heard, anyway."

Too much information; he's too eager.

Ben tried another tack. "So this guy—Specialist Banks—is he okay? Do you like the guy? Ever notice anything sketchy about him?"

"He's all right. Keeps to himself, know what I mean? But yeah, he's straight. Why you wanna know, anyway? Who died? What's so suspicious? It was a woman, right?"

Elijah pounced. "How'd you know it was a woman?"

"You said so."

"No, we didn't."

"So then Tommy—he must have told me. Or maybe I read it in the paper? He has this girl, but I never met her. So this chick from New York came out here to visit him a couple weeks ago, but then she died. I guess it was sudden, he was real broke up about it. That's where I heard it." Kramerwicz grabbed another cigarette and fumbled with his lighter, the flame singing his thumb. "Damn, that smarts."

"He talk about her much?" Ben asked. "Were they good friends?"

"More than good. She was his girlfriend. I think he was in love."

"How'd you know he was upset?"

"Because after it happened, he quit talking to me. He was lying wide awake up there—all night long, just staring at her picture. That was new, cause Banks ain't always around late at night. Some nights, I can't sleep. I wake up, look around, he's not in his bunk."

"He say where he goes?"

"No, man. Never. I got no idea what Tommy gets up to. The man always looks like he's on a mission. Something too important to tell me about."

Ben handed him his card. "Listen up, Kramerwicz—we may need to talk to you again. You remember some detail, no matter how small, no matter how trivial, you call us. Do it right away. You got that, Specialist?"

Kramerwicz nodded back at them, a blank stoner's stare.

36

PERP WALK

30 DECEMBER 1967

When Kramerwicz was back in his CONEX, Elijah turned to Ben. "That troop's a lousy liar. And he's scared to death."

"Yeah. Weird guy, maybe Banks got to him. But we learned something. Our boy's a night owl, apparently."

They went looking for Banks in the huge Long Binh logistics office. It took them ten minutes to reach his section, past rows and rows of clerks staring drone-like into bulky vacuum tube screens. Finally they found Banks's boss in his glassed-in work station in a corner.

"What's that idiot gone and done now?" First Sergeant Moseley asked.

"Routine inquiry . . . we need to ask Banks about a suspicious death in the city. It could be a suicide," Ben said. He saw Elijah flinch; his partner didn't like lies, even little ones.

"He's right over there, have at him," Moseley said, indicating a desk. "I'll take a walk; you can use my office. I wouldn't mind seeing that bastard in the stockade."

"Why, what's he done?" Elijah asked.

"The problem is, most of the time Banks does nothing," Moseley said. "Nada, zilch, zip. Especially lately."

Specialist Four Norman Thomas Banks was staring at the air over his desk, looking angrier than the last time they'd questioned him. He jumped to his feet, menace in his voice. "What you assholes want now?"

Ben took Banks by the arm and guided him toward Moseley's office. "Just a few more questions, Specialist. Let's do this the easy way."

Banks pushed Ben's hand away. "Get off me, man. You can't fuckin' touch me."

Ben closed the door inside the office and arranged the chairs so that he and Elijah could sit behind the desk and Banks faced them, his back to the glass wall and the big room filled with clerks. His face was flushed—he wasn't a big man but he was a very angry one.

"We talked to your bunkmate Kramerwicz today," Elijah said. "About last Saturday night, where you supposedly were during the rocket attack."

"Yeah. So?"

Banks leaned back in his chair, arms crossed tight against his chest, jaw sealed shut.

Elijah took the lead. "Your bunk buddy said some nights you're not sleeping in your hooch. He wakes up, you're not there. Is that right?"

"He's not my buddy. I don't have any buddies. I have insomnia. Then my girlfriend died. You think I can sleep after that? Is that a crime, Sherlock?"

"So what do you get up to every night, soldier?" Elijah raised his voice to match Banks's belligerent tone.

"I walk around. Outside. Grab a smoke on the perimeter. Where the hell else would I go? There's a curfew, this base is secure. You guys know that, right?" Banks's face twitched. He looked away, seemed close to losing it.

Ben tried turning down the temperature. "Listen, Norman, we don't know where you've been. That's why we're asking. This is routine. We'd like to rule you out from our inquiry. Then we can all move on."

"My name is Tommy. Call me by my name, asswipe. How'd Grace die, anyway? You don't know, do you? She was murdered, right? And you got no idea, no clue who did it. Military police, you're a fucking oxymoron, like military intelligence."

"So enlighten us, *Tommy*," Ben said. "Do you know how Grace died?"

"No. I don't. But if I did, I wouldn't tell you assholes."

Elijah got back into it. "What time they rocket you guys last week?"

"You think I keep track? Midnight? I don't know. Maybe later?"

"How many rockets were there?"

"More than one. Less than a hundred."

"You being a smart-ass won't get us anywhere," Ben said. "When did it end, the attack?"

"When it was over."

"Did they call in air support?"

"How would I know? I didn't look; I was in the bunker."

"Why'd the attack end?" Ben pressed. "They called in the F-4s, the fighters bombed the VC positions, right?"

"If you say so. I fell asleep. In the bunker."

That was one lie too far for Elijah. He leaned across the desk, let it fly.

"You killed her, right? You murdered Grace. You killed her and then you threw her in that canal. Disposable—you thought that lovely lady was a throwaway. Like a piece of trash, a pile of garbage. Shit, you didn't love her."

Elijah was rolling now, spittle flew from his lips. "Grace got around, hung out with too many other guys. You were jealous. You couldn't take it, Norman, and you lost your temper. You were nowhere near a bunker that night. The truth, Norman, tell us the truth!"

In one fluid motion, Banks picked up his chair and hurled it at

Elijah. He took it in the chest and fell backward onto the floor. Banks leaped over the desk, straddled Elijah, and started punching him. Ben got behind Banks, locked his arms around the man's neck, and squeezed hard, cutting off his airway.

Pulling Banks's head backward, Ben tightened the choke hold and counted—slowly—to twenty. The man sputtered, fought for air, and then passed out. Ben counted off a few more beats and relaxed his grip. Banks slumped face forward onto the floor and lay gasping for breath.

Elijah got up, rubbing his cheekbone. "Let's throw the slimeball in the stockade, court-martial his ass."

Ben handcuffed Banks and they perp-walked him out of the office. The drone clerks all looked up from their computers; a trooper violently resisting arrest in the middle of USARV's big office, not something you see every day in REMF-land.

When they had Banks secured in the back seat of the jeep, Ben took Elijah aside.

"I don't know if we can charge him," Ben said. "Right now, we're short on evidence. We got no weapon, no witnesses, no real motive. As far as we know, Tommy's got no one to be jealous about. We try to nail him for Grace's murder with what we got now, the JAG guys will laugh us out of the office."

"You're probably right, Louie," Elijah said. "But he's still a liar. He's hiding something."

"It's possible he's just furious that his girlfriend's dead. Let's put him in a cell, let him cool down for a day or two and then talk to him. If we still got nothing maybe we cut him loose. We can watch him, see what happens."

37

THE FALL

30 DECEMBER 1967

Joe Kline hated it when Phuong took the bus down to Vinh Long, it was so dangerous. She always insisted it was safe, claimed that the VC would never dare attack civilian traffic on Route 4 during the daytime—*I can take care of myself, Joe!* Besides, there were always lots of ARVN patrols up and down the road.

Joe didn't believe it. Almost nowhere in South Vietnam was safe now, the MACV pacification program was a joke. Ho Chi Minh was the only one winning hearts or minds, and he captured most of them through threats, intimidation, and targeted murders. The VC moved in and out of villages across the country with impunity. The inflated body counts MACV was infatuated with didn't mean we were winning.

"Be careful, Phuong," Joe said as they stood in the dust outside the terminal. "Stay alert and watch the road. If you get hit, don't run behind the bus. Hide in the ditch between the VC and the bus. Then their RPGs will go over your head, explode on the other side."

"Don't worry, Phuong always careful." To fit in aboard the bus, she'd changed into peasant clothes: a wrinkled white blouse, black pants, rubber sandals and a non la—the straw hat with the big brim the farmers wore.

Phuong always said the war was primarily a political struggle, and Joe thought she was right. She argued that the VC wouldn't murder innocent civilians unless it was obvious they'd been consorting with the Americans or their South Vietnamese "puppets," as the Front called them. Despite her relatively affluent, dependent lifestyle, Phuong didn't think the VC would target her.

"You worry too much, Joe." She took his hands, rose on tiptoe, and kissed him, a daring gesture at a busy bus terminal. "Phuong take extra care of package too." None of the mama-sans noticed, they were busy settling into the jammed minibus, navigating around the cages of pigs and chickens that choked the aisle.

"See you Monday, Phuong. Always remember, I love you."

Joe couldn't see where Phuong found a seat but waved anyway. He watched as the bus was swallowed in the traffic heading south and walked back to the office. Later he hit the five o'clock follies, which his AP buddy Richard Pyle had famously called "the longest-playing tragicomedy in Southeast Asia's theater of the absurd."

Pyle had a point. Every MACV briefing sounded the same, Joe could recite the typical rundown in his sleep:

> *Yesterday, 11 December 1967, throughout the theater, the combined MACV and NVA forces reported 587 Viet Cong killed in action, and another 154 NVA regulars KIA, most of them in I Corps. U.S. and allied forces captured and detained 143 VC and 31 NVA personnel. Our combined air forces conducted 129 sorties against VC and NVA targets in theater, and 67 bombing runs against strategic targets in the North, doing significant damage to arms depots, oil storage tanks, bridges and supply routes. Interviews with Viet Cong prisoners reveal that the enemy's morale*

is very low. They are short on rations, ammunition, and medical supplies. Constant pressure from allied forces on the ground and in the air continues to take a heavy toll . . .

On and on it went. Joe figured if you added up all of the casualties MACV claimed to have inflicted, the total KIAs would exceed the army's original estimates for the total number of Viet Cong in the South.

He decided to dine at La Dolce, got there at 8:30 and tried to read for a while before his meeting—*One Hundred Years of Solitude*, by Márquez. The reviewers had loved it, but Joe was having a deuce of a time finishing the damn thing (who thinks about ice when he's about to be shot?). He thought he'd switch to some bestseller, maybe *Rosemary's Baby*.

The rooftop bar on the Continental's terrace closed at ten, so Joe used the fire stairs, they never locked those. He made it to the roof at 10:15 and stopped to catch his breath, looked for a spot where he could set up his recorder. The climb made him feel his age. The night was hot and cloudy, not much light up here.

No small arms or rockets tonight, just sputtering motorbikes down on the street, nine stories below. He pulled two chairs and a round cocktail table over to the edge of the terrace, where he was partially hidden behind the air conditioning equipment. Then he gazed out at the river and wondered (for about the thousandth time) whether it was time to ask Phuong to marry him.

Joe knew he could find work as a copy editor somewhere, maybe they could even start their own family. Phuong was only twenty-five, and he thought his boys could still swim. There were thousands of Vietnamese expats living in L.A. now; Phuong would have lots of her people around, they'd keep her from getting homesick. His life was starting to make sense. It cheered him, to have a plan.

He took out his little tape player, depressed the start lever, made sure it was rolling, and put it back in his jacket pocket. The light changed; he sensed movement somewhere behind him. He turned to look, rising from his chair, but there was no one there. Then two hands, very powerful, gripped him from behind, lifted him off his feet, and dragged him to the low railing.

A wet cloth came down on his face, clamped over his nose and mouth. It smelled strong. A galaxy of stars—*is that the Milky Way?*—burst across his consciousness. His vision contracted; he tried to hold his eyes open but it was no use. A single push and he tumbled over the parapet. He fell headfirst through the darkness past all the hotel guests in their little rooms, but on his way down Joe never saw a thing.

38

LU WONDER

30-31 DECEMBER 1967

When Ben and Elijah slammed the cell door on Banks Saturday afternoon, he was still screaming at them.

"I'll get you fuckers! Every last one of you. You killed her. You and Hop, you got Grace murdered! You'll get yours. Just you wait."

Banks's anger over Grace's death sounded pretty real to Ben. He was hiding things, sure, but maybe not a murder. And why was he obsessed with this guy called Hop?

"We didn't kill your girlfriend," Ben had said. "And you need a better story about where you were last Saturday night. You keep lying to us, you're looking at thirty years in Leavenworth. Tell us the truth. Then we'll see if we can help you."

Early the next morning, Ben and Elijah started out for LBJ again to see if Banks had found religion after a night in a cell. They'd been in the jeep five minutes when the colonel raised them on the radio, something that never happened on Sundays.

"Lieutenant, how my checkpoints going? Over."

"Very well, sir, we just finished another one, in District 9." *Once the lies start, they keep on coming.*

"Good work. But you two need to get back downtown. Now, to the Continental. We got another weird death, the vic's an American. Lieutenant Lu's been asking for you."

Elijah made a U-turn. When they arrived at the Continental, Sergeant Duc showed them to a second-floor window that led to the roof of the porte cochere above the hotel's entrance. Lu was hovering next to the corpse, which lay face down above the big "P" of the Continental Palace's sign; a passing cyclo driver had noticed the victim's hand protruding over the letter. Lots of blood, coagulating but still moist, surrounded his skull.

The victim was a middle-aged white man in civilian clothes—the tropical-weight khakis Americans favored. Dr. Death's forensics team was late, so Ben and Elijah didn't touch anything. Lu shook their hands and laughed, a high-pitched chortle. The man's laughter reminded Ben of a chickadee, but there was no mirth in it.

"Another dead American, Kin-Kay," Lu said. "Maybe this one special present for your American New Year. Now you even luckier than Lu."

Ben craned his head, looked eight floors up to the Continental roof and its low guard rail. "How far you think he fell?"

"If fall from roof, maybe thirty meters. Head hit first—his brain mush now."

Lu nudged the victim's head with his shoe. There was a pair of eyeglasses underneath, smashed into the man's face. The thick black frames looked like they had a piece of tape on them.

"Oh shit," Ben said. "See the glasses?"

"Yup. Just like Joe Kline's," Elijah said. "The guy's about the right age too. Has to be him. What's that bulge, in his pocket there?"

Ben probed Kline's shirt with his baton. "Looks like a cassette recorder," he said. He nodded to Elijah, who extracted it, put it in a paper bag. "Maybe we will get lucky."

Lu shook his head, trilled his chickadee laugh again.

"So first Grace, then Joe Kline," Elijah said. "Are we seeing a pattern here?"

"Maybe," Ben said.

"You know him?" Lu asked.

"We think he's a newspaper reporter," Ben said. "He worked for the *Chicago Tribune*. He knew Grace Waverly."

"That American Co beaucoup unlucky. Death follow her around."

"Yeah. Hey Lu, your guys make any progress on the Twenty Grand bombing?"

"No luck there, Kin-Kay. VC sappers do it, no doubt. But we no solve case. You know that, right? No one talk, everyone afraid. Any people talk to police, maybe VC kill them. But you already know that too, Kin-Kay."

"Yeah, lost cause."

"Just like Vietnam war, yes? So, my friend, Lu wonder about something. Who you think VC want to target at Twenty Grand? You think they go all that trouble to kill a few GIs? In that bar? No generals, nobody important in there.

"If VC kill Cos from bar, they lose beaucoup spies. No good for them. But you at Twenty Grand when bomb come. You think someone try kill you and Sergeant Jackson? Believe you a threat? Maybe they think you find things, in your investigation. Something they no like."

Ben thought about it, remembering the piece of paper they'd found in Grace's purse. "But that bombing was carefully planned—it must have taken weeks to organize. These two deaths are new; I don't see how they connect to the Twenty Grand."

Lu smiled when he heard that. "Some killers, they act fast."

Ben had noticed that many Vietnamese smiled a lot when they talked to Americans. They seemed determined to please their American guests, even if they hated them. *They always say yes, but they mean no.*

"I find something else," Lu added, a bit reluctantly, Ben thought. "We drag canal, near cemetery. We pull up funny gun. Like pistol, but not pistol." Lu turned to Sergeant Duc for help with his English, said something in Vietnamese.

Duc translated: "Lieutenant Lu, he say they find this strange gun, with two barrels, like this." Duc showed them, held his hands a foot apart. "Two long barrels, but no trigger."

Lu nodded at them. "You come office, I show you."

"Yes, we'd like to see it," Elijah said.

An unmarked jeep rolled to a stop a block away, a civilian driving. Lt. Col. Balderamos got out of the passenger seat, followed by the driver, an American wearing aviator sunglasses—J.B. Darling, Lien's boss. Deep in conversation with Darling, the colonel didn't even look up at them. Ben was too far away to hear anything, but Darling was agitated, kept pointing at the crime scene.

Balderamos put his hand on Darling's shoulder and started to say something but Darling cut him off, his voice rising. Then he jumped in the jeep and accelerated away.

The colonel came upstairs, crawled through the hotel's window, and strode over to them, looking puffed up and officious. "What we got here, Lieutenant?"

Ben and Elijah snapped to and saluted.

"Early days, sir," Ben said, "but we think the victim's a reporter, from the *Chicago Tribune*—Joe Kline. He had some connection to Grace Waverly."

"That's doubtful. What kind of connection?"

"We're not sure, but they knew each other. They talked, several times."

"So he must have fallen, right? Or jumped. Is it a suicide?"

"Or somebody helped him fall," Elijah said. "We think that—"

"Thank you, *Sergeant*," Balderamos said. "When you come up with any *evidence* of that, let me know. Maybe he was drunk. Keep me informed Kinkaid, I don't have time to stick around. I lost my ride, so I'll need your jeep. Have to get over to MACV."

"Who was that civilian you were with, sir?" Ben asked.

"Oh, that's Darling. Old friend of mine. He's with USAID, works for the ambassador."

"He's interested in this death?"

"No, why would he be? He's an ag guy. He just gave me a ride."

"But he looked pretty excited."

Balderamos glared at Ben. "I *play golf* with him, Kinkaid. Some Sundays. When I don't have to worry about bombs you didn't stop, or deaths you didn't prevent. We're in a tournament. I'm looking forward to it."

"Oh, golf. Right." Ben hoped his disdain wasn't too obvious. "I heard he was CIA."

"I don't think so, Lieutenant. You've swallowed too much gossip. Don't be so gullible. Anyone who wears civvies, people always say they're CIA. Too many conspiracy theories flying around Saigon. They're mostly lies, don't listen to them."

"Right, sir." *Time to stop sharing with Baldy.*

"So, Kinkaid, a bit of advice. Don't overthink this. These two bodies—Waverly, Kline—they look like two suicides to me.

"Close it down. Get back on the bombing investigation, ASAP. We need more checkpoints, tighter security . . . focus on that."

Balderamos left the scene in Ben's jeep.

"The colonel's great at telling other people what to focus on," Elijah said.

"Yeah," Ben said, "and he's focused on his golf game."

Lieutenant Lu sidled over from where he'd been eavesdropping.

"Oh, Mr. Darling, he not CIA, no way, GI. He just famous American rice farmer." *Tee-hee-hee.* "You know, Kin-Kay, your Colonel Baldy—he Numbah Ten liar."

"Roger that, Lucky."

Maybe Elijah's right; this is a pattern. It was possible that the vector of violence started with something Banks had done, then went through Grace, then through Kline. The lives of the dead had intersected.

Was Lu right? Were Ben and Elijah the next targets, after Grace? They'd had a very lucky escape. But why would the VC organize such a complicated operation just to rub out two inconsequential MPs? They stole a truck, built a bomb, and found a driver. Why not do a drive-by, use a shooter on a motorbike? *But maybe the perps didn't want anyone to know we were the real targets. Somebody must think we're onto something big, to go to all that trouble.*

And the puzzle of Grace's numbers, what was that telling them?

Ben needed answers. Now, before it got worse.

39

TOO YOUNG TO DIE

31 DECEMBER 1967

Ben decided to go for it and show Grace's list to Lien. Not exactly SOP, to run homicide evidence by a Vietnamese civilian, but he trusted her. It was too dangerous now to tell the colonel about it, especially if Lu was right and Baldy and Darling were obstructing them somehow. He was out of ideas and Lien knew a lot, maybe she could solve the numbers puzzle. But they had to listen to Kline's tape first, which had proved indestructible.

Back in the office, Elijah dug out his portable machine, shoved Kline's cassette into it, and pushed play. Kline's voice was reedy, tremulous. He sounded nervous, pressured.

"Saturday, 2145 hours, December 30. Joe Kline of the *Tribune* here, on the roof of the Continental. Waiting on my source, hope to confirm Grace Waverly's story about the arms shipment . . . if this recording is lost and anyone else finds it, for more details contact my assistant, Miss P., in Vinh Long."

No more words, but Kline had left the machine running. There was a hum, distant traffic sounds, muffled voices. Elijah pushed fast forward until he heard some gibberish, maybe ten minutes further in. He rewound, found the spot, pushed play again.

They heard a scraping sound, a cry of surprise, the *tok-tok-tok* of sharp heels striking concrete, some scrabbling and another gasp. Of what? Surprise? Recognition? Then a whooshing sound, as if the tape was in a wind tunnel, followed by the sound of impact, something soft hitting something hard.

Elijah ran through the rest of the cassette. Nothing—just the whir of tape passing through the player. Ben pushed eject. "So if we heard that right, it sounds like Kline's so-called source threw him off the roof."

"It's strange, he didn't even scream," Elijah said. "We got to find this P person. Who's she?"

"Lien told me once that Kline had a girlfriend. Someone called Phuong. That must be 'Miss P.' Duc says he heard she went home to Vinh Long yesterday. Let's head down there, take Duc to translate. I have to find Lien and ask her about the Twenty Grand again. Meet you back here in an hour. One more thing—grab an M60 from the locker and mount it on the jeep. Make sure Duc knows how to operate it. Take an M79 too."

Lien was working all the time lately, even on Sundays, so Ben hurried over to the embassy. He stopped near the front gate to buy flowers from the mama-san working the sidewalk. Waving the bouquet, he told the receptionist he had a present for Lien and she waved him through. Lien saw him coming and jumped up from her desk.

"Not here. This way."

Avoiding the elevator, Lien led him down a back stair. They crossed Ham Nghi Boulevard and found a table outside the coffee shop. Ben didn't bother to order, got into what was bothering him. "Lien, there's no way Madame Thuy could have known that Elijah and I were going to be in her bar the day of the bombing. We only decided that morning to go over there. You said you met Thuy on Tuesday and she told you that we were coming. That's impossible. So what's the truth?"

Lien offered him a half smile and sighed, her eyes a mix of sadness and amusement. "So you not believe Lien's lies, Benjamin? You good police."

"But why'd you lie?"

"Lien want to save you. You too young to die, Benjamin. Too nice too. So is Elijah."

"Tell me how you knew." Even though he had guessed, Lien's admission that she'd lied to him shocked Ben. He was in love with her, he didn't want to interrogate her, but he had to find out what was going on.

"I know many things, Lieutenant Kin-Kay," Lien said, her eyes steady, her face impassive. She was a strong woman, tough, no wilting flower. "But if I tell all I know, I cannot protect you."

Ben sensed this was going nowhere. *I'll never find out all she knows.* He hated it when people lied to him, although he lied too, if it would advance an investigation. For a moment he wondered if he should give up on Lien, turn her over to Lu's people. But he couldn't do that—if they thought something was up with her they'd press her hard, maybe even torture her. They'd find out what her angle was, use it to their advantage. Maybe they'd try to turn her, make her spy on whatever Darling and the embassy pooh-bahs were up to. Yes, she'd lied, but she'd saved their lives. *Let it go.*

He took the small piece of paper out of his pocket and passed it across the table to Lien. "We found this in Grace's purse. It looks like a code, but it doesn't look that complicated. What do you think?"

48 512s

24 617s

12 213s

06 312s

03 212s

Lien studied the numbers, but shook her head. "You know what one number mean? Any one?"

Some looked familiar, but no bells rang. He recited the numbers on the right: "512, 617, 213, 312 . . . The next one, 212—that could be an area code, for New York City."

"What code?"

"The area code. It's the number you dial to reach a certain area when you telephone long distance, back to the States."

"Oh, I see. Area code for Virginia 703."

"Right." *Lien must call that number often.*

She ran her finger down the numbers on the left side. "These amounts, maybe. Maybe they're 48 of this number, 48 of the 512s. The numbers on this side, they all area codes? What is 512?"

"Oh, right. Texas. That's the code for Austin. In Texas. My aunt lives there."

"So highest number on right side is 48, 48 of the 512s. Smallest number, 3, is next to 212, for New York. You know Grace interested in guns, right? You think this her order, to supplier?"

"You think Grace ordered these guns? It's a shopping list?"

"I tell you before, Grace very interested in black market. But you never check."

Ben studied the list again. "Maybe these are arranged by population, in ascending order. The codes for the smaller cities come first—Austin, then Boston. The largest cities—Los Angeles, Chicago, New York—are last."

"Yes," Lien said. "Maybe this number, 48—how you say in English, unit? Forty-eight units of some small gun—rifles, maybe."

"So it might mean they plan to ship 48 rifles, 48 of the 512s, but only

3 New Yorks, the 212s. They used the codes of the biggest cities for the biggest guns, or explosives, whatever."

Lien searched his face. "Can you tell me what you know? Why did Grace ship guns to Baltimore?"

Ben was surprised, again. "She sent them to Baltimore?"

"I think so, yes. They supposed to be there soon. Early in January. I see part of memo."

Ben leaned back in his chair. So Lien already knew that Grace was in Vietnam to buy guns, knew where the shipment was going, and when it would arrive—she'd read about it at the office. Banks was staying up all night, he must have been helping her. Darling was well aware of Grace's activities and probably Tommy's too. But no spook had tried to stop Banks. Why didn't Darling break up the plot, get them both arrested before the weapons left?

"Maybe Lien help you learn more." She was fingering her mother's necklace, worrying the green gem in the center.

Gazing at her, Ben softened, wanted to quit. *Why don't we just call it a day, head back to your apartment?* He lost focus, began to daydream. He was standing behind her in her bedroom, his hands wandering over her hips, his lips moving to her slender neck, brushing her, touching her lightly.

"Benjamin?"

"I'm sorry, I was on a walkabout. How could you help me, Lien?"

"Listen to me." Her tone had changed, very serious now. "Only one man, one man in Saigon sell beaucoup guns. His name Francois, Frank Nguyen. He have warehouse in Central Market, behind food stalls. I tell Frank you coming, he help you. Maybe he tell you who big buyer is. You know American saying, follow the money?"

"Did Darling teach you that? That's a good tip. Thank you."

"Benjamin, I hear another man die last night. You know him, yes? He American?"

"He was a reporter, Joe Kline. He was murdered. We're trying to find his assistant, someone named Miss P. Maybe she knows something."

"Yes, Miss Phuong."

"You know her?" he asked.

"Pham Van Phuong. I tell you before, she Kline's girlfriend. She say she want to leave Vietnam. Kline say he bring her to America, make her rich. Her name, it mean phoenix. The bird. The one that rise from ashes, be born again. Now Phuong need new patron, to help her rise."

"We're going to Vinh Long tonight to look for her."

"Who go?" She asked, urgent again. "How you go there?"

"In a jeep. Elijah, Sergeant Duc, and me."

Lien frowned, reached across the table and took his hand in both of hers, tracing the long line that ran across his palm.

"Her parents schoolteachers. Ask for Mr. Pham Van Loc, he well-known in Vinh Long. He teach English, in high school there."

Ben laughed, shaking his head. "What don't you know?"

"I grow up in Delta. In Sa Dec, only ten klick to Vinh Long. My cousin, she live Vinh Long, take Mr. Loc class. I visit there often."

She raised his hand to her lips, kissed his palm softly, lingering. "Be very careful, Benjamin. This time, Lien cannot go Vinh Long to help you. Watch out for road, it very dangerous."

"I know," Ben said. *Are we over our heads yet?*

40

WE USED TO IT

31 DECEMBER 1967

The sun was already low in the sky when their jeep cleared the city traffic and rumbled south toward Vinh Long. It was only seventy klicks down Route 4 but the two-lane road was clogged with the usual obstacles: pedicabs poking along, water buffaloes hauling carts laden with mangoes, and farmers bent under baskets of rice hanging from the poles across their shoulders.

Slow progress, but that was okay. Ben wanted to see a lot of people about. When the road was empty, when you didn't see any farmers in the fields, that was when bad things happened. The locals always sensed when the VC were about and *di-di maued* for the exits, hid out in the ditches or sampans, anywhere that looked safe.

"It's New Year's Eve," Ben said to Elijah, trying for a cheery tone. "We should celebrate. You bring the champagne?"

"You sure about this road trip, Lieutenant?"

Ben took his eyes off the tree line. Elijah never called him "Lieutenant" unless he was annoyed, or worried.

"Why you asking, Elijah?"

"You're short, man. What you got, three weeks left in-country? That's low double digits, partner."

"Twenty-two days and six hours." Ben looked at his watch. "And about seventeen minutes, if the Freedom Bird is on time. We're all right. Vinh Long's not that far."

"You know where Phuong lives?" Elijah asked.

"I got a neighborhood. This might be a tough visit. The news about Kline will be a big shock for Phuong. Joe was her ticket to the USA."

Perched behind his M60 machine gun, Sergeant Duc chimed in from the back seat. "No, Lieutenant Kin-Kay. That not right. People we love dying all the time. Phuong, she not be surprised about Joe. We used to it."

It would be dark in fifteen minutes. Ben was never comfortable traversing the boonies at night, and this time they had no air cover, no infantry escort. But tonight luck was with them; after two-and-a-half hours, the last forty minutes in total darkness, they reached the outskirts of Vinh Long, a small town, maybe five thousand people, on the Mekong River. They drove to the village center and asked the mama-sans selling pineapple for directions. Duc got a description of the Phams' house and they found it, a tidy concrete home that faced the town soccer field.

When Duc knocked, an older woman—petite, elegant, with kind eyes—opened the door and gave them a questioning look. Duc started to explain, but Phuong emerged from a room on the left, stepped in front of her mother, and took over.

"Why you MPs here? Joe tell you come here?" She looked wary.

"No, Miss Phuong," Ben said. "I'm afraid he didn't. May we come in? It would be better to do this inside." Phuong hesitated, then stepped back to let them enter.

The living room was dominated by a shrine to the family's ancestors. A large frame mounted on a lacquered red wall displayed more than a hundred small photos, portraits of the Pham family's forebears. From what they wore and the condition of the photos, Ben could see that it included people from at least four generations.

A narrow library table was in front of the wall, covered by red and gold brocade that fell to the floor. A large statue of the meditating Buddha had been placed in the center, flanked by pretty vases filled with fresh flowers and joss sticks. A few still burned, the sweet smell filling the room. Small bowls of apples, oranges, and mangoes, offerings to the Pham family's loved ones who had already crossed over, completed the shrine.

"We honor our ancestors here," Phuong said. "We believe our loved ones who have passed over still living, but they are in spirit world. Their spirits influence our lives."

Ben had read in a Vietnam guidebook that the past and present existed together. For example, the spirit of an upright mother who'd lived a good life could help her earthly children perform good deeds, while an evil ancestor might have a malevolent influence.

"Are those paintings of the Trung sisters?" Ben asked.

"Yes," Phuong said. "We still honor their heroism, so many generations later. May I offer tea?"

She brought tea on a large platter, accompanied by little dishes of candied fruit, and poured it carefully into tiny cups. They sipped it slowly, seated on the floor on pillows with their legs crossed. The position made Ben's legs ache; only Duc looked comfortable. Phuong said something to her parents and they left the room.

Ben took a deep breath. "Phuong, I'm sorry, but Joe's—"

"I already hear news," she said. "On radio, about American who die at hotel. They say it suicide. You find his body at Continental this morning. Joe fall from roof, right?"

"Yes. We're still trying to figure out how he died," Ben said, wondering what to say next. Phuong didn't seem broken up or even particularly upset. She soldiered on, anticipated his next question.

"You wonder, Lieutenant, why I not more sorry, why I not cry? Phuong like Joe, yes. But this no big love story. You have words for it in English—convenience marriage? Phuong never marry Joe, but he good convenience, he help me a lot."

Ben nodded, thinking he should avoid digging around in Phuong's love life.

"We found a tape recording. Joe says on it that if anything happened to him, you would know what he was working on. Can you help us?"

"Yes." Phuong lifted her head, pushed her hair back, touched her eyes. They glistened, maybe she was going to cry. "Joe think he have big story, from that American Co. He give me many pages, to keep safe. But what else you hear on tape?"

Ben ignored her question. "You have the package? Here?"

Phuong rose, turned to the shrine, lifted the heavy red cloth, and removed a large manila envelope taped to the underside of the table. She handed it to Ben.

"This what you want. I no read Joe's story, don't want to know. You can read later. But Lieutenant, Phuong need favor. If you know any American man who need good assistant, you let me know?"

"Yes, I will. Thank you for keeping this safe, it's important. And we're very sorry, about Joe."

They said their goodbyes, drove back to the village center, and parked across the street from the province chief's large villa. It had a lot of security lights and looked like a safe spot to spend the night. There was an unmarked jeep parked in the villa's driveway.

"You were right, Duc," Elijah said. "About Phuong. She's a tough cookie."

"And very businesslike," Ben said. "She made it sound like their relationship was just a transaction. No tears, nothing. But I think I understand."

Ben turned to Sergeant Duc. "You guys are in this for the long haul. I guess you have to be practical."

"Long haul too long," Duc said.

"Yeah, I see that," Ben said. "Probably not a great idea to drive through the boonies in the middle of the night. Let's camp out in the jeep, catch some Zs, and head out at first light." Before he tried to bed down on the hard seat, Ben took out his penlight and scanned Joe Kline's manuscript.

Kline had hung his story on "informed sources"—Grace was never mentioned. The article confirmed everything Ben suspected: anti-war protesters had acquired and shipped a large cache of U.S. Army weapons. Kline's principal source claimed RAW intended to inflict mass casualties on the home front. It fit with what he and Lien had guessed Grace's list was about.

Ben realized he had no choice but to sound the alarm and try to stop them. He had no chance unless he found some big brass who were open-minded and would listen. If he could persuade them that the threat was real, maybe they'd intercept the arms, arrest the bad actors. It would have to be someone way above his pay grade.

41

RUFF PUFFS

01 JANUARY 1968

A rosy hue grew on the horizon as the three soldiers unfolded themselves from their cramped positions in the jeep and tried to stretch, rubbing their limbs. Ben slapped at his cheek and murdered another mosquito before it could draw blood. His leg was numb, it had been jammed under the dashboard for hours. 0530 hours and the village of Vinh Long was waking up—lots of farmers heading to market, pulling carts laden with fresh produce.

"Happy 1968," Elijah said. "If I was back in the city, I woulda camped out in Times Square . . . love watching that ball drop. We shoulda brought a tent. Air mattresses too."

"Why stop there?" Ben asked. "We coulda built a fire, made s'mores, stayed up past midnight, and toasted the New Year. Why didn't you think of that, Elijah?"

"Because all I could think about was how dumb we were driving down Route 4 in the dark. *Alone*, with no escort, *Lieutenant*." Elijah knew their friendship could withstand a little mild criticism. "Let's hope 1968 turns out better than last year."

Sergeant Duc went around the corner and came back with three large cups of Vietnamese coffee cut with condensed milk, very sweet and strong. Elijah took a sip and broke out his winning smile.

"Now, if I had me some scrambled eggs, a pound of bacon, a pile of grits, and a bottle of hot sauce, I'd be set for life, Louie."

As they were getting organized, an ARVN deuce-and-a-half trailed by a jeep carrying two Vietnamese Rangers pulled up beside them. The lieutenant in the passenger seat saluted Ben and asked, "Where you GIs go?"

"Back to Saigon," Ben said.

"You have convoy?"

"No, we're by ourselves."

"You have air cover?"

"No."

"You GIs boo-coo dinky dau," the Ranger lieutenant said. "Road too dangerous out here, VC everywhere. We go together. Safe that way. We take lead. You have M60, you stay rear, behind truck."

"Good idea." Ben gave the ARVNs the thumbs up; Elijah pulled their jeep in behind the big truck and they rolled out, headed north. "Maybe we are dinky dau, loco, crazy," said Elijah. "How come we didn't book air cover, Lieutenant?"

"They'd want to know what we were up to. Baldy would ask a lot of questions."

Twenty klicks north, Ben noticed a change in the atmosphere. They were passing through rice fields, brilliant green in the morning sunshine. Wisps of mist drifted up from the paddies; ripe kernels hung from tender stalks, ready for harvest. Behind the fields, a long tree line stretched across the horizon.

Green on green on more green. If you could ever blot out the war, Vietnam was a very beautiful place. But on this shiny morning all Ben could think about was that there was no one in the fields. Not a single soul.

He pulled the clip out of his black M16, checked for the third time that it was full, punched it back in, heard the round spring into the chamber, and pushed the safety off. Elijah noticed and gave Ben his *Are we ready?* look.

Ben nodded. "Your weapon A-okay there, Elijah?"

"Yes, sir." Elijah kept his left hand on the wheel and pulled his rifle closer until it was against his hip, his right hand gripping the top of the sight. Ben turned to check on Duc. The translator was alert, squinting down the sight of the machine gun. "You ever fired an M60, Duc?"

"Yes, Lieutenant Kin-Kay, Duc fire M60 many times. On range, in basic training. Win medal, for marksmanship. Very strange, Vietnamese give Chinese a medal."

They rounded a corner and saw a checkpoint one hundred meters away manned by a bunch of chattering Vietnamese in black uniforms. They carried older rifles, M2 carbines.

"They look like Ruff Puffs," Elijah said.

These were the Regional and Popular Forces—RFs/PFs, not regular ARVN. Their mission was to defend their home villages. The Ruff Puffs were poorly paid, poorly trained, and often unreliable in a firefight.

The lead jeep with the two ARVN Rangers slowed for the roadblock. The right front wheel hit a pothole and bounced. A flash of light, and the whole vehicle rose in the air as the blast wave from the mine hit them.

The ARVN jeep hovered a moment, tipped over onto its left side, and stayed there. The two Rangers were both hit, stuck in the wreckage, not moving. A fire broke out in the engine.

"Go, go!" Ben shouted at Elijah. He gunned the jeep toward the roadblock.

Ahead of them the deuce-and-a-half driver jammed his brakes, leaped down, and ran toward his wounded comrades. A hail of automatic weapons fire erupted from their right flank, the tree line. A mist of red exploded from the ARVN's head; he recoiled and fell backward, sprawled like a snow angel in the red dust. Shot in the face—finished, probably. The Ruff Puffs behind the checkpoint opened up with their carbines.

Elijah swerved left, went around the ARVN truck, and parked diagonally across the road in front of it.

Ben grabbed the M79 as they scrambled behind their jeep for cover. He shoved a grenade down the barrel, lined up the sight on the roadblock, and fired. The kickback jammed his shoulder but his aim was true. The grenade landed in front of the Ruff Puffs, skipped once, and exploded—they saw body parts fly. The bad guys in the tree line kept firing. Ben registered the distinct *rat-a-tat-tat* of AK-47s as rounds whistled over their heads. Duc held his ground and swept the M60 across the paddy, raining bullets into the water next to the trees. He was on target. They heard screams.

Something moved to their left: four or five Ruff Puffs were on the move, trying to flank them. Ben and Elijah emptied their clips and downed two of them; the rest dove into an irrigation ditch. Ben fired the M79 but missed, overshot the target. He heaved a hand grenade as far as he could into the paddy; more screams, he did some damage with that one. Nothing doing with the Rangers; they weren't moving. Crouching behind their jeep, they laid down another field of fire on the ditch to their left. A solitary cry, then nothing.

"Let's try and get the ARVNs out, before it blows," Ben said.

"I'll go, you cover," Elijah said. He ran ahead toward the wrecked jeep, staying low. It was still quiet on his left, so Ben sprayed the invisible enemy in the tree line. Duc crouched behind his M60, threaded a new ammo belt in and strafed the edge again.

Elijah made it to the ARVN jeep and grabbed the man behind the wheel. He stood up and tried to wrench him free but showed them too much. Elijah's head snapped back and he cartwheeled onto the road, shot in the upper body, probably.

"Keep hitting the tree line, Duc, give the bastards all you've got. I'm going for Elijah." Doubled over, Ben scuttled forward, dove and scrambled behind the bulk of the damaged ARVN jeep. Elijah had managed to crawl behind the overturned vehicle and sit up. He was holding his right shoulder, pressing his hand against the wound. A dark stain seeped through his fatigue shirt and spread down his chest.

The two Rangers in the jeep were in tough shape. Too late for the driver; the right side of his face was missing. The lieutenant looked like he had a chance: he had shrapnel wounds in his legs, but he could talk. Ben heard the jeep radio squawk, somebody yelling in Vietnamese. He low crawled to the passenger side, reached in, and handed his counterpart the transmitter.

"Tell 'em we need air support. And a medevac—a Dustoff." The lieutenant grabbed the mic and yelled for help.

Ben ducked back behind the smoking jeep, pulled off his fatigue shirt, and wound it tightly around Elijah's upper arm, trying to stanch the blood flow.

Elijah managed a wan smile. "How am I doin', Louie?"

"You're gonna be fine, partner. You might lose a little off your fastball, that's all."

The radio crackled. The wounded Ranger listened, looked back at Ben, and gave him the thumbs up.

There was a lull. Elijah was conscious, hurting, but strong enough to keep up the pressure with his left hand against the makeshift tourniquet. Duc kept firing at anything that moved. Ben took another peek over the top of the jeep, popped up, and emptied another magazine on the tree line. A minute or two later, he heard a welcome sound in the distance, the familiar *whoop-whoop-whoop* of a Huey. Probably their Dustoff—the ARVN base was right down the road in Binh Thuy.

Ben crawled around Elijah and edged out to survey the scene. There was a disturbance in the rice; the slender green reeds parted, and a white man in unmarked black fatigues carrying an Uzi jogged from the paddies toward the trees. An American? The guy yelled something, pointed at the sky and the chopper, and began herding his troops back into the jungle. Duc kept his M60 humming, picked off a few of them.

Ben grabbed the binoculars that had fallen out of the ARVN jeep and scanned the tree line. The guy in charge looked familiar. He'd lost his baseball cap and was waving wildly at the gaggle of Ruff Puffs left on the road, signaling them to join the retreat. Ben focused the glasses on the guy's face. Yes, he knew the guy.

It's the colonel's favorite golf partner.

42

THE HIGHER YOU CLIMB

01 JANUARY 1968

The ARVN medevac took longer than Ben expected to land, the pilot circling to make sure the firefight was over. The bleeding from Elijah's wound had slowed and he was in better spirits, gabbing away; he'd figured out this was not his day to die.

"They stop shooting at us?" Elijah asked.

"The fake Ruff Puffs retreated," Ben said. "Gave up. For today, anyway. Here, let me hold that." Ben took over, pressing hard against his partner's wound. "They probably thought our Dustoff was a gunship."

"Yeah. Or the infidels thought Elijah the prophet was about to rain down the wrath of God on them." Right after he'd gotten shot, Elijah had begun to loudly pray: "Please God, help me get through this, and I'll be a better man."

"You shoulda called on the big man earlier," Ben said. "We coulda used the help."

Duc had been a rock, glued to his M60 and firing intermittent bursts into the trees while Ben cradled Elijah in his arms, his back against the overturned jeep. The engine fire had burned itself out. The tourniquet was soaked, so Ben used his knife to cut off a clean piece of his T-shirt and wound it around Elijah's shoulder. The medevac finally landed twenty meters away, its rotors whopping—Ben had to yell to be heard.

"So Elijah, guess who I saw? Running around in the paddy, directing all the action?"

"Santa Claus?"

Ben smiled, thankful Elijah's sense of humor hadn't vanished with a couple pints of blood. "A guy in black fatigues. He's an American, and we know him. J.B. Darling, the so-called USAID guy. He wasn't out here to plant rice."

"That SOB," Elijah said. "The CIA guy was trying to kill us?"

"Looks that way. He must have the local province chief on his payroll—they run the Ruff Puffs. There was an unmarked jeep parked next to the chief's house in Vinh Long last night, must have been Darling's."

"Damn, we must have stumbled onto something important. We need backup, Lieutenant."

"Knowledge is power, Elijah."

"I hope so. Don't feel especially powerful right now."

The ARVN medics arrived, running low with their stretchers. They lifted Elijah onto one, bandaged his shoulder, and started a morphine drip. They took longer with the wounded Ranger lieutenant, trying to stabilize him. The rest of the crew shoved the two dead ARVNs into body bags and secured the four stretchers inside the chopper. The Huey lifted off and turned slowly south.

Silence from the tree line; their enemies had vanished. Ben took a few deep breaths, tried to come off the adrenaline rush. He waved to Elijah's chopper: "Catch you later, buddy."

The nearest hospital was at the university in Can Tho, a mid-sized city in the center of the Delta. It was an all-Vietnamese operation, which meant that it would take a while for Lt. Col. Balderamos to hear about what happened. Ben guessed he had at least twenty-four hours to work with.

He glanced toward the trees and saw a few farmers were already back in the paddies, working the rice. An ARVN company showed up from Vinh Long to deal with the scene, push the wrecked vehicles into the ditch and open the road. Duc climbed back behind the M60 and they took off for Saigon; Ben drove as fast as he could, slaloming through the obstacles. He parked their bullet-riddled vehicle on the street a block away from the office—no point in letting the colonel see it.

Might as well check on the idiot's mood. He grabbed a fresh fatigue shirt from his locker, washed his face, and then knocked lightly on the colonel's door. "Happy New Year, sir," Ben said, firing off a crisp salute.

"Nothing happy about it, Lieutenant. I thought it would be a good idea for us to tour our new checkpoints today, review the security upgrades."

"Great idea, sir. With your permission though, I could use a few days to tie up some loose ends, make sure every detail's in place. Would Saturday morning work?"

"I can't do Saturday."

"How about Sunday, sir?"

"Let's make it next Monday. That should give you time to get everything right."

The asshole's playing golf all weekend.

"Yes, sir, that would be fine. I better get back out there, we have a lot of coordination to work out with the White Mice."

"Good. Any progress on the Twenty Grand bombers?"

"Slow going, sir. Our people and Lu's men have questioned more than a hundred civilians. So far nobody's talking."

"Keep grinding. Someone will crack. You come up with a promising lead, let Captain Lu question the bastard, then you'll see results. It's amazing what a fully charged 12-volt battery can do." The colonel laughed. "Where's Jackson?"

"Sergeant Jackson's on sick call, sir. You know how he loves that Vietnamese stall food—he caught a dose of Ho's Revenge."

"Never touch that shit myself. What's up with your uniform?" the colonel asked, looking at Ben's stained pants. "You been rolling around in the mud or something?"

"Oh no, sir. We hit a pothole yesterday, jeep sprang an oil leak. I had to crawl underneath to get a look. We're going to the motor pool now to sub it out."

"Okay. Keep me posted, Lieutenant. Catch those damn bombers, take down their cell. I want updates every day."

"Yes, sir." Ben found Duc next to his locker and they hustled over to the Central Market to talk to Francois Nguyen.

Duc led the way through the crowded stalls. They were starving. They hadn't eaten since lunch yesterday. A mama-san deep in the market sold them banh mi, shredded pork with carrots in a doughy sandwich, drenched in nuoc mam. They ate the sandwiches standing up, washed down with Cokes.

"You ever been in this guy's warehouse, Duc?"

"No, but I hear it very big."

Ben pounded on the big steel door with the peeling paint. The guard cracked the door open, took a quick peek, and pulled them inside. The big bouncer led them through a dim opium den to another door and into the large showroom; Ben held his breath, trying to avoid a contact high. Dusty sunlight drifted down from the high windows; they stood awkwardly in front of the proprietor, a tall man in a shiny suit who looked half-Asian. He was seated on a raised platform, smoking a cigarette in a long holder. Ben let his breath go and inhaled sharply.

"Your breathing technique is excellent, Lieutenant—I did not realize you were a yogi. I have been expecting you, *mes amis.*

"I am Nguyen Van Francois, at your service. My friend Lien said you might visit. I am very sorry, about what happened to your friend, Sergeant Elijah. He is in hospital? In Can Tho, I think? He is recuperating well, I trust."

How does he know that?

"Nice to meet you, Monsieur Nguyen," Ben said. "I guess you already know our names."

"Just call me Frank, *s'il vous plaît.* Yes, I make it my business to know everyone who comes here, *pour la sécurité.* I would offer you food, but I noticed you have already enjoyed your banh mi. It is excellent here. But how may I help?"

Ben looked around, took in the vast array of arms. He noticed one of Frank's soldiers hunched over a table, staring into three black-and-white TVs that showed views of the market—closed-circuit cameras.

"We're investigating the murders of two Americans."

"We? There are two detectives here? I am happy to hear you have promoted Sergeant Duc. He deserves it." Duc shuffled his feet, uncomfortable around this warlord. "As it happens," Francois continued, "I have some idea of what you are investigating. A young specialist, I believe he is called Tommy Banks—he came to see me.

"This soldier of yours, he purchased a large quantity of arms—rifles, grenade launchers, explosives. The usual menu. He wanted to ship them to America. It is possible he has some connection to your murders."

"What was Banks going to do with the guns?"

"He didn't say. But why would he? And I didn't ask. It may have something to do with the American woman."

"Grace Waverly?"

"Yes. Tommy's *petite amie*. Do you speak French? A few words, maybe? They were very close, Tommy and Mademoiselle Waverly."

"Would he have any reason to kill her, do you think?"

"I don't know. *Cette femme*, she *got around*, I think that is your expression. Perhaps Tommy was jealous? He has a bit of a temper. How did she die?"

"We can't say. But . . . it was unusual."

"Really? What was unusual?"

Frank Nguyen had confirmed the main points of Kline's story, but Ben wasn't going to share more. "I'm sorry, the investigation is confidential."

"*Et Joe Kline. Je comprends qu'il est mort, aussi.* A pity. They say he fell, from the roof of the Continental."

"So they say, yes," Ben said. All he'd understood was that Frank knew Kline was dead. "Did you know him too—Joe Kline?"

"No," Frank said. "I have never been introduced to Mr. Kline. Not formally, anyway. This Monsieur Kline was a reporter, yes? So he would be, as you might say, in the know. Or perhaps he knew too much. What do you think, Lieutenant?"

Ben went at it another way. "Do you know a man, an American, who works in the embassy? His name is J.B. Darling. I don't know what the initials stand for."

"Yes," Frank said, shifting on his perch. "I have met him."

"Do you have business with him?"

"My understanding is that Monsieur Darling—some people call him *Bing*—works for your government. Much of his work is confidential. Or so I'm told."

"Have you talked to Specialist Banks lately?"

"No, not since he collected the merchandise."

"How was it going to get there, to Baltimore?"

"*En bateau, bien sûr.* By ship."

"Do you know when it will arrive?"

"I understand it has been a fast passage. They say it will be there in a few days. On five January perhaps, if the weather holds."

Ben shook his head. *Four days from now. Not much time.*

"What is the name of the ship?"

"It is called the *Trung Nhi,* named for one of our ancient heroes. One of the sisters who repelled our enemies."

"You've been very helpful, Monsieur Frank. I may need to speak with you again."

"Any time. I am at your service. And Sergeant Duc, when next you see her, please say hello to your mother Cam, in Cholon. She is a great lady."

Duc flinched, unnerved that Saigon's leading arms dealer knew his mother and where she lived. Francois threw his best ingratiating smile out over them, proud that he had their undivided attention.

"I hope you catch this killer, this murderer who uses such unusual methods. You and your associates should be careful."

"I have begun to understand that."

"Yes, that was *une catastrophe* in the Delta. Lien told me that you enjoy collecting the sayings of wise men. There is a famous Vietnamese proverb, one you would do well to remember: *The higher you climb, the heavier you fall.*"

Ben looked at Duc and glanced toward the exit. *Time to get the hell out of here.* Francois held their gaze, his eyes lively, intense. Ben drew another deep breath and held it as they retreated through the haze of opium and emerged in the bright sun of the busy market.

43

BEYOND RESOURCEFUL

01 JANUARY 1968

After they left Francois, Ben knew the colonel would still be over at MACV, hanging around the five o'clock follies telling lies about the Urgent Campaign to Double Saigon's Checkpoints, so it would be safe to call Can Tho from the office. The nurse at the university hospital knew very little English, but after their unintelligible exchange, she put a Vietnamese surgeon on the line who'd trained at Texas Christian University—his English was excellent.

"Yes, Sergeant Jackson came through the operation very well. No structural damage, the bullet missed his arteries. His rotator cuff was shredded though. He'll need to convalesce a few months. But this is his ticket back to the States; he should be fine."

"Tell him I'll try to get down to visit. And thank you, for saving Elijah's life."

"Y'all get your boys in here right quick, we'll save 'em," the doctor said. "Most of the time, anyway."

Ben knew it was time to ask for help—he needed a sit-down with the U.S. ambassador. Ben said goodbye to Duc and got to the embassy just as Lien was coming out the door. She was hurrying along, seemed preoccupied.

"You look splendid this evening, Lien."

She stopped, apparently interrupted in mid-thought.

"Your áo dài's very beautiful."

It was the sky-blue one, with gold trim. Ben watched her adjust to his presence; the worry in her eyes eased and she smiled.

"I need to speak with Ambassador Stevens," Ben said. "But I don't want to ask for an appointment. They'll just put me off, and it's something urgent."

Lien turned thoughtful, studied his face. Behind her placid expression he could see her mind working—Lien always had many balls in the air.

"He schedule meeting with Mr. Darling Wednesday—at eleven. You come my desk then, wait. I walk you in at end of meeting."

"Thank you, Lien. Wish I could stay tonight and have dinner with you. But we need to go back to Long Binh, ask more questions."

"You look for Specialist Banks?"

"Yes, the same."

"He not in Vietnam. He fly to States."

"What? How'd that happen? He's in jail and his tour's not over."

"I know. Mr. Darling upset, when he find out this morning. Banks get TDY assignment, take American soldier's body home. For funeral. They say it escort duty."

"We let guys leave Vietnam for that? How'd Darling find out?"

"He read memo, of course. From FBI."

"The FBI? How are they involved in this?"

"Lien not know, for sure. Maybe they worry, in America, about your war protests. Sometimes your agencies, they work together. FBI has secrets too."

Ben didn't get it. What was the FBI up to? If they were tracking Banks, they must know a lot about him. Did they know he was buying guns? The FBI wasn't supposed to operate outside the U.S. That was the CIA's job. Did Darling alert them? It sounded as if the government knew all along this arms deal was happening.

Ben had a hard time believing it, but it appeared the FBI and the CIA wanted the radicals to get their hands on the guns. When two blundering MPs happened onto the plot, they became targets too. Ben was impressed with Tommy's energy, though. He was one hell of a logistics clerk.

"That Specialist Banks, he's quite the operator," Ben said.

"Yes. He is, how you say?" Lien raised her hand to her head, searching. "He is resourced? Is that right word?"

"Resourceful, yes. Banks is beyond resourceful—he's intelligent, clever, and very sneaky. Well, I guess I'm not going back to Long Binh." Ben smiled. "Do you have time for dinner?"

"Yes, but not at restaurant. Saigon not safe at night now. But I make dinner tonight for you. At home, Lieutenant Kin-Kay."

As the soft scented night fell over Saigon, Lien was very tender. She told Ben that when she'd found out they were driving to Vinh Long she'd been frightened, worried something bad would happen.

"You were right," Ben said. "Some Ruff Puffs ambushed us." He told her the short version of the story.

"I am very sorry Elijah wounded," she said, "but very happy you okay."

"Your boss, Mr. Darling, was there," Ben said. "It looked like he was directing the action."

Lien chuckled. "I wonder where he go yesterday. He say he play golf but never call the colonel. He like to play around, think he great commando."

They were resting, naked, on top of the sheets under the mosquito net, looking out her open window across the roofs of the city. She nestled against him, her arm across his chest, rubbed his leg with her bare foot.

"Did you know he was going to ambush us?" Ben asked.

"Not this time," Lien said. "But Mr. Darling unpredictable lately. He disappear a lot, for hours during middle of the day. We need to be very careful."

Lien slid on top of him, pushed his wrists over his head, kissed his neck, and then moved down his body, touching him lightly in all the right places.

"This make sure you sleep tonight, Benjamin. This treatment Number One sleep aid."

Ben had to agree—Lien's methods were foolproof.

He dozed for a couple of hours, then woke up thinking, re-running the chain of events in his mind. One conclusion seemed inescapable. What was really messed up, way beyond all his recognition, was what the evidence pointed to—that two powerful agencies of the U.S. government were handing dozens of deadly weapons to terrorists. And their agents would kill anyone who got in their way.

44

OPEN OR CLOSED

01-03 JANUARY 1968

After two nights in one of LBJ's hot, airless cells, a guard unlocked the door at dawn and escorted Tommy Banks into the sunshine to greet the New Year. Lieutenant Kinkaid's report had noted that during routine questioning Specialist Four Banks had thrown a steel office chair at Sergeant Jackson and punched him in the face. Ben had informed the JAG officer on duty that they didn't have enough to charge Banks with Grace's murder, so the prosecutor cut him loose with a warning: *Cool down and keep your nose clean, soldier. Next time, you'll never get out.* Tommy apologized for losing his temper, said he wasn't himself—he was still grieving, his girlfriend had just died.

The army bureaucracy had not shared the news of Tommy's impending TDY assignment with the military justice system; the JAG prosecutor had no idea Banks was about to leave Vietnam. An hour after his release, Tommy showed up at the USARV office on time, retrieved the TDY form Lieutenant Nelson had been kind enough to approve, and shoved it in front of Moseley before the sergeant could open his mouth to berate him.

"The Lieutenant signed this?" Moseley shook his head. "Fine. Get the hell out, Banks. I hope I never see your sorry ass again."

"Happy New Year to you too," Tommy said. He walked back to his hooch, changed into his dress army greens, and threw some civvies in his duffel bag.

He packed his good jeans, his best Hawaiian shirt, and his black leather jacket with the legend on the back, *When I Die, I'll Go to Heaven Because I've Served My Time in Hell.* Then Tommy headed over to Tan Son Nhut to catch his flight, couldn't wait to accompany his new best dead friend back to the world.

The man's name was Corporal George Miller Junior He'd been walking point with the Air Cav up by Cu Chi, hacking his way through elephant grass with a machete when he'd stepped on a trip wire. The grenade in a can blew Miller's leg off. He'd bled out before the Dustoff could get there.

Tommy felt a certain affinity for the guy. That could have been him; he was one insult to Moseley away from being that guy. The paperwork said the casualty was the son of Peggy and George Miller, RFD #3, Hagerstown, Maryland. A farm boy, Tommy guessed.

The flight to Dover Air Force Base took twenty-four hours. They stopped in Okinawa and Alaska for fuel but wouldn't let anybody off the plane (Tommy asked, twice). At Elmendorf AFB in Anchorage, Tommy watched a dozen mechanics in parkas scurry around the F-4 fighters parked on the tarmac. *I'd rather freeze in Alaska than rot in Vietnam.*

When they landed in Delaware, the pilots taxied the C-141 Starlifter into a huge hangar. Banks and his fellow GIs fell in and watched respectfully as the flag-draped coffins came off the plane, the handlers of the dead making sure each body was unloaded feet first. Lots of brass on hand. He stood stiffly at attention with the others while a full bird colonel reviewed the formation. Tommy saluted and shook the colonel's hand.

"Thank you, Specialist, for volunteering for this sacred mission."

"It's an honor, sir."

The next day Tommy met up with his stateside escort partner, Staff Sergeant Tyrone Talmadge, an army recruiter in downtown Baltimore. Talmadge had been setting enlistment records, persuading young Black men to get off the streets and sign up for the war. They drove together behind the hearse that bore Miller's body to a funeral home out in Hagerstown. The funeral home owner and his son helped them unload the coffin and roll it into the embalming room. It was very cold—the smell of disinfectant was overwhelming. The owner, a small chatty man in suspenders ("The name's Smitty"), had a question.

"Open or closed?"

Tommy didn't get it. "What do you mean?"

"Some boys who come back this way, sometimes just a few body parts are left. Then we keep the casket closed—for obvious reasons, you understand? If the body's mostly intact, we open it. The family likes to see the uniform. How'd this man die?"

"Stepped on a grenade. A booby trap. His leg was blown off, I think."

"Oh, then we keep it open," Smitty said. "We just throw a blanket over his lower half. They'll never know he lost a thing. Let's have a look."

He flipped the latches and raised the lid.

Corporal George Miller looked peaceful, face up, in his dress uniform, his new service medals on his chest—Combat Infantryman Badge, Purple Heart, Bronze Star with V.

Except for a smear of makeup that had failed to completely obscure the shrapnel wound in his cheek, the boy looked fine, very lifelike. "They're so young, aren't they?" Smitty said.

The two soldiers exchanged a look: *Nothing to say; let's get the hell out of here.* They verified Miller's address and left to tell his parents. Half an hour later, their cheap white Ford Cortina with the U.S. government plates pulled up at a small farm ten miles north of Hagerstown. *Windy Acres Farm*, the sign read. *The Millers Welcome You.* A cold day, overcast, old snow showing in the stubble of spent cornfields.

"I've never done one of these," Talmadge said. "I don't know what to say."

"That's okay, Sergeant," Tommy said. "The Millers already got the telegram, they know he's dead. It might get emotional, but it shouldn't be too bad. They coached me, I can handle it."

They headed up the path to a farmhouse—older, its white paint peeling, set on a rise overlooking a field of winter wheat that fell off to the east. Wood smoke drifted from the narrow chimney in the center of the roofline. Lots of farm equipment scattered about, most of it apparently discarded, rusting in the low winter sun. A scraggly mutt ran up to them, barking.

As Tommy mounted the first step, a lean, fifty-something woman in an apron threw open the door—her face looked as weathered as her barn. It took her a moment to realize what she was seeing—two soldiers in their army greens, looking nervous. Tommy saw her begin to understand. The welcoming look fell away, replaced by a wildness in her eyes—fear, fury, anguish.

"No!" she screamed. "No, no, no, I'm not talking to you. You came with his body, didn't you?"

Tommy cleared his throat. "Ma'am, I'm Specialist Banks, this is Staff Sergeant Talmadge, we're here to help you cope with your loss."

He didn't get any further. Peggy Miller leaped from the sill of the front door and fell against him. Tommy staggered backward, held her up. She banged her head against his shoulder and beat his chest with her fists, screaming.

"My boy! He's gone! God damn you! God damn you and God damn the army! He's gone! Dead. And for what? Tell me!"

Things didn't get any better. They managed to help Mrs. Miller inside, got her into a chair at the round kitchen table. Talmadge brought her a glass of water. Tommy sat next to her and held her hand, told her again how sorry he was. Peggy Miller wouldn't look at him. She stared out the window—it was starting to snow.

Her husband, George Senior, having noticed the strange car, came in off his tractor. Big man with a white beard, strong, used to a hardscrabble existence. He lifted Peggy out of the chair and held her as she sobbed. He was trembling, blinking, still trying to take in what had happened to them. Then the tears came; they coursed down his face, washed over the same spot where his son's cheek had been pierced.

45

YOU CAN COUNT ON US

03 JANUARY 1968

Waiting in the small holding area outside Lien's office, Ben was on edge. His left leg kept bouncing up and down—he wasn't sure he could stop it if he tried. Not long after he got there, he'd spotted Darling heading down the hall into Ambassador Stevens's office, carrying an accordion file full of papers.

Ben held his own file on the murders tightly against his chest, half expecting someone to try to rip it out of his grasp. He'd been awake all night, worrying whether he could persuade the ambassador to act. Some of the evidence was circumstantial. Maybe they'd just laugh it off.

He wished he could see the ambassador alone, but that was impossible now. Stevens was an experienced, cautious bureaucrat. If some walk-in lieutenant's message involved anything remotely sensitive, the ambassador would want a witness to hear it, and Darling was already with him. He'd never admit a thing, just try to steer the meeting to some ambiguous ending. *Your betters will look into it. Go away, Lieutenant.*

Ben decided to start with the photo of the cyanide cannon that Lu had recovered. He'd lay it down next to the image of Grace's dead body, that would get their attention. Lien appeared and silently escorted him to the ambassador's office, knocked, and opened the door.

"What is it, Lien?" Ambassador Stevens asked.

"Mr. Ambassador. Very sorry to bother, but Lieutenant Kinkaid here, from the MPs, he say he have something very important to show you, your eyes only."

Stevens looked up, irritated. "We're very busy this morning." Darling was seated in front of the ambassador's desk in his jungle cammies, drumming his fingers on a file.

"I just need five minutes to give you the headlines, Mr. Ambassador," Ben said, stepping inside. "I apologize, but you need to know this. We've uncovered a plot by American terrorists to obtain guns here, possibly even heavy weapons."

In his white tropical-weight suit and bow tie, Stevens looked like the stereotypical buttoned-up New Englander. He hesitated, then tossed the folder he'd been holding across the desk. "All right. Five minutes. And you are?"

"Lieutenant Ben Kinkaid, sir. From the MP Battalion. We're investigating the deaths of two Americans, Grace Waverly, a tourist, and Joe Kline, a reporter."

"Yes, I read about them. This is Mr. Darling, one of my advisors." Darling gave Ben a brief nod. His eyes were vacant, unfocused.

Ben pulled a chair closer to Stevens's desk and launched his pitch before the ambassador could change his mind. "The munitions are on their way, now, to anti-war radicals on the East Coast. We believe they're planning a terrorist act in the homeland, possibly very soon. We need to alert stateside authorities."

Ben paused and studied their faces. Darling swiveled his chair so he could stare out the window at the big banyan tree, no doubt thinking about how he could deep-six the whole story.

Stevens gestured for Ben to continue.

He laid his pictures on the table: Grace's naked body, the cyanide cannon, Joe Kline in a pool of blood, headshots of Frank Nguyen and Tommy Banks, a copy of Grace's list, and several views of the cornucopia of arms inside Frank's warehouse, which Duc had snapped with his tiny camera.

Talking fast, Ben walked them through it. Waverly and Banks met at an anti-war protest in New York organized by a hardcore group called RAW. Banks fell in love with Grace, she wrangled a tourist visa, followed him here, and gave him her shopping list. Banks bought most of the guns from Frank Nguyen and then bribed ARVNs to fill in the rest. Unclear where the money came from. The shipment left Saigon before Christmas and was due to arrive at the Port of Baltimore any day now. Could the ambassador alert the FBI? Could they intercept it, seize the arms, and arrest the perpetrators?

As Ben told his story, Darling smiled and shook his head, perhaps impressed that two dimwit MPs knew so much. He didn't look worried though, and the ambassador kept his own counsel, his face blank. Ben thought his ace in the hole was the draft of Kline's article; he saved it for last, handed it to Stevens.

The ambassador scanned it but gave away nothing. Darling leaned in over the desk, trying to read it. His cheeks reddened; he looked like he wanted to burn it, reduce Ben and his evidence, to ashes right there.

"Yes," Stevens said. He paused for several beats, considering his response. "Well, thank you, Lieutenant. I'm so glad you stopped by. Very fortuitous, that you managed to discover this story before it was printed. I'd like to run it by a couple of key people in D.C. May we make a copy?"

"Yes, sir. But it's evidence. I'll need the original for the investigation."

"Of course." Stevens pushed a button under his desk and Lien appeared. He handed her Kline's story. "Please type this and make a carbon copy."

She nodded and left the room.

"I will look into this," Stevens said. "Could you come back here on Friday, say 1100 hours? I'll return the article and let you know what we've found out."

"Yes, sir," Ben said, thankful he'd made several copies of the story.

Darling met Ben's eyes with a cold stare and spoke for the first time. "One question, Lieutenant—does your supervisor know about this?"

"Colonel Balderamos?"

"Yes."

"Not yet, sir. I thought the information was so sensitive that we needed to get it to the very highest level, as soon as possible."

"You did exactly the right thing, *Lieutenant*," said Darling, emphasizing Ben's modest rank. "Very prudent, not to involve the colonel. You can count on us. We'll get to the bottom of this."

Ben rose, saluted, shook their hands. He figured if Stevens hadn't been there, Darling would have thrust a combat knife between his ribs and sliced his aorta into little pieces on the spot. The man radiated darkness. Ben walked out, feeling uneasy.

Did I screw up? Should I have gone to MACV, used army channels? More people would know. The higher you climb, the heavier you fall.

46

REPOSE EN PAIX

04 JANUARY 1968

Bing appreciated Frank's latest invitation; he'd been saying yes to their "meetings" whenever his friend called, which was every couple of days lately. He'd leave the office around noon, take a leisurely stroll down to the market, and meander through the stalls. He made a show of looking at the expensive electronics and the cheap Japanese clothes, but he never bought anything. After a few diversions down blind alleys and covert scans of the scene (you could never be sure who was watching) he'd end up on Frank's doorstep.

This Thursday was no different. He was agitated; the unscheduled meeting with that pushy MP yesterday had been concerning. More than concerning, it was a threat to their carefully constructed plan. Yes, the ambassador was still on board, but the time frame was tight. If Stevens decided to tell some FBI higher-up in D.C. what the MPs were onto, and asked for guidance—well, who knew what would happen? But he couldn't risk taking another shot at the MPs now, that would ring far too many alarm bells. Stevens knew President Johnson too, referred to him as *my friend Lyndon* all the time; he might even decide to tell LBJ about it, try to take credit for quashing a harebrained scheme.

It was an election year. Opposition to the war was mushrooming, Johnson was under a lot of pressure. The president wouldn't want to be anywhere near a potential scandal like this. He might shut down the operation five minutes after he heard about it. That would be the prudent thing to do—by far the best move, politically.

Hoover would be pissed the op had leaked. The FBI chief might even open his big bag of tricks to keep the plot alive, deploy some of the dirt he'd amassed on anyone in Washington who possessed a smidgeon of power. Bing feared this project was turning into a clusterfuck. He and Del had been trying to accomplish the mission—*git her done*—for the big picture, the greater good and all that. He could imagine what his mother would say if she knew about this. *It's a train wreck, Bing. Get yourself back on the straight and narrow.*

Bing had reached the door to Frank's den. The little voice in his head was telling him not to succumb, to stop right here and walk away. But his body was on autopilot. He needed a hit, couldn't stop thinking about it, had to have it. Was he addicted? Of course not, that was impossible. He was Jarvis Bingham Darling, CIA Chief of Station, Saigon. He wasn't a doper, a junkie. He was too smart, too careful, too important to get sucked into that life. *I just like the occasional jolt. A man has to relax sometime.* He needed to kick back and calm down. One hit, maybe two. That would help him sort this out.

Frank was always so gracious. *I shouldn't be so hard on him.* He felt safe in the den. Behind the red curtain, the other men there never noticed a thing. Bing loved the way Frank comforted him, guided him through the process.

"Mon ami!" Frank said, greeting him at the door. He put his arm around Bing and shepherded him to his favorite corner.

When Bing was settled in, Francois began to heat the opium. He loved molding the little balls, shaping the dose so it would give his mark the maximum rush. The perfect hit. He passed the pipe into Bing's hands; he drew hard on it and sank into the cushions.

"Welcome to Xanadu," Francois whispered.

Bing closed his eyes as Francois took a second plastic bag from his pocket and pressed a new reddish-brown mound into the pipe.

"I saved the best for last," Francois said. "This is the Burmese variety, from the Golden Triangle. Very pure, the essence of the poppy."

Bing drew deeply—once, twice, three times. When he inhaled the fourth time the pipe slipped from his mouth. Francois caught it before it hit the ground. He cradled Bing in his arms and pressed a napkin against his mouth so the milky drool wouldn't stain his jacket. He waited a moment, then checked for a pulse. Nothing. He gently lowered the body to the ground, pressed the eyes shut. A very neat result, just the way the Eel liked it.

Repose en paix, mon ami.

47

UNTOUCHABLE

04 JANUARY 1968

"How did meeting go?" Lien asked Ben.

They stood in the high sun outside the cafe by the embassy on her lunch break. Lien was her usual cool collected self, shading her face with a deep red parasol.

"The ambassador listened. He said he'd make some inquiries, but I didn't see a lot of urgency. We're supposed to meet again, at 1100 tomorrow."

"How Mr. Darling seem?"

"Hard to tell. He stared at your favorite banyan tree a lot. He seemed amused, almost. A little out of it, not all there. I couldn't tell what he was thinking."

"Hmmm."

Ben loved the way she bit her lower lip, the tip of her tongue showing—her mind was humming, contemplating the next move. It was unsettling, how much he'd come to rely on her. "Maybe Mr. Darling surprised, how much you know."

"Yeah. But my guess is they'll do nothing. Maybe Stevens is part of it too, some idiotic plan to promote the war. What do you think? What should I do now if they ignore me?"

"Joe Kline's article, you have more copies, yes?"

"Yes."

"So you can use that. Maybe some other paper interested. Mr. Whittlesey, you know him? From *New York Times*?"

"Yes."

"If Mr. Stevens no help, maybe Whittlesey write story, then police in U.S. can stop shipment—no one else die."

"You think I should show up for tomorrow's meeting?"

"You should not skip meeting. I meet you in lobby, 1030 hours."

"I could bring you coffee."

She flashed a radiant smile. He moved closer, thought he could hug her. She slipped gracefully under his arms, blew him a kiss, escaped, and crossed the street. He watched her for a long time, wishing they had more time for each other.

Back in the MP office, Balderamos was nowhere to be found, probably out practicing his short game. Ben called Lieutenant Lu and told him he needed help organizing extra checkpoints on all the major roads leading into the city.

"You have good idea, for more checkpoints," Lu said. "We hear some rumor, VC maybe plan big attack, later this month."

"Any truth to it?"

"Our people up north see lot of traffic on Ho trail. Sapper squads, many VC on the move. They carry beaucoup explosives to south."

"But there's supposed to be a cease-fire," Ben said. "For Tet." The Year of the Monkey: the VC had agreed to a three-day truce at the end of

January. "Half the ARVN will be on leave. Sergeant Duc's going to visit his mother in Cholon."

"You think VC stop their fight for Tet, Kin-Kay?" Lieutenant Lu trilled his chickadee laugh. "Tet no holiday for VC. No, it Number One opportunity. Lu help you with checkpoints, for sure. But no ARVN be here to guard them, maybe."

They arranged to set some skeletal roadblocks so Ben and the colonel would have something to see Monday afternoon. Lu agreed to ride along.

"Lu have other news for you. We figure out who drove truck, into Twenty Grand."

"Really? How'd you manage that?"

"Driver, his wife no see him. He gone four days, she report him missing. We show her picture. He burned, but not on face."

"Who was he?"

"His name Do Van Khiem. He AWOL, from ARVN. Frank Nguyen give Khiem job, protect him. Probably Frank force him to drive truck into bar. Khiem not know it explode, maybe."

"You sure about the ID, Lu?"

"One hundred percent."

"When are you going to arrest Frank and question him? I'd like to be there."

"No way, GI. White Mice never arrest Frank Nguyen. He know many people, high places. Vietnam prime minister, for example, he Frank's friend. Minister's wife, also. She very powerful too. Lu think you have American word for Monsieur Frank. *No touch*, maybe?"

"Pretty close, Lu. I think you mean, *untouchable*."

"Yes, that right." Lu was giggling again. "Frank Nguyen untouchable, like gangster in American movie. White Mice no question him, never. He like Al Capone of Vietnam. No way we point finger at *Bac* Frank, arrest go nowhere."

Ben was starting to lose hope. Whatever avenues he had left to solve the murders, reveal the corruption, and recover the guns, he could feel the doors closing. There might not be any light left at the end of any of these tunnels.

48

GEORGE JUNIOR'S FUNERAL

04 JANUARY 1968

After all the emotion with the Millers, Tommy had no desire to attend their son's funeral. He'd seen enough grief for one week. But if he blew it off, some army doofus might find out and ask a lot of questions—he didn't need that. So there he was on Thursday night, seated in the second row of the mortuary chapel right behind Peggy Miller and right next to George Junior's Aunt Flo, trying to hum along to hymns he didn't know.

Grace deserves a funeral too. I won't even know if she gets one.

Bringing George's body home had hit him harder than he'd expected. He was sick of the war and depressed about his situation; it felt like his life was spinning out of control. This war was going to ruin them all.

When the service ended they trooped by the casket to pay their respects. Tommy could only manage a nod as he passed by. The reception was in a crowded room on the second floor. Sergeant Talmadge had gone back to Baltimore to sweet talk more teenagers into risking their lives, so

Tommy was on his own, stuck in a corner slugging down a sweet, cherry-flavored alcoholic punch from a plastic cup, the only liquor available. He downed about six, one after the other.

George and Peggy stood in a receiving line, stiff in their Sunday clothes, accepting condolences from their neighbors. They looked crushed, inconsolable. Tommy shook their hard, calloused hands, tried to hold their teary eyes. He couldn't even imagine how bad it must be.

He was chugging another cup of punch when a young woman touched his arm. "Thank you. For bringing Georgie home. You're the escort soldier, aren't you?"

A petite, attractive brunette—ponytail, rosy cheeks, short black dress—looked up at him—her face was a blur. He blinked, woozy from the punch.

"I'm Tommy," he said, managing a wan smile.

"I'm Sue; Georgie's my boyfriend. I mean, he was my boyfriend." She smiled, apologetically, like it was her fault, what had happened to him. "We were together a while ago, before he went away. Overseas."

She reached for the punch cups, leaned closer, ran her fingers down his arm, let her hip touch his. Not that pretty, but eager. *Might as well be kind.* "Would you like some punch?"

"That would be great." Tommy was too unsteady to fill her cup, so just handed Sue his. *What the hell am I doing? This is the poor schmo's girlfriend.*

In the end, he didn't care. Sue seemed like a sweet girl but was probably just as fucked up as he was. She asked a lot of questions, and it felt good to tell the truth for a change. They talked about where he'd grown up, where Hell's Kitchen was, how many people you could jam into a tenement apartment, how he loved to go as a kid to Coney Island to ride on the big Ferris wheel. He'd ride it three times in a row, mesmerized every time by the lights of Manhattan. Sue had grown up on a farm, had never been to New York, would love to see Broadway.

"Maybe we can go there, some day," he said. She smiled up at him, her breasts taut against the little black dress. No great beauty, but something real seductive about her.

After ten minutes of small talk they slipped away; Sue drove them back to his rundown motel on U.S. 15 outside Frederick. In the car Tommy turned to her, pushed his hand up her dress, and pressed his palm against her panties. He unlocked the door to his crappy room, and Sue was halfway out of her dress before he could kick the door shut. He threw her on the bed, pinned her down, and screwed her. Pounded her as hard as he could, still wearing his uniform shirt. She cried out, must have enjoyed it, but as he finished all he could think about was Grace. He felt like she was in the room, looking down on them. He thought he heard her sigh.

I'm such a wreck. Fuck this war, I got nothing to look forward to.

They rested and shared a smoke. He turned on the radio to pass the time. It played the latest by the Beatles—"Hello, Goodbye." The DJ said the thermometer was down to zero; no wonder the room was so cold. Sue got up, started to put her clothes on. "I have to get home, my mother will worry."

"Take care, Sue," Tommy said, his hands on her bottom. He kissed the top of her head, the way he had with Grace. "Maybe I'll see you around."

Tommy heard the car drive off, the tires crunching on the snow. He got back in bed, doused the light, and thought about heading down to the port later to collect his package. After that it would be time to line up his partners, if he could call them that.

49

GONE FOR GOOD

05 JANUARY 1968

After he crawled out of bed and drank three glasses of water Friday morning, Tommy called a cab and rode to the Baltimore airport to pick up his rental car—a black Ford Galaxie 500, the big four-door model. It was the FBI's sedan of choice; if anybody questioned why he was parked someplace maybe they'd think he was police. Then he headed over to the Port of Baltimore, just twenty minutes away.

Tommy found the harbor master's office, showed him the invoice Lieutenant Nelson had signed authorizing the shipment, and completed all the paperwork. "Just follow Boris, the guy on the forklift," the harbor master said.

"We'll be back in a few days to get the rest," Tommy said, pointing to the manifest for the other twelve boxes. He drove slowly behind Boris to a vast field of steel containers stacked next to the cargo ships docked nearby. Boris checked Tommy's form, found the right CONEX, and lowered it to the ground. Then he pried it open and extracted two long wooden boxes, which they stacked in the Galaxie's big back seat.

"Pretty heavy," the big stevedore said. "What you got here? Steel pipe?"

"Bingo," Tommy said, smiling. "My mother's house in Catonsville has a drainage problem. She's on Social Security. Figured I'd help her out, do it myself and save her a few bucks. I bought the pipes cheap, they came all the way from Vietnam."

"Okay," Boris said, unconvinced. The box had "Coconuts" printed on it, but maybe Boris's English was not so good. Tommy waved goodbye and drove off, surprised at how easy it was. He felt proud, capable, like some movie assassin with a poker face and a huge revolver who knew what the fuck he was doing. He made sure Boris was well out of sight and then backtracked, eased the big Ford in behind a warehouse.

He donned the yellow hard hat he'd bought in a construction supply store, grabbed his clipboard, and walked briskly toward the ship, looking official. A crane was off-loading CONEXes from the Trung, dozens of them; the dock workers placed them in neat rows on the pier. He spotted a couple boxes on the ground with the labels he was looking for: "Perishable—Fresh Fruit—Republic of South Vietnam."

Off to his left Tommy noticed another cluster of steel containers with a ladder propped against them. He walked over, moved the ladder to the far end where the stevedores wouldn't see him, and climbed up. He crawled to the edge of the CONEX and looked out. He had a clear view, impossible to miss from this range. He imagined the look on their faces when they figured out what was going down.

When Ben showed up in the lobby of the U.S. Embassy at 1030 hours Friday morning, Lien wasn't there. She'd never missed a meeting with him before; he was worried.

He talked his way past the guard: "I have an appointment with Ambassador Stevens. First Lieutenant Benjamin Kinkaid with the 18th MPs. I was here two days ago, you remember?"

Upstairs, the ambassador's assistant was dismissive. "Oh, yes. I'm sorry, Lieutenant—you were on the calendar but the ambassador was called away. A last-minute thing. He had to go up to Nha Trang."

"Did he leave any message?"

"No, I'm very sorry. We're usually very careful not to break appointments. Would you like me to arrange something for later?"

"I'll have to get back to you."

So Ambassador Stevens was gone, three hundred klicks away. Even if the ambassador had believed what Ben had told him, he apparently didn't think a quick response was required. The assistant's phone rang. When she turned to reach for a file, Ben wandered off down the hall. He came to Lien's glass-walled office first, but she wasn't in it. Darling was gone too. But both their offices were full of people. Tough-looking American civilians had taken over, guys he'd never seen before. They had buzz cuts, maybe ex-military. Ben dipped into the men's room across the hall, held the door open a crack, and watched for a while.

They emptied drawers, pulled out files, took pictures, and studied computer screens. They were very thorough; it appeared they were going to root through every document and appointment book in Darling's office. No point in sticking around. Stevens's aide was still on the phone, he waved as he walked out the door.

No Bing, no Lien. Looks like they're gone for good.

50

A CERTAIN PURITY

05 JANUARY 1968

The agency types weren't going to say a word, so Ben decided to search for Lien. He knocked hard on her apartment door, called her name. No answer. Ben took out his little tool, checked to see no one was around, and slid it into the lock. He jiggled the pick until it clipped the tumblers and the lock gave way. He walked the rooms—all empty. Her bed was made, everything clean and neat, but there were no clothes in her closet.

All of her mother's paintings—the green-on-green scenes of the countryside—were gone from the walls. *She didn't even say goodbye.* He picked up a pillow and pressed it against his nose, caught a trace of her scent. He put it back, smoothed it, tried to think. Then he closed up and left.

By 1430 he was pounding on the door to Francois's opium den. The big Montagnard with the Uzi opened the door a crack but kept his finger on the trigger. As he walked through the dark room, Ben noticed that the heavy red curtain Francois used to screen the corner seat had been left open, and the pillows were scattered around. Odd, Ben had noticed on his first visit that Francois was quite fastidious. Ben's eyes were still adjusting to the light when Francois materialized from the back of the building. He paused to straighten his tunic and smooth his dark hair.

"So happy to see you, Lieutenant. Will you have tea?"

Francois took his time, immersed himself in the ceremony. They settled into their places, sipped green tea from tiny cups. Ben noticed a tremor in his host's hand when he poured.

"How may I be of assistance, *mon fils*?"

"I can't find Lien," Ben said.

"You were going to meet the ambassador again—when was that?"

"This morning, but he didn't show."

"I understand Mr. Stevens was called away. He is giving a medal to the province chief in Nha Trang, a man called Nguyen Van Dông—he is part of your Phoenix program. Have you heard of it? Mr. Dông has killed many VC. Perhaps *killed* is not the word. No, Mr. Dông has *murdered* many people, usually while they were sleeping. Your intelligence people tell him which ones to kill. Dông is an excellent assassin. You Americans are very proud of his work."

Ben nodded, noting Francois's disgust. Phoenix was a joint effort by MACV and the CIA to decimate the National Front's rural leaders. Ben had seen a *Times* story that said Vietnamese "Provincial Reconnaissance Units" had murdered nearly twenty thousand VC. *Say hello to Bing and Dông, Vietnam's leading serial killers.* But Ben knew neither side had a monopoly on evil. The VC had tortured and killed a similar number of soldiers and civilians by now.

"Thank you, *Bac* Francois," Ben said. *Bac* meant uncle, which was as much respect as he could muster. "Mr. Darling wasn't there either. His office was full of American civilians; they were searching everything."

"Really? So soon?" Francois said, raising an eyebrow. "If they are looking for your Mr. Darling, I don't think there will be much to find."

"What happened to him?"

"I understand that he is missing. Unfortunate, of course. I fear Mr. Darling's war is over, Lieutenant Kinkaid."

"You sound pretty sure of that."

Francois gave him a sad little smile.

"Mr. Darling and his friends have a favorite phrase they use when they move against those they decide are their enemies. *Terminate with extreme prejudice* . . . that's it."

"Can you tell me, Bac Francois—do you consider Mr. Darling to be your enemy?"

Francois drew deeply on his cigarette, tapped the holder so the ash dropped neatly into an antique blue-and-white dish. He gazed off, ignoring the question. Ben let the silence stand for a few moments, but the subject was closed. He looked around the room. Most of the tables were empty, just a few rifles and sidearms left. Either business was booming and his stock was depleted, or Saigon's big-ass gun store was shutting down. No wonder Francois seemed a bit frazzled.

"Yes, mon fils," Francois said, chuckling softly. "My cupboard is bare. Well, not quite, but diminished. I am downsizing. Business has not been so good lately."

"What happened?"

"It is the way of the world, I suppose. As we Catholics say, there is a time for every season. A time to live, a time to die, and so on. More people have been noticing, lately, what we do here. Attention is bad for business—it is better to remain discreet. I think it is time for a sabbatical."

Ben took a chance, blurted out his question: "Did you kill Grace, Monsieur Francois? And Joe Kline, Mr. Darling?"

Francois fixed Ben with a long look—implacable, his eyes cold, lifeless. He paused for several seconds and then spoke slowly.

"Our war in Vietnam, it has killed a lot of people, Lieutenant. Millions of souls have departed this earth. Some of them good, some not so good. If some of the very worst had to die, is that not a good thing?"

Ben thought about it. Not an outright admission, but close. And were Grace Waverly and Joe Kline among the worst? But what was the point, to press Francois now? This awful war had a momentum of its own; a few mere humans couldn't change its course, no matter how good their intentions.

He probably killed them. Was he ordered to? Who gave the order? In the larger scheme of things, what difference did it make? He'll have to answer for it, someday, somewhere.

"What happened to Lien?"

"May I ask you something personal, Lieutenant? Are you in love with Lien?"

Ben was taken aback. *I thought I was.* Francois spoke gently, as if he was about to break bad news, something catastrophic.

"Do you know what *Lien* means?" Francois asked. "Her name—the word, I mean. In Vietnamese, the symbol associated with *Lien* is a lotus. A lotus flower. It suggests a certain purity, divinity. I think that was an appropriate name for our friend. It was pure, her love for our people."

"You speak of her in the past tense," Ben said, his voice breaking. He fought back tears. "Is she dead?"

"No, no, Lieutenant, forgive me. She is alive. Very much so. She is just not here in Saigon, at the moment."

"Where is she?"

"I don't know, precisely. A little farther north, I think. They are very busy now."

"'They'? Who are 'they'? What are you talking about?"

Francois reached back and pulled a small parcel from behind his chair. He held it out with both hands, like an offering.

Ben nodded his respect and opened the red box, removed the tissue paper. It was a framed picture of Lien, a younger Lien, maybe about twenty, in a North Vietnamese Army uniform. She was looking up, smiling—adoringly, he thought—at a tall, slim man with kind eyes and a narrow wisp of a beard, kept in the ancient Annamese style. He was handing her a piece of paper, in a frame. A diploma, perhaps?

"You recognize her, of course," Francois said.

"Yes." Ben choked on the word, the pressure rising behind his eyes. He wiped away a tear.

"And do you realize who that man is?"

"Yes." The picture of Ho Chi Minh and Lien was the same size, the same shape as the bright patch of paint he'd seen on the wall of Lien's apartment months ago—a photo that had been in a place of honor for some time and then removed.

"Your friend Lien, your *amour*, she is a colonel," said Francois. "A full colonel in the National Front, much decorated. She was one of Ho's favorites—you see, how Bac Ho is smiling. This is her graduation picture, from her training in Hanoi."

Ben had no words. He'd had no idea. But there she was, smiling up at Ho.

"Lien has been one of the best spies the National Front had. Can you imagine, the access she had to your army's plans? She knew where you were strong, where you were weak, everything you were planning, what you would do next, and when you would do it. But now, as James Bond might say, her cover has been blown. Perhaps because of you, *l'affaire* with you. Lien has had to return to the field, you see. But please, keep the picture. It will remind you of her."

"And take this as well," Francois said, handing Ben a mini-cassette tape. "You may share it with your friends in the press." Francois said, his eyes hard, "But you will leave my name out of it."

What a fool I was.

51

TYGER, TYGER BURNING BRIGHT

06 JANUARY 1968

Ben was in the office early again. He'd been running around so much there'd been no time to do a thorough report on the investigation into Grace's death. If the cover-up was underway, he wanted to document everything he and Elijah had found out, get it all on the record.

He was weary. He'd lain awake again last night, going over everything he knew about Lien, trying to understand everything she'd done and why she'd done it. It had been so easy for her to deceive him—he was so naive and besotted that she'd barely had to lie. He'd caught her in a lie or two of omission but had never punctured the veil. The obvious conclusion was that she was just using him. But she'd saved their lives. Now he didn't know what to think. The brass were always complaining that the VC seemed to know in advance where American troops were planning to attack. Saigon had to be riddled with spies—he was just another easy mark.

Ben had typed one sentence when the phone rang.

"Lieutenant Kin-Kay, your friend Lucky Lu here. You no believe what I see here this morning, at zoo. Big crime scene. You come now, meet at Hung Kings Temple? You think this very interesting—Lucky give you money-back guarantee."

When Ben drove onto the grounds of the zoo, he passed a gaggle of cars and utility vans with U.S. government plates. They were parked at strange angles with the doors open. A dozen White Americans in short sleeve shirts and khakis were scurrying around the tiger cage. One man was still in his car, talking into a radio telephone.

Ben turned away from the scene and parked behind two big trees and a thick line of bushes on the far side of the temple, three hundred meters away. When he got out of his jeep, Lucky Lu stepped out from behind the foliage, holding his binoculars.

"Hi, Lu. What's going on?"

"Can you guess?" Lu asked. "They not my guys, that for sure. This crime scene, yes, but very unusual. Look."

They crept forward and crouched behind the temple wall. The sun was rising behind them and Ben and Lu were a football field away—it would be a long shot for the investigators to spot them. Ben raised the glasses and focused on the scene. The door to the big tiger cage was open. There were three guys inside clustered around something; two knelt in the dirt while the third took photos. There was a lot of blood on the ground. One of the kneelers—Ben pegged him for a forensics specialist—lifted something out of the cage with a forceps and studied it.

It took Ben a moment, but then he got it—it was a fragment of an arm, severed at the elbow. Only three fingers were left on the hand, which hung by a strand of skin from the victim's wrist. The investigator dropped the body part into a clear plastic bag. Two other guys wearing gowns and gloves squeezed into the cage and slowly lifted what appeared to be a male torso, still dripping, and deposited it in a body bag. Pieces of shredded rope dangled from it; the corpse had been wrapped in heavy rope, similar to a mummy. Ben saw gaping wounds where something had broken through the ropes and ripped apart the victim's flesh.

Then the chief investigator extracted a scrap of white cloth. It had ruffles, like a Cuban-style shirt. Ben scanned the scene and recognized a couple of the Americans—they were the same guys who'd been turning over Darling's office.

A smear of color caught his eye, a dusky orange mass off to the side. There were black stripes on it. Ben realized he was looking at the carcass of the Saigon Zoo's only tiger—*Shere Khan*, chief among tigers, the creature's name taken from the Kipling poem. Shere had apparently eaten his last meal.

"You guess, Kin-Kay, who that is?"

"My money's on Mr. J.B. Darling."

"That what Lu think. Those guys all CIA. Who else could body be? Why go all this trouble for anyone else? When I get here, I go over, ask if they need White Mice help. They get beaucoup excited, yell at me: 'Di-di mau! Di-di mau, papa-san! This U.S. operation, no place for slope cops.' I tell them I see a lot more than they do," Lu said, laughing. He had thick skin and had heard every insult imaginable.

"What your guess, Kin-Kay?" Lu asked. "You think Mr. Darling take dancing lesson with tiger?"

"Killed somewhere else, probably," Ben said. "That's more likely, don't you think?"

"For sure, Kin-Kay. Maybe killer try to make it harder for anyone to find things in autopsy. Also, this send message. Killer say, you mess with me, I tear you up, big time."

Ben didn't know the Kipling poem that well but some William Blake came to him.

Tyger, tyger, burning bright,
In the forests of the night;
What immortal hand or eye,
Could frame thy fearful symmetry?

"A poem?" Lu asked. "What that mean, Kin-Kay?"

"In this case, I think it means don't screw around with God. He might feed you to a tiger."

52

THE SETUP

08 JANUARY 1968

Parked across from her apartment building in Harlem, Tommy watched as Makeba—a.k.a. Patience Jefferson, Hop's ex-colleague in the RAW cell—hustled down the steps of her apartment in the light snow, carrying her car keys. Makeba grabbed the door handle of her battered '56 Chevy and it swung open before she could put in the key. She took a step back, shook her head, and got in. Tommy figured she must have forgotten to lock it.

He looked up and down the street for watchers but it looked clean. Tommy got out of his big black Ford, walked over, and knocked on her frosty window. Makeba rolled it down and glared at him. "How'd the hell you find me?" she demanded.

"Pretty simple. Your man Lavarious is still in the phone book. Under 'L. Prince.' Grace said you were in New York."

"How is that feisty chick anyway?" Makeba asked.

Tommy winced. "Grace is dead. Hopkins got her killed. He sent her to Saigon. He knew how dangerous it was, but he did it anyway. He didn't give a shit what happened to her. We need to talk."

She sighed but got out of the car.

"Don't forget your letter," Tommy said, pointing to the envelope on the front seat.

"What the—?" she asked. "Damn, it's cold. C'mon, I'll open it inside."

"So he screwed you too, huh?" Makeba asked Tommy when they were inside the one-bedroom flat she shared with Lavarious. She'd stepped into the bathroom to read the letter, so Tommy struggled out of his black hooded sweatshirt and sat down on the worn orange velour sofa that faced an ancient TV. He noticed a document on a TV table, with the heading "Brink's Armored Car Co., Inc." It was a list of times and places, mostly banks. It looked like a delivery itinerary.

Makeba came out, brushing her sleeves and tossing her hair to shake off the remaining snow.

"They found Grace in the Saigon River, a couple weeks ago," Tommy said, his voice breaking. "It looked like a suicide, but I know it wasn't. The MPs are all over it. They think I did it. They'll arrest me if I go back there. They're so stupid. I loved Grace."

"Yeah, I can see you're torn up. I'm sorry."

Lavarious walked in from the bedroom in his work clothes, a one-piece fresh green coverall. "You guys need coffee?"

"Yes!" Tommy and Makeba said in unison. Lavarious stepped into the galley kitchen to put the kettle on.

"You a mechanic now?" Tommy asked.

"Plumber's apprentice," Lavarious said. "Plumbers make good money, you know."

"Turns out I prefer good-looking plumbers to selfish eggheads," Makeba said.

Tommy laughed. "I gotta confess something," he said to Makeba. "When this all started you were suspicious of me, asked a lot of questions. Wondered if I could be trusted. Well, you were right. I was an informant. But I'm not one, not now."

"I knew something was off."

"The FBI blackmailed me . . . forced me to help them. I was at that protest in Maryland last year with those priests. I helped them burn some draft records. Dumbass that I am, I did it wearing my uniform. I didn't know it was a federal crime. The feds said if I didn't cooperate, I'd go to jail."

"So they set you up," Lavarious said, sipping from his mug that read "Make Coffee, Not War."

"What'd they want?" he asked.

"To help Hop get guns," Tommy said. "The FBI plans to arrest everyone who shows up Sunday at the Baltimore pier. They got it all arranged. They're gonna bring the newspapers and TV stations along to take pictures. They call it Operation Ricochet."

"I should have guessed," Makeba said, glaring at him. "Some army guy appears out of the blue to help us. And the fucking FBI, they're everywhere. Look at this letter, Lavarious . . . I found it on my front seat." He scanned it, shook his head, and gave it to Tommy.

"Makeba, my friend—just thought you should know" . . . was the first line of the typewritten message that followed:

> *I hate to be the one to tell you, but Arthur Hopkins is setting you up. He's a spy, for the FBI. He's going to give you guys your share Sunday night and let you drive off. Then he's going to rat you out, tell the feds where you live. He wants to wipe out your whole cell. Don't let it happen! My best to L.*
>
> *Power to the people!*
>
> *Your friend, D.*

"That bastard," Makeba said. "I trusted Hop, slept with him, washed his socks, even brought him his fucking coffee every morning. And now he does this? To us? What a snake. At least Deborah had the guts to warn us."

Tommy remembered Deborah: the redhead who'd told Hop he was nuts to attack all those cops in Washington Square.

"Thank goodness I managed to get my hands on Hop's precious heirloom," Makeba said. "We're gonna need it."

Tommy didn't buy it. *They had me, they didn't need Hop.* He didn't think Deborah would come all the way up to Harlem, throw a letter in Makeba's car, and then split. No, she'd warn them in person. And why a typewritten note? Too formal, too weird. Maybe they didn't want to forge Deborah's handwriting, thought Makeba would suss that out. But he kept his mouth shut. *This way she'll hate him more than I do.*

"Hop's been trying to get me to move back in with him," Makeba said. "That's why he offered to let us have half the guns. He has some scheme to blow up something. But why'd the FBI let him get them in the first place?"

"Because they're devious bastards," Lavarious said. "They want to discredit the protesters and the Panthers, in one fell swoop."

"You got it," Tommy said. "Their plan is to parade you around on TV, label you as violent anti-war terrorists, Communist sympathizers, whatever.

"They think when the public sees a few Black Panthers and White radicals with all those guns it will scare the shit out of everyone, increase support for the war."

Lavarious laughed. "The feds didn't need to go to all that trouble. We're planning our own stuff now. They're gonna find out how scary we are."

They're after Brink's trucks. That's one way to fund the movement.

53

I DON'T GET MAD

14 JANUARY 1968

On the ride down I-95 Sunday to the Port of Baltimore in their U-Haul van Makeba and Lavarious talked pretty much non-stop. It was good to have no distractions, just the two of them.

Lavarious held the van's speed to 63 miles per hour on the Jersey Turnpike, checking the mirrors frequently for cops. That was the last thing they needed, one of those "We pulled you over because you're negroes" traffic stops. The cops would assume two young Black people, one with a big Afro, were crooks. Something had to be illegal about them. In this case that happened to be true, but the turnpike pigs would never latch on to their hustle.

Tommy had told them to allow an extra hour for the ride. He'd get there first and find a firing position where he could cover them.

"You think we should have let Tommy in on this?" Lavarious asked. "You trust him?"

"I know he loved Grace and he despises Hopkins," Makeba said. "He hates the feds, and the army too. He's armed and dangerous and he's volunteered to be our backup. Seems okay to me. If he was going to blab to the feds he would have already done it, stayed away from this scene."

Lavarious nodded. He'd driven to Baltimore a few days earlier, checked out the port. He was surprised how you could drive right up to the pier. A dockworker told him there was a skeleton crew after three p.m. on Sundays—just two guys in an office near the main gate, which they didn't close until midnight. They could park facing the exit, throw their boxes in the back, and run like hell.

Makeba didn't think escaping would be much of a problem, after they'd dealt with Hop. One look from Lavarious and Hop's crew of chumps would be scared shitless; they were too soft for this kind of work. His acolytes tagged along because they were into the easy sex, pot, and LSD. They had this naive notion they could change the world, but they weren't serious players.

Lavarious touched the brakes as a state trooper flew by in the left lane, then reached over to rub Makeba's neck. "You ready for this, baby?" he asked, his wide grin lighting her up.

"Totally," Makeba said. "This is gonna be a day that shit Hopkins will never forget. We're lucky Deborah told us what he's really up to."

"The FBI probably promised him the moon," Lavarious said. "He gives us up, then walks on all the charges. They roll up his whole cell, give him a new identity, move him to some shithole state school in Illinois where he can pontificate all day and screw coeds all night."

Makeba let out a long sigh. "I don't know what I was thinking, all that time I spent with him. I thought he cared about Black people."

The meet was set for nine p.m. and their van rolled through the main gate just after seven. Lavarious found the *S.S. Trung* and parked next to the stack of containers, the van pointed toward the exit. A full moon poked through the clouds, cast a pale light on the cargo. Makeba paced around, rubbing her hands to stay warm. She looked around for Tommy but couldn't see him. She left the tailgate open, Hop's heirloom within easy reach.

Hopkins and his crew showed up at 8:30. He pulled his U-Haul box truck up and flashed his headlights twice, the pre-arranged signal. Three other people were with him: Deborah, Carleton, and a new skinny blonde—Grace's replacement.

Looking happy to be there—excited, high on the danger—Hop bounced out of the truck in his fringed leather jacket and jogged over, opened his arms to welcome her. Makeba stepped in front of him so he wouldn't see his father's shotgun.

Hop hugged her and grabbed her ass with both hands. "Just like old times," he said. She fought back the urge to kick him in the balls. *Your time is coming.*

"It's been too long, Makeba. How are you?"

"Just fine. Okay if we load up first? Lavarious and I have to get back to the city tonight, get this stuff squared away before it gets light."

"That will work," Hop said, as if he had to approve every little thing Makeba contemplated before she could do it. "I really appreciate it, that you're going to help with the main event. You're the key to it all."

"Right," Makeba said, ignoring his flattery. "I signed on yesterday. It was easy."

In the prone position on top of his CONEX seventy-five meters away, Tommy sighted his sniper rifle on Hop. The M79 was right beside him, five grenades at the ready, plus one in the chamber. Three smokes ready to go too, to cover his exit.

He'd been there since 1500, when most dockworkers had gone home. It was chilly, in the mid-twenties with a cold wind off the bay, but Tommy had dressed for it in long underwear and the used parka he'd bought at a war surplus store. His position was perfect, he was close enough to see and hear everything. And the green tarp he was under matched the color of the CONEX; nobody would spot him.

The FBI had arrived at 4:30 p.m. in two black vans and three black Ford sedans. They'd parked behind the big warehouse to the south, maybe a quarter mile away. Del wanted to preserve the big surprise. They might have more watchers somewhere, but Tommy couldn't see them. He knew the agents would be lightly armed, handguns and shotguns—they weren't expecting a full-fledged firefight. Tommy felt good about that, because he had enough ordinance to blow away a platoon. And it would be easy to take out Hop from here, if Makeba somehow lost her nerve, got out of the way.

When the agents moved in, Tommy would lob a couple of M79 rounds in their general direction, drop a few smokes to cover his trail, and the three of them would be long gone before Del and his entourage knew what hit them. Pretty foolproof, really.

I don't get mad, I get even.

54

HOLY SHIT

14 JANUARY 1968

Right after Hop's crew arrived, Tommy watched Del exit the lead black van. A tall, silver-haired man followed him and they stepped behind a pile of containers. It was that WBAL anchorman from the six o'clock news—Del was setting the scene for him.

"Get off me, Hop," Makeba said, pushing him away. "We got work to do." Hop finally noticed Lavarious glaring at him and released her.

"Okay, let's crack these open," Hop said, pointing to the containers. "Make two piles, we'll split the boxes fifty-fifty."

Lavarious and Makeba took a quick peek at the contents—M16s, M60s, M79s, and some Claymores—and then lugged their boxes to the van. When the last one was in Makeba turned and waved to Deborah, who was resting on the bumper of Hop's truck.

"Thanks, Deborah. I appreciate everything you've done."

Deborah shook her head, puzzled. "What'd I do?" she asked.

Hop ambled over to Makeba. She stood with her back to the van's cargo bay, one hand behind her, touching the shotgun.

"You're coming home with me, right, Makeba?" Hop asked. "The peace movement needs warriors like you."

Makeba reached back, pulled out the shotgun, and pointed it at Hop's legs.

"I'll tell you one thing, you fucking asshole. The movement—anyone who's fighting for racial justice or an end to the war—we don't need scumbags like you. You took the feds' money, then you ratted us out. You *spied* on us, Hop."

"Whoa there! What you sayin', girl?"

Tommy was sure Makeba was going to shoot him.

"Holy shit!" Del yelled into his radio. "Gun! Gun! Go, go, go! Return fire if fired upon!"

Tommy shifted his rifle away from Hop toward the agents who had spilled out of their vehicles and ran toward the protesters waving their pistols.

"FBI! FBI!" they yelled. "Drop the weapon! Get your hands up!" The reporters and photographers in the FBI's media pool were right behind the agents, TV cameras rolling.

One agent aimed his pistol at Makeba. Tommy didn't hesitate and squeezed off a round. The guy cartwheeled backward, hit in the mid-section. Tommy grabbed his M79 and launched a grenade toward the rest of them. The agents fired back.

Hop tackled Makeba and rolled on top of her, shielding her from the small arms fire. Deborah took a round in the upper body and fell over in front of the truck. Carleton and the new girl ran past her and tried to take cover. Lavarious scooped Makeba up with one arm and Hop with the other, threw them into the back of the van and peeled off toward the exit, his front door swinging free.

Tommy fired a smoke grenade toward the feds, followed up with two more. A thick white curtain billowed up from the pier, creating a wall of white between the feds and Hopkins' U-Haul. "Hold your fire!" someone yelled. "Wait till it clears."

Tommy shoved his gear in the duffel bag, reverse crawled off the CONEX and lowered the ladder. He was two warehouses away when the FBI agents emerged from the smoke and surrounded Hop's three leftover accomplices.

"Get down! Put your hands on your heads!" they yelled. But no more gunfire; Lavarious and his passengers had a big head start.

Shouldering his load, Tommy melted away to the north back to his car.

Time to find a hidey-hole, study my options.

55

TOO LATE

15 JANUARY 1968

Ben was still waiting for his meeting with Ned Whittlesey late Monday morning when Pham Van Phuong entered the *New York Times'* office, looking *tres élégant* in a black áo dài with silver accents.

"Hello Phuong, this is a surprise. Why are you here?"

"Hello, Lieutenant Kin-Kay. I have appointment to talk to Mr. Whittlesey. He Joe's friend. Maybe need good assistant now."

"I hope he hires you. How are you?"

"I miss Joe. He not most beautiful man, but he very kind to me. Always."

"Yes, everyone said he was very nice."

"His story, can you publish it?"

"I'm trying. That's why I'm here."

"Cheerio," Whittlesey said, looking sharp in his starched khakis. Ben figured he probably had more than one maid. "I'll be with you soon, Miss Phuong."

Whittlesey showed Ben around his inner sanctum. It was a pretty cushy place, clean and modern, filled with the latest communications equipment: telephones, telexes, a separate darkroom, and lots of tall shelves filled with reference books. A couple of Vietnamese assistants scurried around; the *Times* was a prosperous newspaper.

Ben noticed the large portrait of Churchill over Whittlesey's desk. "Is Winston one of your heroes?"

Whittlesey twisted one end of his mustache. "He is indeed. As it happens, I've taken my motto from Churchill—KBO."

"What's that mean?"

"Keep Buggering On. Winston's mantra, during the Battle of Britain. It reminds me that a chap can't pack it in, even when the Huns are bombing your lights out. Even in a place as depressing as Vietnam can be. Don't give in to cynicism. Never surrender."

Is that what I've done?

Maybe Whittlesey was a great correspondent, but he struck Ben as an odd one, very full of himself. *Am I just like him, quoting famous people?* Ben continued, launched his pitch.

"I have the article that Joe Kline was working on when he died. It reveals government malfeasance that people need to know about. I'm hoping you can get it published—this story could affect the course of the war.

"Phuong is out there waiting to see you. She can tell you how important he thought this story was. In a way, he gave his life for it."

Whittlesey drew on his pipe, shook his head. "Doubtful I can help, Lieutenant. I'm sorry that Joe died, of course. But I can't rely on other reporters' sources. Printing Joe's stuff as is would be a bridge too far. The *Times* has standards; we'd have to confirm everything. But crack on, give me the headline."

"Kline found out that the FBI and the CIA encouraged an anti-war group to acquire weapons here to attack stateside targets. J. Edgar

Hoover's trying to brand all peace activists as monsters who want to blow up America. To increase support for the war, re-elect Johnson."

Whittlesey recoiled, incredulous. "You want me to believe that our government would organize an illegal arms shipment just to frame some peace activists?" He chuckled. "Preposterous."

"I had my doubts too, but we strongly suspect that the CIA was behind the two murders here—the Waverly girl and Kline. They knew too much, so the agency had them killed. Maybe we can still save lives. *If* you expose it, make it all public."

"Did you tell your superiors about this, Lieutenant?"

"I took it to Ambassador Stevens. J.B. Darling was at that meeting; I'm sure you've run across him."

"Yes. And I understand he's gone missing," Whittlesey said.

"That's one way to put it. They pretended to listen to me, but they didn't follow up. Wanted nothing to do with it. Which makes me think it's all true. That's off the record, by the way. You can't print anything that suggests I met with them; that would be a career-ending event for me. Just write 'sources say highly placed U.S. officials knew about it'—something like that. So, are you interested?"

"Maybe," Whittlesey said. "Leave it with me. I'll make some calls, see if I can confirm anything."

Ben sighed. He was tired, frustrated, worn down by too many dead ends the past three days, the past three weeks. He wanted answers, satisfaction, justice, but he had nothing.

A machine beeped behind them. Then three bells sounded, in quick succession.

"It's a bulletin," Whittlesey said. They walked over to the telex machine: the paper from the roll fell to the floor as the machine's typewriter clacked out a wire service story.

URGENT BULLETIN

RADICAL ANTI-WAR CELL PLANNED MAJOR ATTACK ON NATION'S CAPITAL, FBI SAYS

U.S. AGENTS SEIZE HUGE ARMS SHIPMENT ON BALTIMORE DOCK. SHOTS FIRED, FBI AGENT AND ONE TERRORIST SERIOUSLY WOUNDED. THREE RADICALS ARRESTED TWO ALLEGED BLACK PANTHERS AND CELL'S LEADER ESCAPE WITH DANGEROUS WEAPONS. STATE OF THE UNION ADDRESS WAS PRESUMED TARGET

Whittlesey whistled, tore off the piece of yellow paper with the headlines.

"I'm afraid you're too late, Lieutenant. The guns have arrived. Give me Kline's article, I'll get on it."

56

AWOL

15 JANUARY 1968

After the FBI shoot-out in Baltimore, Tommy Banks drove the black Galaxie carefully through the back streets of Dundalk. A depressing neighborhood where every third house was boarded up. He stayed off I-95, took the Pulaski Highway northeast and crossed the Chesapeake at Havre de Grace. Harbor of Grace. *No safe harbors for my Grace.* He continued on U.S. 1 toward New Jersey. He only saw one cop, parked at a sleepy diner outside Elkton.

Tommy got a kick out of tailgating the few cars that were still on the road. His fellow travelers inevitably hit their brakes when they discovered a black Galaxie 500 on their tail (352 horsepower, with Cruise-O-Matic). He caught up with Makeba and Lavarious a little after one a.m. in a low-down bar in Wrightstown, a block from the main gate to Fort Dix. He'd told Lavarious he knew a good spot in the Pinelands where they could ditch the van. They'd be fine; the guns would fit in the Galaxie's trunk.

"Where's Hop?" Tommy asked, pulling up a chair.

"We dropped him at a truck stop in Elkton," Makeba said. "He's not going back to New York."

"Why the hell didn't you shoot him?"

"Got distracted when the feds started up," Makeba said. "Your fault, Tommy. You lit everything up with your damn grenade gun." He worried when she said that but then saw she was grinning.

"If Hop hadn't hit the deck and taken me down with him, the feds probably would have killed us all," Makeba said. "That's when I realized that Hop is a Grade-A asshole but he's no rat. That letter in my car was a fake. Must've been the feds, trying to mess with our heads. They want us to kill each other instead of the real war criminals."

"True," Tommy said. "I hate Hop for what he did to me and Grace. But I never pegged him for a traitor. The FBI had me—why would they need Hop?"

Lavarious nodded. "Makes sense."

"Why'd you aim at his legs?" Tommy thought he knew the answer but wanted to hear Makeba say it.

"I thought a quick end was too good for him," Makeba said. "Figured it would be better to kneecap him, let him spend the rest of his life stuck in a chair. Won't be screwing many coeds then."

"Pretty evil," Tommy said, smiling.

"When you heading back to Nam?" Lavarious asked.

"Not sure I will. I have unfinished business."

Makeba raised an eyebrow but didn't press him. "Thanks for backing us up," she said. "I know you didn't have to."

"To tell you the truth, I was thinking about blowing Hop away myself," Tommy said. "But then Del unleashed his agents and I had to get busy. What's next for you guys?"

"Still working on that," Lavarious said. He looked around to see if any of the drinkers at the bar were paying attention. "We can't go back to Harlem . . . obviously they know about that crib."

"I'm thinking D.C.," Makeba said. "I grew up down there. We could get an apartment in Southeast. Rents are low in Anacostia, and the pigs ignore that neighborhood."

"Well, we're all on the run now," Tommy said. "You up for another roommate?"

"Why not?" Lavarious said. The man's smile was magnetic.

"I can dig that," Makeba said. "We can save money, watch out for each other."

"I'm still curious," Tommy said. "What was Hop gonna do with his half of the shipment?"

"Okay," Makeba said, lowering her voice. "I guess we can trust you now. Listen to this."

Tommy was impressed when he heard the plan. Now he understood what Grace was always hinting about. Hop was a snake, but he was a smart snake, ambitious and imaginative. If Tommy thought about the big picture, he could see that the professor wasn't the only American who'd put him in this fix, murdered his girl, ruined his life.

Justice, now that's a cause worth fighting for.

57

THE BIG INVITE

17 JANUARY 1968

Arthur Pierpont Hopkins Junior arrived early for his lunch date. The Army and Navy Club didn't open its restaurant until noon, so Hop bought that morning's *Post* and walked over to Farragut Square to wait on a bench beneath the statue of the Union admiral and his famous quote: "Damn the torpedoes, full speed ahead!"

Although he was born here, Hop had never warmed to Washington. Except for the museums and monuments, he thought D.C. was a shabby town, a southern backwater populated by a mixture of crackers and Blacks not that far removed from slavery days, all trying to make ends meet sucking on the government teat. For many it was a subsistence living: there was a huge income gap between the janitors who polished the Senate's floors and the power brokers like his father, who spent their days consuming expensive lunches and greasing the wheels of commerce.

After Makeba had left him at the truck stop, he'd caught a ride with a trucker headed to New York Avenue who dropped him next to a cheap motel. He'd found a barbershop yesterday on Benning Road NE where everyone was Black and minded their own business. He'd gotten a radical buzz cut and took the bus downtown to Hecht's—cabs generated receipts—where he picked up a tuxedo for Makeba's waitress gig. Then he bought a gray flannel suit, two white shirts, a red tie, and a pair of Florsheim wingtips. Hop felt he'd been transformed overnight, from a Jesus look-alike into a perfect copy of a mid-level Justice Department lawyer.

FBI headquarters was two blocks down Pennsylvania Avenue; Hop wondered if agents frequented his father's club. He'd been stunned when Makeba had pointed his own shotgun at him, but when she explained the letter from "D," he forgave her. It had to be the FBI's work. They'd broken into her car and left it, no one else had a motive.

Time for my free lunch. He left the newspaper on the bench and went back to the club. His father spotted him right away, did a double take.

"Well, well, you finally cut your damn hair," Arthur Senior said, extending his hand. "It's been years since I've seen you in proper clothes. I wondered when you'd wise up. Those hippie clothes aren't good for your career."

Hop laughed. *He finds me easier to love in Hickey Freeman.*

They made their way into the dining room where their fellow diners, almost all men, were gathered at round tables with white tablecloths and fine china. Most looked like retired military, not completely comfortable in their crisply pressed suits. A smattering of colonels and generals were in uniform, their chests covered in service ribbons. Arthur Senior smiled and waved at several of them; he had a prodigious memory and was convinced he knew everybody who was anybody. He paused to chat with General Earle G. Wheeler, chairman of the Joint Chiefs.

"Good to see you, Bus," Senior said, using the general's nickname. "This place sure beats the food at Long Binh, right?"

"Better than ham and lima beans," the general said, a nod to the MRE most GIs detested.

"General Wheeler's just back from a fact-finding trip to Saigon," Arthur Senior explained.

They sat down, and when his martini arrived Arthur Senior took a hefty sip. "Perfect," he said. "So how are things at Columbia?"

Hop thought his father had gained thirty pounds, was becoming the quintessential fat cat; the buttons of the starched white shirt he wore under his dark blue suit were about to burst.

"Columbia's fine," Hop said, the lie coming easily. He wasn't going to tell his uptight father he'd quit. "It's a relief to have tenure; you can pretty much do what you want." He tried his iced tea, which was sickeningly sweet. "Do you ever get any exercise, Dad?"

"Play golf twice a week," Arthur Senior said.

"That's not really exercise."

Hop watched him douse a jumbo shrimp with cocktail sauce and take a huge bite—a few drops fell on his tie. Arthur Senior plunged his napkin into his water glass and dabbed at the stain. "This is why I wear dark ties. Have the T-bone," he said, gesturing to the menu. "It's great here. They truck it in overnight, from Nebraska."

"I think I'll stick with the salad," Hop said.

His father snorted. "That figures. I'm paying, you know. In case you're short on cash."

"I like salad, Dad."

"What do your students say about the war?"

"They think it's a disaster," Hop said.

Their meals arrived, and Hop picked at a cherry tomato while his father took a large bite of his steak. "A lot of them have joined the protests. And of course, all the young men are scared to death they'll be called up."

"Fucking draft dodgers," Arthur Senior said. "They belong behind bars, the whole damn lot of them."

"The war doesn't seem to be going that well," Hop said. "It's starting to look like a stalemate to me."

"It wouldn't be, if Lyndon had listened to LeMay," Senior said. "Bomb the bastards back to the Stone Age. That's the only way you win a guerrilla war. But I shouldn't complain. Vietnam's going swell for me. It's a gold rush for my defense guys."

"Right," Hop said. "Except the North Vietnamese haven't advanced much past the Stone Age, Dad. It won't matter how many bombs we drop. The North has the political will to win. The South doesn't. By the way, are you going to the Gridiron this year?"

"Wouldn't miss it. Would you like to come?"

"Love to," Hop said. "I get a kick out of the skits."

"Yeah, it's a long night, but I get a lot of business done. What are you down here for anyway?"

"A conference at Georgetown, an examination of Stalin's role in ending WWII."

"Your fellow eggheads are there to praise his performance, I assume."

"We wouldn't have won without the Russians, Dad."

"Maybe. But the man was the greatest butcher of the century. Deserves to rot in hell."

"Hell's a busy place," Hop said. "Quite a few Americans are going to get in too."

"Yeah. But we didn't start WWII, or Vietnam, either."

"That's debatable. Nobody really knows what happened in the Gulf of Tonkin. Working for peace isn't a crime, you know."

"Well, I see you haven't wised up entirely. Remember this, kid:

we live in the greatest country in the world. We have responsibilities. Those young people you're coddling, they need to show some respect for authority."

"Uh-huh," Hop said. *We'll give them something to respect.*

58

A LITTLE IN LOVE

18 JANUARY 1968

A Thursday in late January, almost 1900, and Ben was still in the office—dead tired and a little depressed. He only had three days left on his one-year tour, and he hadn't solved much.

Yesterday the big brass had handed Lt. Col. Balderamos an official reprimand for the Twenty Grand bomb, having come to the brilliant conclusion that he'd failed to protect GIs on liberty. The MPs stood at parade rest for fifteen minutes while a bird colonel from MACV yelled at them: "The enemy bombed that bar in broad daylight, Colonel! Where was the security? Where the hell were your people?"

Angry and embarrassed, Balderamos was forced to pay more attention, had even skipped his Thursday afternoon golf game today. He'd spent most of the month micromanaging Ben, dreaming up make-work adjustments to their long-delayed checkpoints. The bigger security problem—when all the ARVNs had gone home for the Tet holiday and the supposed truce—was still unsolved. But Ben didn't bring that up; he'd be home by then.

Ned Whittlesey had managed to publish his story about the plot in the *Times*, emphasizing the probability that government agencies arranged an illegal arms shipment. Ben had slipped Whittlesey the tape of Darling blackmailing Frank, and Ned loved it. He got great play, the lead story in last Monday's edition, and Congress was going to hold hearings. Red-faced again, the MACV generals had to do something, so they dropped another ton of shit on Baldy, demanding to know why his patrols were unable to intercept this huge, embarrassing contraband arms shipment before it ever left Saigon. Somehow the ambassador's role escaped scrutiny.

Ben had lost all hope of clearing the two murders. He had wandered over to the Central Market once, but heavy steel bars had been welded across the door to Frank's warehouse—nobody home.

He'd had time for a catch-up call to Elijah in the Can Tho hospital.

"I'm doing fine, Louie," Elijah said. "They're flying me home tomorrow, for more therapy."

"I'll see you back in the world, partner," Ben had said.

Part of him was itching to get home, decompress, and veg out in some safe harbor. But there was another part, a larger piece than he'd expected, that would miss Vietnam. Not the mortars, the carnage, or the constant danger. It was something else—intangible, hard to pin down.

Saigon, Vietnam, the city, the people, the countryside—the place had seduced him. Sometimes he thought he was beginning to love it: the myriad shades of green, the muddy brown wide rivers, the strange but delicious food, the exotic smells. The kids everywhere who ran laughing through the dusty streets, shining shoes and hawking Cokes. The resilience of so many of the souls who soldiered on, managed to smile through the hardships and the endless suffering. And Lien, of course. He would miss Lien forever.

To lift his spirits and keep from thinking about her, Ben had been playing a long list of short-timers' favorites on the little phonograph next to his bunk, like "The Letter"—the number one song by The Box Tops—who opened the song with "Gimme a ticket for an aeroplane." His other go-to 45 rpm disc was The Animals' 1965 hit—"We Gotta Get Out of This Place"—every short-timer loved that one.

He finally left the office at 1945, thinking he'd go home, have a beer, play some records, and finish packing. He'd gone a couple of blocks when a shiny black Citroen DS-21 pulled up beside him. A young Vietnamese man in a gray suit was behind the wheel; he glimpsed a young woman in a glistening dark tunic in the back seat. She cranked the window down, pushed her sunglasses into her hair, and offered a gentle smile.

Ben's heart skipped a beat—he broke out in a smile, he'd thought he would never see her again.

"You like ride, Lieutenant Kin-Kay?"

"Lien—what are you doing here?"

"Get in, I tell you. Hurry."

As he stepped around to the other side he heard a whir, the smooth sound of machinery working. The cabin of the car lowered itself four inches to ease his entry; an invisible mechanism could move it up and down. *Where did she get this?*

Ben got in, took both her hands. "You disappeared. I thought you were gone, Lien. Forever."

He admired her all-black silk outfit, a Mandarin tunic with a standing collar over wide trousers, just a touch of lipstick. "You're so beautiful. I've missed you. A lot."

"Sorry, Benjamin, that I not say goodbye, before. Lien have problem. Temporary, but still problem. Agency wonder how Mr. Darling die, ask many questions. Better if Lien unavailable, care for sick mother."

"I understand. I talked to Francois."

"Yes, he tell me. Sorry you find out truth, that way."

"He said you are very busy, just now."

"Yes. Good you go home soon, Lieutenant Kin-Kay. War come to Saigon soon. Very dangerous now, for everyone."

They drove away from the city center, out along Sông Saigon toward the Ben Nghe Canal. The driver parked in front of the Mac Dinh Chi Cemetery, where Grace Waverly had been murdered. Lien got out, took his hand with her light touch, and led him to the bench in front of Grace Cadman's grave. She sat silent for a moment and closed her eyes. Perhaps she was praying, Ben couldn't tell.

In the distance a handsome Vietnamese woman stood with her small son in front of a grave, holding some flowers. She made the sign of the cross, handed the flowers to her child, said something. The boy placed them in front of the stone. His mother dabbed at her eyes with a tissue, then reached down to do the boy's.

"That his father's grave, maybe," said Lien, looking up. "So many fathers, they all dead now. So many of my people, they have no graves. No place to remember them."

"A thousand tragedies."

"No, no, Benjamin. Many, many more than that." She was quiet for a moment. "The Waverly girl, she like this place, yes?"

"I think so. That's what Specialist Banks said."

"Two Graces," she gestured to the grave. "They share name. And they both believers. Different causes, revolution and Christianity, but both believed. Lien sorry girl die. She mean well, just want to end war."

"Did Francois Nguyen do it?"

"I think so. He being blackmailed, by Mr. Darling. Francois think he have no choice."

"What did Darling have on him?" He knew but wondered if she'd elaborate.

"I think you already know. Lucky Lu, he give you hint before, and then Francois give you tape, yes? Our friend involved in dangerous love affair."

She smiled, shook her head. Ben thought she was trying not to laugh, perhaps at herself. "Just like Lien."

"Thank you for saving us, Lien, for protecting Elijah and me. I still have a couple of questions though. If you will allow it."

She reached across the seat, took his hand in both of hers and stroked his wrist. He wanted to lift her into his arms, carry her off, and stash her on his Freedom Bird. He'd take Lien back to Washington, where they'd buy a nice little house, he'd find something to do, they'd live peacefully ever after. *Never happen, GI.*

"Yes, Benjamin. Ask me anything."

"I understand why you couldn't tell me the truth. About the Twenty Grand and about what you really do, for the National Front. But I need to know, was what we had, together—was it just part of the job for you? So you could find out what Elijah and I were up to, warn your people if we got too close to the truth? Did you care about me at all?"

Lien frowned, took a while to organize her thoughts.

"Answer very complicated, Benjamin. At first, Lien think, too much risk, way too dangerous for me, get involved with any American soldier. My life very complex, you know. Have many things I try to balance. 'Too many balls in the air!' That what Mr. Darling always say." Lien laughed softly.

Did she actually like working for that nut job?

"But then we go on our date—first date, to zoo."

"That changed things?"

"Yes, Lien fall a little in love. With you, Benjamin. You know that, yes? Then I think, maybe is good, for Lien to know American MP. Might help me sometime, in my work. So yes, Lien care about you, Benjamin. Care a lot. I tell you before, love . . . it is very hard to love someone, in time of war. *Impossible, peut-être.* You understand, yes?"

Of course he did. He knew it was inconceivable for them to go on the way they had been, or go on in any way at all. But he couldn't accept it—he never would. He teared up again. She reached over, held his face in her hands, brushed his tears away. He wrapped his arms around her, pulled her close, kissed her forehead.

"So how did you use me? Did it help you, Lien? Knowing me, in your work?"

"No, Lien never use you. You did not know very much that would be useful." She smiled, amusement in her eyes. "Sorry, but that is truth.

"But Lien learn a lot about what Mr. Darling up to, by watching you—where you go, what you ask. You know Mr. Darling missing now, right?"

"Missing. That's a good word for it," Ben said. *Missing a lot of body parts.*

"Your flight home, when is it?"

"In three days, on 21 January."

She nodded, ran her hand lightly across his cheek, traced his lips with her fingers.

"Timing, it is . . . everything. That something else Mr. Darling like to say." Lien rose from the bench, touched her eyes, and smoothed the wrinkles from her silk tunic.

Is she crying?

"May I give you ride?" Lien asked.

"No, thank you. I need to walk, I think. Thank you . . . thank you for loving me. I love you too, always. I'll never forget you."

She leaned in, took his head in her hands, brushed his lips with hers, and turned away, went back to the car. Ben sat on Grace's bench for a long time, waiting for the sun to set.

59

BACK IN THE WORLD

14 FEBRUARY 1968

Now that he was finally home and unscathed—physically, anyway—Ben tried, like all of his brothers-in-arms, to come to terms with the war. The first word that occurred to him—and it wasn't even a word—was FUBAR. That was the right term, for the whole Vietnam experience. GIs had coined the acronym to describe WWII, which certainly produced more than its share of fuckups and catch-22s.

Ben knew that tragic mistakes were routine in wars but thought there was a key difference between WWII and Vietnam. Those who fought for their country in the 1940s knew why they were risking their lives. They knew, in their bones, that stopping Hitler and his allies from enslaving the world was a righteous cause. But Vietnam? Who knew? It was hard to imagine anything more screwed up than Vietnam, from beginning to end and along every step of the bloody way. Nobody understood it all, not even the Vietnamese. He shook his head in bitter amusement every time he heard a politician refer to the "Vietnam conflict." Congress didn't even have the balls to declare war. The pols knew admitting we were embroiled in a long war would be seriously unpopular and force a deeper examination of what we'd gotten ourselves into—oh no, we can't have that. *To hell with them all.*

When he got back to California, he had a month left to serve on his army commitment. He took some leave, thought about whether he wanted to stay in the army.

He didn't feel like going home immediately, so he got a room at the YMCA and spent his first few nights back in the USA at a bar on the Oakland waterfront, studying the reflection of the Bay Bridge lights and getting reacquainted with Johnnie Walker Black on the rocks. He sat in the same seat every night, the last stool on the right, facing the mirror behind the bar—the same spot he'd held down at the Twenty Grand. At first, he'd been content to luxuriate in his new sense of safety, not having to study every new patron to see if he was a determined terrorist with a bomb. But he still jumped out of his skin every time a truck backfired. Inevitably his mind drifted back to Saigon. He went over every event, thought about Grace, Joe Kline, Madame Thuy, Lucky Lu, Bing Darling, Francois.

He lay sleepless, reliving the whole mess. Francois had been the only one who'd told him anything, until Lien finally admitted her role. *My life very complex, Benjamin.*

I'll say. Lien had been the conductor, pacing about the stage with her baton. She must have orchestrated some of it, while simultaneously working for the CIA and the VC and posing (at least some of the time) as his girlfriend. A very busy woman, and he'd barely noticed, had no clue what she was up to. *What kind of a cop are you?*

Ben and Elijah had never caught up with the arc of the case. *Forget about it*, he told himself, he was well out of it now, he might as well lick his wounds and get sloppy, sleepy drunk.

Easy to say, impossible to do. Lien was never far away, in his daydreams and his nightmares. All of his contemplations began and ended with Lien. *I'll never get over her.*

He let a couple weeks pass, bumming around the Bay Area, checking out Haight-Ashbury, the funky bookshops, the Golden Gate, and Fisherman's Wharf. He left the Y, moved to a rundown rooming house out in Vallejo owned by a family from Bombay. He invaded his savings and splurged on a late model red Chevy convertible, drove around to see the more distant sights: the giant redwoods in Muir Woods, the Jack London museum in Glen Ellen, the wild coast up by Point Reyes. He bought a Valentine's Day card and signed it "Love, Ben" but never sent it, slow to realize he'd left with no idea how to get in touch with Lien.

Then his father wrote, said his old MP buddy at Fort Dix, Steve Orsino, had telephoned the house, wanted to tell him about a job opening at the Pentagon. Given Ben's spotless record as an MP it would be easy to get a job with Department of Defense security, Orsino said. So Ben informed the army he would not be accepting their generous offer to re-enlist. *No Re-Up Bird for me.* Then he drove home to get reacquainted with his family and apply for the job.

Orsino's prediction was correct: "Your service record is excellent," said the retired MP colonel in charge of DOD security. "Colonel Balderamos vouched for you, says you're an excellent officer. He's nominated you for a Bronze Star with V—for your actions in Vinh Long province." Ben guessed Baldy was quite grateful he'd been left out of the *New York Times* story about the weapons. He told his new boss he could start next week and spent hours driving around Maryland, looking for an apartment.

60

THE GRIDIRON BURNS

11 MARCH 1968

"Watch what you're fluffing up back there, bub!" the woman yelled. "That's not a pillow!"

Ben jerked his hands away from the lady's ample hips and reached for the sky in the classic *I'm innocent* gesture.

"Precious cargo," she said with a wink. "You won't know what hit you, you push my buttons like that."

The crowd waiting to be searched started laughing. Ben wasn't sure if the dame was going to kiss him or punch him. He would have passed the job to a woman, but DOD security didn't have any female searchers.

"Be careful with Miss Thomas," Ben's supervisor said.

Ben hadn't realized he'd been frisking Helen Thomas, UPI's White House reporter and the only woman member of the Gridiron Club. She was always badgering LBJ about the war at the White House briefings from her front row seat. *Do you know who you're bombing, Mr. President?*

Women, children, and babies? Is that United States policy, to murder young families?

Ben sighed and waved her through. He was tired of digging into the pockets of dinner guests who could barely conceal their disdain. He'd been told to keep the line moving, just do the guys who looked nervous or scruffy. But there weren't many of those, the Gridiron Dinner was a very formal event, so Ben searched everybody.

He'd expected to be happier in his new job, but the past few weeks had been stultifying, waiting around babysitting bigwigs. Pulling security involved boys with guns and lots of coffee cups sitting around in black cars. Sometimes it was so boring he got nostalgic for the Tan Son Nhut Road. But Ben thought he should stick with it. The money was pretty good and you could retire in twenty years and have a second career.

Finally, a little before seven, the last guest passed through security. As the band struck up "The Star-Spangled Banner," Ben entered the ballroom and took his assigned position next to the dais, thirty feet to the left of the raised platform. He had a good view of the middle-aged men at the head table as they ate, drank, and guffawed their way through the skits onstage.

Secretary McNamara was in the third seat down the line, so Ben wasn't far away if there was an emergency and he had to hustle him out. The secretary was having an intense conversation with the FBI director—Ben was surprised how small the G-man was. Small, but powerful: people said J. Edgar Hoover knew all of Washington's secrets.

It had been a long day. The security detail, led by the Secret Service, had completed their search of the Statler Hilton's ballroom that afternoon around three-thirty, but then a waitress had reported a plumbing issue in the VIP bathroom next to the head table.

Ben was nearby and looked in. The waitress, a young Black woman, pointed to a big puddle on the floor. "I'll call maintenance," she said. Ben thought she looked familiar but couldn't place her.

A few minutes later she came back with a huge guy in green coveralls and a baseball cap who looked like he could play for the Redskins. "This is Mr. Douglas; he'll take care of it," the woman said. Ben saw the guy take a wrench out of his big bag and kneel down next to the leaky toilet.

Tommy had a new getaway car.

He'd been so impressed with the rental, he'd emptied his savings and bought his own black Ford Galaxie, got the big Thunderbird 352 engine. He didn't tell anyone he'd made a few modifications to the trunk and the back seat. The three of them—Tommy, Makeba, and Lavarious—had left the Anacostia apartment about noon, headed downtown for the Statler Hilton.

"So, how's it feel to be helping out Hop?" Tommy had asked Lavarious.

"I didn't dig it at first," he said. "But I didn't realize then who was going to be there. Hop made a good case. This is our chance to hit Hoover and all those other racists who keep on abusing and murdering Black people."

"You straight with your plan?" Tommy asked.

"I took a good look at them Claymores," he said. "Once I'm in the bathroom it's a cinch to slip under that skirt below the head table. I point the mines up at their chairs, set the timers for 11:05 p.m. and plug 'em in. Whole thing should take three minutes."

"And I'll be his lookout," Makeba said.

"Then I mop up the water and find a place to hide till it's over," Lavarious had said with a smile. Tommy smiled back but kept quiet—*only one loose end left.*

After he'd dropped Makeba and Lavarious at the Hilton he drove over to the new Marriott just across the Key Bridge. It was his last-minute brainstorm to pick up Hop and personally deliver him to the scene of the crime. There was a certain symmetry to it. He didn't intend to kiss the motherfucker though, the way Judas had.

"It's great you showed up to help, Tommy," Hop said. "It's a bitch to park in the District."

"Happy to be of service. Your picture is still on those FBI flyers in the post office, you know. You worried someone will recognize you?"

"With my new buzz cut? In this get-up?" Hopkins asked, tugging on his white bow tie. "No chance."

"Isn't your name on the guest list, to get in? You gotta show ID, right?"

"Nah, they never check. White guys in tails . . . they wave us right through."

"Cool. I'll be parked right here in the alley when you're ready," Tommy said.

"Makeba and I will be hustling out that back door a little before eleven. Did she tell you we're getting back together? Gonna leave that lout Lavarious in the dust. Don't lock your doors. This is a night to remember."

"You know it, Hop."

Back inside the ballroom, a chorus of flabby reporters took the stage in cowboy clothes, complete with chaps and spurs, and belted out an off-key version of an old Gene Autry song, the lyrics changed to skewer the president.

I'm back on my bronco agin,
Gunnin' for ole Mister Minh.

Fighting' Reds ain't no sin,
Just watch Sheriff Lyndon win.

Ben was dog-tired. *They think that's funny?* It was almost eleven p.m. and he'd been on his feet since lunch; his sense of humor had evaporated hours ago.

This dinner was endless, going on six hours. How many courses could these people eat? After the Davy Crockett nonsense there was yet another break before the president was scheduled to speak.

Everyone was out of their seats again, milling around, chatting up friends, enemies, and sources. He decided to do a few deep knee bends to stay loose—he'd watched Bonnie Prudden's "15 Minutes to Fitness" when he was a kid.

Ben was on his third knee bend staring at a narrow crack in the white table skirt on the head table when a light caught his eye. Something under there had flashed amber. He strolled over and pulled the skirt back. Two lights were blinking, one at either end. The lights were in square boxes wired to two gray trays with slight concave bends in them. Each tray had been mounted on a small tripod, so it faced up toward the torsos of the assembled VIPs. *What am I looking at?*

It dawned on him. He slipped under the table and low crawled until he could get his head next to the face of the device nearest him. "FRONT TOWARD ENEMY," the inscription read. He thought about getting a flashlight, see if he could figure out what it would take to disarm them—two Claymore mines with enough C-3 explosive to obliterate most of the United States government. The dinner was scheduled to conclude in a few minutes; he guessed that the mines would be set to explode soon, no time to call the bomb squad. Ben scuttled out, dragged the nearest Secret Service agent over, and pointed.

"Those are bombs under that table. Claymore mines. On timers. We gotta get everybody out."

The agent bent down for a closer look.

"I gotta tell my supervisor."

"Forget your supervisor, there's no time!"

Ben scanned the back wall and spotted the red box mounted behind the dais. *Yes.* He ran to it, smashed the glass, and yanked the handle. The fire alarms did their *whoop-whoop-whoop*, and floodlights flashed at rapid intervals around the room.

"This is a fire emergency," a disembodied voice proclaimed through the ballroom's PA system. "Please make your way to the nearest exit."

Groans rose from the audience, but no one moved. Most of these guys figured they were too important to jump to when a fire alarm sounded.

Ben bolted onto the dais, shoved his way past an elderly Supreme Court justice with a colorful bow tie, yanked the microphone from its stand, and yelled, "This is not a drill! Evacuate the room immediately! I repeat, this is not a drill. There is a suspicious object in the room. It may be a bomb. Please leave the room. Immediately."

When Ben said "bomb," people began moving toward the exits. Slowly at first, but gathering momentum, like the proverbial snowball. The lead element broke into a run; seconds later there was a mad dash for the exits. Ben hustled over and helped Secretary McNamara down from the dais and out the side door. Hoover had scuttled out ahead of them and was already halfway down the exit stairs, his bodyguards running to keep up.

Tommy was nestled in the Ford's partially disassembled back seat in the prone position, his Winchester 30.06 with the sniper scope poking out of the hole he'd made in the cavernous trunk. He heard sirens and announcements, but no bomb had gone off. Not good. They must have discovered the mines. He'd been hoping for a triple play, McNamara to Hoover to Hop, but that wasn't going to happen. He thought about leaving, but figured Hop would stick to the plan, show up soon.

Thirty seconds later, the hotel's emergency exit door to the alley banged open and a wave of guests surged out in their white-tie penguin suits. Tommy spotted Hop with his arm around Makeba, pushing her out of the building. She shook him off, didn't want help. Then Lavarious caught up with Hop, shoved him to his knees on the dirty concrete. As Hop struggled to his feet Tommy settled the crosshairs on his head, then remembered Makeba's words. *Let the FBI goons have him.*

He swung the Winchester's scope down to Hop's right knee and pulled the trigger. The hollow-point bullet obliterated his knee; he screamed and fell on his side, clutching his leg. Tommy worked the bolt, squeezed off a second shot. Sparks flew as the round ricocheted off the pavement and struck Hop in the upper arm. *Oh shit, just finish him.* Tommy fired a third time; the white-hot bullet shattered the man's forehead. *That one's for Grace.*

He heard explosions and two windows of the hotel's kitchen blew out, showering glass into the alley. The crowd in the street hesitated, caught between a shooter and a bomb, then scattered in all directions. Tommy backed out of his position and was behind the wheel when Makeba and Lavarious tumbled into the front seat. He floored it around the corner, ran the red light at 15th and L, and headed northwest.

"I thought you were gonna let Hop live," Makeba said.

"He knew everything," Tommy said. "He could have really screwed us down the line."

Lavarious chuckled. "Not happening now, man."

61

NO KNOCKOUTS

24 MARCH 1968

A couple of weeks later, once he was settled in his spiffy new studio apartment in Silver Spring, Maryland, Ben called Elijah's mom on Long Island to see how his old partner was.

"Elijah's still in rehab," Jalissa Jackson said. "At Walter Reed in D.C. Thank you, Lieutenant Kinkaid—Elijah says you saved his life."

"Not really, ma'am," Ben said. "Your son's a hard man to kill, and the Vietnamese surgeon did a great job."

So here he was on a sunny Sunday afternoon in front of the big red brick army hospital in Bethesda that housed hundreds of wounded Vietnam veterans—Elijah had been convalescing for three months. The orderly directed him to Ward 17, where he found his friend in a chipper mood, sitting up straight on his bed with the neat hospital corners, in a big ward next to two guys in wheelchairs.

"Well, take a look at Staff Sergeant Jackson," Ben said. "Congrats,

Elijah, I see you're an E-6 now, a staff sergeant. You ready for our big outing?"

"Lieutenant Kin-KAY." Elijah welcomed his friend with a big shit-eating grin. He was ready to go in his starched khakis adorned with his brand-new decorations: the Combat Infantryman Badge, his Purple Heart, the Army Commendation Medal, and the Vietnam Service Medal, the yellow bar with red stripes. His right arm was in a bright blue sling, and he'd let his hair grow out some.

"That's a swanky sling you got there," Ben said. "I like the new haircut—you're looking like Muhammad Ali."

Elijah stepped toward Ben to shake hands. "I'm a southpaw now," he said, extending his left hand. Ben shook it and gave him a brief hug.

"No way am I floating like a butterfly," Elijah said with a sad smile. "Not yet anyway. The Donut Dollies gave me the sling. You look right at home in the new civvies."

"Still feels awkward wearing them," Ben said. "I'm not brave enough to let my hair grow."

"Good you got home before that Tet shit show though." Ben nodded, and Elijah introduced his friends in the wheelchairs, Mark Dorfman and Ron Hansen. Dorfman's upper body was erect, chin up, shoulders back, his elbows rigid against the arms of the chair. A blanket was draped around his waist; Ben noticed he couldn't see the man's feet, and the blanket had collapsed where his lower half should be. He realized that Dorfman was a double amputee; they'd removed his legs just below his hips.

Hansen's body was all there, but half his face was obscured by a large white bandage plastered in several layers. His head lolled against his chest, eyes closed.

"Who were you guys with?" Ben asked.

"The Big Red One," Dorfman said, referencing the U.S. Army's First Infantry Division. "It was an ambush up near the Michelin

Rubber plantation. We walked right into it, NVA machine gun cut me to pieces. I'd been in-country just 39 days—thought I was dead, man. Medics and the Dustoff saved my sorry ass. Trouble is, now I don't know if it was worth saving."

Dorfman gave them a rueful smile, the expression of a man who'd lost the life he'd expected to live and knew it.

"How's the rehab going?" Ben asked Dorfman.

"Okay, I guess. We're still waiting for the prosthetics. Then I try to learn to walk again. They keep telling me the new fake legs are better than gimping around on crutches. The worst thing is my brain thinks my legs are still there. My toes—I think I can still move them, man. At night they get all tingly, and I get these ghost pains in my knees. 'Course I don't have any knees or toes, but they hurt like hell anyway."

"Weird," Ben said, trying to think of something better to say. "That's gotta be tough."

"The medicos say the phantom pains—that's what they call them—they claim they'll go away, over time."

"How long?" Ben asked.

"They didn't say."

Ben looked over at Hansen. His head had rolled to one side and lodged against the chair. It didn't look like he would be awake anytime soon.

"Hansen was in an APC," Elijah explained. "VC got 'em with a B40, the round hit the fuel tank. It blew and set the whole damn thing on fire. Hansen stayed with the fire, tried to pull his lieutenant out, burned up half his face and lost an eye. Got a Silver Star for his trouble. He's still in a lot of pain, so they got him on a ton of morphine."

Ben shook his head, thought Hansen would trade his medal in a New York minute if he could get his face back.

"Maybe we should get going," Ben said. They said their goodbyes and went out to the car. "Pretty tough scene in there, Elijah."

"Sure, but sitting around a hospital is a damn sight better than gettin' shot at. No rockets at night here. And I don't have to worry where my bunker's at. But it ain't easy. We got a lot of casualties, man. Bad ones. You saw it, in there. We got burn victims, amputees, paraplegics. A ton of shell shock too.

"Those troops, they have nightmares all the time, some of 'em scream all night long. A lot of our guys, I don't think they're ever gonna get over this war. It's the loss that lasts a lifetime. Their lives are ruined."

"Yeah. The good news about the Dustoffs is our boys get to the docs in record time. The bad news is, what do they have left to live for?" Ben asked. "So . . . what are they saying about your recovery?"

"Like you said, I got no future in baseball. But I can still whisk up a mean dressing for a noodle salad. Do that left-handed, no problem."

"You're making me hungry. I found this bar over in Takoma Park, not far from my pad. Place reminds me of the Twenty Grand, only thing missing is the pretty Cos. And there's a nice Vietnamese-Chinese joint around the corner."

"Let's go have a drink," Elijah said, "then find us some funny noodles. I don't have to be back on the ward until nine."

They headed over to Ben's new favorite bar. The place was popular Friday nights, filled with tough guys in dirty work clothes who'd come from a nearby construction site, plus a smattering of University of Maryland students, would-be hippies who looked like they were slumming, searching for an authentic proletarian experience.

They settled in on the stools. Elijah ordered Jack Daniel's on the rocks to go with Ben's Johnnie Walker. "Top shelf booze, Elijah. Glad to see you've kept your taste for the best."

The CBS *Evening News* was playing on the boxy TV above the bar. Walter Cronkite had just completed a weeklong trip to Vietnam. America's most popular newsman had decided tonight to offer his assessment of how the war was going, in a rare personal commentary. The bar went quiet, everyone staring at the screen.

Tonight, back in more familiar surroundings in New York, we'd like to sum up our findings in Vietnam, an analysis that must be speculative, personal, subjective. Who won and who lost in the great Tet Offensive against the cities? I'm not sure. The Vietcong did not win by a knockout but neither did we . . . We've been too often disappointed by the optimism of the American leaders . . . both in Vietnam and Washington, to have faith any longer in the silver linings they find in the darkest clouds.

For it seems now more certain than ever, that the bloody experience of Vietnam is to end in a stalemate. To say that we are closer to victory today is to believe, in the face of the evidence, the optimists who have been wrong in the past. To say that we are mired in stalemate seems the only realistic, if unsatisfactory conclusion . . .

It is increasingly clear to this reporter that the only rational way out then will be to negotiate, not as victors, but as an honorable people who lived up to their pledge to defend democracy, and did the best they could.

This is Walter Cronkite. Good night.

"Wow," Ben said. "I've never heard Cronkite show his cards."

"You think he's right?" asked Elijah. "Was it all for nothing, what we did?" He rubbed his shoulder, fussed with his sling.

"Nah, I don't think so," Ben said. "Maybe it ends in a stalemate, or maybe we will lose. Sometimes it sure feels that way. But if nothing else, we fought for one another. We were brothers, brothers-in-arms. And we fought well—there's honor in that. Like Cronkite said, we did the best we could." He smiled, gave Elijah a pat on his good arm. "Let's go eat our noodles."

They were halfway to the door when a young longhair from the U of M crowd jumped up from his booth, his beer stein still in his hand, and got in Elijah's face.

"How many kids did you kill over there, *Sergeant*?" The hippie spit out the word. "How many babies did you bomb? How many did you napalm, huh? Those innocent people you killed—did you even notice they were brown people? You're a murderer! A traitor to your race, you fucking Uncle Tom."

The hippie spat in Elijah's face and threw the beer at him. Elijah took a step back, shaking the brew from his curls like a wet dog. Ben coiled his arm to deliver a right cross but before he could launch it, a burly workman tackled the hippie, slammed him to the floor, and landed two straight rights to his face, breaking the guy's nose.

The bar erupted in chaos; the hippies and the construction crew squared off in a tangled scrum in the middle of the room, throwing punches and chairs and anything else they could get their hands on. Ben grabbed Elijah and they double-timed out the door.

"We don't need that shit, Louie," Elijah said. "We already fought our war."

They rounded the corner, cleaned up in the restaurant's men's room, and ordered some beers, taking their time to calm down. Elijah ordered them spring rolls, garlic eggplant, grilled pork with rice noodles, and General Tso's chicken, a dish Ben had never heard of. Not exactly Vietnamese, but delicious.

"It's good," Elijah said. "Carries some heat, good for your digestion."

"A lot more interesting than chop suey," Ben said, mixing his chicken with fried rice to cut the spices a bit. "You could drink a lot of beer with this."

"So," Elijah said, "I read the news today, oh boy."

"Didn't know you were a Beatles fan, Elijah."

"I ran across that story Whittlesey wrote a couple weeks ago about the bombing at that fancy press dinner. You're an American hero now, man. You think those Claymores came from that shipment we couldn't stop?"

"Maybe," Ben said. "The guy who died, the one who got shot in the head—did you see his name was Hopkins? That ring a bell?"

"I remember," Elijah said. "Grace was always going on about some guy named Hopkins. Said he was the leader of her goofy group. She thought he was God's gift."

"Right, in the paper it sounded like he was that guy, an ex-professor. I think I actually met him, a couple years ago at that same dinner. You see the shooter kneecapped the poor bastard before they put him out of his misery? I don't know much about the investigation. The FBI bigwigs are all over it. It's way above my pay grade. It was just dumb luck that I happened to see the flashing lights on the timers, had time to pull the alarm."

"Can you believe the FBI? Helping a bunch of deranged hippies get guns and heavy weapons? Unreal. They're supposed to uphold the law, not break it."

"And that asshole J.B. Darling—he got you shot, Elijah. That day in Vinh Long could have been the end, for both of us. The Twenty Grand bomb was him too."

"What happened to Darling?"

"Frank Nguyen got to him. OD'd him and fed him to a tiger. Shere Khan, the only one, at the Saigon Zoo."

"Was Darling still alive?"

"I don't think so. The agency guys probably put the tiger down after he'd chewed on Darling's corpse for a while. Then they covered the whole thing up. As far as the world's concerned, Darling just disappeared."

"That's a shame . . . about the tiger. Why would Frank kill Darling?"

"Darling was blackmailing Frank. Threatened to tell the prime minister Frank was screwing his gorgeous wife every Sunday. That would have been the end of Frank's business, and maybe his life. Frank had Darling on tape, making the threats."

"I'll be damned," said Elijah. "We knew some stuff, but it was never enough."

"For sure, GI. You Numbah Ten sleuth, Elijah. Just like me."

"So what happened to Lien?"

"She was a spy, Elijah. Frank said she's a colonel in the National Front, one of their best operatives. She's apparently one of Ho's favorites. Who knows how many secrets she passed on. Working for Darling, she could see everything we were doing, mess up our whole war effort."

"No shit? Damn, we were out of our depth over there."

"Far, far out, as our hippie friends next door might say. I thought she loved me, Elijah. How stupid is that? The wise men always say humility is a virtue. You know what Einstein said about that, right?"

"You know I don't."

"A true genius admits that he knows nothing."

"Okay, I admit it—we're true geniuses. We were never going to solve this."

"Right," Ben said. "Never happen, GI."

Elijah laughed. "And Tommy Banks, what happened to him?"

"As far as I know, he's back in Long Binh. Must be a short-timer now. He wrangled some kind of cushy TDY assignment, escorted the body of a GI back to Maryland. I think he was near Baltimore when the arms fiasco went down at the port, but then my tour ended. I bummed around California, never heard another thing about Banks."

"Another mystery," Elijah said. "What a nut job. That's Nam for you, a thousand mysteries, a million tragedies."

"Even more than that, partner."

They ordered their last round, opened their fortune cookies. Elijah's read, "Good health is in your future."

Ben read his out loud: "You will be lucky in love, again."

"Good to know there's always hope," Elijah said. "Maybe we should accentuate the positive."

Ben raised his Tsingtao, clinked the bottle against his friend's: "To better days, Elijah."

"I'll always drink to that, Lieutenant."

AUTHOR'S NOTE

Like Ben Kinkaid, after I graduated from college in 1966 I had no idea what to do with my life. I had a naive notion that I could become a writer, but the Vietnam War was ramping up and draft boards across the country were combing the population of 18-to-25-year-olds to meet the army's needs.

I was indifferent about the war's purpose. President Johnson's rationale for it sounded semi-reasonable to me and in those days Americans usually gave politicians the benefit of the doubt. But after I watched four professors stand on the steps of Dartmouth Hall and announce they were mailing their medals from two World Wars back to the president as a protest, it dawned on me that I could get killed in a steaming jungle 12,000 miles away, before my adult life even started.

So I tried to evade the draft. Despite my meager qualifications, I managed to get a job teaching English to high school seniors, many of whom were more mature than I was. That won me a nine-month deferment, but it was a disastrous year.

One winter evening after watching play practice I fell asleep at the wheel and totaled the Chevy station wagon my dad had given me, so I replaced it with a brand-new Triumph TR4 purchased with a loan that left me bankrupt. Then in May 1967, the school fired me for failing to correct my students' papers, a fate I richly deserved. My Minnesota draft board promptly tracked me down, and by July I was doing push-ups at Fort Dix; on January 6, 1968, I stepped onto the runway of Tan Son Nhut AFB outside Saigon, scared to death.

Like Tommy Banks, I was a clerk. We were "intelligence" advisors, and one of my jobs was to type up orders for B-52 strikes. "Rolling Thunder" was what we called them. Although I never had to fire my M2 carbine, I still ask God for forgiveness for my contribution to the death and destruction this undeclared war caused. I was lucky to survive. In the end, my nearly fourteen months in a combat zone proved to be a blessing, because it helped me grow up and get serious about life.

This book is meant to be an "entertainment," as Graham Greene called his Vietnam novel, *The Quiet American*, but I hope it also makes a point or two about the wisdom of going to war in uncertain circumstances.

Several million human beings were killed, wounded, poisoned, or psychologically maimed by the Vietnam War. May the dead rest in peace, and the suffering be comforted.

ACKNOWLEDGMENTS

I'm grateful to Greenleaf/River Grove for publishing this book, and especially thank their excellent editor, Erin Brown, for her wisdom, guidance, and many suggestions on how to improve it. And thanks to Eric Denzenhall for introducing me to Erin and opening the door to publication, which is so hard these days.

Killing Grace is fiction, but it is inspired by the great body of literature the Vietnam War produced. Along those lines, I'm grateful to Don Luce and John Sommer for their fine 1969 book *Vietnam: The Unheard Voices*, which recounted the anecdote when Secretary McNamara tried to say, "Long live Vietnam" in Vietnamese but it didn't come out that way. I hope this book captures some of the truths of the Vietnam experience and the tumult of the 1960s, but I have played with dates, times, units, and places, and undoubtedly made mistakes. I apologize in advance for them all.

Thanks to the great authors and creators, living and dead, whose works have illuminated the lasting consequences of this "epic tragedy," as the British author Max Hastings called it in his recent history. A partial list would include Bernard Fall, Graham Greene, Stanley Karnow, David Halberstam, Neil Sheehan, Horst Faas, Peter Arnett, Eddie Adams, Nick Ut, Liz Thomas, Dickey Chapelle, Peter Braestrup, Jim Webb, Phil Caputo, Frances Fitzgerald, Robert Olen Butler, Wallace Terry,

Hal Moore, Joe Galloway, Tim O'Brien, Mark Baker, Michael Herr, Jan Scruggs, Jack Wheeler, Nancy Smoyer, Jim Wright, Robert Jay Lifton, Laura Palmer, Ken Burns, Geoffrey Ward, Lynn Novick, Duong Van Mai Elliott, Viet Thanh Nguyen, and many others.

I'm also deeply grateful to the generous battalion of friends and supporters—you know who you are—who took the time to read the book, correct mistakes, write blurbs, and tell their friends about it.

Finally, a heartfelt thank you to my lovely and literate wife of nearly 52 years, Ann O'Donnell Prichard, who made many wise contributions and waited patiently while I was MIA upstairs for a few years writing.

GLOSSARY

AIT – Advanced Infantry Training

APC – Armored Personnel Carrier used by U.S. forces

ARVN – Army of the Republic of South Vietnam

Áo Dài – a long, split tunic worn over silk trousers

Bac – literally, "Uncle," a Vietnamese term of respect for older people

Choi Oi – pidgin expression of amazement, like "Oh my goodness"

C.I.D. – Army Criminal Investigation Department

Claymore – anti-personnel mine used by U.S. Army

Co – pidgin for a young woman

CONEX – standard steel container used to ship goods

Cyclo – Vietnamese open-air taxi, powered by a bike or small engine

Deuce-and-a-half – two-and-a-half-ton cargo truck used by U.S. forces and ARVN

Di-di mau – pidgin for "hurry up" or "get out of here"

Dinky dau – pidgin for "crazy"

DOD – Department of Defense

Dustoff – medical evacuation helicopter used by U.S. and ARVN forces

Freedom Bird – the chartered plane that took GIs home

FUBAR – an acronym for Fucked Up Beyond All Recognition

I Corps – military designation of the South Vietnamese area that bordered North Vietnam

KIA – Killed in Action

Klicks – short for kilometers

Louie – slang for lieutenant

MACV – Military Assistance Command, Vietnam, the unified U.S. command structure

M16 – standard automatic rifle for U.S. troops

M60 – standard machine gun used by U.S. troops

M79 – standard grenade launcher used by U.S. troops

MIA – Missing in Action

Mama-san – slang term GIs used for older Vietnamese women

National Liberation Front – formal name for the Viet Cong

NCO – Non-commissioned Officer, e.g., a sergeant

NVA – North Vietnamese Army regular soldiers, as differentiated from Viet Cong guerrilla soldiers

Number Ten – pidgin for "the worst," as opposed to Number One, "the best"

Papa-san – term GIs used for older Vietnamese men

REMF – Rear Echelon Mother Fucker, a support soldier not in daily combat roles

RFs/PFs – Regional and Popular Forces, South Vietnamese militia, mostly based in the countryside

R&R – Rest and Recreation

SBA – U.S. Small Business Administration, where Ben's father worked

Saigon The – The watery alcoholic drink served to GIs in bars

TDY – Temporary Duty Assignment

USAID – United States Agency for International Development

USARV – United States Army Vietnam command structure

WIA – Wounded in Action

ABOUT THE AUTHOR

PETER PRICHARD served in South Vietnam for thirteen-and-a-half months in 1968–69 and was awarded the Bronze Star for service. He was the top editor of *USA Today* from 1988–95, and later was chair of the Newseum, the Freedom Forum's museum of news in Washington, D.C. He is also the author of *The Making of McPaper: The Inside Story of USA Today.*

Made in United States
North Haven, CT
19 September 2023